A collection
the world's

**International bestselling
award-winning author**

Lynne Graham

*has written more than 50 books, appeared on
numerous bestseller lists, and sold more than
15 million copies of her novels.*

**"Lynne Graham spices [things] up with
good character development, a strong
conflict and hot tension."**
—Romantic Times

**"Lynne Graham blends her trademark
Latin lover, sensual scenes and gripping
storyline into top-notch entertainment."**
—Romantic Times

Available in the

Queens of Romance

collection

17th March 2006

7th April 2006

21st April 2006

5th May 2006

Collect all 4 superb books!

Lynne Graham

Claiming His Wife and Child

Containing

**One Night with His Wife
Duarte's Child**

M&B

*M&B™ and M&B™ with the Rose Device
are trademarks of the publisher.
Harlequin Mills & Boon Limited, Eton House,
18-24 Paradise Road,
Richmond, Surrey TW9 1SR*

ISBN 0 263 85034 X

109-0406

*Printed and bound in Spain
by Litografia Rosés S.A., Barcelona*

One Night with His Wife

LYNNE GRAHAM

Lynne Graham was born in Northern Ireland and has been a keen Mills & Boon reader since her teens. She is very happily married with an understanding husband, who has learned to cook since she started to write! Her five children keep her on her toes. She has a very large dog, which knocks everything over, a very small terrier which barks a lot, and two cats. When time allows, Lynne is a keen gardener.

Lynne Graham has a fabulous new novel available in May 2006.
**Look for *The Greek's Chosen Wife*
in Mills & Boon Modern Romance®.**

CHAPTER ONE

'THE account no longer exists…' Star repeated that shattering announcement shakily under her breath as she walked back out of the bank.

In her hand, she still gripped the cheque she had tried unsuccessfully to cash. Beneath her shining fall of copper hair, her delicate features were stamped with shock, her aquamarine eyes bemused. She climbed back into Rory Martin's elderly classic car.

'Why were you so long?' Rory asked as he drove off.

Twisting round in her seat to check that the twins were still fast asleep in their car seats, Star muttered, 'I had to see the assistant manager—'

'That'll be because you're a lady of substance now,' Rory teased, referring to the money which Star had proudly paid into the bank only a few weeks earlier.

'And he told me that the account no longer exists,' Star confided abruptly.

At the traffic lights, Rory's fair hair swivelled. 'What are you talking about?'

'Juno has closed the account—'

'Your mother's done what?' Rory interrupted incredulously.

'There must be something badly wrong, Rory.'

'You're telling me. How could your mother close your account?' he demanded.

'It was *her* account.'

At that revelation, Rory sent Star a bewildered glance. 'Why didn't you have a bank account in your own name?'

'Because until last month when I sold those canvases, I

5

wouldn't have had anything to *put* in an account of my own,' Star stressed defensively. 'Juno was keeping me!'

Looking unimpressed by that argument, Rory pulled away from the traffic lights again. 'It was still *your* money in that account, the proceeds of the first couple of pictures you sold—'

His persistence made Star bristle with annoyance. 'Juno and I work on a "what's mine is yours" basis, Rory. We're family. We stick together. If she drew out that money, she must've needed it.' Then a further cause for alarm assailed her. 'Do you realise that it's over two weeks since I even *spoke* to my mother? Every time I call, all I get is that wretched answering machine!'

'I wouldn't be surprised if she's simply moved the account elsewhere and just forgotten to tell you about it,' Rory suggested in a soothing tone. 'Let's stop worrying about it. This *is* my day off. Where do you want to go next?'

Still in a bemused state, Star slowly shook her head. 'I can't go shopping without money—'

'So, I'll give you a loan to tide you over,' Rory slotted in with an easy shrug.

'No, thanks,' Star told him hurriedly, determined not to lean on him that way. 'You'd better just take us home again. I need to phone around and try to get hold of Juno to find out what's happening.'

'Be sensible, Star. She's hardly ever at home. Meanwhile, you *still* have to eat,' Rory pointed out with all the practicality of a male whose considerable family fortune was built on that same fact of life.

However, Star was immovable. Half an hour later, Rory drew up in the cobbled courtyard of a dilapidated fortified house complete with a tower surrounded by rusting scaffolding. Star lived rent-free as caretaker at Highburn Castle. The owner lived abroad. A friend of Juno's, he didn't have the money to maintain his inheritance, or the interest to apply for the grants available to repair a building listed as being of historical significance.

Star detached the belts from the baby seats in the back of the car. Rory unlocked the sturdy rear door of the castle and transported the first twin inside. Venus sighed in her sleep but remained comatose. Mars loosed an anxious little snort and shifted position. Both Star and Rory stilled until her restive son settled again. Mars had yet to prove the perceived wisdom that a baby could sleep through anything.

'They're great kids.' As they entered the big basement kitchen, Rory scrutinised the sleeping babies with the interest of a male who, as an only child, had had little contact with young children. 'I can never get over how tiny they are. When you think how premature they were, they're a right little pair of miracles!'

Having noticed the winking light on the answering machine which her mother had installed, Star gave him an abstracted nod. She switched on the tape and a familiar voice broke into speech.

'Star, it's me…I've got into some real hot water,' Juno gasped breathlessly into the sudden silence greeting her message. 'I haven't got time to explain, but I have to go abroad in a hurry and I had to borrow your money to pay for the flights! I'm absolutely skint. If I've left you in a hole, I'm sorry, but maybe you could contact Luc and get him to pay his dues for you and the twins…*please*, darling—'

'Who's Luc?' Rory demanded abruptly.

Star wasn't looking at him. She had jerked violently at the sound of that name. Her stomach somersaulting, she turned a whiter shade of pale. With an unsteady hand, she stopped the tape to absorb what she had so far heard and forcibly repressed all thought of Luc Sarrazin… Luc, her estranged husband, and the unwitting father of the twins.

What on earth had happened to the art gallery Juno was about to open in London? Only six weeks ago, Juno had been so confident of success. For goodness' sake, she had borrowed a small fortune to open that gallery! At the time, Star had been secretly astonished that *any* bank would give her mother such a large loan. Investing in Juno was a risky venture. Twice before, her mother had set up businesses which had failed.

And now it seemed that once again everything had fallen through. Star sighed. Where Juno was concerned that was nothing new. There was nothing new in her sudden dramatic flight from trouble either. That was vintage Juno, Star reflected sadly. When things went wrong, Juno panicked.

But now she urged her daughter to approach Luc Sarrazin for child support, Star simply cringed. Her mother might be desperate to justify her bahaviour, but that particular suggestion had been *way* below the belt. Juno knew what a disaster her daughter's short-lived marriage had been. Hadn't it been partly *her* fault that Luc had felt constrained to marry Star in the first place?

'Star…' Rory said again more forcefully.

'Shush! I need to hear the rest of this message.' Star switched the tape back on.

'I know you're trying to tune me out because I'm not saying what you want to hear. *Yes*, I hate Luc because he's a Sarrazin, but you made *babies* with him! He's got no heart or imagination but he ought to be keeping his own kids.' Juno paused. 'You see, I don't know how long it'll take to sort this mess out, or even if I'll be successful. But I promise you that *if* I am, I'm going to have the most wonderful surprise for you when I get back again!' she forecast in a bright but not very confident tone. 'Byee!'

'Luc…so his name's Luc,' Rory continued in a sharp, flat tone unfamiliar to Star's ears. 'I've never understood why you won't talk about the twins' father, but now that I've finally got his name, maybe you could tell me who he is.'

'My husband…well, sort of…' Star's voice just petered out again.

Rory's jaw had dropped. He pushed a dismayed hand through his fair hair, making it stand on end. 'You're saying you're married? But I thought—'

Star gave an awkward shrug. 'Yes, I know what you thought, but I couldn't see the point in contradicting you.'

'You saw no point?' His suntanned face was flushed, his hazel eyes bemused. 'There's a big difference between being a single mother and someone's *wife*, Star!'

'Is there? It wasn't a proper marriage and it only lasted a few weeks. The twins were an accident…*my* accident, *my* mistake,' Star stressed tautly. 'It wasn't something I wanted to talk about. It's something I just want to forget.'

'But you can't just *forget* you've got a husband!' Rory's dismay at that revelation was unconcealed. 'My parents will hit the roof if they find out that you're a married woman!'

It was make-your-mind-up time, Star conceded ruefully an hour later as she settled the twins into the wooden playpen with their toys. She had made a snack for their lunch from the few provisions that remained in the fridge. So where *was* she going with Rory?

Almost without her noticing, he had crossed the boundary of being just a good mate. But she could now pinpoint the exact date when that subtle change had begun. It had been the day he took her home to meet his family. Even though he had introduced her purely as the casual friend she had been at the time, his wealthy parents had seen her as a threat and acted accordingly. Rory had been embarrassed, and then furious at their behaviour. He was a decent guy, a really decent guy, and he had been a terrific friend.

They had met in the hospital canteen some weeks after the twins were born. The twins had been in the special care unit for a very long while. At the same time, Rory's beloved grandmother had been seriously ill. When he had realised that Star had to walk miles just to catch a bus to the hospital, he had started synchronising his visits to his grandmother's bedside and offering Star a lift home.

He'd been twenty-two then, and he had told her he worked in a supermarket. He hadn't mentioned that it was his year working out to complete a degree in business management, or the even more salient fact that his father *owned* a vast chain of supermarkets which was a household name in the UK.

When she had angrily accused him of not telling her the truth, he had said straight off, 'You've got a real prejudice against people with money.'

To be fair, she had not been very frank with Rory about her own past. She had told him that she had been a charity child, raised at a rich and reluctant French guardian's expense. The child had been kept rigorously at arm's length, lest she contaminate her guardian's good name and reputation with her unconventional background and questionable parentage.

Luc Sarrazin's father, Roland, had been that guardian.

And Star had only met Roland Sarrazin twice in her entire life. Once when she had first become his ward, at the age of nine, and the second and final time just over eighteen months earlier, when the old man had been dying. She had flown out to France to stay at the Sarrazins' magnificent family home, the Chateau Fontaine, and dutifully pay her respects. Her conscious mind now recoiled from remembering the other events which had taken place that winter.

Instead she recalled her years of separation from her mother, Juno Roussel. Nine years of prim and proper imprisonment in a boarding school for a child who had once known what it was to run free. Nine years deprived of even written contact with her mother. She had spent the school holidays in London, as the guest of Emilie Auber, an elderly childless widow related to the Sarrazin family. Only Emilie had given Star affection during those years, but Emilie had also made the appalling mistake of encouraging Star to love Luc Sarrazin.

Dear sweet Emilie, with her sentimental dreams of romance…

'Luc needs someone like you, but he doesn't know it yet,' Emilie had said.

No, Luc definitely *hadn't* known. And he hadn't needed her either. Indeed, Luc had given Star a taste of humiliation which she would never, ever forget.

'You're not in love with me. You're in love with sex. Find a boy the same age and experiment on him!'

As Star stared into space, she shivered and hugged herself. The chill inside her seemed to bite right through to her bones. It had been eighteen months, and she hadn't yet followed Luc's advice and experimented. First she had discovered that that single reckless night in Luc's bed had got her pregnant. Then she had become the mother of two tiny premature babies. The twins' tenuous hold on life had sentenced her to months of tortured fear and anxiety. But now Venus and Mars were home, safe and healthy, and slowly catching up with their peers. And Rory was *still* here, being caring and supportive. He loved the twins and he wanted a girlfriend, not just a mate. He wasn't likely to wait for her to make up her mind for ever…

His kisses were pleasant. They didn't burn. But then being burned *hurt*, Star reminded herself fiercely. No more dancing too close to the fire. No more dizzy adolescent fantasising. The guy she loved, the only guy she had ever loved, had spent their wedding night in the arms of his exquisitely beautiful mistress, Gabrielle Joly. As rejections went, it had been pretty final. It had told her all she should have needed to know. But Star had always been a fighter, and stubborn with it. She hadn't been willing to let go of her dream. Hating Luc, loving Luc, and determined to hang onto him by any means available, she had got down and dirty in the trenches of fighting for her man.

Getting him into bed had felt like a major coup. She had thought she had won; she had thought he was *hers*; she had thought surrender meant acceptance. She hadn't really cared how *he* felt about it. After all, men didn't always know what was good for them. In fact men could be pretty thick about recognising their soulmate if she came along in an unfamiliar guise. And Luc, even possessed as he was of an IQ of reputedly sky-high proportions, had been a really slow and exceedingly stubborn learner.

'Look—'

Star glanced up.

Rory was watching her with a rueful smile. 'I've got some things to do. I might call back later this evening.'

For a split second, Star studied him with blank eyes. Then she coloured and finally pulled free of her troubled thoughts. 'OK…sorry, I was miles away.'

As she saw Rory out, she was conscious of a guilty sense of relief. Thinking about Luc had shaken her up and filled her with angry frustration. But regretting her mistakes was currently an unproductive waste of time. She would be far better occupied worrying about how she was to feed herself and the twins when Juno had left her literally penniless!

It was going to be a wild night, Luc Sarrazin acknowledged. On the exposed hill road, the wind buffeted his powerful car, forcing him to keep a hard grip on the steering wheel. But the gale-force wind was a mere breeze in comparison to the cold and lethal anger Luc was containing behind his habitually cool façade.

The day before, Emilie Auber's accountant had flown to Paris to request an urgent meeting with Luc. Robin Hodgson had been the anxious bearer of bad news. Without consulting her accountant, or indeed anybody else, Emilie had loaned practically every penny she possessed to a woman called Juno Roussel.

Luc had been furious. But he had also been grimly amused that even in such trying circumstances Emilie had not admitted the embarrassing reality that Juno Roussel was in fact *his* mother-in law! The mother-in-law from hell, Luc conceded with a curled lip. He hadn't been remotely surprised to learn that Juno had since disappeared without repaying the trusting Emilie any of the money she had borrowed.

'I believe that from the outset of this unpleasant business there was a deliberate intent to defraud your father's cousin,' Hodgson had then gone on to contend heavily. 'Emilie was first introduced to Juno Roussel by a young woman she had known as a child—the Roussel woman's daughter, Star.'

That information had genuinely shaken Luc. The suggestion that Star might have been involved in ripping off Emilie had turned his stomach; Star had always been so honest.

However, what had truly shattered his legendary nerves of steel during that interview was hearing the entirely incidental news that Star had apparently become the mother of twins. Infants still in hospital at the time of Star's visit to Emilie last autumn. A *mother*...Luc's teenage bride, Luc's runaway wife. Star had given birth to another man's children while she was still *his* wife!

Luc had been incandescent at that revelation. He recalled little beyond that point. And he *still* felt wild with rage. He wanted to smash something; he wanted blood to flow. How dared Star do something so sordid? How dared she run around sleeping with other men while she was still legally married to him? But then she was faithfully following in her mother's footsteps, wasn't she? Juno, whose dangerous influence he had impulsively tried to protect her from. What a fool he had been to have any faith in the daughter of a blackmailer!

No doubt Star currently believed herself safe from retribution. In spite of all his efforts over the past eighteen months, Luc had been unable to find out where his runaway wife was living. But that very morning Luc had obtained entrance to the art gallery which Juno had abandoned. There he had found the address book which the older woman had left behind in her hasty departure...

That evening, Star had just finished settling the twins into their cots when the ancient front doorbell shrilled noisily on the old servants' call board in the kitchen. Only a stranger would go to the front entrance, which was hardly ever used. Indeed, the bolts had long since rusted into place. But, even though there was a sign directing all callers to the rear entrance, it was amazing how many people chose to ignore it.

Not in the mood to rush out of the back door and trudge all the way round to the front, Star groaned. The bell shrieked again in two long, ferocious bursts. She tensed, wondering if urgent need lay behind such unreasonable impatience. Perhaps a walker had been injured or a car had crashed out on the road.

She raced out into the teeth of the wind that had been rising steadily throughout the day. It blasted her copper hair back from her brow and plastered her long fringed skirt to her legs, making it difficult for her to move quickly. As she struggled round the wall into shelter, she winced at the racket the scaffolding was making as it rattled in the gale.

The first thing her attention centred on was a stunningly expensive sports car, with a sleek golden bonnet. With disconcertion, her gaze whipped from the car to the tall, dark male positioned by the Victorian bellpull. Luc…it was Luc! But how *could* it be Luc? With Emilie Auber sworn to secrecy about her whereabouts, how could he possibly have found out where she was living?

The sheer shock of recognition stopped Star dead in her tracks. A wave of disorientating dizziness currented through her. She rocked back unsteadily on her heels and shivered violently in reaction. Registering her presence, Luc strode towards her, his devastatingly dark and handsome face hard as granite.

Huge aquamarine eyes fixed to him as her head tipped back to take in all of him. He was so big. Somehow she had forgotten *how* big. There he stood, six feet three inches of potent masculine intimidation, exuding a twenty-two-carat sophistication that came as naturally to him as breathing. He was, after all, one of the most powerful investment bankers in the world. He had the sleek, honed elegance of a prowling jaguar and a physical presence that was sheer intimidation.

Eyes dark as midnight glittered down like shards of ice crystal into Star's. A pulse at the base of her slender throat beat convulsively fast and made it impossible for her to catch her breath.

'Shock…horror,' Luc enumerated with a sibilant softness that trickled down her sensitive spine like a hurricane warning. 'You still wear every thought and feeling on your face, *mon ange*.'

While *he* still showed nothing, Star reflected in feverish abstraction, her attention glued to the smooth, hard planes of his lean, strong face. 'Luc…' she managed in a choky little voice before the tidal wave of horribly familiar guilt engulfed her and reduced her to squirming silence instead.

'*Oui*, your husband,' Luc drawled, his husky French accent dramatising every syllable with the most incredibly sexy edge.

A tide of colour washed over Star's triangular face. She shut her eyes in dismay at that last forbidden thought about his accent and struggled to get a grip on herself.

'Surely you expected me to track you down sooner or later?'

'Not really, no…' Star mumbled, eyes shooting wide again to telegraph a look of naked panic. She was trying to picture herself telling him the most unwelcome news he would probably ever hear. That he was the father of twelve-month-old twins.

Luc's beautifully modelled wide, sensual mouth compressed into a hard line. 'Guilt is written all over you!' he ground out in icy disgust.

He *knew*. He knew about the twins! What else could he be talking about? He must have leant on poor Emilie and browbeaten her into spilling the beans. And he wasn't wrong about the guilt. At that moment, Star was just eaten alive by that sensation, and at the same time savagely hurt. It had been one thing to imagine how Luc might react, quite another to be confronted with the brutal reality of that rejection.

CHAPTER TWO

'*ALORS!*' Luc slung the noisy scaffolding girding the castle frontage a grim appraisal. 'Take me inside,' he instructed in imperious command.

'The front door doesn't open...you'll have to come round the back.' Alarmingly conscious of Luc powering along beside her, impatiently curtailing his long stride to her smaller steps, Star hurried breathlessly back round to the rear of the castle.

'I'm so s-sorry, Luc...I really am,' she stammered truthfully in the dim passageway which led past several doors into the basement kitchen. It was her only reception area, and although daylight was only just beginning to fade she already had candles lit, because it was a dark room, and the place needed rewiring.

One step into the kitchen, Luc surveyed her with dark eyes colder than frostbite. 'By the time I have finished taking this betrayal out of your useless little hide, you'll understand the *true* meaning of what it feels like to be sorry!'

Shaken by such a level of condemnation, Star turned even paler. Did he think that she should have terminated her pregnancy? Was that what he was getting at? Had it been a betrayal of trust to give birth to children he would not have wanted her to have? Her tummy muscles knotted up. 'Sometimes things just g-go wrong, Luc—'

'Not in my life they don't...not once until *you* came along,' he completed with icy exactitude.

In the face of an accusation that she was aware had more than a smidgen of truth, Star braced herself with one nerveless hand on the back of the sagging armchair by the range and stared helplessly at him, registering every detail of his

16

appearance. His superb charcoal-grey silk suit sheathed his broad shoulders and the long, powerful length of leg in the kind of fabulous fit only obtainable from extremely expensive tailoring. His luxuriant black hair had been ruffled by the wind, but the excellence of the cut had ensured that the springy dark gleaming strands just fell back into place.

Briefly engaged in sparing his humble domestic surroundings a grim, lip-curling appraisal, Luc turned his attention back to her without warning.

Flash! As Star collided with the long-lashed brilliance of his stunning dark deep-set eyes, it was like finding herself thrust into an electric storm. Heat speared through her slight frame. Feverish pink sprang up over her slanted cheekbones. She trembled, every sense awakened to painful life and sensitivity, an intense awareness of her own body engulfing her to blur every rational thought.

Silence banged thunderously in her ears, her heart thumping a frantic tattoo against her breastbone. A wanting so powerful it left her weak had seized her, dewing her skin with perspiration, stealing her ability to breathe or vocalise. What was it about him? She had asked herself that so many times. The obvious? He *was* fantastically good-looking. So tall, so dark and beautifully built. His maternal grandmother had been an Italian countess. That heritage was etched in his fabulous bone structure, the blue-black ebony of his hair and the golden hue of his skin.

Was that really the *only* reason she yearned for him with every fibre of her being and when deprived of him, felt only half alive? It had to be the only reason, she told herself frantically.

'So you have nothing to say for yourself,' Luc drawled.

'I'm still in shock,' she mumbled truthfully.

Shock. *Her* shock was nothing to *his*, Luc decided with sudden ferocity. To find her living like this in abject poverty, candles lighting a room Gothic in its lack of modern conveniences or comfort. She was dressed like a gipsy and thin

as a rail. Bereft of the support of Sarrazin money for just
eighteen months, she'd clearly sunk without trace. Just as he
had expected; just as he had forecast. He studied her bare
feet, recalled that she had almost run across the rough gravel,
and the most extraordinary ache stirred inside him. Frustrated
fury leapt up to engulf and crush it out. Not enough sense to
come in out of the rain, Emilie had once said of Star.

Emilie... Luc's quick intellect zoomed in on that timely
reminder at supersonic speed, but his hooded gaze was nonetheless still engaged on roaming up over Star's veiling skirt
with its silky fringe. Memory unerringly supplied a vision of
the slender, shapely perfection of her legs. He tensed almost
imperceptibly, his appraisal rising higher, finding no escape
in the pouting thrust of her small braless breasts beneath her
velvet wrap top.

As she flung her head back, his lean, powerful body hardened in urgent all-male response. Her hair glowed in the dim-
ness, bright as beaten copper in sunlight, dancing round her
triangular face. Her pallor highlighted exotic eyes, alive with
awakening sensuality, and a wide, soft, voluptuously pink
mouth.

And *this* was the woman he had spent over a hundred
thousand pounds trying to trace over the past eighteen
months? Tiny, skinny, irredeemably different from the rest
of her sex. There was nothing conventional in her mercurial
changes of expression, her fluid restive movements, her jangling bracelets, her outrageous earrings shaped like cats or
her ridiculous clothing. She wasn't beautiful either. There
was nothing there that he admired or looked for in a
woman—nothing but the drugging, earthy sexuality that was
as much a part of her as her dusty bare feet, Luc told himself
with driven determination.

Star had the soul and spirit of a small wild animal, always
ready to fight for survival and use whatever she had to get
what she wanted. Or *trade*? Why else was she surveying him
with that melodramatically charged look of undeniable hun-

ger? No, there was no doubt in Luc's mind that Star knew exactly what he was here about. To look so ashamed and desperate, she had to have been involved up to her throat in persuading his father's elderly cousin to part with her money!

'How could you have done such a thing to Emilie?' Luc demanded icily.

A frown line indented Star's smooth brow. Colliding with his glittering dark gaze, she froze as if an icy hand had touched her heart. Perspiration beaded her short upper lip. Gooseflesh sprang up on her exposed skin. The chill he emanated was that powerful.

'Emilie...?' Star's frown line deepened.

'The loan, Star.'

'What loan...what are you talking about?'

'*Si tu continues...*' Luc swore so softly that the tiny hairs at the nape of Star's neck rose.

It was a threat. If she kept it up, he would get angry. But, Emilie and what loan?

'I honestly don't know what—'

Luc slowly spread the long brown fingers of one expressive hand. The atmosphere was so charged she could almost feel it hiss warningly in her pounding eardrums. 'So that's the way you're trying to play it,' he spelt out, framing each laden word with terrifying emphasis. 'You're acting all ashamed because of the two little bastards you've managed to spawn while you were still married to me?'

The offensive words struck Star in the face like a blow. She fell back in physical retreat. 'Bastards?' she whispered tremulously.

'Illegitimacy seems to run very much in your family genes, doesn't it?' Luc pointed out lethally. 'Your children... you...your mother—not one of you born with anything so conventional as a church blessing.'

Registering in disbelief that Luc believed that their twin babies had been fathered by some other man, Star gazed back at him with haunted eyes of bewildered pain. 'No...*no*, Luc...I—'

'Surely you don't think I require an explanation?' Luc elevated a winged ebony brow, studying her with sardonic disdain. 'I shall divorce you for adultery and will *not* pay alimony, I assure you.'

Divorce...*divorce*! Even in the midst of her appalled incredulity that Luc should believe her capable of giving birth to another man's children while still legally joined to him, that single word tore into Star like a bullet slamming into her body. And like a bullet rending tender flesh it brought unimaginable pain. Divorce was for ever and final. She stared back at him, eyes shadowing, slanted cheekbones taut with tension beneath her fair skin.

A roughened laugh escaped Luc. 'You seem shocked.'

The atmosphere sizzled, hot with high-voltage tension. She sensed his rage, battened down beneath the icy façade he maintained. And aching, yearning sadness filled her to overflowing when she saw the grim satisfaction in his hard, dark gaze. Now he had the perfect excuse to be rid of her. But then he'd had excuse enough in any case. Not wanted, not suitable. Too young, too lowly born, possessed of embarrassing relations, unfit to be the wife of the chairman of a bank.

'You should never have married me...' Anguish filled Star as she remembered her ridiculous optimism against all the odds. Her manipulation, her manoeuvres, her final desperate attempt to force him to give her a trial as a real wife. What did it matter if he now chose to believe that the twins belonged to some other man? It had to be what he wanted to believe. He didn't care; he had *never* cared.

Luc had swung away. His strong profile was rigid. He clenched his hands into fists and then slowly uncurled them again. But he could still feel the violence like a flickering flame darting along the edge of his self-control. She was a little slut. He despised her. In the circumstances, he was being wonderfully polite and civilised. Only he didn't feel civilised. He wanted to punish her. He wanted to punish her even more when she stood there like a feckless child, who never, ever thought of the damage she might be doing. But he didn't dare risk acting on that urge.

For eighteen endless months he had had Star on his conscience. He had worried himself sick about her. How she was living, *where* she was living, even whether or not she was *still* living. In Luc's opinion, anyone with her capacity for emotional intensity had to be unstable. She had too much emotion, the most terrifying amount of emotion, and it had all been focused solely on him.

Eighteen months ago, in more anger than he had ever known, he had lashed out and ripped her apart with the force of his rejection. And she had taken off like a bat out of hell, leaving all her clothes behind, not to mention a letter which Luc had considered dangerously close to thoughts of self-destruction. He had had the moat dragged at the chateau, he had had frogmen in the lake day after day...

Sarrazin Bride Driven to Suicide by Unfeeling Husband. He had imagined the headlines. Over and over again, he had dreamt of her floating like the Lady of Shalott or Ophelia surrounded by lilies. He had been *haunted* by her! Freed of her ludicrous expectations, he should have found peace. Instead, he had got his nice quiet life back, and his freedom, but he had lived in *hell*!

Star studied Luc with pitying aquamarine eyes and tilted her chin. 'You weren't worthy of my love. You were never worthy of my love. I can see that now.'

Luc swung back to face her as if she had plunged a dagger into his strong back. Black eyes cold as charity assailed hers.

'You're unreachable. You're going to turn into a man as miserable and joyless as your father,' Star forecast with a helpless shake of her copper head. 'You don't even *like* children, do you?'

Luc stared back at her in silent derision, but the slight

darkening of colour over his spectacular cheekbones, his sudden tension and the flare of hostility burning from him told her all she needed to know. Oh, yes, some day a recognised son and heir would be born to his next wife, Star reflected painfully. And Luc would naturally repeat all the cruelties of his own lonely childhood. What else did he know? That child would be banished to a distant nursery and a strict nanny. He would be taught to behave like a miniature adult and censured for every childish reaction until he learned not to cry, not to shout, not to lose control…indeed that emotions were messy, unnecessary and unmanly. At least that poor stifled child would not be Mars, Star told herself wretchedly.

'Emilie…' Luc reminded Star with icy bite. 'How *could* you introduce Emilie to a vulture like your mother?'

Thrown into total confusion by that abrupt and confusing change of subject, Star had to struggle to recall the loan which Luc had mentioned earlier, but she could not stretch her mind to comprehend how anyone could possibly call Juno a vulture. Juno would give her last penny to anyone in need. 'I don't understand—'

'*Bon! Cela suffit maintenant*… OK, that's enough,' Luc incised harshly, his darkly handsome features cold and set. 'Lies are going to make me even angrier. In fact, lies may just prompt me to calling in the police!'

Lies? The police? *The police?* Star's lashes lowered to screen her shaken eyes as she fought to concentrate her wandering thoughts. How much more did Luc expect from her? All right, so he acknowledged few human feelings and therefore could not understand what she was going through right now. But he arrived here without warning, disgustingly referred to their children as having been 'spawned', simply assumed that they had been fathered by a lover and then he announced that he wanted a divorce! Wasn't that enough to be going on with?

'I don't tell lies,' she stated.

'That should make life simpler. So, you and Juno collaborated to persuade Emilie to loan your mother everything she had—'

'*No*…' Star stepped forward in aghast disconcertion at that charge.

'Yes. Don't you dare lie to me,' Luc intoned in a low, vicious tone she had never heard or thought to hear from him. 'Yesterday, Emilie's accountant told me the whole story. Emilie cashed in her investments and gave Juno the money to open up that art gallery.'

Star froze. The pieces of the puzzle finally fell into place. Juno had borrowed from Emilie, *not* from a bank!

'And now Juno's vanished. Are you going to tell me where she is?'

'I don't know where she is…' Horrified by what she was now finding out, Star spun away in an uncoordinated movement.

As she reconsidered the message which Juno had left on the answering machine, her temples tightened with tension. Now she knew why her parent had fled the country at such speed. And no wonder Juno hadn't explained the nature of the 'hot water' she was in! Her mother would have known just how shocked and disgusted her daughter would be at her behaviour.

Juno had lied by omission, deliberately concealing the fact that her loan had come from Emilie. Had Star had the smallest suspicion that Emilie was considering backing the art gallery venture, she would have stepped in and stopped it happening. But how could Emilie have been so naive? Emilie was neither rich nor foolish. So why on earth had she risked her own security to loan money to a woman she hardly knew?

'You're not prepared to rat on Juno, are you?' Luc condemned harshly.

'I'm not in a position to!' Star protested.

Luc studied her with hard, dark eyes. 'Emilie has been left without a sou.'

'Oh...*no!*' Distress and shame filled Star to overflowing. She loved Emilie Auber very much. That her own mother should have accepted Emilie's money and then run away sooner than deal with the fall-out when things went wrong truly appalled Star.

But she had one minor comfort. Luc would not allow Emilie to suffer. He would replace her lost funds without question or hesitation. His reputation for ruthless financial dealing would not get in the way of his soft spot for the kindly older woman. Juno would have known that too, Star reflected bitterly. Was that how her mother had justified herself when she had borrowed money which Emilie could ill afford to offer?

'If you tell me where Juno has gone, I might begin to believe that you have nothing to do with this disgraceful business,' Luc murmured very softly.

'I told you...I don't know!' Star flung him a shimmering glance of feverish anxiety. 'How could I have anything to do with this? How could you even *think* that I would have encouraged Emilie to loan money to my mother?'

'Why not?' Luc dealt her a grim appraisal. 'Aside of that one visit you made with your mother in the spring, Emilie has neither seen nor heard anything from you since you left France. That doesn't suggest any great affection on your side of the fence, does it, *mon ange*?'

Star braced slender hands on the scrubbed pine table and stiffened with instant resentment at that accusation. But she could not admit that she had maintained regular contact with Emilie without christening Emilie a liar for pretending otherwise to Luc.

'I can't believe that you think I could've been involved in this in any way,' Star reasserted with determined spirit.

'You're not that innocent. How could you be? You're Juno's daughter. And living like this...' Luc cast a speaking glance round the bare kitchen. 'It must've been very tempting to think up a way of hitting back at me.'

'I don't think like that—'

'Your mother does. She hates my family. Emilie may only be a cousin of my late father's, but she is still a member of my family.'

'Luc...I wouldn't let anyone harm Emilie in any way!' Star argued frantically.

'So why did you introduce her to Juno?'

'Why wouldn't I have? Emilie had always wanted to meet her. I could never have dreamt Juno would ask her for a loan, or that Emilie would even *consider* giving her money!'

Star raised unsteady hands and pressed them against her taut face in a gesture of frustration. Why would Emilie have loaned money to Juno when she *knew* that Juno was hopeless with money? It didn't make sense.

'Do you want to know why Emilie gave your mother that money?'

Star nodded slowly.

'Emilie thought that if the gallery got off the ground, you would move up to London and live with Juno. Emilie was hoping to see more of *you*.'

Every scrap of remaining colour drained from beneath Star's skin. She twisted away on driven feet, her face stricken. She wanted to cover her ears from Luc's derisive tone of condemnation. She also wanted to get her hands on her irresponsible, flighty parent and shake her until her teeth rattled in her pretty blonde head.

'I hold you responsible for all of this,' Luc delivered in cold completion.

Star's slight shoulders bowed. 'I honestly didn't know about the loan—'

'I don't believe you. When you first saw me this evening, your guilty conscience betrayed you.' Luc strolled fluidly towards the door. 'Since I'm not getting any satisfaction here, I'll go to the police.'

Star whirled round, aquamarine eyes aghast. 'Luc... no...*please* don't do that!'

Luc shrugged a broad shoulder. ' "Please" doesn't work with me any more. I want blood. I want Juno. If you can't deliver her, I'm just wasting my time, and I don't like people who waste my time.'

'If I knew where she was, I'd tell you...I *swear* I would!' Star gasped, hurrying across the expanse of worn slate floor that separated them.

'No, you wouldn't. You'd protect her. You'd hide her from me—'

'No... If she got in touch...' Star snatched in a shuddering breath, her eyes overbright with unshed tears. 'I'd tell you. I swear I would. I wouldn't like doing it, but what Juno's done to Emilie hurts and angers me very much. My mother was in the wrong—'

'The police can deal with her. I've got enough to hang her with.'

'No...you can't do that!' Involuntarily, she stretched out her hand and pulled at his arm in an attempt to hold him back as he opened the door that led into the passageway.

Luc gazed down at her, eyes glittering black and cold as ice in warning. 'Don't touch me...'

Her throat closed over. Her fingers dropped jerkily from his sleeve. She trembled in shock, a mortified wave of hot colour sweeping up her throat. For an instant, she sank like a stone into a bottomless pit of remembered rejection. Their wedding night, which Luc had spent with his beautiful mistress. The unbelievable anguish of loving without return. In a split second she relived it all, aquamarine eyes darkening with pain and veiling.

'I'll crucify Juno in court and I'll divorce you,' Luc murmured with velvet-soft sibilance.

'Do you want me to get down on my knees and *beg*?' Star flung at him wildly.

Luc raised a withering aristocratic dark brow.

'I'll do *anything*—'

'Begging doesn't excite me.'

Startled by that husky assurance, Star lifted her head and looked up at him again. Luc gave her a dark smile, brilliant eyes shimmering beneath his lush black lashes. Heat curled low in the pit of her stomach, jolting her. She quivered, drawn like a moth to a flame.

'But then I like my women tall and blonde and rather more sophisticated,' Luc completed with dulcet cool.

Star flinched, stomach turning over at that lethal retaliation.

In the simmering silence the door at the foot of the dim passageway was suddenly thrust noisily wide. Rory strode in, carrying several bulging supermarket carrier bags. He came to a halt with a startled frown. 'Sorry. When you didn't hear me knock, I tried the door. I didn't realise you had company.'

Disconcerted by Rory's appearance, Star breathed in deep. 'Rory, this is Luc…Luc Sarrazin. He's just leaving—'

'Like hell I will,' Luc incised, half under his breath, still as a statue now by her side.

Not believing her ears at that intervention, Star glanced at her estranged husband in astonishment.

'Luc…?' The bags of groceries in Rory's hands slid down onto the stone floor as he released his grip on them. 'You're…you're Star's *husband*?'

Luc ignored him. His attention was on Star. 'Does he live here?'

'No, I don't,' Rory stated curtly.

Luc turned his arrogant head back to study Rory. '*Fiches le camp*…get out of here!'

'I'm not leaving unless Star asks me to…' The younger man stood his ground.

'If you stay, I'll rearrange your face,' Luc asserted with cool, unapologetic provocation.

'Stop it, Luc!' Star was aghast at Luc's unashamed aggression.

Luc angled back his proud dark head and lounged back

against the doorframe like a big powerful jungle cat ready to spring. 'Stop what?'

'What's got into you?' Star demanded in hot embarrassment.

'This little punk got my wife pregnant and you dare to ask me that?' Luc launched back at her, his husky accent scissoring over every syllable with raw incredulity.

'Rory is *not* the father of my children!' Star slammed back at him shakily.

Rory shot a thoroughly bemused look at both of them.

Luc had stilled again. His nostrils flared. His breath escaped in an audible hiss of reaction at that news. 'So how many experiments did it take?' he derided in disgust.

Star was ashen pale. She said nothing. Turning away, she closed a taut hand over Rory's arm and walked him back outside. 'I'm sorry about this, but it's better if you go for now. Luc and I need to talk, sort some things,' she explained tightly.

'Obviously you haven't told him about the twins yet.'

'No...but he wants a divorce,' she heard herself advance, because she was too ashamed to tell Rory what her mother had done to Emilie.

Rory sighed. 'Probably the best thing in the circumstances. He seems a pretty aggressive character. I couldn't see you ever being happy with someone like that.'

Happy? She almost laughed. What was happy? Being separated in every way from Luc had been like living in a void. It hadn't cured her. Forcing a brittle smile, Star said, 'Tomorrow, I'm going to have a row with you about buying food for us.'

Closing the back door again, she leant against the solid wood, mustering all her strength. She had assumed that Luc had gone back into the kitchen. So as she moved back in that direction she was surprised to see that the twins' bedroom door had been pressed more fully open.

Luc was poised several feet from the foot of the cots.

Venus was curled on her side, an adorable thatch of copper curls screening her tiny face. Mars was flat on his back, silky dark hair fringing his sleep-flushed features, one anxious hand gripping the little bunny rattle which he never liked to get too far from him.

'They're what? Five…six months old?' Luc queried without an ounce of emotion.

After the number of setbacks the twins had weathered, they were still quite small for their age. Star studied her children with her heart in her eyes, thanking God as she did every time she came into this room that they had both finally been able to come home to her, whole and healthy. She glanced from under her lashes at Luc. His bold dark profile was grim.

'Would you have liked them to be yours?' she heard herself whisper foolishly.

'Tu plaisantes!'

You must be joking! Star reddened fiercely at that retort. What a stupid question to ask! Instead of asking it, she should just have told him the truth. Whether Luc liked it or not, Venus and Mars, fancifully christened by Juno, *were* his son and daughter.

Luc strode out past her. Leaving the door carefully ajar, Star followed him back into the kitchen.

'In fact, I'm extremely grateful that they are *not* my children,' Luc drawled in level continuation as he took up a commanding stance by the hearth, his lean, dark, devastating features cool as ice. 'It would have complicated the divorce and made a clean break impossible. Considering that we have about as much in common as oil and water, joint custody would have been a serious challenge.'

Star was pale as death now. His reaction shook her to her very depths. All right, so he had never thought of her as his wife. Yet when Rory had walked in Luc had been angry, aggressive, powered, it had seemed, by some atavistic all-male territorial instinct. She had never seen that side of him before, but now she had to accept that his reaction to Rory had simply stemmed from his savage pride.

Didn't he have any normal feelings at all? How could Luc just stand there telling her that he was relieved and grateful that her babies were supposedly nothing to do with him? In pained fascination, she searched his face, absently noting the very faint sheen of moisture on his dark golden skin, the unyielding blank darkness of his hooded gaze.

'Luc…I—'

'I was leaving…' Luc studied his diminutive wife, struggling to distance himself, black fury like a thick, suffocating smoke fogging his usually ordered thoughts. Suddenly he understood why so many unfaithful wives had ended up losing their heads to Madame Guillotine during the French Revolution. Feeling the slight tremor in his hands, he dug them rawly into the pockets of his well-cut pants. *Nobody will ever love you as much as I do.* Such soft words, such empty promises. He was *not* a violent man. But he wanted to remind her who she belonged to. No, she did *not* belong to him, he adjusted at grim speed. He did not *want* her to belong to him. He had meant every word he had said.

Star moved anxious hands. 'Could we just talk?'

'Talk?' Luc growled, not quite levelly, watching the way the flickering candlelight played over her porcelain-fine skin, accentuating the distinctive colour of her eyes and the full, inviting softness of her ripe mouth.

'About Juno?' Star moistened her dry lips with the tip of her tongue and watched Luc tense, his stunning dark eyes welding to her with sudden force.

'No.'

'No?' Colour mantled Star's cheekbones as the raw tension in the atmosphere increased. Her heart skipped a beat and then began to thump against her ribcage. Her mouth running dry, she tensed in dismay as she felt her breasts lift and swell, the rosy peaks tightening into mortifying prominence.

Luc's brilliant eyes flamed over her. 'If you spend the night with me, I'll let you both off the hook...'

'I b-beg your pardon?' Star stammered dizzily.

'I won't put the police on Juno's trail.' He gazed back at her steadily, not a muscle moving in his lean, strong face. 'One night. Tonight. That's the price.'

Her soft full mouth fell open. She closed it again, and tried and failed to swallow. She felt as if the ground had suddenly fallen away beneath her feet. 'You're not serious...you can't be!'

The silence shimmered like a heatwave between them.

Star trembled.

'Why shouldn't I be serious?' Luc angled his well-shaped dark head back, a hard smile slanting his wide, sensual mouth. 'One night only. Then tomorrow you travel down to London with me to see Emilie. Together we reassure her that she has nothing further to worry about. After that, we never see each other again in this lifetime.'

Her stomach twisted at that clarified picture. 'But you don't want me—'

'Don't I?' Luc moved a slow, fluid step closer, dark eyes mesmerically intense as they scanned her bemused face. 'Just one more time...'

'You don't want me. You never did! I'm not your type,' Star argued, as if she was repeating a personal mantra, a fevered, disbelieving edge to her voice.

'Except in bed,' Luc extended without hesitation.

Star stilled in astonishment. Then she jerked in reaction to that revelation. He was finally acknowledging a fact he had refused to concede eighteen months earlier. Luc *could* find her desirable. The night the twins had been conceived, Luc had genuinely responded to *her*, not just to the anonymous invitation of a female body in his bed. The following morning, his cold silence on that point had shattered what little had remained of her pride.

Anger and regret now foamed up inside her in a bewildering surge. 'Couldn't you just have admitted that to me eighteen months ago?'

'No,' Luc drawled smoothly. 'It would have encouraged you to believe that our marriage had a future.'

The heat still singing through Star's blood suddenly slowed and chilled. Such cool calculation stabbed her to the heart and unnerved her.

'But that was then and this is *now*,' Luc stressed with syllabic sibilance.

Now, she repeated to herself in reminder. Now, when Luc had knocked her sideways by suggesting that they spend one last night together. Why not? With his customary cool he had already boxed her in with cruel, unfeeling boundaries to ensure that she didn't misunderstand the exact tenor of his proposition.

He had told her he wanted a divorce.

He had told her that after tomorrow they would never meet again.

Star's throat constricted. Her wretched body might quicken at one glance from those stunning dark eyes of his, but did he really think she held herself that cheap?

'You don't want me enough...' Even as that impulsive contention escaped her Star tried to bite the words back, for they revealed all too much of her own feelings.

Luc surveyed her steadily, devastating dark eyes fiercely intent. 'How much *is* enough?'

She wanted him on his knees. She wanted him desperate, telling her that never in his life had he experienced such hunger for any woman. If she couldn't get into his mind, it would be the next best thing. Hot colour warmed her cheekbones.

'How much?' Luc repeated huskily.

'M-more...' The current of excitement he generated in her as he moved closer literally strangled her vocal cords.

More? What did that mean? Familiar frustration raked through Luc. He felt like a man trying to capture a dancing shard of sunlight. He felt out of his depth, which infuriated him. He had expected her to grab that offer with both hands. She never looked before she leapt. She was as hot for him as he was for her. He saw it in her, he could *feel* it in her, only this time she was holding back. Star, exercising restraint? Why? What more could he offer?

'Cash inducement?' Luc enquired with lethal cynicism.

Her eyes widened, and then she couldn't help it. A nervous laugh bubbled from her dry throat.

His superb bone structure snapped taut, hooded dark eyes glittering. He reached out a lean brown hand, closed it over her narrow wrist and tugged her close, so close she stopped breathing. 'You think this is funny?'

Belatedly, Star saw that *he* didn't. He thought she was laughing at him, but sheer disbelief had made her laugh. She gazed up into the night-dark depths of his eyes. The wickedly familiar scent of him washed over her. The faint tug of some citrus-based lotion overlaying warm, husky male. She wanted to bury her face in his jacket and breathe him in like an intoxicating drug.

'Not funny...*sad*.' Star struggled to retain some element of concentration even as his raw magnetism pulled at her senses on every level. 'I think you'd prefer it if I asked for money.'

He released his breath in a stark hiss. 'That's rubbish—'

'You could call me greedy then. You could judge me, stay in control.'

'I'm not *out* of control.'

'You like paying for things...you don't value anything that comes free,' Star condemned shakily, fighting not to lean into him.

'*Ciel!*' Luc countered with roughened frustration and impatience. 'Since you and your mother entered my life, everything has had a price!'

At that charge, which had its basis in actual fact, Star paled. Simultaneously from somewhere in the distance there was the most almighty screeching sound, followed by a loud crash. As she jerked back from him, Star's eyes flew wide with dismay.

Luc swung away with a frown. 'What was that?'

Star groaned. 'It sounded like the scaffolding coming down.'

Loosing an impatient expletive in his own language, Luc headed for the door. Star only then recalled that he had parked his car *beneath* the scaffolding surrounding the tower. Pausing this time to thrust her feet into the leather toe-post sandals lying on her bedroom floor, she hurried outside after him.

When she reached Luc's side he was poised in silence, scanning the huge heap of twisted metal framing and rotten splintered wooden panels which had come down on top of his gorgeous sports car. The car was all but buried from view on three sides.

'Pour l'amour du ciel...' he ground out in raw disbelief, abruptly springing back into motion to stride towards the still accessible driver's door.

'What are you doing?' Star cried in panic, grabbing his sleeve to hold him back.

'I need my mobile phone!' Luc launched down at her.

'Are you crazy?' Star pointed to the single tier of scaffolding still hanging at a precarious angle above the destruction below. 'That could fall at any minute!'

'Oui...I'm crazy.' Luc flung her a grim slashing glance. 'When you last looked into your little crystal pyramid, did you put a *curse* on me?'

Star stiffened until her muscles were as tight as a drum skin. After that derisive response, she resisted the urge to tell him that many people believed in the value of crystal healing. 'There's a phone in the kitchen. You're welcome to use it.'

She walked away, but before she disappeared from sight she stole an anxious glance back. She could see that Luc was still calculating the chance of that last section of scaffolding falling at the exact moment he retrieved his phone from his car.

'Don't you *dare*, Luc Sarrazin!' Star screamed back against the wind, infuriated by his obstinacy, that indefinable male streak which could not bear to duck a challenge.

And in that split second, with a wrenching noise of metallic protest, the remainder of the frame leant outward and came tumbling thunderously down, forcing Luc to back off fast.

Well, that took care of that problem, Star reflected gratefully, and hurried back indoors again.

Luc followed her into the kitchen and approached the huge built-in dresser where the phone sat. 'Who owns this Gothic horror of a dump?' he demanded in a flat tone of freezing self-restraint. 'I intend to sue the owner.'

'Last I heard, Carlton was on a Caribbean island repairing boat engines for the locals. He's poorer than a church mouse,' Star proffered ruefully.

At that news, Luc breathed in so deep she marvelled at the capacity of his lungs. 'That structure was in a very dangerous condition—'

'Yes. An accident waiting to happen.'

His glorious accent was so thick it growled along her nerve-endings like rough tweed catching on the smoothest silk. He was furious, she recognised, outraged by the owner's irresponsibility, not to mention any circumstance which could maroon him in a dilapidated dwelling at the back end of nowhere. She watched him shoot a granite-hard glance of displeasure at his homely surroundings and the strangest feelings began blossoming in Star.

At that instant, Luc was just so human in his fury and his exasperation he provoked a huge melting tide of sympathetic warmth within her. His control over his emotions was so engrained he would not allow himself to shout and storm like most other men would have done. Yet he would be feeling so much less tense and angry if he let himself go. Of course, he wouldn't let himself go, she conceded wryly. But such infuriating events as collapsing scaffolding did not figure much in Luc's life.

He rarely drove himself anywhere. He was a brilliant banker with immense power and influence. A fabulously wealthy but driven workaholic, who had his routine as slavishly organised for him as a prisoner locked up behind bars. His daily existence was smoothed by servants, efficient bank staff, a fleet of chauffeur-driven limos and helicopters and a private jet. In his world of gilded privilege, disaster was invariably kept at a distance, and the irritating, time-consuming repercussions dealt with by someone else.

'I'm really sorry about this…' Star sighed heavily.

Luc lifted a candle to enable him to see the numbers on the phone. 'This is medieval,' he complained with slashing incredulity. 'Did the storm bring down the power supply?'

'No. The lights don't work in here. The whole place needs rewiring, but Carlton can't afford to do repairs. However, the phone's still working.' That was why the original caretaker had moved out, and the only reason why Star had a rent-free roof over her head.

She watched Luc stab out a number on the phone with an imperious forefinger. He'd be calling for another car. When he walked out, she'd *never* see him again. Her thoughts screeched to a bone-jarring halt on that realisation. Like an addict suddenly forced to confront the threatening horrors of denial ahead of her, Star was aghast at that reality. That sense of total loss felt so terribly final she wanted to chain him to the wall, to hold onto him for just a little longer. But she didn't need to chain him, *did* she? He had already offered her a time extension, a little slot, a ridiculously narrow little slot.

Why had he asked her to spend one more night with him? Was it to be his treat or her supposed punishment? My goodness, she thought headily, that one night at the chateau must've been something reasonably acceptable on his terms.

For here was the proof she had never expected to receive. Luc was asking to repeat that night, asking the *only* way he knew how, asking the only way he would allow himself to ask…bargaining from a position of strength and intimidation. Stripping everything bare of emotion, foreseeing every possible future complication but, with a remarkable lack of foresight, risking those same complications. Whooshing tenderness swept over Star like a tidal wave: Luc was acting out of character.

'Why are you looking at me like that?' Luc shot at her with a dark, questioning frown. 'This phone is acting up!'

'It's the storm…put the receiver down and try again,' she advised quietly.

One more night, she bargained with herself. It would be pure and utterly foolish self-indulgence. She would make no excuses for herself. It wasn't sensible, but then loving and wanting Luc Sarrazin had never been sensible. Tomorrow she would *have* to face up to the divorce and the fact that they were like two different planets, forever condemned to spin in separate orbits. Just not meant to be.

Luc was now telling someone at the other end of the line that he wanted a limo to pick him up as soon as possible.

Awkwardly, barely crediting the decision she had reached and instantly terrified that if she lingered on that decision, she might decide against it again, Star cleared her throat, desperate to commit herself.

'*Tomorrow morning…*' she contradicted hoarsely, her mouth feeling as dry as a bone, her tongue too clumsy to do her bidding. 'You won't need the limo until tomorrow morning.'

CHAPTER THREE

LUC was not slow on the uptake.

Tomorrow morning! Star had changed her mind. Or had she? Had she merely been playing games with him all along? His lean, powerful frame tautened. On the phone, his chauffeur was asking for directions. Without any expression at all, Luc gave the details and altered the timing of the arrangement, but his thoughts were already light-years removed from the task at hand. He replaced the receiver in a quiet, controlled movement.

Yet Star tensed like a restive small animal scenting a predator down-wind. As well she might, Luc conceded in febrile abstraction. He wanted to rip her lithe quicksilver body out of those absurd clothes and enjoy the kind of raw, urgent sex he hadn't fantasised about since he was a teenager. But even as the hot blood coursed to his loins, innate caution held him back.

'Tomorrow, we part again.'

'No problem...fresh start for both of us,' Star pointed out shakily.

It was what she needed, Star told herself urgently. The opportunity to draw a final line beneath her disastrous marriage. The chance to rescue a little of her shattered pride at his expense: *he* was the one asking, not she. That was a most ironic first in their relationship. All of a sudden, she had power. He had given her that power. Why shouldn't she use it?

In answer to that defiant question, she tensed as she thought of one very good reason why not for herself. 'Are you involved with anyone else right now?' she asked tightly.

'No,' Luc murmured drily.

Her eyes veiled, Star let her breath slowly escape again. So his mistress, Gabrielle Joly, who had caused her so many sleepless nights of anguish, had finally got her marching orders. Relief quivering through her, she lifted her head again.

Luc was as poised and still as an ice statue, his dark, devastating features unreadable. As he began moving towards her, her heart thumped like a giant hammer inside her.

'Tell me…do you sleep curled up in the hearth here, like Cinderella?' Luc enquired lazily.

'No… Well,' Star qualified tensely, 'I did sleep in here over the winter because my bedroom was too cold.'

He reached for her slowly, as if he was afraid an abrupt movement might startle her into retreat. He wasn't far wrong, Star admitted to herself. Nervous tension already strung her every sinew taut. It had just occurred to her that there was a vast difference between sneaking into Luc's bed when he was asleep…and inviting him to her own bed when he was wide awake and fully in control.

'Luc…?'

'Don't talk…' He lifted a silencing forefinger to trace her parted lips with silk-soft sure delicacy.

She trembled, his merest touch awakening the intense hunger she had fought every day for eighteen months. Aquamarine eyes rested on his lean, dark face with a sudden flare of defiance. 'I won't let you hurt me again—'

'I never meant to hurt you,' Luc ground out, his dark, deep-set eyes flaring to lambent gold.

But how could he have done anything else when he hadn't loved her? He hadn't asked her to love him either, Star reminded herself ruefully.

'It's all in the past,' she swore, as much for her own benefit as his.

Luc curved strong fingers to her exotic cheekbones and tipped her ripe mouth up to his.

As his hands slid down past her slight shoulders to lift her up to him, the sheer power of anticipation made her head spin in a dizzy whirl. He found her mouth, and for the time-less space of a heartbeat she lost herself in the hot, hard hunger of his lips. The most terrifying excitement laced with undeniable greed currented through her slim body. She linked her arms round his broad shoulders and pressed herself against the muscular hardness of his powerful physique, a fevered gasp of urgency torn from her throat.

He set her down on something hard. She wasn't rational enough to care what or where. All that motivated her was the overpowering need to stay physically linked to him. One kiss and he lit a fever inside her. She burned, heart racing, pulses pounding, as he dug his fingers into the silky tangle of her copper hair. He drove his tongue deep in an intimate invasion as incredibly exciting as it was rawly sexual in intent.

At the height of that explosive passion, Luc dragged his mouth from hers and gazed down at her with smouldering heat. *'Diabolique...'* he muttered thickly. 'You're on a table...'

So what? an impatient voice screamed inside her head. As he lifted his proud dark head bare inches from hers, Star reached for him with determined hands, sinking her fingers into the springy black depths of his hair and forcing him back to her. With a ragged groan of male appreciation, Luc melded his sensual mouth roughly to hers again, his hands sliding to the base of her spine to jerk loose the ties of her wrap top.

Hauling her back up into his arms, he lifted his tousled dark head again, colour scoring the fabulous cheekbones that lent his face such power. 'Where's the bedroom?'

Star blinked. She was in another world, in which neither language nor reason existed.

Luc elbowed back the kitchen door. 'Bedroom?'

'First right...*no*, first left!' Every pulse in her treacherous body was thrumming on a high, making it a challenge to think.

Luc dipped the tip of his tongue in a provocative flicker

into the tender interior of her mouth, making her jerk with reaction. 'You have the most gorgeous mouth, *mon ange.*'

The sun was going down, intense light flooding through the window to illuminate the small cluttered room. He settled her down on the side of her bed. Her heart was jumping to such an extent she had trouble keeping air in her body. She studied him with passionate intensity. His lean, hard-boned features were half in light, half in shadow. Taut cheekbones, eyes the colour of midnight, straight, arrogant nose, hard, masculine jawline.

She watched Luc cast off his beautifully cut jacket, pull loose his tie and peel off his crisp cotton shirt. He discarded the items with the same controlled cool with which he did everything. Yet she quivered, insidious heat rising from deep within at the sight of his muscular brown chest, the sprinkling of curling black hair hazing his pectorals, the satin-sleek smoothness of the skin over his flat, taut stomach. The strength of her own craving shook her.

'I just love your body,' she whispered, knotting her fingers together, nerves and anticipation headily mingling to keep her ferociously tense.

Luc flashed her a slightly uneasy glance. 'That's my line.'

Star frowned in dismay, taking him literally. 'We don't have to have lines, do we?'

'We don't need to talk, do we?' Evidently even more threatened by that idea, Luc strode forward at speed and raised her upright. The edges of her loosened top fell apart. His hands tightened hard on hers. The silence sizzled. He gazed down fixedly at her bare pouting breasts crested by swollen pink peaks that stirred with her every quickened breath. A tide of colour washed her face as she resisted her own self-consciousness with all her might.

'Sensational…' Suddenly, Luc was dragging the sleeves of her top down her arms, freeing her of the garment and backing her down on the bed with a lack of cool that she found intensely gratifying.

'Say it in French,' she urged breathlessly. 'Say everything in French.'

Momentarily, Luc stilled. 'Try to smother the urge to tell me what to do.'

Star gave him a hurt look of confusion.

He lifted her up against the pillows so that she was level with him. Excitement glanced through her, sharp as a knife, but the pained light in her eyes lingered. He closed a soothing hand over her taut fingers, forcing her to release her death-grip on the corner of the duvet. 'Just keep quiet,' he practically begged. 'Don't talk…when you talk, you drive me crazy.'

Very slowly, Star nodded.

Eyes burning gold swept over her. He snatched in a ragged breath. 'You just always say the wrong thing.'

Tears stung her eyes behind her lowered eyelids.

Luc gazed down at her in frantic frustration. She was lying there like a corpse now, still as death in human sacrifice mode. He curved not quite steady hands to her delicate cheekbones. '*I* always say the wrong thing,' he contradicted in desperation.

Star opened her wonderful eyes and nodded forgivingly.

Without hesitation, he captured her lips again with potent driving passion. She stopped thinking, as if he had punched a switch. He slid lithely down the bed and closed his mouth urgently over one thrusting tender pink nipple. She gasped and jerked, every muscle straining in reaction, and instantly she was on fire again. The tormenting sensitivity of her own flesh made her moan helplessly and melted her quivering body to hot liquid honey.

'I want to taste you…' Luc muttered raggedly, wrenching her out of her skirt, his mouth travelling down over her slim, twisting length with a hot, devastating sensuality that over-whelmed her.

There was no escape from the raw force of her own need. Her heart racing, she flung back her head as he found the hot moist centre of her. A low, keening cry of reaction erupted from her. She was out of her mind with excitement, lost in the domination of an expert sensualist and increasingly frantic as the nagging, terrible ache for fulfilment built ever higher. Her fingernails scored his shoulders in a wild passion of impatience.

'Luc!' she sobbed in despair.

He came over her then, and slid between her trembling thighs. She couldn't get him there quick enough. The fire inside her was all-consuming. He sank into her on one powerful thrust, and the pleasure was so tormentingly intense she almost passed out at the peak of it. Nothing had ever felt so good. And there was more and more and more, and she was hugely desperate to hold onto every sensation and make it last as long as she possibly could. Out of control, she let that mad spiral of tormenting excitement gather her up and send her sobbing and mindless to the intense height of a climax that totally wiped her out.

Afterwards, the first thing she was conscious of was the silence. Luc was still holding her, every damp, hard, muscular line of him welded to her smaller, slighter frame. For a moment she luxuriated in that feeling of intimacy and closeness. Then her mind awakened again, and with a sinking heart she recognised her own weakness.

'Star…' Luc husked in an indolent tone of satiation. 'It's never been like that for me.'

She hoped it never would be again. In fact she hoped she would be a tantalising memory that infuriated him until the day he died. Mustering every scrap of self-discipline she possessed, she forced herself to pull away from him. Unexpectedly, he caught her back to him. In the half-light, dark golden eyes appraised her flushed triangular face, her lowered lashes which betrayed only a wary glimmer of aquamarine.

'You can talk now,' he murmured, almost teasingly.

'I've got nothing to say.' Once she would have told him

she loved him. And that recollection of her old self now made her cringe.

Luc came up on one elbow, stunning dark eyes level. 'Star—'

'We left the candles burning in the kitchen.' She snaked out of his hold before he could guess her intention. Stretching out a frantic seeking hand for the wrap lying on the chair by the bed, she got up, keen to make her escape.

In the kitchen, she shivered, cold as ice without him, even colder when she looked into the future. Yet her body still thrummed and ached from the glorious possession of his. How dared he make it even better than she had remembered? How dared he tell her that that was the best sex he had ever had? He didn't have a sensitive bone in his entire body. But then what did that matter now?

She felt anguish beckoning like an old friend, but she turned away from it, older and wiser now. Making a meal of misery wouldn't change anything. She forced herself to put away the groceries which Rory had brought. The prosaic task dragged her down from the heights, gave her the chance to get a grip on her turbulent emotions.

It was past time that she faced up to the truth she had spent such an impossibly long time evading. Their marriage had been a fake! She had known that from the outset but had stubbornly refused to accept the fact. Luc had never wanted to marry her; Luc had simply felt that he *had* to marry her, Star acknowledged painfully.

That winter his father had been dying, Star had enjoyed a long-awaited and very emotional reunion with her mother. Only one awkward fact had shadowed that reconciliation: Juno hated the Sarrazin family and had been desperate to persuade Star to leave France. But Star had been head over heels in love with Luc...and quite incapable of choosing to remove herself from his immediate radius.

On an unannounced visit to the chateau, her mother had been genuinely appalled to walk into a room and find Star in Luc's arms. Accusing Luc of taking inexcusable advantage of her teenage daughter's naivety, Juno had threatened to create a major scandal. Determined to protect his sick father from the distress of such sordid publicity, Luc had insisted that they get married. It was ironic that Juno had been even more outraged by their marriage.

But Star had entered their marriage of convenience with a hidden agenda the size of a jumbo jet. She had honestly thought that if she prayed hard enough, tried hard enough, she could *make* Luc love her! Every scrap of misery she had suffered since, she decided, she had brought on herself.

Fortunately, she didn't love Luc any more, she told herself fiercely. He was her first love. It was understandable that she would never be *totally* indifferent to him. But here, tonight, she promised herself that she would say goodbye to that humiliating past and move on. When the dawn came in tomorrow, there would be no looking back.

Having got her flailing emotions back under control, Star drifted back to the bedroom and lodged uncertainly in the doorway, striving for a cool stance. In the moonlight, Luc was lying in a relaxed sprawl on his side, his skin vibrant gold against the pale bedding. He looked like an incredibly gorgeous oil painting. Her heart gave a treacherous lurch. She waited for him to lift his handsome dark head and say something. When he didn't, she moved slowly closer. She couldn't believe it. He had gone to sleep! But then when had Luc *last* slept? She swallowed a rueful laugh, bitterly amused by her own intense disappointment. He followed a relentless schedule. He would have had to make time for a trip to England. To do so he might well have worked through most of last night. And now, tension released by a rousing bout of entirely uncommitted sex, he had given way to exhaustion and fallen asleep. How touchingly, uncharacteristically human! It shocked her that she was really tempted to wake him up again.

Refusing to give way to that degrading desire, Star sat in

the kitchen by the light of one candle. She didn't trust herself to get back into bed with him. She didn't even trust herself asleep in bed with him. Around Luc she did things she would not have dreamt of doing with any other man. Of course this time it was only the lure of his sexual magnetism, his heartbreaking good-looks, his lithe, beautifully built body. In other words, sex—and he was very, very good at sex; that was the only reason she was still tempted...

The limousine arrived at eight the next morning. The chauffeur delivered a garment bag and a small case to the door and then retreated back to the car.

By then Luc was already up, although Star had yet to see him. Minutes earlier she had heard the shower running in the bathroom, and had marvelled at Luc's staying power under that freezing cold gush. Her own record was three minutes, and she always boiled the kettle for hot water to wash her hair. She put the garment bag and the case into the bedroom and went back into the kitchen to wait.

She had already fed the twins and dressed them in their best outfits: Venus in a pink velour top and leggings, Mars in navy dungarees with a checked shirt. They looked cute. At least, Star thought they did. Hopefully, at some stage, a vague memory of the twins looking cute and cuddly would slightly soften the blow of paternity coming Luc's way. When the divorce proceedings began she would have to get a solicitor. She would then tell her solicitor to tell Luc's solicitor that Luc was the father of her twins.

Star could see no reason to confront Luc with the fact that he was a father face to face. Luc was going to be furious. Luc was going to feel trapped and resentful. Luc liked everything to go to plan. Only he hadn't planned on succumbing to her the night she'd sneaked into his bed, and she hadn't planned as far as him actually succumbing, so she hadn't taken any precautions against pregnancy. Why *should* she put herself through a humiliating scene like that? Nothing she could do or say would make the fact of the twins' existence any more palatable to him, she reasoned painfully. It would be much easier all round if he received the news from a third party.

Just then, she heard Luc's steps in the passageway. Her tension level shot so high she felt light-headed. She fixed a really bright and friendly smile to her face. Luc strode through the door as immaculate and elegant as if he had just strolled out of the Sarrazin bank in Paris. Charcoal-grey suit, burgundy silk tie, pale silk shirt. He looked spectacular, and very, very intimidating.

'You should have wakened me earlier,' he drawled smoothly.

Encountering brilliant dark eyes as cool as ice, Star hung on gutsily to her smile. 'Do you want some breakfast?'

'I'm fine, thank you.' Luc glanced at his watch. 'If you're ready, we should leave now for London.'

The horrible silence stretched. But he wasn't touched by it. Or by her discomfiture. She could see that. Inside himself, Luc was already so far from her he might as well have been back in France. There wasn't a hint of warmth or intimacy. There was nothing. It was as if last night had never happened. And Star, who had believed herself prepared for whatever he might choose to throw at her the morning after, just could not cope with that complete denial.

'Do you think I'm going to cling to you now or something?' she heard herself demand rawly.

Luc froze, but on the way to freezing he winced.

Hot-cheeked with fury and pain, Star stepped forward. 'I'm *over* you!' she launched at him.

'We haven't got time for a scene,' Luc murmured deflatingly.

Star trembled, and her hands squeezed into defensive fists. 'Saying how I feel is not creating a scene!'

Luc elevated an aristocratic brow. 'Doesn't it occur to you that I might not be interested in how you feel?'

The angry colour drained from her skin, her expressive eyes shaken.

As Star spun away, Luc gritted his even white teeth. That sunny smile she had greeted him with had filled him with volcanic rage. The Star he remembered would have been self-conscious, shy. Not this one. Involuntarily, he recalled the wild sweetness of her response the night he had consummated their marriage. His body reacted with a surge of fierce arousal, infuriating him.

As a punishment, he made himself focus on the shabby playpen and its tiny occupants. Both babies were watching him with surprisingly intent expressions. The littlest one, with the explosion of copper curls, the colour of which jarred horribly with her pink outfit, gave him a big, gummy winsome smile. That smile was so hopeful and appealing that in spite of the mood he was in he very nearly smiled back. Focusing on the little boy, with his solemn dark brown eyes and slightly anxious air, Luc was astonished to find himself thinking that they were remarkably attractive babies. He looked swiftly away again, but not before he had reminded himself that those children were now *his* responsibility as well. Who else was there to support them?

Star turned back, determined to stand her ground, no matter how much his attitude upset her. 'We had a good time in bed last night. It was just sex. I *know* that,' she told him fiercely. 'But it was my way of saying goodbye to you. I will not be treated like some sleazy one-night stand.'

Luc surveyed her with dark, deep eyes and remained maddeningly silent.

Star squared her slight shoulders. 'Believe it or not, I'm really happy now that we're getting a divorce. I have someone in my life who cares about me and now I'll be free to enjoy that relationship. *He* has a heart, and an imagination…and he talks as well.'

Luc's narrowed gaze chilled her to the bone. The atmosphere seemed to have dropped in temperature to the level of a polar freeze. 'Are you finished?'

Star compressed her lips and spun away, wondering why she had bothered to try and get through to him. 'I'll get the twins' car seats—'

Luc frowned. 'You're planning to bring them with us?'

Star spun back in bewilderment. 'What else would I do with them?'

It was clear that it had not occurred to Luc to wonder what else she might do with the twins. But then in his world young children were invariably in the convenient care of a nanny.

'You just didn't think, did you?' she said witheringly. 'Where I go, Venus and Mars have to go too.'

Luc stilled, his ebony brows drawing together. 'Venus…and Mars?'

'Juno christened them in their incubators.' Star hated the defensive edge she heard in her own voice. 'I know their names sound a little fanciful, and I may have put Viviene and Max on their birth certificates, but Venus and Mars are names which gave them good luck when they really needed it.'

'Venus and Mars,' Luc repeated with a sardonically curled lip.

Cheeks warm with angry colour, Star scooted past him to fetch the car seats from the twins' bedroom. As she emerged, Luc lifted them from her hands with easy strength. 'I'll take these outside.'

As the limousine drove towards London, Star worked hard at not looking in Luc's direction. But she remained agonisingly conscious of his all-pervasive presence. Their relationship, it seemed, had turned full circle. Once again, Luc was taking her to Emilie Auber and then planning to walk out of her life again. Her mind roamed back to their first fateful meeting eleven years earlier…

Her stepfather, Philippe Roussel, had died when she was

nine. In his will he had named Roland Sarrazin as her guardian. Since Philippe hadn't had contact with the Sarrazins since his own childhood, he could only have chosen Luc's father in the hope that the wealthy banker might feel obligated to offer his widow and her child financial help.

By then, Juno and Star had been living on the breadline in Mexico. Philippe had been charming, but hopelessly addicted to gambling. Only after his death had Juno shamefacedly admitted that she had fallen pregnant with Star *before* she'd met Philippe, and that he had not been Star's real father.

Roland Sarrazin had sent Luc to Mexico to track them down. At the time, Juno had been feeling a failure as a mother.

'I had no job, no money, no proper home for you, and you were missing out on your education. I thought that the Sarrazins would take care of you until I got my life sorted out. Then I would bring you back to live with me,' Juno had shared painfully years later, when mother and daughter had finally been reconciled after their long separation. 'How could I ever have dreamt that it would be nine years before I saw you again?'

Juno was still very bitter about that. Roland Sarrazin had applied to a French court to gain full custody of her daughter.

Luc had only been twenty then, but he had had an authority and a maturity far beyond his years. Star had waited outside their shabby one-room apartment while Luc talked to her mother. Within a couple of hours of that meeting Star had found herself accompanying Luc on a flight back to France.

Luc hadn't had a clue how to talk to a child, but he had made a real effort to be kind and reassuring. He had also appeared to believe that she was coming to live with his family, and he had described Chateau Fontaine, their fabulous seventeenth-century home in the Loire valley.

But on their arrival there his father's air of frigid disapproval had frightened and confused Star. Apart from commenting that she was a astonishingly plain little girl, Luc's beautiful mother, Lilliane, had displayed no more interest in her than she might have done in a stray cat.

'My parents are very busy people.' Luc had hunkered down to Star's level to explain when she'd looked up at him with big hurt eyes welling with tears.

'They don't w-want me,' she had sobbed helplessly. 'Why did you bring me here?'

'My father is your legal guardian.'

'What about my mum?'

'Right now your mother can't look after you the way you need to be looked after, and she wants you to catch up with your schooling.'

The following day, Luc had flown her over to Emilie in London. She had been greeted with open arms and home-made lemonade and biscuits.

Of course, how *could* Luc have explained that his father had been outraged at being landed with responsibility for her? A formidably correct man, with immense pride in his own respectability, Roland Sarrazin had had a pronounced horror of scandal. Years earlier, Philippe Roussel had disgraced his own family. The circumstances in which Star and her mother had been living, not to mention the discovery that Star was *not* Philippe's child, had convinced Roland Sarrazin that to protect himself from any further embarrassment he should ensure that Star's mother, Juno, was kept out of her daughter's life.

Emerging from the memory of that cold-blooded and entirely selfish decision, Star glanced at Luc. He had a desk in his limo: that really said it all. He was using a laptop computer while simultaneously talking on the phone. They had shared not a word of conversation since the journey began. The twins, initially eager to attract Luc's attention, had finally given up on him and dozed off.

Star found herself watching the way stray shards of dimmed sunlight flickered through the tinted windows, glinting over the springy luxuriance of his black hair, shadowing a hard cheekbone and accentuating the lush length of lashes longer than her own. One lean brown shapely hand rested on the edge of the desk. Dear heaven, even his hands were beautiful, she thought, suddenly stricken to the heart and sucking in a steadying breath so deep it left her dizzy.

A phone buzzed. Luc lifted his arrogant dark head, a slight frown line etched between his winged brows as he recognised that the phone ringing was not, in fact, his. Star dug into her capacious bag to produce the mobile which Rory had given her for her recent birthday, thinking how unfortunate it was that she had never got the chance to give her mother the number of her mobile phone.

'Star, where *are* you?' Rory demanded anxiously. 'I drove up and saw that car buried under the scaffolding. I was afraid that you'd been hurt!'

'Oh, no, I'm fine…really I am, Rory.' Star smiled with determination, grateful for anything capable of distracting her from Luc's intense visual appeal. Just like the night they had shared, such reactions belonged in the past now, she reminded herself doggedly. It was Rory she should be concentrating on. Rory, who was steady and caring. Rory, who would probably never seek a mistress who resembled a supermodel…

'Luc's taking me to visit Emilie. I was sort of rushed out the door and I forgot to call you.' Star faltered on that last enervating recollection of Gabrielle Joly.

'When will you be home?' Rory prompted.

'Soon…' Looking up to meet Luc's eyes, which were as cold and dark as the river Styx, reputed to lead into the underworld, Star swallowed with difficulty. 'Look, I'll call you when I get back. I'll make a meal,' she proffered on the spur of the moment.

The boyfriend was history, Luc decided without hesitation. A relationship in which neither fidelity nor loyalty appeared to figure was very bad news for Star. And if she couldn't work that out for herself, it was obviously *his* job to do it for her. What Star needed was a fresh start. For that reason, he would make his own generous financial support conditional on Rory's exit from her life. A case of being cruel to be kind. For her own good, and that of her children, Star would have to learn to like a quieter, more conventional lifestyle, he reflected with grim satisfaction.

But she had changed. Last night he had been waiting for her to tell him she still loved him. He could not understand why her failure to do what he definitely hadn't wanted her to do should have irritated the hell out of him. Quite deliberately, Luc dredged up purgative memories of their six-week marriage. Star calling him every hour on the hour…Star reading poetry out loud over breakfast…Star waiting for him every night when he came home, even if it was the next morning…Star, outrageously sensitive and vulnerable but as subtle as an army tank, and yet so loving, so incredibly loving and giving…

His hooded gaze chilled on that final reflection. Over the last eighteen months she had been loving and giving with how many *other* men?

At that moment, the limo pulled in at the tiny mews house where Emilie had lived for over forty years.

'Is Emilie expecting us?' Star asked awkwardly.

'*Bien sûr*…I contacted her before I arrived with you last night.' Luc watched Star lean forward with the evident intention of undoing her daughter's seat restraint. 'Why don't you leave the children sleeping? My chauffeur will watch over them. I don't expect this to be a long visit.'

Star frowned. 'But—'

'Indeed, I imagine that you will be relieved when this meeting is at an end.'

Star stiffened. 'I'm very fond of Emilie. I may be upset and embarrassed about what's happened, but I'm still looking forward to seeing her.'

Luc looked singularly unimpressed by that claim. Star

tilted her chin. Emilie was already waiting at her front door, a tall, spare woman with soft white hair and a remarkably fresh complexion for a lady of seventy-two years.

'I was delighted when Luc told me that he would be bringing you with him.' Emilie greeted Star with a warm and affectionate hug and whispered, 'Thank goodness you've finally told him about the twins.'

While Star reddened at that misapprehension on the older woman's part, Emilie went to peer into the limo at the slumbering babies. 'I do hope they wake up before you have to leave.'

In the pretty sitting room, Star sat down opposite Emilie.

'I was most annoyed when I found out that my accountant had dragged you into this, Luc,' Emilie confided, disconcerting both her visitors.

'I wasn't dragged, Emilie…and Hodgson was only doing his job.'

'But he completely misread the situation. I *offered* Juno my money; she didn't ask me for it and she didn't want to accept a loan from me. I persuaded her to accept my help. Now that the gallery had failed—through no fault of hers, I might add—I will not have the poor woman hounded as if she's a criminal!'

That spirited defence of her mother took Star entirely by surprise. Luc's dark, devastating features betrayed no reaction whatsoever.

'Juno's a kind and decent woman who's had a very difficult life and more than her fair share of bad luck.' Emilie proclaimed in determined addition.

Tears stinging her eyes in a hot, emotional surge, Star reached across and grasped Emilie's hand with very real gratitude. 'My mother means well…she always means well…but nothing ever seems to go right for her,' she agreed shakily.

'Or for anybody else in her vicinity,' Luc completed in a gritty undertone.

'I *know* that she shouldn't have run away like this,' Star acknowledged tautly, ignoring that comment.

'But Juno didn't run away. She came to see me first.' Emilie's smile of recollection was wry. 'Full of crazy ideas about how she might rescue us both from ruin…bless her heart. She does try *so* hard!'

'Bless…her…heart?' Luc studied his father's elderly cousin much as he might have studied someone intellectually challenged.

'A well-known artist had agreed to exhibit at the gallery opening night,' Emilie explained with a sigh. 'But last month he pulled out. I'm afraid the other artists backed out then too. By then, all the money had been spent on setting up the gallery and funding the advance publicity. It really wasn't her fault.'

'Only Juno could emerge from this fiasco white as driven snow,' Luc commented icily.

Star flinched.

Luc met Emilie's anxious blue eyes and produced a reassuring smile. 'However, I'm relieved that you've not been as upset by this business as I had feared, Emilie. And, believe me, you have nothing further to worry about. As Juno is my mother-in-law, I will naturally replace the money you've lost.'

Emilie frowned. 'I really couldn't allow you to do that, Luc.'

'Of course you could.' Luc did not take that claim seriously.

But, conscious of the level of Emilie's discomfiture, Star was now studying the older woman with questioning concern.

'This is a family matter,' Luc pointed out with impressive conviction.

'*Is it?*' Emilie pursed her lips. 'Families live together and support each other, Luc. But you and Star have been apart for a long time now. In those circumstances, how could I possibly allow you to repay Juno's loan? I can't think of her as your mother-in-law when I know that your marriage must be over.'

A silence in which a dropped pin could have been heard had spread while Emilie explained her reasoning. That the older woman was serious about what she was saying was clear.

Star stole one fleeting glance in Luc's direction. His pronounced stillness suggested that he was as stunned by this development as she herself was. It had not occurred to Luc that Emilie, who invariably agreed with everything he said and did, might flatly *refuse* an offer of financial restitution! And why was Emilie refusing? Emilie believed that their broken marriage meant that she could not consider Juno's debt as being either a family concern *or* Luc's responsibility.

'On the contrary, Emilie,' Luc countered with brilliant dark eyes, a faint smile curving his wide, sensual mouth. 'Our marriage is not over. Star and I were about to tell you that we've just embarked on a trial reconciliation.'

CHAPTER FOUR

LIKE a woman caught up in a sudden polar blast of bone-chilling cold, Star simply froze in position.

Her stunned gaze fixed to Luc's bold, masculine profile while he focused his entire attention on Emilie. *A trial reconciliation?* Star could not credit her own ears! Luc was famed for his ice-cool nerves and fast reactions in times of crisis. How could a male as clever, cautious and controlled as Luc have made such an insane announcement?

'That is the most wonderful news I've ever heard!' With a sudden smile of surprise and pleasure, Emilie scrambled up to clasp Luc's hand and extend her other hand expectantly in Star's direction.

'Star...' Luc prompted, in probably much the same commanding tone he employed with slow-moving junior employees at the Sarrazin bank.

But Star stared at Emilie's extended hand and found she simply couldn't move a muscle. Of course, she knew what Luc was *trying* to do. She understood why he had suddenly pulled that whopping fib like a rabbit out of a magician's hat. But how did Luc think that such an enormous lie could be carried off? Pretending that they were having another go at their marriage would demand far more of a convincing show than Luc could fondly imagine.

No doubt he thought he was telling a little white lie which he could easily shrug off again with a regretful sigh at some stage in the future. But then he wasn't aware that Emilie and Star had remained in too close contact for such a pretence to work. And Star was furious at the idea that she might be forced to stay out of touch with Emilie to support that same pretence!

57

Star collided unwarily with Luc's intimidating dark gaze. Get up and play your part, that hard, warning scrutiny urged. When she failed to move, he bent down and closed his other hand over hers to literally *lift* her up into doing his bidding.

'I'm so very happy for you both.' Emilie folded Star into her arms. 'Although,' she added hesitantly, 'I'm not quite sure I like the sound of that word "trial", Luc. Particularly with young children involved—'

Star jerked back into life and interrupted the older woman by pressing a harried kiss to her cheek. 'I'm so sorry, but we really do have to rush off now, Emilie. You know what Luc's schedule is like! I hope you'll allow Luc to sort out this financial thing for you.'

'Of course Emilie will,' Luc asserted.

'Yes, and then I shall visit you all in France this month,' Emilie announced with an even brighter smile of anticipation, seeming not to notice that Star's expressive face fell by a mile in shock. 'Now I can really look forward to spending the summer at Chateau Fontaine with Star and those beautiful little children of—'

'Gosh, got to run...love you so much, Emilie. See you soon!' Star carolled wildly, yanking on Luc's hand with desperate determination to drag him out of the room before the older woman could spill the beans about the twins' parentage.

Shell-shocked by the experience of visiting Emilie when Luc was in an inventive mood, Star climbed back into the limo and just sat there like a stone effigy, her bemused dismay as to how Emilie's expectations could possibly be met etched in her face.

'We'll fly back to France this evening,' Luc drawled without skipping a beat.

A faint frown line indented Star's smooth brow. 'Sorry...you said...?'

'You heard what I said,' Luc informed her drily.

'I'm *not* coming to France just because you've landed us

in a heck of a mess with that stupid lie!' Star exclaimed in vehement accusation.

Faint colour darkened the superb angles of Luc's hard cheekbones. 'Scarcely a "stupid lie"', *mon ange*. It was the only option left. If Emilie won't allow me to repay that money, she'll be homeless by the end of the month. Without the income from the investments she cashed in she can't even pay the rent on that house, never mind hope to keep herself with the smallest degree of comfort!'

Star had paled as he spelt out those harsh facts. 'But—'

'Just for once...concentrate that brain of yours,' Luc advised grimly. 'Your mother reduced Emilie to this level. Emilie's very proud, and she might be talking very bravely at the moment. But at her age how do you think she will cope with such a drastic change in lifestyle? Worry and distress will affect her health and will most definitely shorten her life.'

Star lost even more colour. And by the time Luc had finished speaking she saw that there *were* no other options. Just as suddenly she felt as if she was in a trap. She loved Emilie; she loved Emilie very much. But it seemed awesomely cruel to Star that she should be forced into such a situation on the very day she had finally mustered the sense and courage to say goodbye to Luc and her feelings for him for ever.

'You can spend the summer at Chateau Fontaine,' Luc continued levelly. 'It will be a small price to pay for Emilie's peace of mind. I will stay in the Paris apartment and make occasional weekend visits. Emilie will soon see for herself that you are being sadly neglected. She'll be disappointed, but I'm sure she'll understand when you decide that you *do* want a divorce.'

'Magic...not only do I get to spend three months away from my boyfriend...but I also get to be the one who demands the divorce. Thanks, but no thanks!' Her bright eyes shimmered with angry pain. 'You'll have to come up with something an awful lot better than that!'

Luc dealt her a cool, considering appraisal, dark eyes diamond-bright. 'So you'll have to do without sex for three months. You'll live.'

Star shivered with sheer rage.

'Let me be even more frank,' Luc continued in a tone as smooth as cut-crystal. 'Your life is a disaster zone. You're only twenty and already you have two children. Where's their father?'

Eyes aflame with defiance, Star stared back at him.

'Do you even know who the father is?' Luc drawled.

Furious colour lashing her cheekbones, Star snatched in a ragged breath to steady herself. She wanted to shout back at him, but she didn't want to waken the twins and distress them. 'How dare you ask me that?'

Unmoved, Luc raised a winged brow. 'Is that a yes or a no?'

'Of course I know…and I deeply resent the suggestion that I might *not* have known!' Star dragged her attention from him and focused instead on Venus and Mars. 'But they weren't conceived in what you might call a lasting relationship—'

'You had a one-night stand,' Luc assumed in derisive interruption.

Star breathed in so deep she wondered that she didn't simply explode. 'Yes, I suppose that *would* be the most apt description,' she conceded unevenly. 'The twins weren't planned—'

'So they just happened along, much like you did yourself? Doesn't that strike you as a very irresponsible attitude?'

'Their father was irresponsible too,' Star pointed out dulcetly. 'And the reason he's not helping me to support the twins is that he doesn't know that I got pregnant because I decided not to tell him.'

Luc shifted a broad shoulder. The slight, elegant Gallic shrug of dismissal suggested his waning interest in the subject.

Cut off in full swing, and feeling incredibly snubbed by his apparent lack of normal human curiosity, Star thrust up her chin. 'I can't fly to France this evening.'

'You must,' Luc contradicted. 'You can pack what you need for tonight. I will have the rest of your possessions cleared and flown over tomorrow. We can't afford to appear lukewarm about our reconciliation at this stage.'

'It just gets worse and worse...' Star groaned. 'We're getting sucked deeper and deeper in.'

'I'm afraid there won't be time for you to cook for Rory.' Without the slightest warning, Luc's wide mouth curved into a startlingly charismatic smile.

Her heart jumped like a bemused bird smashing itself against a windowpane. That so rare smile stole her breath from her throat and sent her treacherous pulses pounding. Her colour fluctuating, she collided unwarily with stunning dark eyes alight with amusement, and her sense of impending tragedy simply mushroomed. Her whole body was taut as a bow, every muscle so tight it hurt, and all Luc had done was smile, filling her with intense awareness of his masculinity and all the raw-edged emotions she had sworn to put behind her.

'Unless you've been polishing up your catering skills since we last met, Rory may well live to be grateful for the cancellation,' Luc extended silkily.

At that explanatory reference to an incident from their own past, Star's over-taxed emotions responded by simply flooding her eyes with tears. 'You are *so* insensitive!'

'After last night, I could hardly be expected to appreciate that you are *that* keen on the guy,' Luc murmured with cool, contemptuous clarity.

Humiliated by that rejoinder, Star's hands knotted into fists and she twisted her bright head away, fighting to get herself back under control. He could think what he liked! And as usual he'd read her wrong! Eighteen months ago, in one of her many attempts to persuade Luc to see her as a proper wife, she had given the chateau chef a night off and made dinner one evening. And it had been an absolutely mortifying total fiasco. Anything that hadn't been overcooked had been undercooked. And, worst of all, Luc had attempted to eat those pathetic edible offerings because he'd felt sorry for her.

'My chauffeur will take you home to pack and bring you to the airport in time for the flight this evening,' Luc drawled some minutes later.

Startled by that announcement, Star glanced up and registered that the limousine had already drawn to a smooth halt outside the Sarrazin bank in central London.

'I have several appointments to keep.' His brilliant dark deep-set eyes were cool as ice. 'But, as requested, I've come up with a better explanation with which to satisfy Emilie when our charade of a marriage disintegrates all over again. On this occasion, you can just tell her the truth!'

Star studied him in bewilderment. 'Sorry, I—'

'Did you really think that I wouldn't work out that Emilie appears to believe that your children are *mine*?' Luc demanded with sardonic bite.

Since Star had been guilty of thinking exactly that, she was taken entirely by surprise. A split second later, she found she could not meet his hard, challenging gaze either. Her own shrinking reluctance to tell him the truth about the twins had created this particular misunderstanding.

'You never think anything through to its likely conclusion,' Luc said very drily.

In this particular case he was undeniably correct, and Star was stung. 'How did you guess?' she heard herself asking.

'Emilie would not have welcomed your children had she not believed that I was their father,' Luc pointed out.

And, once again, he was quite right, Star acknowledged with gritted teeth. Had the twins been the result of an extramarital affair, Emilie Auber would have been very distressed by their birth. Nor, in such circumstances, would she have been so willing to believe the story of their supposed reconciliation.

'Whatever lies you employed to persuade her into crediting that cosy little fiction are your own responsibility,' Luc continued. 'But let me warn you now that while I appreciate the shock which Emilie will suffer when you admit the truth, I won't allow that lie to stand even temporarily in my own home. No matter what discomfiture it causes you, I have no intention of playing along with that particular pretence.'

Star scanned his lean, strong face with sudden aghast intensity. 'But everyone will think I'm a real tart!'

'You said it,' Luc murmured with lethal cool.

Pulverised by that final comment, and furious at herself for giving him that opening, Star watched him swing out of the car with predatory grace and stride towards the entrance of the London headquarters of the Sarrazin bank. Somewhat belatedly, it occurred to her that she had been foolish to allow Luc to continue believing that their children had been fathered by another man, foolish to place her own pride ahead of what was, after all, an unalterable fact. And the sooner she told Luc the truth now the better.

When Star boarded the Sarrazin private jet, she was clutching a squirming Venus under one arm and a clinging Mars under the other. Her floaty blue skirt and white cropped top were sticking to her damp skin. After rushing through the airport, she was feeling really harassed.

Luc strode out to greet her. Sheathed in a formal navy pinstripe suit embellished with a silk geometric print tie, he looked shockingly sexy. A guilty little tremor ran down her backbone.

'Do you realise how long we've been waiting for you?'

Her backbone became suddenly less sensitive. 'I'm sorry.'

She could have bitten her tongue out as soon as she said it. Unfortunately, Emilie had trained her too well, to always apologise for being late. However, Star had had a very difficult afternoon. With no prior preparation, packing for herself and the twins and closing up Highburn Castle had been serious hard work.

She had phoned Rory as soon as she'd got home. He had arrived while she was still struggling to get organised. He had been shattered when she'd told him that she was flying back to France with Luc. While she had still been trying to explain Emilie's financial situation, he had walked out in a temper. Now she could not imagine how she had ever thought she could hold onto *any* kind of relationship with Rory when Luc had stolen her life and her freedom for months to come.

'Who disabled the car phone?' Luc enquired glacially.

'I did.' Star owned up straight off. 'I told you we were stuck in a traffic jam. I didn't see the point of five-minute bulletins.'

Luc breathed in very deep. A combination of relief and raw exasperation powered through him. Punctual to a fault himself, he found her laid-back attitude infuriating. Star could leave a room promising to be *just* five minutes and then forget to come back at all. She was very easily distracted. But when telephone contact with the limousine had abruptly been severed, Luc's stress level had rocketed. He had wondered if Star had changed her mind about their arrangement and gone for the sort of sudden vanishing act her flighty mother excelled at.

'Do you think you could offer to take one of the twins for me?' Star prompted as the ache in her arms at the combined weight of the babies reached an unbearable level.

'Take one of the...?' Luc just froze.

Star shifted closer and indicated Venus with a downward motion of her chin.

'Where do I take hold of it?' Luc demanded.

'Just grab her before I drop her!' Star urged.

Luc clasped Venus between two stiff hands and held his daughter in mid-air like an unexploded bomb. Initially delighted by the transfer, Venus then picked up on that adult uncertainty and let out an anxious wail of fright. In response, Luc extended his arms to put an even greater distance between them. Venus squirmed and yelped in panic, clearly thinking she was on the way to being dropped.

'Hold her close, for goodness' sake…you're frightening the life out of her!' Banding both her arms round Mars, Star sighed with relief at the easing of the strain in her muscles.

Luc grated, 'I've never held a baby before!'

'Well, it's about time you learned. Babies are very touchy-feely and like to know they're secure.' Out of the corner of her eye, she watched Luc draw Venus closer with such pronounced reluctance she could have kicked him.

'Why's she going all slack?' Luc enquired in a driven undertone.

'Because she's in cuddle mode.' She watched Venus snuggle her curly head down on Luc's shoulder and just sag, the way very tired babies do.

'She's got little bones like a bird,' Luc drawled flatly. 'I was afraid I might hurt her.'

In the luxurious working area which made up only about a sixth of the passenger space available on the extensive Sarrazin jet, Star settled Mars into one of the baby seats awaiting occupancy. Luc bent down for her to peel Venus off his shoulder.

'Cots have been organised for them in the rear cabin,' Luc advanced.

Star strapped herself in beside the twins. Minutes later, the powerful jet taxied towards the runway. Luc was already perusing a file at the far side of the cabin. Star suppressed a rueful laugh. She had planned to tell Luc during the flight that Venus and Mars were his *own* flesh and blood. But she was exhausted, and what difference would another few hours make? She would be calmer and better equipped to deal with making that announcement in the morning.

As soon as they were airborne, the stewardess approached her and showed her down to the rear cabin, mentioning that a meal was about to be served, but Star said that she wasn't hungry. Having settled Venus and Mars into the cots, she decided to take advantage of the bed beside them and get some rest.

About ten minutes later, the door opened with quiet care. 'You should eat something,' Luc informed her levelly.

Half asleep, Star flipped over, copper hair tumbling over one exotic cheekbone, aquamarine eyes heavy. Light spilled in from the passage to glimmer over the satin-smooth skin of her slender waist where the crop-top had ridden up. As she stretched unselfconsciously, the extended length of one long shapely leg emerged from the folds of her skirt.

She studied Luc from below her dark lashes, the perceptible tension in the atmosphere tugging at her senses.

'You look like a gipsy,' Luc murmured.

The dark, deep pitch of his accented drawl quivered along her nerve-endings, awakening treacherous warmth low in the pit of her stomach.

'*Sauvage*...wild,' he breathed in husky addition.

Suddenly her every muscle was taut. She stared helplessly at him. So tall, so dark, so extravagantly, breathtakingly gorgeous. Hunger surged up inside her with such greedy immediacy she could barely breathe. In a split second she relived the urgent passionate force of his sensual mouth only just over twenty-four hours earlier, the hard, powerful pressure of his expert body moving on and in hers. Sensual weakness cascaded like melting fire through her, her breasts now full and swelling, their pointed peaks tightening into aching prominence. But then, just as suddenly, she remembered how Luc had behaved after he had got out of her bed. Cool, distant, dismissive, all intimacy forgotten.

Star lifted her bright head from the pillow, aquamarine eyes glinting now with angry self-loathing. 'Wild...but not free...not free to you *ever* again,' she told him.

Luc surveyed her with glittering intensity. 'This has the feel of a negotiation—'

'*Ever* the banker,' Star heard herself chide, but she was on a high from the excitement electrifying the atmosphere, a high that increased to the level of a stunning power surge when Luc bent the entire force of his concentration on her.

'The situation has changed—'

'Has it?' Star let her head tip back, soft, full mouth in a slight considering pout. 'I don't think so. I just think you always want what you believe you shouldn't have. But leave me out of it. It'd cost you too much.'

'*How* much?'

'Your problem is that you can't think of cost except in terms of money,' Star sighed without surprise, knowing that he would definitely run a mile if he suspected that further intimacy might well persuade her to stick like glue to him and refuse a divorce for as long as she could.

Luc dragged in a roughened breath.

'And anyway,' Star purred, like a little cat flexing her claws as she sent him a sidewise languishing glance, 'I'm not tall *or* blonde *or* sophisticated. So we can't possibly have a problem, can we?'

Without the slightest warning, Luc bent down and hauled her slight figure all the way up into the strong circle of his arms. A startled gasp of disbelief was wrenched from Star. He welded her into every angle of his hard, masculine physique and crushed her soft mouth with savage hunger under his. He stole every scrap of air from her quivering body. Burning fire leapt up at the very heart of her, a sweet, desperate ache stirring to make her slender thighs tremble.

Luc lowered her very gently down onto the bed again. Before he left, he scanned her flushed and bemused face with slumbrous amusement. 'It's not a problem for me, *mon ange*.'

He was right; it was *her* problem, Star acknowledged in shaken honesty. He had shot her to the height of excitement so fast she was still reeling from the extent of her own weakness. She hadn't realised that her limited ability to resist Luc might be tested again. Only now did she see that in acceding with such apparent ease to Luc's request that she spend one last night with him she had given him entirely the wrong impression. About her, about her attitude to sex...

Indeed, the very *worst* impression that she could have given him now that they were pretending to be reconciled for Emilie's benefit! Star cringed, embarrassed and angry with herself when it was far too late to change anything. Luc assumed that what she had done with such seeming casualness *once* she would surely be eager to do again. And evidently Luc was more than willing to take advantage of any such eagerness on her part. Yet that reality left Star in even deeper shock. Luc was *finally* awarding her adult status, but only in the most basic field a woman could qualify in.

But their marriage was over, and she didn't believe in casual sex. The night before, she had genuinely been saying goodbye to Luc and her love for him. But a male as unemotional as Luc couldn't possibly understand such reasoning. He had simply noted that his soon-to-be-ex-wife had demonstrated little reluctance to jump into bed with him again. In fact they might never have got beyond the kitchen had it been left up to her. So why didn't she just face the ugly truth head-on? Luc now thought she was not much better than a tart...

Didn't say much for *his* morals, did it? Naively, she would have believed that Luc would be too fastidious to want a woman who might make herself so freely available to men. Just showed how much she knew about his sex! Just showed how much she knew about the man she had married! Suddenly, Star was in a white-hot rage with Luc, and very, very grateful that they would be getting a divorce...

As the limousine travelled down the thickly wooded approach road to Chateau Fontaine, Mars finally fell asleep again.

Star could have wept at her son's sense of timing. Mars

had cried from the minute he was rudely removed from his cosy cot on board the Sarrazin jet. He had wailed like a howl alarm all the way through Nantes Atlantique airport. Working himself up into a state of inconsolable misery, he had kept his mother far too busy to worry about anything else.

But now, when she finally had the peace to consider the timing of the trip which she and the twins had been forced to make, her resentment overflowed. 'Mars will probably be crying half the night.'

Luc elevated a winged brow, a perceptible air of self-satisfaction in his level dark gaze. 'I doubt it. I have an extremely competent nanny awaiting the children at the chateau.'

Star's jaw dropped.

'I should have asked Bertille to meet us at the airport—then we might all have enjoyed a more relaxing trip.'

Star's jaw would have hit the floor had it had not been securely attached to other bones. 'I don't believe I'm hearing this. *You*—'

Luc frowned. 'What's wrong?'

'What's *wrong*?' Star gasped incredulously. 'You organise a nanny, over the top of my head...then you suggest that *she* could've managed my son better than I have!'

Registering his error as the limo filtered to a halt in front of the chateau, Luc shifted a fluid hand, intended to soothe Star. 'You misunderstood me—'

'Did I heck!' Star shot back at him fiercely. '*You're* the one responsible for my son's distress—'

'If you don't keep your voice down, you're likely to wake him up again,' Luc countered in icy warning just as the passenger door beside Star swung open with a thick, expensive clunk.

'Who was it who *insisted* on travelling with two babies until this hour of the night?' Star demanded. 'Of course Mars has been upset. All he wants is to be home in his *own* snug little cot—'

'In a building which should be condemned, "snug" is scarcely the most apt word! Your so-called *home* is unfit for human habitation!'

Pained condemnation filled her disconcerted gaze. 'I didn't notice you being half so fussy last night!'

As she spoke, Luc noticed the passenger door standing wide. He frowned like a male emerging from a dream, his lean, dark devastating features setting into unyielding lines. The chauffeur was nowhere to be seen, presumably having decided that desertion of his duties was more tactful than hovering to listen to the happily reunited couple having a thunderous row.

His brilliant eyes glimmered like a banked-up fire ready to flame. 'I suggest we drop the subject. There's no reason for this dispute. It is irrational—'

'Irrational? You insulted me. You, who can't even hold a baby for five seconds without panicking, *dared* to deride my maternal abilities,' Star enumerated shakily as she tugged Venus out of her car seat. 'You insulted me, my home, my hospitality. Yet it was your arrogant refusal to rearrange your schedule, your stupendous ignorance of childcare, your absolute conviction that everybody has to jump to do exactly what you want when you want which was at fault.'

'If you don't keep quiet, I will treat you like a child having a temper tantrum, because that is how you are behaving,' Luc condemned with freezing restraint.

'How difficult it must be to deal with someone who has no respect for you, no fear of you and no dependence on your good will. Yes, I can see it must be a real challenge when someone like me dares to fight back. What are you doing with Mars?'

Emerging from the limo in a state of frozen fury, Luc pressed a shielding hand to the baby's back, where he was now carefully draped over Luc's shoulder still fast asleep. 'He's a sensitive child. He doesn't need to be swung about like a little sack of potatoes.'

Star's frown of surprise that he had lifted Mars faded at that point. Her attention was finally grabbed and held by the sheer vast magnificence of the building before them. The Chateau Fontaine was illuminated by what appeared to be around a hundred lights, both outside and inside. On her last visit, Star absently recalled how Emilie had strictly warned her not to leave on any unnecessary lights as her guardian paid close attention to all matters which related to household expenditure.

'Of course, Emilie would never have said it, wouldn't even *think* such a disrespectful thing about any member of your illustrious family,' Star found herself musing out loud.

'What are you talking about?' Luc demanded as they crossed the superb arched seventeenth-century bridge that led to the huge and imposing front door.

'Your father was as rich as Croesus, but he was as tight with his wealth as any miser,' Star reflected. 'That's so sad. His only real enjoyment in life seemed to be saving money.'

It was perfectly true, but it had never, ever been said to Luc's face before.

'I suppose he'd have been apoplectic if he'd ever seen all these lights blazing…' Star drifted into the chateau without a backward glance.

Bertille, the nanny, was young and warm and wonderfully appreciative of the twins. Only the meanest and most possessive of mothers could have objected to her assistance, Star conceded ruefully. A bedroom on the first floor had been rearranged as a nursery, and neither Venus nor Mars wakened again as they were settled into comfortable cots. As Bertille was to sleep in the adjoining dressing room, Star said goodnight and wandered back out into the corridor.

It was after midnight, and she was embarrassed to find the housekeeper had been patiently waiting for her to reappear. Self-conscious with such personal attention and the assurance that her humble wardrobe of clothing had already been unpacked for her, Star stiffened uneasily every time she was addressed as a married woman. Even so, it was quite a shock when the older woman opened the door of Luc's bedroom and stood back, leaving Star little choice but to enter.

For the duration of their six-week long marriage, Luc had left her in a bedroom at the foot of the corridor. It had not occurred to Star that anything might be different this time around, but then she really hadn't had time to consider the ramifications of returning to the chateau as Luc's acknowledged wife. One of the bedrooms *next* to his, she decided, would be the most suitable choice.

However, sooner than be seen walking straight back out again, Star lingered. The vast and magnificent room was centred on the superb gilded four-poster bed which sat on a shallow dais. Luc had slept in that incredible bed since he was eight years old. And so might a medieval merchant prince have lived, with glorious brocade drapes, fabulous paintings and the very finest antique furniture.

'Luc was never like other children,' Emilie had once confided. 'He was a very serious little boy.'

But what else could he have been? An only child, born to parents who had inhabited different wings of the chateau and led entirely separate lives.

Lilliane Sarrazin had died in a car crash shortly after Star had met her. Reading between the lines of Emilie's uncritical description, Luc's mother had been as committed to extravagance as her husband had been to saving, but had shared his essentially cold nature. Was it any wonder that Luc, with every natural instinct stifled in childhood, should be so reserved, so controlled, so inhibited at showing either affection or warmth?

And yet Star could remember times when Luc had broken through his own barriers for *her* benefit. He had comforted her when she was nine years old and missing her mother. He had done so again—fatally—when she was eighteen and a half...

Star's memories slowly slid back over eighteen months to

her last stay at Chateau Fontaine. Emilie, who could not bear to think badly of anybody, had worked hard to give Star the impression that Luc's terminally ill father was really a caring man, whom she had misjudged at their only previous encounter. It had not been the wisest idea.

Shortly after her arrival with Emilie, Star had been summoned to her guardian's sick room for a private meeting.

'You've done very well out of this family.' Roland Sarrazin regarded her with sour disapproval.

'I really appreciate everything that you've done for me—'

'Just be grateful that Luc took pity on you,' the older man urged. 'I had no intention of accepting you as my ward when I sent Luc to Mexico. But when he met your mother she was so drunk she could barely stand. Decency demanded that I do my duty by you.'

Devastated by that cruel, demeaning candour, Star spoke up in an angry defensive rush. 'My mother was really dreading giving me up that day. She was terribly upset...it *wasn't* normal for her to be like that!'

'Your stepfather was a weak, pathetic wastrel. You have no idea who your father is and your mother *is* a drunk,' Roland Sarrazin repeated with crushing distaste and contempt. 'With a sordid, shameful background of that kind, how *dare* you raise your voice to me?'

Humiliated and distressed by that counter-attack, Star fled. She ran into the woods that surrounded the chateau to find the privacy to cry. Nine years earlier, Luc had taken her down to the riverbank there to tell her about Emilie and stress how very lonely and sad Emilie had been since losing her husband. Indeed, so successful had he been at impressing Star with those facts that she had been a lot older before she'd appreciated what a huge debt she owed to the older woman.

And, nine years later, somehow Luc knew exactly where to find Star that evening. An hour earlier she had watched his helicopter flying in, had known that soon she would be missed, but she hadn't been able to face the prospect of sitting down to dinner with Luc and Emilie and whoever else might be staying in the vast house.

A Ferrari pulled up on the estate road that ran to within yards of the river. Fresh from a day of high-powered wheeling and dealing at the Sarrazin bank in Paris, Luc climbed out, his appearance one of effortless elegance and supreme sophistication in a beautifully cut charcoal-grey suit.

Nothing could have prepared Star for that first emotional meeting with Luc Sarrazin that winter. Luc, with the remote air of self-containment which surrounded him like an untouchable aura. As he moved with fluid grace towards her, arrows of pale sunlight broke through the overhanging canopy of trees to illuminate his stunning dark deep-set eyes. For Star, it was like being struck by lightning.

He looked so extravagantly gorgeous that he simply took her breath away.

'My father is very ill,' Luc drawled tautly. 'Confined to the sick room as he now is, his temper has suffered. Unfortunately, he tends to lash out at those least able to defend themselves. I must offer you my apologies—'

'Your father despises me...he thinks I'm the lowest of the low!'

'That is not true,' Luc countered with impressive conviction.

And Star sensed how very much Luc wanted her to accept that unlikely assurance and, even more crucially, how *very* difficult he found it to set aside his forbidding reserve and attempt to both explain and apologise for the episode in as few words as possible.

'My mother is *not* a drunk!' Star protested in driven continuance as she moved closer in open and desperate appeal for his agreement. 'And my stepfather may have been a gambler but he was a lovely, lovely man!'

Luc studied her with a tension he could not conceal. 'You touch my conscience. Had I been less frank with my father when I brought you back from Mexico, you might not have been deprived of your mother for so long.'

'No, that wasn't your fault. You didn't know her; of course you got the wrong idea... But that was the *one and only* time I ever saw her drink like that...' Star sobbed as her turbulent emotions overcame her again.

Luc reached out and put his arms round her, very, very slowly, like a newly blind man needing to feel his way with care and caution. There was still a good foot of clear space between them. Star swiftly closed that space. He was as rigid at that physical contact as a living, breathing rock.

'I think it's time you had the opportunity to get to know your mother again,' Luc murmured.

Gently peeling her from him, Luc opened up the space again, but lost his ascendancy as Star flung herself back close and gazed up at him with wondering eyes of hope. 'You actually *know* where Juno is?'

'I do.'

'But how can you?'

'You're eighteen. Strictly speaking, you're no longer my father's ward. If you want to see your mother, I will arrange it.'

'You really mean it?'

'I don't make promises I can't keep.'

And that was the moment when Star fell head over heels in love with Luc Sarrazin. The moment when she pictured how her infinitely less inhibited nature might magically mingle in a perfect match with his. The moment when Luc Sarrazin, temptingly packaged with the hidden vulnerability of his utterly miserable, loveless childhood, became nothing short of an overwhelming obsession for Star.

She only saw Luc being incredibly kind and considerate of her needs. She didn't know that it was imperative Luc ensured that she forgave his father's behaviour and stayed on at the chateau. Why? Roland Sarrazin enjoyed Emilie's restful companionship. Had Star insisted on returning to London,

Luc wasn't convinced that he could depend on family loyalty to keep Emilie in France.

As a door closed softly shut behind her, Star was shot back to the present. She was bemused to find herself still standing in Luc's huge bedroom where, on the night of the twins' conception, she had crept round removing lightbulbs from the lamps to create a more intimate atmosphere. The memory made her cringe.

'I thought you would've been in bed by now,' Luc drawled with the most staggering lack of expression. He said it lightly, casually, as if they had been sharing a bedroom for years.

Star spun round. Her brow furrowed, her eyes bewildered as she ran that sentence back through her brain. 'You think I'm going to sleep in here...with *you*?'

A very faint smile tugged at the edges of Luc's wide, sensual mouth. 'Why so shocked?'

CHAPTER FIVE

STAR gaped at Luc, aquamarine eyes at their widest. She could not credit that he could actually expect her to share a bedroom with him.

'No more drama, *please...*' Luc urged with soft, silken derision as he loosened his well-cut jacket and shrugged out of it to stroll in the direction of the dressing room.

'We'd both be very uncomfortable in the same room!' Star folded her arms together in a jerky movement. 'I'll use one of the rooms next door—'

'*J'insiste,*' Luc responded very, very quietly.

The sheer appalling arrogance of that assurance that he would not take no for an answer shook Star. 'It's quite unnecessary for us to—'

Brilliant dark eyes cool as ice, Luc swung back from about thirty feet away and moved back towards her at a leisurely pace that was oddly intimidating. '*Ecoutes-moi...*listen to me,' he commanded with natural authority. 'As I will not be here very often this summer, the very least we can do in support of this charade is occupy the same room. When it is time to demonstrate waning enthusiasm for that intimacy, you can move out, but *not* before that point.'

'Emilie would never dream of enquiring into our sleeping arrangements!' Star argued.

'But she will certainly notice them. I am not a demonstrative man. I am no actor,' Luc disclaimed with growing impatience. 'That we sleep in the same bed is likely to be the *sole* evidence she sees of our supposed reconciliation!'

Star's chin came up. 'I'd rather settle for you bringing flowers home on Friday evenings. Surely even you could manage that!'

Luc sent her a gleaming glance. 'The flowers are your department. I got a dozen red roses every day of the six weeks we were together. They were delivered to the very door of my office with cute little handwritten cards attached. My staff took extraordinary steps to get the chance to read those cards before I did. Surely you don't think I could have forgotten that experience?'

A crimson blush now flamed over Star's taut cheekbones.

'Should you be thinking of repeating that romantic gesture, do you think it would be possible for you to put the cards into sealed envelopes?'

Fury and intense mortification were licking like flames through Star's slender length. 'Don't worry about it...I'll never ever send you flowers again!'

'And while we're on the subject, you're not getting my mobile phone number until you assure me that it will only be used in an emergency.'

'I've grown out of any desire to keep hourly tabs on your whereabouts!' Star bit out between gritted teeth, eager to escape the dialogue and turning away. 'Well, if I'm going to be stuck in here with you, I'm sleeping on the sofa.'

Luc surveyed the gilded sofa which had been in the family since the late eighteenth century. He said nothing. He knew a marble slab would have offered as much comfort.

Star stalked into the dressing room and rattled and banged through loads of drawers and closets before she found her own small stock of clothing. Gathering up nightwear, she headed for the bathroom. Stripping off her clothes with trembling hands of angry frustration, she switched on the shower. She yelped as enervating jets of water hit her tense body from all directions. Her hair soaked, she threw herself down on the seat in the corner. It was typical of Luc to have a shower with more confusing controls than a rocket ship!

She pictured him as she had last seen him in the bedroom. Tailored silk shirt partially unbuttoned to show a riveting triangle of golden brown skin, taut, flat stomach, lean hips

and long hard thighs encased in charcoal-grey trousers cut to
enhance every lithe masculine line of his tightly muscled
length. A treacherous burst of warmth low in her belly made
her tense up even more. She clenched her teeth, hating herself
for being so weak. She'd stood there arguing with him and
burning for him at the same time. It was sick, indecent.

But Luc had always made her feel like that. Everything
about him pulled at her senses, awakening the most tormenting hunger. His dark, deep voice, his husky accent, his
beautiful eyes, his sexy mouth. She listened, she looked, she
went weak at the knees with lust. *Lust.* She latched onto that
word with intense relief. It definitely wasn't love any more;
it was lust. A greedy, mindless, wicked craving which she
had to control, stamp on, stamp *out*!

No longer did she crave that rare smile, that devastating
little glimmer of gold in his eyes when he was amused, the
sense of achievement she had once enjoyed when he laughed.
No, she didn't, she absolutely didn't, she told herself with
ferocious urgency. Which was just as well, she reminded herself. Luc might not have been exactly delighted to believe
that the twins had been fathered by some other man, but he
was likely to be even less happy when she told him the truth.
It was going to be a very long and miserable summer, and
tomorrow, when she informed Luc that he was a father,
promised to be the very worst day of her life...

Star emerged from the bathroom and stopped dead, heart
hammering so hard against her breastbone she felt faint, like
someone in the grip of a severe anxiety attack. And no wonder! Luc had evidently made use of some other bathroom.
Black hair still damp and gleaming, he was in the act of
shedding a short silk robe. From across the room, Star
watched the collar dipping, the light fabric drifting down to
expose what had to be the most beautiful male back in the
world. Smooth brown skin stretched taut over well-honed
muscles. She shut her eyes tight in shame, denying herself

any more of a view. Averting her head, she scuttled over to the bed to haul the spread from it.

'Goodnight,' she said in a tight little voice.

Luc climbed into bed, tossed back the duvet and threw himself back against the pillows. Star was wearing an over-size T-shirt with a large yellow duck motif back and front. It wasn't remotely seductive. But his body seemed to think otherwise and reacted with unquenchable enthusiasm. Star bent down to arrange the spread on the sofa, revealing slender legs to the top of her thighs, the cotton jersey of the T-shirt stretching with provocative fidelity over the shapely curve of her bottom...

His breath escaped in a soft hiss of reaction, the ache of frustration becoming so powerful he clenched his long fingers. The anger still pent-up inside him began to smoulder again. She was playing the tease deliberately. Star was no longer the adoring little virgin he had, with commendable adult restraint, contrived *not* to touch for the first six weeks of their marriage.

'A little schoolgirl...' Gabrielle had composed her perfect face into a pained grimace. 'Men who prey on schoolgirls are *sick*, aren't they? But Star does ask for it. Those big soppy puppy eyes of hers follow you about like you're a god or something. How can you stand it?'

Surprisingly easily.

Snatched from that unwelcome recollection by the enervating sight of Star raising her arms high to comb her fingers through her wet hair, Luc went rigid. The T-shirt pulled taut over small breasts as firm and round as apples. Not free to him *ever* again, Star had said. Smugly. The rage he had been keeping a lid on for two and a half days surged higher still. She was on the market and he would buy. Why not? He would get her skinny, shameless little hide out of his system. Long before the summer was over, he would be sated. No woman had ever held him beyond a couple of months...and one in a duck T-shirt had less hope than most.

Star could feel the silence buzzing around her like an electric storm. Goosebumps came out on her arms as she got into the makeshift bed, wishing Luc would switch out the lights. Then she could lie in the dark, hating herself without an audience. The dulled ache low in her stomach and the painful tightness of her sensitive breasts were a source of utter misery to her. She didn't trust herself to look back near him again, lest the craving get stoked to a level that he might notice. He noticed most things, did Luc. He missed nothing. He read her like a book when she could least afford to be read.

'*D'accord*...OK, now that you've given me the benefit of seeing what's on offer from every conceivable angle, I want the T-shirt off. And forget the sofa. I want you in this bed for the rest of the night,' Luc spelt out with crystal-clear clarity.

Totally disbelieving the evidence of her own ears, Star very slowly picked her head up and attempted to focus on Luc across the depth of the room. 'S-sorry?' she stammered helplessly.

Luc hauled himself off the pillows with one powerful hand. 'Don't you dare play games with me,' he warned in low-pitched but forceful continuance. 'I'm not in the mood for what you fondly imagine figures as verbal foreplay!'

Star sat up with a jerk, clutching the bedspread to herself. The pool of light round the vast bed illuminated the hard cast of his stunning dark features, the perceptible tension in the knotted muscles of his wide brown shoulders. The sheet was at his waist, startlingly white against his magnificent torso. He looked startlingly handsome and startlingly intimidating. Angry too. About what? She could feel that anger. Why was he so angry? What had she done?

'You seem to have the idea that I've been angling for some sort of approach,' Star breathed with hot cheeks, her annoyance with him somewhat tempered by the fear that she had somehow been putting out sexually inviting vibes as easily read as placards. 'But I honestly haven't been…at least, *not* knowingly.'

'You are as hungry for me as I am for you, *mon ange*,' Luc breathed in impatient interruption.

Star tore her dismayed eyes from his challenging scrutiny. 'You're very up-front about this sort of stuff, aren't you? Can I use an analogy here? If I ate as much chocolate as I'd like to, I wouldn't fit my clothes, so I control myself. Wanting to rip your clothes off all the time…well, it's much the same thing.'

'*Mon Dieu*…God give me strength,' Luc growled half under his breath.

'It *is*, whether you can see it or not,' Star persisted, pleating the spread between her restive, taut fingers and not looking at him lest she lose the thread of what she was trying to say. 'Last night we should just *leave* in the past—'

Luc groaned out loud.

'You're like too much chocolate, you're bad for me, and I really don't want to be tempted to do what's bad for me…and bad for *you* too.'

Luc sprang out of bed. As he crossed the room, Star kept her head down and talked faster than ever. 'Now I could be really angry with you for phrasing your invitation to join you the way you did…but I'm making allowance for the fact that maybe you're annoyed with me for still seeming attractive to you. And maybe you're tired and just not used to having to *ask* with all these women throwing themselves at you…*what are you doing?*' she squealed in disconcertion.

Luc clamped his hands to her waist and lifted her off the sofa to hold her in mid-air. 'I am not bad for you. I am probably the sanest man you ever shared a bedroom with. Whether I'll still be sane at the end of the summer is anybody's guess. Think of me as a chocoholic, wholly at the mercy of ungovernable greed. Be compassionate,' he urged thickly.

Star remembered wanting him on his knees with lust for

her. Her own feet were dangling a good foot and a half off
the floor. He wasn't quite begging but he was certainly on
the road to very, very keen. And there was something in
those stunning dark frustrated eyes that just filled her to overflowing with sympathy and longing and...?

As he interpreted the dreamy look in her aquamarine eyes
with the instant recognition of a male who had once seen no
other expression but that in her gaze, a blazing smile of satisfaction flashed across his lean strong face. Her heart literally tilted on its axis.

'Indulge yourself with me, *mon ange*,' Luc invited in a
husky tone that made every nerve-ending in her treacherous
body sit up and sing.

Common sense made a mighty and praiseworthy attempt
to be heard inside her head. 'I can't...I *mustn't*!'

Luc laid her down on the bed with the sort of achingly
tender care she had not experienced since his accidental con-
summation of their marriage. The thoughts in her head started
seeming detached from reality.

Luc gazed down at her with glittering dark eyes of hunger
and then stilled, a more grave expression forming on his
darkly handsome features. 'Obviously I will look after you
and the twins for as long as you need me to do so.'

'Look after me?' Reality was retreating so fast for Star
that nothing short of a lightning strike was likely to bring it
back. She was trembling, her pulses racing. The gloriously
familiar scent of him was washing over her. After the emotional devastation which had followed their lovemaking the
night before, there was now a sharper, needier, more desperate edge inside her; she had given him up and now he was
back. She couldn't help but be caught up in a sense of how
precious that was.

'*Naturellement*...I also believe that I can find you a house
to live in here in France,' Luc mused with growling sensual
huskiness, a whisper's breadth from her parted lips.

Her braincells surged together on the belief that something

enormously important was being said. Was he teasing her?
A house in France? My goodness, how stupid she was being!
Was he…could he be asking her to stay on at Chateau
Fontaine? What *else* could he be doing? A tide of pure joy
roared up through Star and left her feeling totally intoxicated.
Her fingers slid into his luxuriant black hair and curved down
to his magnificent cheekbones.

'House here in France?' she echoed like an obedient child,
eager to encourage further revelations but scared of the big
prize being withdrawn if she seemed too pushy or greedy or
impatient.

'You'd like that…' Luc gathered, lowering his proud dark
head to sensually taste her full lips.

Liked that, liked *everything*! The hunger he expressed with
one kiss sent heat hurtling through her at storm-force po-
tency. She kissed him back with all her heart and soul and
let her palms rove with wondering delight over his powerful
shoulders. Mine, mine, *mine*, she wanted to yell to the roof-
tops, but she also wanted to live out every fantasy of eighteen
months away from him.

She pushed at his shoulders with as much force as she
could muster, grateful enthusiasm leaping through her. She
wanted to show him just how much she could learn if he
would only give her the opportunity and the time to pick up
more experience. Then he would never, ever think that he
needed a mistress like Gabrielle Joly in his life again.

Luc fell back against the pillows, a slight hint of disconcertion in his intent dark gaze. 'What's wrong?'

'Nothing…absolutely nothing!' Star was just a little shy
now, on the spot, as it were, with all those lights on while
being aware that Luc was very much a sophisticate. She was
absolutely terrified of doing something wrong and spoiling
the moment. After all, sex had to be of crucial importance to
Luc if just one night with her could persuade him to ask her
to forget that theirs was supposed to be a fake reconciliation
and make it a real one instead.

'Star...?' Luc curved a hand to her downbent head. 'I want you to be happy. I want to *make* you happy—'

'Oh...you're making me s-super-happy, because I—' Just adore you. She swallowed it back hastily, not wishing to show herself too keen too fast. Goodness knows, that hadn't got her very far before. Luc needed to believe that he had to make an effort to get those kind of results.

'You *need* someone like me.' Letting his fingers lace into her hair, Luc claimed a devouring kiss that left her quivering.

Intent on ensuring that he needed *her* even more, Star let an uncertain hand slide down over his taut stomach, fascinated by the way his muscles suddenly clenched and his equally sudden exhalation. She shifted position and bent her head, and let the tip of her tongue trace the intriguing little furrow of hair that ran down over his stomach and disappeared beneath the sheet. He jerked with satisfying responsiveness. Damp answering warmth surged at the very heart of her.

'*Later*...' His eyes blazing gold with desire, he tugged her up to him again, a ragged edge to his dark drawl. 'But now there's a couple of conditions to this arrangement that I need to be sure you understand and accept.'

Arrangement? In the act of drifting down to meet that wide sensual mouth like a programmed doll, Star found herself unexpectedly stayed by Luc's hands on her arms. 'Conditions?'

'I expect total fidelity from you for the duration.'

Her lashes fluttered over bewildered eyes. She was really fighting to concentrate now, because Luc was wearing that deadly serious look which always intimidated her into listening.

'Duration?' she repeated dutifully, rather like someone knowing only about five words of a foreign language but working hard to follow and comprehend.

'Inevitably this attraction will burn out.'

As Star stiffened, Luc locked both arms round her, brilliant megawatt eyes intent on her now troubled face. 'On the other hand, it could last for *ages*,' he extended, quick as a flash. 'But the other little condition I need to mention is that you'll have to be more discreet as my lover than you were as my wife. Emilie must *not* know.'

Star worked out the significance of that assurance very, very slowly, because her brain was functioning very, very slowly. And when it came to working out something that crucial to her life and her happiness, and she saw with stricken insight that nothing but sheer pain and disappointment awaited her, she didn't want to *think* any more.

But comprehension still marched on at supersonic speed. She had picked Luc up wrong. And wasn't that huge misapprehension as to his meaning entirely self-inflicted? She had been pathetically eager to believe that Luc was willing to give their marriage a real chance. But he had no intention of doing that. He *still* wanted a divorce.

Yet, in spite of that, he could ask her to stay on in France as his lover. *Lover?* A euphemism. Without love, she would just be his sexual partner, his mistress. Did he really think that she was that desperate to hold onto him? Enormous hurt enfolded Star like a blanket, chilling her overheated body to ice.

'Let go of me...' she said unsteadily.

'Yes...switch off that blasted phone of yours!' Luc agreed in exasperation, and willingly released her.

'Phone?' Star blinked, and only then did she hear the irritating buzz. She peered blankly at her bag, which was lying in a heap where she had left it earlier.

'I'll do it!' Luc offered.

'No...*no*!' Suddenly Star was flying off the bed and running to answer that phone as if her life depended on it.

In a sense it *did*. As the pain of renewed rejection settled on her, she just wanted to run and run from Luc. She snatched the mobile phone from her bag. Rory's voice greeted her. The tears came in reaction then, great, unstoppable rivulets pouring down her quivering cheeks. 'Rory...oh Rory!' she sobbed, and raced for the bedroom door to take the call in private.

CHAPTER SIX

STAR paced the floor of the giant front hall at Chateau Fontaine. 'I've got to be honest, Rory... I still care about Luc. I can't lie about that. All I've got to offer you is friendship, and you'd probably be better off without it while I'm feeling like this...'

'You're not short-changing me.' Rory's sigh carried down the phone line. 'You've never offered anything else; you've always held back.'

Still in the act of zipping up a pair of beige chinos, Luc reached the galleried landing above just as Star spoke again.

'I'm so grateful you're still speaking to me...you know, after everything I've just told you. I really, really love you for that!' Star admitted with tears stinging her eyes again.

'You married a really smooth rat—'

'I know he's a rat, but maybe that was the attraction,' Star muttered. 'I imagined I saw all sorts of other things, but now I see how stupid I was, and that has to be for the best, hasn't it?'

This was not eavesdropping, Luc told himself. He was in his own home listening to his wife telling her boyfriend she loved him. *Loved* him. The way she had loved *him* once? He wanted to yank the phone out of her hand and smash it to bits. Star was *his* wife! Wheeling round in his tracks, Luc strode away again, suddenly knowing only one thing for sure. He had no desire to hear any more.

But the strangest sensation of cold had begun spreading through Luc. He didn't like it. It was as if a big black cloud was rising at the back of his mind. In the space of little more than twenty-four hours, Star had got under his skin to the extent that he felt he wasn't in control any more. He liked

88

that suspicion even less. But the inexplicable gap between what he was thinking and what he was actually doing could no longer be ignored. How else did he rationally explain asking Star to be his mistress? Where had that *insane* idea come from? Exactly when had a concept that far removed from reality crept into his subconscious mind?

It would be sheer madness. He wanted a divorce. He did not want to stay married to her. He didn't care if she loved another guy. He just wanted to kill the other guy…he just wanted to kill her. No, not her, *him*! That black cloud kept on rising; he couldn't concentrate. Perspiration beaded his skin. He clenched his fists in angry frustration. He didn't want to think. Suddenly, he understood that much. In the grip of the powerful nebulous feelings closing in on him, he felt alarmingly unstable. What he needed was a drink.

Star switched off the phone and sank down on one of the hall chairs. All she could think about was what an idiot she had been to imagine even briefly that Luc might want their marriage to continue. So he had asked her to be his mistress instead. Well, there was no prospect of her lowering herself to that level.

But then what other kind of offer could she have expected him to make? She *still* hadn't told Luc that he was the twins' father! Just when had she stopped remembering that? Why hadn't she paused to consider that letting Luc go on believing that Venus and Mars were another man's children was to fatally colour his view of her and change their relationship?

Oh, golly, gosh, what relationship? she asked herself painfully, her head in her hands as she sniffed. That winter, over eighteen months earlier, Luc had reunited her with Juno. Star and her mother had met first at Luc's Paris apartment. Afterwards, Luc had taken Star out to lunch. She hadn't realised then that there was already a woman in his life: Gabrielle Joly had been the ultimate in discretion.

'I think I fell in love with you the minute I saw you again,' she had announced over that lunch.

Luc dealt her an arrested glance.

'I didn't know anything could feel *this* intense,' she continued unsteadily. 'I suppose you're used to your looks knocking women flat, but what I notice most about you is how lonely you are—'

'I've never been lonely in my life,' Luc responded drily.

'I don't think you ever get close to anyone. I've been watching you. You freeze people out; you can't help yourself. Anything personal or emotional and you're really challenged to stay within a mile of the experience. Like now. You just want me to shut up and you want to escape without hurting my feelings,' she said guiltily. 'Well, thanks for listening to me. You can leave now if you like.'

He was trapped then for a little longer. She knew it, and had planned it that way, but her conscience twinged as she watched his long, beautifully shaped fingers close very tautly round his wine glass.

'You're just a child,' he began.

'No, I'm not a child. I seem like a child to you because I say things out loud that you wouldn't scream under the worst torture. I'm sorry, but this is the only way I had of getting through to you. You quite like being with me,' she pointed out shyly. 'Haven't you noticed that? And I notice you look at me, and then look away like you shouldn't be looking, and—'

'*Bon! Ca suffit maintenant.*' Rising from his seat, Luc glowered down at her from his impressive height. 'If you're not embarrassed for yourself, I am.'

'I know. But when you love someone as much as I love you—'

'You don't know what love is at your age,' he drawled with sudden lethal derision.

'I know more than you do. I don't think you've ever been in love in your whole life,' Star protested. 'Love's messy, and you're not. Love would make demands you wouldn't like and wouldn't want to spare the time for—'

Taking her by the arm when she knew that what he was really desperate to do was gag her into silence, Luc dragged her out of the exclusive restaurant, seemingly blind to the fascinated stares his unusual behaviour was attracting.

Out on the pavement, she whispered, 'I'm not expecting you to love me back, but doesn't it give you a warm feeling to know that someone loves you?'

Brilliant dark eyes hooded, Luc thrust her into the back seat of his limo. 'All that you're suffering from is adolescent hormones—'

'No, even if I could never, ever sleep with you, I would still *care* about you!' Star argued vehemently.

Luc studied her with even more glacial cool. Star got redder and redder, and eventually dropped her head. 'I'm sorry.' She hesitated, and then rushed on, 'Are you going to avoid me now? I couldn't *bear* that!'

'Of course I will not avoid you,' Luc rebutted in exasperation. 'But nor will we discuss this subject again. Is that understood?'

That same week, Luc had taken Emilie and Star to a dinner party held by some friends of his. Gabrielle Joly had been a guest as well, seated close to Luc and regularly engaging him in conversation. Gabrielle, with her endless legs, gorgeous blonde hair, exquisite face and svelte sophistication. Star felt so sick at the sight of what she feared might be the competition that she just couldn't eat.

'Tell me what you know about that Gabrielle woman,' Star urged Emilie later that evening.

Emilie reddened almost guiltily. 'I believe she was once a fashion model.' The older woman hesitated. 'I know no other way of putting this, Star...Gabrielle is Luc's mistress, and has been for quite some time.'

'His...*mistress*?' The bottom fell right out of Star's world.

'Don't look so horrified, Star. Frenchmen have always made convenient arrangements of that nature. Luc will never ask his mistress to play hostess at the chateau, but he'll socialise freely with her everywhere else. Gabrielle would've been invited for his benefit this evening. She uses a house just a few miles from here.'

Pale as death, hearing the hollow note in Emilie's recitation, Star produced a ragged laugh. 'I wish you'd mentioned her existence sooner, Emilie.'

'I didn't want to put you off Luc,' Emilie admitted ruefully. 'Whether he realises it or not, he's already very much attracted to you. Your warmth draws him like a magnet. When he walks into a room, you're the first person he looks for, and if you're not there he can't settle until he knows where you are.'

'But he already has *her*—'

'Oh, well, if you can't accept that a man of almost thirty comes with some worldly experience, you'd be wise to give up on him. And that would be a shame. We all need to be loved. If he doesn't meet the right girl soon, the kind of girl who's not afraid to fight through those barriers of his, he's likely to end up as unhappy as his poor father is now.'

Was it any wonder that with such constant eager encouragement Star continued to love Luc to distraction? And Emilie might have known how Star felt about Luc, but Star didn't confide in her mother, who was by then renting an apartment in Nantes. Determined to have nothing to do with the Sarrazins, Juno refused to visit Star at the chateau. For her daughter to love Luc Sarrazin would have seemed the ultimate disloyalty. So Star kept quiet.

But then fate took a hand: Roland Sarrazin had a heart attack and was rushed into hospital with Emilie by his side. In all the fuss, Star forgot that she should have visited her mother that day. That evening, Luc returned from the hospital, looking exhausted. Star rushed to offer sympathy.

'Do you want to talk about how you feel?' she asked.

'No.'

'Do you want me to talk about something else?'

'No.'

Luc nodded grim agreement.

'But you *can't* want to be on your own!' Closing her hand over his sleeve to prevent him from moving away, as he always did when she got too close, Star looked up at him with pleading eyes. 'Isn't there *anything* I can do to make you feel better?'

Glittering dark eyes gazed down into hers. *'Go—'*

'Luc, *please—'*

And then he just grabbed her, literally grabbed her up into his arms and brought his mouth down hot and hard and hungry on hers. The shock of that sudden onslaught knocked Star sideways, but his explosive passion blazed up through her like a bush fire. She couldn't get enough of him and clung like superglue. When Juno was shown into Luc's library by the housekeeper, Star was welded to every available inch of Luc in enraptured surrender.

There was the most awful scene, with her mother hurling all sorts of ridiculous accusations and threatening to go to the newspapers. After Juno stormed out again, Luc, who had uttered not a single word in his own defence, turned to Star, where she was cringing with shamefaced guilt. 'We'll have to move fast to spike your mother's guns.'

'She didn't *mean* those things she said!'

'She's very bitter, and right now my father's peace of mind is of paramount importance. A sordid scandal would destroy him. Since I invited this situation, I must ensure that there are no repercussions,' Luc drawled flatly, no emotion of any kind showing in his lean strong face. 'The only way I can do that is to marry you as quickly as possible. Your mother can get no immoral mileage out of that development.'

'M-marry me? You're asking—?'

'Not a *real* marriage,' Luc emphasised drily. 'When the need for a cover story is past, we'll get an annulment. So don't get excited, *mon ange*. Nothing has changed.'

Star clasped her trembling hands together. 'Do I get a wedding ring?'

Luc gave a grudging nod.

'A dress?'

'No.'

'What's wrong with me *pretending* it's a proper wedding?'

'Your imagination doesn't need encouragement.'

They married in a civil ceremony in Nantes, attended only by Emilie and Luc's lawyer. It was not a secret marriage, but neither was it publicised, and, with Roland Sarrazin so ill, people might have questioned their timing, but not the quietness of the ceremony.

Her father-in-law asked to see her after the wedding he had been too weak to attend.

'I would not dream of questioning Luc's choice of bride,' the older man sighed, surprising Star with that assurance while simultaneously appraising her with a morose dissatisfaction that ensured she would not get a swollen head. 'I hope I know better than to interfere in my son's private life.'

Before Star's thoughts could stray on to the devastating disillusioning reality of having been abandoned on her wedding night for another woman, the cold marble beneath her bare feet became uncomfortable enough to dredge her out of her memories. But she still found herself recalling when, later, a minor car smash had put Luc into Casualty with concussion and sent her running panic-stricken to his side. Flatly refusing to be hospitalised overnight, Luc had come home with her. She had just adored fussing round him, insisting he go to bed and getting her crystals out, determined to heal his headache away.

Now she shied away from the recollection of how appallingly immature she had been just eighteen months earlier, and stood up in sudden decision. It might be the middle of the night, but it was time she came clean with Luc about their children at least. Maintaining that fiction was unfair to him.

But when Star returned to the bedroom, Luc was nowhere to be seen. Too worked up now to settle again, Star pulled on jeans and a top and went off to find him. Her troubled reflections marched on. How did she stop craving what Luc could never give? A man couldn't be forced into loving. So why did she keep on letting her emotions get the better of her? Why had she kidded herself that she was strong enough to spend one last night with Luc? That one night had plunged her back into emotional turmoil. That one night had convinced Luc that she would quite happily settle for sex if she could have him no other way. And Luc, ever the banker, was programmed to take advantage of the best deal he could get. Instead of crying like a drippy wimp, she should have lifted one of those giant ornate lamps in the bedroom and simply brained him with it!

Star had worked up quite a temper by the time she saw the light burning under the door of the library on the ground floor and walked in.

Luc was by the window, a brandy goblet clasped in one lean hand. His hair-roughened chest and his feet were bare, a dark green shirt hanging open over his well-cut chinos. Dressed so casually, and with his jawline darkened by stubble, he looked incredibly unfamiliar to her disconcerted appraisal.

'Go back to bed,' Luc advised flatly.

Even though he was standing in the shadows cast by the desk lamp, Star recognised his seething tension and came to a halt several feet away, scanning the fierce angularity of his dark golden features, the warning flash in his eyes before he veiled them and the rigidity of his broad shoulders.

'Just for once, do as I ask!' Luc raked with sudden unconcealed fury.

Startled into taking a backward step, Star studied him in honest bewilderment. 'What have *you* got to be so angry about? I certainly didn't ask for this situation with Emilie to develop.'

'My anger dates back a lot further than yesterday. There

was no ''situation'' until you decided that you were in love with me and refused to back off.'

Her natural colour receded under that surprise attack. 'But—'

'Before I married you, I saw only your youth and vulnerability. I didn't appreciate how far you would go to get what you want!' Eyes burnished gold with anger sought out and held hers. 'The first time you approached me I should have squashed you beyond all hope of recovery! But I was reluctant to hurt you. You *played* on that—'

'No…' Star made a tiny awkward movement of appeal with her hand. 'Not deliberately—'

'I thought you were sweet, essentially harmless…' A roughened laugh was wrenched from Luc. 'But from the minute you came into my life you've been as destructive as an enemy tank!'

Star was paralysed to the spot by the shattering effect of Luc casting aside his reserve and getting truly personal. The anger and bitterness he was revealing really shook her up.

'I'm drunk…' Luc breathed grimly, as if she had asked a question.

Luc drunk? That struck Star as so extraordinary she just gaped at him. He didn't look drunk, but he certainly wasn't behaving with his usual chilling self-command. He had compared her to an enemy tank. She tried to force a smile at that colourful image, but she couldn't. Shock went on spreading through her, and beneath it only guilt was rising in strength.

'A lot of men would have taken you up on your invitation that winter.' Shimmering dark eyes welded to her in unconcealed condemnation. 'You were very sexy. I was never unaware of your attraction. I was never indifferent, but I kept my distance.'

'Luc, I didn't kn—'

'I went against my father's wishes when I reunited you with your mother. And *how* was I rewarded?'

At that unwelcome question, Star's tummy just flipped.

'One lousy kiss and I end up having to get married,' Luc framed jaggedly, pale with sheer outrage at that recollection. 'But that wasn't the end of it, was it? You *still* wouldn't take no for an answer.'

'Please don't say any more, Luc...' Star urged in desperation. 'If I could go back and change things, I would, but I can't! I was obsessed with you...and I'm sorry...but I couldn't help that, nor could I see how selfish I was being.'

'You waited until I had a concussion,' Luc continued between gritted white teeth, his husky accent fracturing audibly. 'Then you slunk into bed with me when I was asleep. How *low* can a woman sink?'

Star studied the rug and watched it blur under her filling eyes. Seen through *his* eyes, framed in *his* words, her behaviour seemed even worse in retrospect. Yet after that night she had judged herself equally harshly. That was why she had left France. She hadn't run away; she had simply seen that the very least she could do was get out of Luc's life and leave him in peace.

Momentarily, she was tempted to mention the role which Gabrielle Joly had played in that final decision. But now that Gabrielle was gone from Luc's life Star was too proud and still too sensitive on that subject to admit how disillusioned and hurt she had been by the other woman's apparent hold on Luc. In those days, their marriage had been very much a fake, she reminded herself.

'And when I finally dared to tell you that no woman was going to trap me into a marriage I didn't want with sex, what did you do?' Luc's dark deep drawl had dropped to a seething whisper of what sounded like near uncontrollable rage.

'The only thing I could do. I went away,' she answered heavily.

At that response, Luc shuddered. 'You went away,' he echoed unsteadily. 'You did *not* just go away!'

In bewilderment, Star stared at him. 'What are you getting at?'

'You left me a letter telling me you couldn't *live* without me and vanished into thin air!' Luc shot at her in savage condemnation, devastating her with the force of his anger.

'What was wrong with that?'

'*What was wrong with that?*' Luc practically whispered his incredulity at that response, black fury emanating from him in blistering waves. 'I thought you'd gone off to drown yourself! I had the moat dragged…I put frogmen in the bloody lake!'

She regarded him as if he had taken leave of his wits.

'If you laugh…if you *laugh*…' Luc warned her thickly.

But Star was already picturing the extreme anxiety it would have taken to persuade Luc to embark on such a search. Her stomach turned over sickly. There was no risk of her being amused.

'Not once did it occur to you that I might be concerned for your welfare. Not once in all those months we were apart did you even phone to tell me that you were *all right*!' Swinging away from her, Luc sent the goblet in his hand flying into the fireplace, where it exploded noisily into crystal fragments.

Star studied those gleaming fragments in deep, deep shock. 'I…I didn't think—'

'You don't *ever*. You live every day like it's going to be your last. You don't look back, you don't look forward, you just do what you *feel* like. That's a luxury some of us have never known,' Luc stated glacially, his anger clearly spent.

Trembling in the face of all those sins he had piled up into a giant weight with which to crush her, Star was parchment-pale. Irresponsible, selfish, flighty. It seemed she had no re-deeming graces. She was guilty as hell, she conceded wretch-edly. She had thrown herself at him. She had also allowed him to marry her when she should have confronted her mother and at least tried to persuade her into withdrawing her unjust threats. During their brief time together after their marriage, she had refused to accept rejection. But, surprisingly, it appeared that in Luc's eyes her biggest sin had been vanishing and failing to contact him in all the months that had followed.

'You even persuaded Emilie to pretend that she didn't know where you were all that time,' Luc concluded grimly. 'Do you think I didn't realise that today? Emilie who might have been my mother, had my father had the courage to stand by her!'

Her utter confusion at that allusion made him release a weary laugh.

'You see nothing but what relates directly to you.' Luc shook his proud dark head in despair. 'Why do you think it was so important for Emilie to be there for my father when he was dying? Why do you think her presence was such a comfort? When they were young, they were in love. But my grandfather disapproved because Emilie was a poor relation. My father was afraid of losing out to his younger brother in the inheritance stakes and he gave Emilie up. She went on to make a happy marriage; *he* didn't.'

Listening to Luc spell out what she felt she should have sensed or worked out for herself made Star feel even worse. It was like the missing piece in a puzzle, which she had been too self-absorbed to recognise as a puzzle... Emilie's constant attendance on Roland Sarrazin that winter, her quiet, but undeniably deep grief when he finally passed away.

'Emilie felt sorry for him, desperately sorry for him, because he never stopped caring for her. After my mother died, my father would have married Emilie, but she turned him down.'

'You're right...' Star mumbled ruefully. 'I don't see anything that's not directly under my nose. I thought I was so perceptive too.'

'Go to bed...it's three in the morning.'

Star still hadn't told him about Venus and Mars. Now the prospect of making that announcement loomed over her like a death sentence. If he didn't hate her yet, he could only be a hair's breadth from doing so. She saw that in so many ways Luc had been amazingly tolerant of her behaviour. And she didn't think tolerance came naturally to him. Indeed, with his legendary reputation for cold rationality and ruthlessness, all of a sudden it was very hard to grasp *why* Luc had allowed one foolish teenager to cause him so much grief...

'Just one more thing...' Luc remarked flatly, breaking into her thoughts. 'What I said about buying a house here for you? It was a foolish impulse, and I apologise for making the suggestion.'

'Maybe you wanted revenge...' Star suddenly felt as if she had been smacked in the face with the ultimate of rejections. His apology was undeniably sincere. Evidently one good long look at the catastrophic results of having her in his life had cured Luc of the smallest desire to continue their relationship in any form. And she really didn't feel that she could blame him, which felt even worse.

'I don't think like that...'

Luc watched Star sidling backwards out of the room with a kind of blind look in her eyes and wondered why he didn't feel better. He wondered why he suddenly felt like the sort of male who was brutal to small children and animals. He wondered why, when it was natural for him to be extremely tough on those who surrounded him, being tough on Star had demanded the spur of eighteen months of pent-up rage finally breaking its boundaries. But sanity had reasserted its natural sway, he told himself in grim consolation, wincing as Star bashed one slight shoulder on the corner of the bookshelves before finally disappearing from view.

He was amazed that she hadn't shouted back at him. Strange how dissatisfying an experience that had proved. But then alcohol was a depressant; he had lost his temper and he loathed being out of control. Possibly he had been a little too tough on her. But revenge? Trust Star to come up with that angle! He was *above* that sort of nonsense.

Upstairs, Star collapsed down on the bedroom sofa without

even taking off her clothes. Her life seemed to stretch before her like a desert of grey desolation. Luc just about hated her and had no reason whatsoever to think well of her. Yet she did find herself questioning why Luc had held onto his anger for so long. Flattened by exhaustion, however, she slept for four hours, and woke up feeling unrefreshed.

Luc's bed was empty, untouched from the night before. It was seven. She headed straight into the bathroom, peeling off clothing as she went. After a frantically quick wash, she donned the black sand-washed silk hooded summer dress which her mother had given her for her birthday. It felt suitably funereal.

With the twins' birth certificates clutched in one nerveless hand, she went straight downstairs. Her steps getting slower and slower, she entered the imposing dining room. Luc was seated in aristocratic isolation at the far end of the polished table. He lowered his newspaper, revealing hooded eyes and a grim cast to his dark good-looks. Immaculate in a silver-grey suit worn with a silk shirt and a burgundy silk tie, he looked formidable, but he still stopped her susceptible heart clean dead in its tracks.

'I didn't expect to see you up this early,' he admitted with complete cool.

'I…I needed to speak to you before you left for the bank.' Star sucked in a deep, deep breath and forced herself to walk down the length of the table towards him.

Luc folded his newspaper and rose with lithe grace. 'I'm afraid you left it too late. I'm about to leave.'

'Luc…these are the twins' birth certificates,' she practically whispered, pale as milk.

'Of what possible interest could they be to me?' Luc didn't pause even to spare the documents a glance as he strode down the other side of the table in the direction of the door.

Star turned again, her rigid backbone tightening another painful notch. 'The twins were born *more* than six months ago, Luc. They're twelve months old…they just don't look it because they were premature—'

Luc swung back with a frown of complete exasperation. 'Why are you unloading all this stuff on me?'

'Venus and Mars are twelve months old, you see,' Star continued in a fast fading voice. 'That night…you know, when I "slunk", as you put it, you-know-where…well, that night had consequences. I'm really sorry.'

CHAPTER SEVEN

LUC studied Star, absently noting that she was wearing a nightie that resembled some sort of mourning apparel and that she lacked her usual glow.

His brain had shrieked to a sudden halt on her second reference to the age of her children. Twelve months...*twelve months old*? What were they? Miniature babies? What was she trying to tell him? Premature? Born too early, he rephrased for his own benefit. Was there something wrong with the twins? Were they ill? A momentary image of those helpless little creatures under threat gripping him, Luc paled as if a spooky hand had trailed down his spine.

'They're your kids,' Star framed unevenly. 'I should have put you right the minute I realised you thought otherwise. But I was shocked, and annoyed that you could think that they were some other man's. Since you didn't seem that bothered by the idea, I didn't contradict you.'

'*My* kids...' Luc echoed in the unreacting manner of a male who had not yet computed what he was being told. 'What's the matter with them? Are they sick?'

Now it was Star's turn to look confused. 'No, of course not. They're fine now, and catching up great. Luc...do you understand what I've just told you?'

'You said they were my children,' Luc repeated back to her, still without any change of expression, although his winged ebony brows were beginning to pleat.

'I really don't know where you got the idea that they *weren't*—'

'Emilie's accountant said the twins had only got out of hospital in the autumn. He assumed that they were newborns

103

then…*certainement.*' His usual level diction rose in volume, a dark frown slowly building.

For Star, who was feeling nauseous with nerves, that silence was unbearable.

'*J'etais vraiment fâché…*' Luc murmured in fluid French.

I was angry as hell, Star translated, watching Luc, bracing herself for a sudden massive explosion, every muscle in her slender length straining taut. Without warning, he moved again, and she jerked, only to look on in utter bewilderment as he headed towards the housekeeper, who was standing about thirty yards away in the hall, positioned by the front door in readiness for his punctual exit.

Luc was engaged in recalling the way Star had used to see him off every morning, no matter how early the hour of his departure, no matter how discouraging his mood. Chitchat at breakfast wasn't his style. Star had been impervious to the message of his silence. She had torn up his croissant for him in the most infuriatingly invasive and messy manner, poured his coffee, and talked and talked with endless sunny good cheer, deflated not one jot by his monosyllabic replies.

She had been waiting for him when he'd come home as well, surging across the bridge to greet him, always hurling herself at him as if he had been away for at least a month. It had never mattered who was with him either. A party of important diplomats or high-ranking bankers, he mused, all of them had been instantly fascinated by her quicksilver energy, her innate charm, her incredible legs…

Now he was undoubtedly confronting a future of having his croissant mangled… *Ah, c'est la vie,* Luc conceded with a sigh. Congratulating himself on his self-control, not to mention his remarkable cool in crisis, he informed his housekeeper that he would not be flying to Paris after all. He then strolled out into the fresh air, where he breathed in slow and deep to counteract the infuriating light-headed sensation assailing him.

Had he considered himself to be an emotional individual,

he might have wondered if what he was experiencing was shock combined with the most intense relief. But a complete stranger to all such self-analysis, and a male who reasoned solely in practical terms of cause and effect, Luc decided that he was suffering for his alcoholic indulgence several hours earlier.

Striding in the direction of the heli-pad, he was even more happily engaged in rationally reviewing obvious facts which might not immediately appear as obvious to Star as they were to him. Point one, he thought, smiling at the prospect, Rory would now sadly be nothing more for Star than a fleeting thought of what might have been, but was *not* to be. All children deserved two caring parents living under the same roof.

Frozen in position by one of the tall dining-room windows, Star watched Luc approach the waiting helicopter with eyes of complete incomprehension. He spoke to his pilot, sunlight glinting off his luxuriant black hair, one lean hand thrust with casual nonchalance in the pocket of his well-cut trousers. Star could not credit what she was seeing. He looked so relaxed, not at all like a male who had just been given a revelation of earth-shaking magnitude. Maybe he had walked outdoors in an effort to keep a tight rein on his temper. Maybe *she* just couldn't read body language. When had she ever known what was happening inside that tortuously complex brain of his?

Striding back through the front door, emitting a strong air of decisiveness, Luc headed straight for the stairs. Star hurried across the hall in his wake. 'Where are you going?'

'To see my children.'

The sound of the possessive pronoun he used off-balanced Star.

Bertille had already fed and dressed the twins, and as soon as she saw their parents appear, she smiled and slipped out. Luc stilled in the centre of the room, just staring at the two babies playing on the carpet, his bold profile taut.

Venus cried, 'Mum-mum!' and began to crawl towards Star.

'They can move independently…and *talk*?' Luc breathed in almost comical amazement.

'Well, Venus knows two words…those two.' Star was watching Mars. Her son could only crawl backwards. Brought to a halt by the barrier of the wall, he loosed a plaintive wail, big brown eyes filling with tears of frustration.

As Star went to help, Luc startled her by getting there first. Hunkering down with athletic ease, he lifted Mars and spoke to him in husky French. A total pushover for all affection and attention, Mars's tears dried up like magic. Beaming, he snuggled into the shelter of Luc's arm with the air of a baby who would be quite happy to spend the rest of the day there.

'He's so trusting…' Luc commented in a roughened aside, torn between the child he held and Venus, who, intrigued by his presence, had switched direction from her mother to make a beeline for him instead.

Planting herself back on her bottom, Venus tugged at the tassel on one of Luc's shoes. Then she threw her bright curly head back and looked up at him with a playful smile of challenge.

Luc extended his free hand in welcome. Venus gripped his thumb. Then she let go to make a frantic grab at the gold watch she had just noticed gleaming on his wrist. At that sudden switch of focus, Luc's rare smile broke out, amusement lighting up his lean strong face. 'She's like a miniature clone of her mother.'

Her heart rocked by that intensely charismatic smile, Star's mouth ran dry. 'Well, Mars takes after you.'

In fact it was as if their respective genes had known better than to try to mix in their offspring, Star reflected ruefully. Mars got upset if his routine was disrupted, and when he played his ability to concentrate was already noticeable. Venus did everything at high speed and took life just as it came.

As the minutes passed, with Luc wholly engaged on interaction with the twins, Star's tension steadily increased. She just couldn't believe what she was seeing. Careless of his beautiful expensive suit, Luc was now seated on the carpet with Venus and Mars swarming over him as if he was a large and novel toy. Little hands were snatching at his tie, digging into his pockets, pulling at his hair and exploring his face.

Star had never dreamt that Luc might drop his dignified reserve to allow all that close bodily contact and over-familiarity. In fact she would have sworn that he would run a mile from such treatment. Nor had she appreciated that learning that the twins were his might enable Luc to relax and handle their children with much greater confidence than he had shown before.

Indeed, the most awful biting jealousy surged up through Star as she stood there. She was totally ignored by all. She had even been denied her usual enthusiastic early-morning welcome from her babies. And she was now an unwilling audience to the birth of what appeared to be a mutual admiration society for three.

'They're both yawning,' Luc commented a whole twenty-five minutes later, his disappointment audible.

'You've overtired them,' Star heard herself snipe, although she was well aware that after their disturbed night the day before both children would have a much greater need for a long morning nap.

Star settled the twins back into their cots, but not before quite a few hugs and kisses had been exchanged.

'I didn't expect such young children to accept me so easily,' Luc finally drawled, finding himself as ignored as Star had felt ten minutes earlier.

Star turned her head, shining copper hair framing the tight expression on her triangular face. 'They're very fond of Rory, and because of him they like and trust all men,' she said dismissively.

Luc gazed steadily back at her, stunning dark eyes un-

readable as an overcast night sky, but his magnificent bone
structure was taut beneath his smooth golden skin.

'So can I expect to see a lot of you in England after the
end of the summer?' Star asked brittly. 'You know, I'm
homesick already.'

'We'll discuss that downstairs,' Luc informed her, and
strode out.

I just bet we will, Star thought, resenting the way Luc
automatically assumed charge and closing out the little voice
that warned that she was being mean and nasty. After all,
just at that minute she felt like being *horribly* mean and
nasty. It felt better than dwelling on the physical ache of
painful yearning which Luc could rouse in her just by being
in the same room. She could even justify nastiness as a necessary defense mechanism against a male who had hurt her
as much as Luc had hurt her during the early hours of the
morning...

First wanting her, then rejecting her, but not before he had
picked out every one of her failings and held them up to her,
so that she could know what an awful person she was. That
seemed to be a pattern with Luc too. It was as if every time
he felt he might be getting too close to her he just instantly
switched off again and dragged up every reason under the
sun to keep his distance.

And what she had said about Rory *was* true...up to a point,
she reasoned. Rory was fond of the twins, but he really saw
them as an extension of Star, while Luc had instinctively
responded to their son and daughter as individuals and had
awarded them and *not* Star his full attention. Was that a sin
or a virtue? she asked herself bitterly.

Coffee had been laid out in the main salon when Star finally came downstairs again. While he'd entertained Venus
and Mars, Luc had appeared more relaxed than she had ever
seen him. Now she absorbed his cool and distant expression
and veiled eyes. In a split second her nervous tension mushroomed. So Luc had accepted the existence of his children

and had spent some time with them, but that certainly didn't mean he was *pleased* that the wife he was planning to divorce had made him a father.

And if Luc was about to throw recriminations, Star wanted them over with as soon as possible. 'Well?' she said baldly, giving him the opening.

'Coffee?' Luc proffered smoothly.

'Coffee makes me sick when I'm nervous!'

Luc poured himself a cup with the kind of cool that set her teeth on edge.

'Well?' she prompted a second time. 'Just go on. *Say* it!'

Luc raised a politely enquiring brow. 'What is it you wish me to say?'

In a whirl of sand-washed silk and frustration, Star spun away again, bangles jangling on her slender wrist in tinkling accompaniment. 'If I hadn't sneaked into bed with you, you wouldn't be a father now!'

'I knew what I was doing, *mon ange*.'

Star whirled round again, aquamarine eyes confused.

'Did you notice me struggling?' Luc enquired drily.

Her cheeks warmed.

'Naturally not,' Luc answered for himself. 'I was enjoying myself far too much to call a halt, and I didn't protect you from pregnancy. The responsibility for the conception of our children is undoubtedly *all* mine.'

His absolute self-command disconcerted Star just as much as what he was saying. After all, the enemy tank he had likened her to had taken surprise hostages. And possibly Luc was still in shock at that development.

'You don't have to take the blame,' she began, sounding more like her usually fair self. 'I knew—'

'You knew *nothing*,' Luc stressed with a wry twist of his sensual mouth. 'Isn't that the definitive point?'

Her face burned at that incontrovertible fact. She might have known about the birds and the bees the night the twins had been conceived, but the combination of boarding school and Emilie's careful supervision had given Star little opportunity to experiment. A few over-enthusiastic clinches with teenage boys had not prepared her for the distinct but delicious shock of sharing a bed with a fully grown adult male possessed of the ability to give her the ultimate in pleasure.

Luc moved to lift the birth certificates which she had last seen in the dining room from the magnificent mantelpiece. Although only he could have been responsible for having moved them, he perused the certificates afresh with a decided hint of fascination. 'Viviene and Maximilian…Viviene and Max Sarrazin,' he sounded out softly.

'*Known* as Venus and Mars,' Star stressed, pausing in her restive movements round the room.

'But my son and my daughter, who will naturally be brought up here in their family home.' Luc was very still, the long, lean flow of his powerful body perfectly poised by the superb fireplace.

Taken aback by that confident statement, Star dropped dead and stared. 'What are you talking about?'

His brilliant dark eyes were steady as a rock in his lean strong face. 'I think you should sit down and have some coffee. All this frantic pacing up and down must be making you dizzy—'

'Look, I'm not dizzy!' Star folded her arms tight. 'I don't want to sit down either.'

'And I don't want to argue with you, but if you force the issue, you'll find yourself on a losing streak,' Luc warned.

Her eyes fired with quick resentful anger. 'Will I indeed? Five minutes after finding out you're a father, you start making outrageous statements and trying to lay down the law.'

'And I should add that the law—French family law, at least—will come down on my side,' Luc drawled with cool exactitude.

Goosebumps rising on her bare arms, Star went rigid. 'What are you trying to say?'

'That a description of the home environment in which you

were keeping my children in England would be very much in my favour in a French court.'

Star turned pale. 'You're threatening me...'

'You're shocked,' Luc noted. 'Why? Sadly, the twins are more entitled to tender treatment right now than you are, *mon ange*.'

'You *are* threatening me...' Shaken disbelief was splintering through Star.

'You should know where you stand. Between a rock and a hard place,' Luc told her helpfully, lest she be too slow to have absorbed that message. 'No way are you removing my children from beneath this roof at the end of the summer and taking them back to England with you!'

'You *can't*—'

'I *can* stop you. I would dislike the means I would have to utilise, but I would do it,' Luc countered levelly. 'You've made some unwise decisions since our children were born—'

'Like what?' Star slammed back at him ungrammatically, thrown into a greater panic by every word he voiced with such intimidating calm.

'In spite of the fact that you were existing below the poverty line, you didn't inform me of their birth nor did you ask for my financial support. Now even *I* am aware of the accepted authority which states that the needs of the child should always come first.' Luc sent her a winging glance of reproof. 'In attempting to raise our children in an undesirable environment, while also denying me my rights as a father, you failed to behave like a mature and responsible parent.'

Star's soft lips fell open in appalled incredulity at that judgement.

Luc screened his penetrating gaze and spread his lean hands in a wry, dismissive gesture. 'Now, I don't believe it would be fair to judge the teenager you were at the time of their birth against that particular yardstick. But you must accept that in any custody dispute you will be compared to me,

and my worst enemy couldn't label me as either immature
or irresponsible.'

It was a terrifyingly impressive conclusion. By the time
Luc had finished speaking, he had succeeded in seriously
scaring Star. A custody dispute in which what she could offer
their children would be measured against what Luc could
offer? Luc, with several centuries of solid family respectability behind him and every one of his gloomy ancestors born
in wedlock. Luc, with his immense wealth and with his opin-
ions on global financial problems sought by the highest
placed politicians in Europe. Star's blood simply ran cold.

'I just don't understand any of this…' Star was fighting to
keep a grip on her turbulent emotions. 'The instant you find
out that the twins are yours, you immediately start threatening to take them from me—'

'No, that's not either my wish or my intention. But, ironically, it is exactly what you did to me before I came downstairs again,' Luc drawled very quietly. 'Were you expecting
me to jump for joy when you announced that you were already homesick and you talked about returning to England?'

Star reddened and looked away with extreme awkwardness. 'No…but—well, OK, maybe it was a threat,' she muttered in an undertone.

'Thank you. But although you've finally told me that the
twins are my children, you don't appear to have the slightest
grasp of how much that fact is going to impact on *all* our
lives.'

'But why should it change anything?' Star demanded. 'I'm
quite happy for you to see them as much as you want—'

'Will you please explain to me why you can't accept that
I should want my own children as much as you want them?'
Luc enquired, with what appeared to be sincere incompre-
hension.

Her bewilderment and fear flipped into total panic at that
announcement. 'Because you didn't want *me*, didn't want to
be *married*, for goodness' sake!' Star practically shrieked

back at him. 'Why would I ever think that you would welcome being saddled with two kids from that same stupid *fake*
marriage? I thought you'd be furious if you found out I was
pregnant! I thought you'd want me to have a termination! I
thought you'd be outraged with me for creating such an ongoing problem…'

'So you made some very wild assumptions and created a
really huge ongoing problem. That doesn't make any kind of
sense to me,' Luc admitted with the strangest half-smile of
evident acceptance. 'But then not a lot of what you do makes
sense to me, so it doesn't matter. What *does* matter is that
you're becoming very upset.'

Star gulped back the thickness of tears in her throat. 'And
you're surprised?'

Luc took a slow, fluid step closer. 'How can I be a father
to two children living in a different country? I can't agree to
that. Perhaps I came on too hot and heavy, but you have ties
back in England that I want you to put behind you now.'

Star blinked, her breath snarling up in her throat. Ties?
What ties? What had she to put behind her? Four hours of
sleep had left her brain less than agile, but Luc appeared to
be firing on all four cylinders, like a Ferrari ready to roar
down a race track.

'I'm referring to Rory,' Luc clarified without hesitation. 'I
won't stand back and allow a casual lover to take *my* place
with my children.'

She almost told him that she had never slept with Rory,
but then angry defensiveness and pride overcame the desire
to be that honest. What business was it of his? How many
women had he slept with since she had last been in France?
Gabrielle might be old history but that didn't mean that Luc
had become celibate. And what right did a male set on divorcing her have to dictate what she did in her own life? The
right of power and influence, her intelligence warned her at
that point. Luc had already said that if she tried to take the

twins home he would go to court and, at the very least, prevent her from removing them from France.

Star jerked in even greater confusion as Luc suddenly reached for her fiercely clenched hands to draw her to him.

'What are you doing?' she gasped.

'Once you told me that the only thing in the world you would *ever* want was to be my wife, and that if you couldn't have me your life wouldn't be a life any more…it would just be an existence, shorn of all sunlight and happiness, because inside yourself you would just want to die,' Luc recited in his rich, dark accented drawl.

Star just froze. The words were vaguely recognisable. Her note, her goodbye note eighteen months earlier! Her lashes fluttered and then stayed deliberately down low, because at that precise moment she could not have looked Luc in the face to save her life. The cringe factor of that cruelly sharp memory of his was high, indeed sufficient to make her entire bodily surface blush.

'And you wonder *why* I had the moat dragged…' Luc murmured gently. 'But now I'm asking you to put your money where your mouth is.'

Star blinked. 'P-put my money where my m-mouth is?' she stammered helplessly.

'Yes, and live up to all those heartfelt sentiments…*ah, non*,' Luc scolded softly as she suddenly attempted to wrench free of his determined hold.

'You're trying to send me up!' she condemned hotly.

'No. For the sake of our children, I'm challenging you to forget Rory and concentrate your attention back on me and our marriage,' Luc contradicted tautly. 'I accept that that will *be* a challenge for you. But I'm hoping that even if you can't recover that original enthusiasm, some day you could be happy with me again.'

For the sake of our children? Concentrate on our marriage? Those were the only two phrases which Star absorbed from that speech. All the rest of what he said might as well

have been directed at a brick wall. A heady mix of anguished
pain and humiliation engulfed her like a drowning tidal wave.
So that was what he was after now! Total possession of
Venus and Mars, with her as a useful adjunct on the home
front. Violent hurt shuddered through Star. All of a sudden
Luc didn't want a divorce any more. But *she* herself had
played no part in his change of heart! What she had wanted
and prayed for through eighteen endless months he was ready
to give after spending only half an hour with their children!
That was an unbelievable cruelty.

'Are you cold?' Luc demanded anxiously. 'Why are you
shaking?'

'You insensitive toad!' Star hurled rawly, her head flying
up, aquamarine eyes blazing with outraged pain as she jerked
free of him and stalked towards the door. 'How dare you ask
that of me after all you've put me through? You know, you
may be the cat's whiskers of a brain at the bank, but I don't
think you know diddly-squat about anything else in life!'

Luc reached the door first and slammed it fast, while he
attempted to identify what he had said wrong. He had worked
out that speech while he was playing with the twins, satisfied
that it covered every potential rock on which he might run
aground. He could have told her he thought she was like a
butterfly, lighting on whichever male was within closest
reach at any given time. He could have told her that her great
love for Rory would enjoy as much longevity as her love for
himself evidently had. And that when it came to loyalty in
love she was horrendously unstable, and that for as long as
he was her husband, he wouldn't be trusting her out of his
sight. But he had carefully avoided voicing a single superior
or deflating opinion, and he really couldn't understand why
she was all wild-eyed and going over the edge screaming at
him.

'Calm down,' Luc instructed steadily.

'Get away from that door or I'll throw something at you!'
Star threatened.

'If wilful destruction gives you a juvenile thrill, go ahead,' Luc invited.

That provocative response sent such a flame of fury hurtling through Star she shuddered again. 'You're worse than a revolving door—'

'A revolving...door?' Stunning dark eyes rested on her with galling cool. 'Come on, don't leave me in suspense, *mon ange*. In what way do I remind you of a revolving door?'

'One minute you're there, the next you're not and then you're back again...you keep changing your mind and my head's *spinning*!' Star cried in shaking condemnation. 'I don't think you know what you want, but the minute I start wanting you back, you push me away again—'

'Control yourself,' Luc commanded.

'Control myself?' Star echoed, a whole octave higher. 'Gosh, that's a good one! Control yourself, but don't do it in bed. Do you think I want to end up a buttoned-down control freak like you are? I don't think you even *know* what goes on inside your own stupid head. I think around me you're totally controlled by your over-active male hormones! And you don't like that, do you? That gives me a certain power, doesn't it? And that annoys the *hell* out of you, Luc Sarrazin!'

She saw the sheer rage in his eyes and it went to her head like pure alcohol, because at last she had hit home and, if not hurt, had outraged him, which was probably as close as she could get to getting a rise out of Luc. In an abrupt movement, he stepped away from the door.

Assuming he was backing off, shocked rigid by the kind of verbal attack he had never dreamt of receiving from her corner, and feeling incredibly triumphant, Star sashayed out through the door. She paused then, and sent him a shimmering glance of naked incitement over one slight shoulder. 'And it didn't take me to be tall, blonde and sophisticated either, did it? That gets you most of all, doesn't it?'

'If you want to hear what I really think, keep on talking,' Luc ground out.

Star moved out into the hall and turned back again. 'I bet you could have swallowed me as a wife if I'd—'

'Shut up?' Luc slotted in rawly.

'No, if I'd been legitimate, rich and real snobby, you'd have thought I was really special!'

'Would your mother still have been part of the deal?'

'You pig…how dare you insult my mother?' she launched at him in a tempest of renewed fury.

Luc strode forward and just swept her up off her feet into his arms. 'Now where did you find an insult in such a simple question?' he probed, angling a razor-edged smile of grim amusement down at her confused face as he strode for the stairs.

'Put me down, Luc—'

'So that I can chase you all round one of the largest chateaux in the Loire? You must *really* think I am stupid, *mon ange*.'

'I think you're very stupid thinking that a caveman display of brute male strength is likely to silence and subdue me back into doormat mould!'

Luc said nothing, but his jawline took on an even more aggressive slant as he carted her up the stairs and across the landing.

'I hope you put your back out doing this!' Star goaded, wanting him to react again.

'In spite of a temper that would grace a fishwife, you don't weigh any more than a doll.' Shouldering open the door of his bedroom, Luc kicked it shut again behind them, crossed the room and tumbled her down on the bed in a heap. 'But if you get me mad enough, I'm not so buttoned down that I can't match you!'

Righting herself into a sitting position, Star slung back her head and directed a scornful glance at the tall dark male standing over her. 'What did you bring me up here for? An argument where the staff are less likely to hear us?'

Backing off several steps, Luc wrenched off his tie and pitched his jacket down on the floor.

That very unexpected development grabbed Star's entire attention. 'If you think for one moment that I have any intention of letting you—'

'*Letting* me?' Luc queried with an insolent appraisal that was so blisteringly confident it made her teeth grit. 'You'd let me have you in a thunderstorm, with lightning hitting the ground round us and a full orchestra playing beside us.'

'Why, you—'

'And you wouldn't notice the storm or the music because you would be *that* lost in what I can make you feel,' Luc derided, ripping off his shirt with such impatience that several buttons went skimming in all directions. 'And you call my hormones over-active? Even before I married you, you were eating me alive with the strength of your desire for me.'

'I never once approached you that way!' Star raged back at him, her cheeks red as fire.

'Approach me? What would you need to approach me for when your eyes did your craving for you? Then I thought you didn't realise what you were doing; now I suspect you knew *all* along.'

'I was a virgin!' Star proclaimed with embarrassed but infuriated reproach.

'There was nothing remotely virginal about the way you looked at me.'

'How many virgins have you tripped over?'

'*One* was quite enough,' Luc assured her wrathfully.

'It gave you a kick being lusted after, though, didn't it?' Star hissed like a spitting cat. 'I mean, you certainly did *not* avoid me—as you *should* have done if you didn't want to encourage me.'

'*Mais c'est insensé*…that's crazy! I assumed that the more you saw of me, the more you would appreciate that I was far too old for you and far too boring to be an object of such excessive adoration!' Luc slashed back at her.

'It was not excessive. I *loved* you! And you were only boring when you started rabbiting on about that stupid bank.'

A line of dark feverish colour rose over his taut cheek-bones at that less than tactful confirmation.

He could actually look *hurt*, Star registered in absolute total shock as she saw the shaken flash in his beautiful dark eyes. 'I mean, I didn't understand what you were talking about, so it was bound to be less than totally absorbing…and my mind used to drift away all the time, until I was just listening to the s-sound of your voice.'

The wobble in her own voice developed as he peeled off his trousers.

'Only a fool marries an airhead, so I got what I deserved,' Luc enunciated.

'I'm not an airhead…' But her mind was certainly drifting, Star acknowledged in deep shame. Not six feet from her stood the almost naked embodiment of every female fantasy come true, and her only fantasy—even *with* his clothes on. So with them off, barring an exceedingly cool pair of black silk boxer shorts, well, reasoning became a challenge. The twisting curl of heat low in her tummy made her go rigid with rejection.

'An airhead who thinks of nothing but sex,' Luc purred with awesome contempt. 'Who, after a separation of over eighteen months, went to bed with me again within an hour of my appearance back in her life.'

'Oh…*oh*!' Star gasped, the very oxygen squeezed from her lungs at that inexcusable taunt.

'OK, so I *asked*…but if you had any morals at all you would have said no to that proposition,' Luc condemned as he came down on the side of the bed. 'I was ashamed for you when I woke up the next morning.'

'The *next* morning?' Star forced a brittle laugh, so mad, so hurt she could happily have strangled the love of her life to death. 'Doesn't history repeat itself? Just like the only other night you ever spent with me. You're so mad you succumbed to me you punish *me* for it!'

'That is not true…' Luc emphasised that statement by pulling her round to face him. His dark eyes were forthright as flames on her surprised face. 'I got up the morning after our first night together and I looked down at you and you opened your eyes—'

'Gosh, how daring of me! Was I supposed to be hiding under the sheet in shame after spending the night with my own husband?'

Luc released his breath in a sharp hiss. 'I saw a teenager so besotted with me she couldn't see or think straight. I was angry, and ashamed that I had had so little control that I had taken advantage of you—'

'Don't tell me you felt like that!' Star wailed, aghast. 'It was wonderful…it's still a wonderful memory…and you didn't take advantage of me in any way!'

Luc studied her with unconcealed frustration. 'You don't see, do you? That morning, I really badly needed to look at you and see a grown woman, but all I could remember was the vulnerable little girl I first met in Mexico…' He hesitated, and frowned. 'It didn't strike me then that in some ways you'll probably never grow up, at least not in the way less passionate personalities do.'

'Oh, thanks a bundle.' Star exclaimed. 'Well, if you thought helping me to grow up was telling me to go off and experiment with boys my own age, I don't think much of your advice.'

'I said that in anger. Only you could have taken it so literally!' Luc gritted.

'How literally did you *want* me to take it?' Star asked with a teasing sidewise glance.

'You just never know when to quit, do you?' Without warning, Luc tugged her fully into his arms and stood up.

He held her fast and tumbled her back down onto the comfortable bed with him.

The heat of his big powerful body penetrated the fine silk of her dress. She quivered against him. She knew she wasn't going to say no. She knew *he* knew she wasn't going to say no either. Male amusement glimmered deep in his dark eyes and it made her want to slap him, but it didn't make her want to push him away.

'*D'accord*…OK, I gather I can assume that we're staying married.' Level dark eyes zeroed in on hers in enquiry.

Star tensed, lashes screening her gaze as she focused on a smooth brown shoulder instead. Stay married only for the sake of their children? Outside the bedroom he seemed to have as much grasp of *her* needs as the average block of solid wood. Or solid steel, she acknowledged, her weary mind running back over the enervating passage of events that had taken place during the past thirty-six hours. Her batteries required recharging. Yet Luc seemed able to take constant stress in his stride.

So damn him for making that statement which was really a direct question right now! Right now when there wasn't an atom of her treacherous body lacking contact with the awesome promise of his. Right now when she was suffering from this shockingly lowering need to cling and stop thinking and fighting. If she said no, that wasn't a sufficient reason to stay married, was he likely to chuck her out of bed?

Star rested her forehead down against Luc's shoulder. 'Talk about that later,' she mumbled.

'Why has your nightdress got a hood?' Luc enquired.

'It's a dress, Luc.'

Smoothly rearranging her so that she sat astride him, Luc eased it over her head and tossed it aside. 'Better off, than on, *mon ange*,' he mocked, but his intent gaze shimmered over the bare curves of her pouting breasts with smouldering appreciation.

Her face reddened as her nipples pinched into straining

tautness. Luc tensed and suddenly hauled her down to him. 'I'm so glad you're all argued out,' he groaned, closing his mouth hungrily to a thrusting pink peak.

As he did so, a wave of such intense excitement clenched Star that she stopped breathing. She shut her eyes, moaning as he caught the other bud between thumb and forefinger and gently tugged on her achingly responsive flesh. Her whole body was electrified with need as he rolled her over onto her back, skimming off her briefs with sure hands.

He scrutinised her with satisfied eyes. She opened her own, collided with that appraisal and snatched in a sob, just desperate for him to touch her again, and suddenly the amount of power he had over her weak physical self mortified her. 'Don't look at me like that—'

'I always get a high out of your response to me. Can't help it,' Luc muttered hoarsely, still scanning her slender naked curves with devouring attention. 'On your last stay here, I spent the entire time wondering, burning, fantasising...'

'About me?' Her sultry smile was as natural to her as breathing.

'And trying to work out what it was about you that got to me.' Luc ran a caressing hand down over her sensitive breasts, smiling slumbrously as her back arched.

'Oh...?' Her voice emerged strangled.

'You're very small, but you're in perfect proportion. Your eyes are a wonderful colour, and your mouth...when I look at your gorgeous mouth, I just get...' Luc framed the words thickly, sinking lower with every driven word as if the more he said, the more unbearable it became to resist that part of her.

She got the message when he kissed her with all the hunger she craved, but for a split second her brain got its act together and a solitary thought emerged. Luc was talking to her, Luc was *finally* talking to her, but it mightn't be a good idea to mention it because he probably didn't realise what he was doing. And then the primal thrust of his tongue inside her tender mouth just drove her wild. Her mind emptied as she held him to her, fingers laced in his hair, heart pounding in concert with his, the thrumming pulse-beat of desire running like a tightening hot wire through her slender length.

'You excite me beyond belief,' Luc muttered raggedly, pulling back from her to remove his boxer shorts.

Star blinked. My goodness, he was *still* talking. She gazed at him with slightly worried eyes and decided that it had to be stress that was making him talk so much. He came back to her, all rippling muscles and magnificence, and all-pervasive weakness radiated through her lower limbs. She reached up without even the guidance of thought and ran her palms down over the curling dark hair that hazed his pectorals, loving the heat and the roughness of him, the glorious differences that made him so male and made her feel so incredibly feminine.

He shuddered and crushed her eagerly parted lips under his, sensually exploring and tasting her until tiny little quaking tremors were rippling through her.

'You're so quiet,' Luc breathed, sounding almost disappointed, which she could not credit.

If he wanted intellectual stimulation, he was going the wrong way about it. 'I...I can't think when you're this close to me, Luc...I can only *feel*.'

And what Star was feeling was shivering, desperate impatience, her skin hot and tight, the terrible ache he could arouse with such ease sending taunting little throbs of frustration along every single nerve-ending.

'A man should take time making love to his wife.' Luc sent her a winging smile of pure devilment.

The combination of that smile flashing across his lean, dark, devastating face and that teasing reference to her as his wife shook her. He pulled her to him like a guy who had all the time in the world and who planned to enjoy making her wait. Her fingers bit fiercely into his shoulder, and he laughed in a way she had never heard him laugh with her before, and then he sealed her mouth again with his and the hunger took her in an explosive surge again.

He touched her in every place but the one place craving his touch. She discovered she had erogenous zones all over her. He let his sensual mouth nip at the extended line of her throat and she was convinced she would burst into flame. He licked her fingers and her very bones seemed to liquefy. He smoothed his palms with aching slowness along the outside of her slender thighs and she burned in absolute torment. And when he started shaping her squirming hips, she clawed him down to her in a tempestuous movement.

'If you don't...' she moaned.

And then he did, and nothing from that point on could have wrenched her from the grip of such torturous excitement. Not thunder, not lightning, not even a full orchestra. Sounds escaped her that she didn't recognise as her own, and she twisted and she writhed until at last he came over her.

And Luc was trembling too then, dampness sheening his golden skin, the hands that spread her beneath him taut and impatient, dark eyes burnished with raw desire. He entered her in a hungry surging thrust. She cried out loud, out of control, loving it, loving him with such fevered intensity that the pleasure seemed more than she could bear. And as he drove her deeper into that pleasure with long, hard strokes, she felt the great gathering ultimate surge taking her in its hold and just let go, gasping, shuddering, sobbing out his name at the height of ecstasy.

'I think, *mon ange...*' Luc groaned indolently into her hair. 'I think I shall adapt to being *really* married with remarkable enthusiasm.'

She shifted indolently against him, enfolded by the most marvellous sense of peace and satiation. Lifting his head, Luc gazed down at her abstracted expression and he laughed softly. 'You're still out of it.'

Out of everything, she conceded happily as he traced the relaxed fullness of her reddened lips with a fingertip and gave her the sort of megawatt smile that made her heart sing. 'Just keep on smiling at me…'

'I believe I can definitely promise you that.' His dark drawl husky with sensual amusement, Luc rolled over into a cooler patch of the tumbled bed, but he kept her welded to him with one powerfully possessive arm and covered her mouth very softly with his again.

It felt as if the whole world stood still while he kissed her. Glorious contentment enveloped Star. She closed her arms round him in helpless hunger, revelling in the damp, hard feel of his relaxed length and knowing that she already wanted him again.

Lifting his tousled head, Luc scanned her with stunning dark eyes ablaze with the same awareness. 'It's hard to believe that in the early hours of this morning. I was angry and drunk and climbing the walls with sexual frustration…and look at us now.'

Yes, look at us now, Star suddenly thought, tensing at the reminder of that upsetting confrontation during the night. It was as if Luc had pressed a panic button inside her head. Luc seemed to be suggesting that now everything was sorted, as it were. He thought, he had actually just assumed, that he had got what he wanted and that she had now agreed to stay married to him. And why *shouldn't* he have made that assumption? Hadn't she just fallen at abandoned speed back into bed with him again?

'For the sake of our children,' he had drawled piously, when he had stated the case for finally making their marriage a real and binding commitment. And didn't she still love him? Wasn't this probably the very most Luc was ever likely to offer her? What was she holding out for? Red roses and romance? Chance would be a fine thing! But how much could she even *trust* in what Luc was saying right now?

'You know…' she said uneasily, pulling away from him in a move that took an amount of will-power that embarrassed her. 'Only last night you were talking like you hated me…'

Faint colour surfaced over his hard cheekbones and he frowned. 'I still believed that the twins had been fathered by some other man! You never put yourself in my place, *mon ange*.'

No, now that he said it, she had to admit that she hadn't ever tried. But then she had never managed to work out what went on inside Luc's head. However, she suspected that when his emotions became involved Luc's sense of proportion and his pure logic went out of the window, leaving him vulnerable. How else did she explain an overwhelmingly practical guy who, on the basis of a goodbye note, had had the moat and the lake dragged for her body?

'But ever since you tracked me down all you've been talking about is divorcing me. It was like it was a real mission with you…'

'So *that* is what is worrying you. But naturally my priorities have changed,' Luc countered without hesitation. 'We have the twins to consider now. They need their mother just as much as their father. You and I both enjoyed less than idyllic childhoods. By staying together we support each other as parents and we can ensure that our children enjoy a different experience.'

Star's heart was steadily sinking. She had put him on the spot again when he hadn't been expecting it, but couldn't he just have lied and pretended that *she* figured in this reconciliation as something more than the mother of his children? No, she was better off with that honesty, she decided miserably. Even she couldn't romanticise deeper meanings into words and phrases like 'priorities' and 'supporting each other as parents'.

Luc was determined to hang onto Venus and Mars. First he had softened her up with the threat of a custody battle, then he had tried to talk her back into a marriage he had previously been keen to escape. All for the benefit of the twins. But children and good intentions were not enough to hold a marriage together. Why on earth was Luc the logical being so *illogical*? Her head whirled. It was as if they had suddenly switched characters. *She* was supposed to be the one who chased idealistic windmills; *he* was supposed to be the one grounded in the solid rock of realistic expectations!

Star dropped her head and murmured heavily, 'I think we should just take stock of our marriage at the end of the summer...and not make any hard and fast decisions before then.'

Luc threw back the sheet and sprang out of bed.

That got her attention all right. She watched him hauling on his boxer shorts and then snatching up the chinos lying on a nearby chair. His long, smooth brown back expressed hostility in violent waves. In the space of ten seconds the atmosphere had churned up and charged like dynamite ready to explode.

'Luc?' Star prompted apprehensively.

Luc swung back, dark eyes grim. 'Explain exactly what you mean by that suggestion. I want to be sure I haven't misunderstood.'

'Well, we just see how we get on over the summer—'

'You keep your options open until then?' Raw incredulity edged his dark accented drawl.

Star nodded. That way she wouldn't get her hopes up too much. That way if he discovered he couldn't hack being married to her, she would be prepared and she wouldn't be quite so hurt.

Studying a point slightly to one side of her, Luc breathed in very deep, so deep she could see his impressive chest expanding. '*Rien à faire*...nothing doing!'

She stiffened. 'But—'

With a slashing motion of one powerful hand, Luc silenced her. 'When you went to bed with me again, you *knew* that I believed you had agreed to my terms!'

Star quickly dropped her head again, wincing, wishing he

wasn't quite so clever. 'I just wanted you so much...can't you accept that?'

'You're my wife and you're behaving like a wanton little slut!'

'You don't mean that,' she told him, looking up hopefully but meeting hard, challenging eyes across the depth of the room and shrinking.

'I heard you telling Rory you loved him last night,' Luc ground out.

'Oh...' Her mind occupied with something which was to her way of thinking much more pressing, Star said, 'Are you about to apologise for calling me a slut?'

'Not on my deathbed!' Luc roared, which seemed fairly comprehensive.

'Fine...this dialogue is over until you say sorry.' Beneath his arrested gaze, Star flopped back on the pillows and shut her eyes.

'Rory was not on your mind that night in England...*and* he was a very distant memory not ten minutes ago, when you were having a hell of a good time under me!'

Star whispered frigidly, 'And when you were having a hell of a good time *over* me. So that leaves us about equal.'

'How can you be so crude?' Luc had the nerve to sound genuinely shocked.

'I just learnt it from you. But at least I have never in my life eavesdropped on someone else's private phone call...' It was a lie: on their wedding night she had listened to him call Gabrielle and say he was coming over. That recollection just choked her. 'But I love Rory like a friend...OK?'

'No, it is not OK!' Luc thundered back at her. 'You will have no further contact with him. And if you think for one moment that I intend to be put on trial as a stud for the summer, you are out of your crazy mind!'

Star felt frozen from neck to toe. She looked up at the superb ornate ceiling, exhaustion creeping over her. 'I wouldn't worry about that if I were you. I have no plans to ever sleep with you again, Luc Sarrazin. Are you going to apologise? Because if you're not, you can leave.'

As the silence lingered, Luc closed his eyes and counted to ten, then to twenty. This terrible rage she evoked. He felt as if he was coming apart at the seams. He felt gutted. He strode into the dressing room and flipped the door shut. She *loved* Rory like a friend? She had to have slept with the guy. Of course she had! All those months when he himself had been... He just could not stand to think about that, rammed that thought train back down into his subconscious. It leapt out again like an evil genie. Who was the smartass who'd told her to experiment?

Star wakened a couple of hours later, amazed that she had just dropped off to sleep. There was a note on the pillow beside her. She lifted it with a frown, everything that had happened between her and Luc flooding back.

'Urgent appointment to keep. Sorry, Luc,' the note ran.

He was gone. She had chased him back to Paris. Her eyes stung like mad with tears. It had been thirty-six hours of mostly hell, but she couldn't bear him that far away from her—especially after a violent row. All she had done was fight with him. What had got into her? He couldn't stand scenes. All right, so it hadn't been the most tempting invitation to stay married, but she could have been more tactful. He had been shocked when she'd announced that she would prefer to go for the trial reconciliation rather than the for ever and for ever challenge.

She didn't even have the number of his mobile phone. She didn't even know when he was coming back. Six lousy words, and one of those his own name. She buried her face in the pillow and sobbed her heart out.

CHAPTER EIGHT

BY THREE that afternoon, Star was dry-eyed. As Luc had promised, all the rest of her possessions had arrived and she was in the midst of organising a workroom for herself.

She had picked a room on the ground floor, where the light was particularly good and the view from the windows inspirational. The shop which had bought her first small embroidered canvases had indicated an interest in seeing more of her pictures. As she didn't know what was likely to be happening between her and Luc at the end of the summer, she needed to be every bit as disciplined at forging a career as an artist as she had been at home. The ability to be self-supporting, whether it was necessary or not, was important to her self-esteem.

Her body had a slight, definite ache, which was as strong a reminder of Luc's infuriating absence as it was of her own weak physical self. Of course Luc had been furious with her. Luc always thought he knew best. But he didn't necessarily know what was best for *her*. Luc could be terrifyingly self-sufficient, and she needed more than she had naively wanted eighteen months earlier. She hadn't even understood that herself until he had suggested staying together solely for the twins' benefit.

Granted, Luc wasn't *ever* going to fall madly in love with her: no longer did she wish for the moon. But if Luc couldn't love her, he had to respect her, care for her well-being and stop treating her like an overgrown child who couldn't be trusted to express a sensible opinion of her own.

A maid appeared at the door to tell her that there was a call for her.

Star swept up the phone.

'It's Luc.'

Star stiffened, still furious at the unfeeling way he had vanished while she was asleep. 'I know. Don't tell me. You're too busy to come home for dinner?'

'I'm afraid that I somehow overlooked an emergency meeting on the current stockmarket crisis—'

She didn't believe him. He never overlooked anything. He just didn't want to come home. 'So where's the meeting?' she enquired very coolly.

'Singapore.'

Singapore? Aghast, she studied her own white-knuckled grip on the phone. How many hours did it take to fly to Singapore? Was he even likely to make it back for dinner tomorrow evening? She didn't think so. The fight went out of her. She went limp

'It isn't possible for someone else to attend in my place,' Luc imparted with audible tension. 'I know that this is a case of extremely bad timing as far as *we* are concerned, but I have a duty and responsibility as Chairman to attend this conference. I'll be home next week—'

'Next week?' Her horror escaped her this time in a shrill exclamation. She clamped a frantic hand to her parted lips, furious at her loss of control.

'I would prefer to be spending time with you and the children. Please understand that sometimes I don't have a choice,' Luc breathed stiffly.

'Oh, don't worry about us. We'll be fine, and I'm sure you're really busy, so I won't keep you. Have a nice time!'

She sank down on the nearest seat, feeling as if Luc had yanked the very ground from beneath her feet. Next week. All those days to be got through. There were twenty-four hours in every day, sixty minutes in every hour. What was the matter with her? She had managed without Luc for a long time. All right, so she hadn't been happy, but she had stopped feeling dependent. It made her mad that the passage of barely two days could make such a difference.

*   *   *

Luc phoned at odd hours during the following week.

There were awkward silences. Then one or both of them would rush into speech, usually to say, or in his case ask, something about Venus and Mars. The phone was a business aid to Luc. He didn't chat. He didn't share the experiences of his day. And Star was too mortified to press him on the latter subject after her pretty much unforgivable crack about how bored she had once been when he mentioned anything relating to the Sarrazin bank.

A little over eighteen months ago she had thought she was so mature for her age too. Now she was looking back and wincing for her younger self, appreciating how much she *had* matured since becoming a mother. Before the twins' birth she had been as self-absorbed as most teenagers. Luc's workaholic schedule had just made her resent the Sarrazin bank and she hadn't ever attempted to understand anything he tried to explain.

The day before Luc was due to return, Star took the twins into the woods for a walk and a picnic. It was a heavenly afternoon. Drowsing early summer heat seeped down through the tree canopy into the grassy glade where Star had spread a rug. With the twins dozing in their pram, Star was in a dreamy daze when she heard a slight sound and lifted her head. Her expressive eyes widened, her throat constricting.

Luc came to a halt several feet away. In an elegant cream suit that accentuated the stunning darkness of his hair and the vibrant gold of his skin, he looked drop-dead gorgeous. Her mouth ran dry and her heart leapt.

'Luc…how on earth…? I mean…I wasn't expecting you!' Scrambling up, the folds of her many-shaded long green skirt fluttering round her slender frame, she surged off the rug in her bare feet, only to jerk to a sudden halt about eighteen inches from him as she recalled her original intent to greet his return with frozen cool.

'No, don't spoil that welcome!' His amusement uncon-

cealed as he recognised her dismay, Luc reached out and
urged her the rest of the way to him.

A lean hand splaying to her slim hips, to pin her in place,
he gazed down at her, lush lashes screening all but a dark
glimmer of his eye. 'I think you missed me—'

'I was just so surprised to see you standing there. I got a
fright!' Star's cheeks were red as fire.

'With those eyes, you can't lie...you really can't lie to me,
mon ange,' Luc chided, his other hand curving to her chin
to push up her face, his fingers slowly sliding into her hair.
'And why should you lie?'

The touch of his hand on her sun-warmed skin sent a wave
of undeniable awareness tremoring down her taut spinal cord.
She fought the sensation with all her might, only to succumb
to the sudden passionate force of Luc's mouth possessing
hers.

After a week of deprivation, he had the same effect on her
as a flame on dynamite. Her whole body leapt in sensual
shock. She closed her hands over his shoulders to keep herself upright as she leant into him, the heat and strength of
his hard, muscular frame a powerful enticement. Wildly excited by the taste of him, she closed her arms around him,
quivering as she registered his potent arousal.

Suddenly Luc dragged his mouth from hers, bracing his
hands momentarily on her shoulders to steady her, and
laughed softly. 'We have an audience...'

He strode away. Blinking in bemusement, Star spun round.
Luc was now hunkered down by the pram, all his attention
directed at Venus, who was holding out her arms and making
little excitable noises of welcome. Feeling like a third wheel,
Star stiffened and bit her lower lip.

'Star...' Luc extended his hand.

'What?'

'I have time to make up with you, but time to make up
with our son and daughter as well,' he murmured smoothly.

Her face burned like a house fire. She had never been so

grateful that he wasn't looking at her. If she had been sixteen, she'd have stormed off in furious embarrassment. Four years older, she compressed her lips and approached the pram. Tugging her down beside him, Luc curved a strong arm round her.

'This is what I want them to see. You and I together and relaxed,' he shared softly. 'Aside of weddings and funerals, I never saw my parents together. They despised each other. If they had to communicate they used the phone. I thought that was normal. I thought all families lived like that…each of them entirely separate under the same roof.'

Her discomfiture was forgotten. The images Luc evoked chilled her.

'That's why I want something better for our children,' Luc continued in the same level tone. 'Because I know the cost of getting something less. I'm not prepared to *play* at being married while you make up your mind about what you want to do.'

'I wasn't suggesting we—'

'You *were*…and if you start out with the belief that it's all right to fail, failure becomes that much more likely.' Releasing her from his light hold, Luc vaulted back upright.

'That's not how I see it.' Her aquamarine eyes frustrated, she scrambled up.

Luc gave her a cloaked scrutiny. 'I won't be put on trial.'

'I'm not putting you on trial, for goodness' sake!'

His eyes glittered like ice-fire in a shaft of sunlight. 'I've already lost out on the first year of my children's lives and yet you're expecting me to spend the next few months wondering whether we're likely to end up fighting over them in court!'

Taken aback by that statement, Star swallowed uncertainly.

'And not only that,' Luc continued with glacial cool, 'At the same time you actually expect me to behave as if our marriage is normal and treat you as my wife—a bond which requires a sense of trust and security. What do you think I am? A split personality?'

'How long did it take you to work out that argument?' Star asked with helpless curiosity, eyes now wide with wonderment.

Disconcerted by that offbeat question, and by the way she was studying him, Luc frowned.

Star gave a slow, rueful shake of her bright head. 'Never mind. I have to admit that I'm torn between resentment and admiration. You've made a very good point and pretty much trashed my argument.'

Without another word, she threaded her feet into her sandals and then whisked up the rug and carefully folded it. She planted the rug into his surprised hands and then, retracing her steps, wheeled the pram in the direction of the path. She glanced back, noting Luc was still poised like a devastatingly handsome statue in the same spot.

'Aren't you coming?' she asked in surprise.

'What you just said…' Luc drawled as he strode onto the path. 'What did it…*mean*?'

'I'll tell you when I work it out. Mmm…' she sighed with a sunny smile. 'I love the smell of the woods.'

'Star, we need to sort this out—'

'Relax…unwind…loosen your tie,' Star urged pleadingly.

He wanted to organise their marriage along the strict lines of his daily schedule. Nothing unexpected, nothing outside normal boundaries, everything under his rational, structured control. He couldn't help himself. His brain was like a steel trap. And arguing with him was a waste of time. She wasn't about to be browbeaten into changing her mind on the spur of the moment. She was a lateral thinker who worked on gut instinct. Luc was just going to have to accept that.

When they got back to the chateau, they entertained the twins for an hour. After that, Venus and Mars had their tea and Bertille helped Star to bathe them. By the time the children were tucked into their cots Star was hungry, and, since

Luc was now home again, she went to change for dinner. Clad in a floaty lemon dress that skimmed her ankles, she went downstairs and joined Luc in the drawing room.

To her surprise, Luc wasn't wearing his usual formal evening dress. Dressed in beautifully cut khaki chinos and a toning shirt, he looked very elegant, yet very much more casual than she was accustomed to seeing him. In that split-second first encounter with his brilliant dark gaze, her tummy clenched and her pulses quickened. Her awareness of his devastating masculinity intensified to a degree that made her suddenly self-conscious.

'Where's your dinner jacket?' she muttered in a rush to fill in the silence, shifting from one foot to the other, her cheeks warming as she hurriedly lowered her eyes from the downright lure of his.

'Do you remember telling me that when I wore a dinner jacket I reminded you of the men who appear in old black and white movies?' Luc enquired gently. 'Since then, for some reason, I've never felt quite the same about dressing up for dinner.'

'Well, times do change, although they never did *here*, did they?' Star started talking in mile-a-minute mode. 'Your father was a real old stick-in-the-mud for living the way your ancestors did. The last time I stayed here it was like I'd strayed back into the eighteenth century and was living history!'

Luc scanned her simple dress with its delicate embroidery. 'But in spite of that, you're now dressing for dinner.'

Star just grinned; she couldn't help it: it was just typical that they should be out of step. But as she connected with his magnetic dark eyes a second time, that thought drifted from her again, more elemental responses taking over. All she really wanted was to be in his arms, and she felt she ought to have more control over herself.

'You do look gorgeous in that dress,' Luc extended softly. 'And it's going to be the perfect foil for my present.'

'Present?'

Luc swept a gift-wrapped box from the table behind him and settled it into her hands.

In genuine surprise, Star sat down hurriedly to open the box. When she lifted out a chakra necklace, she studied it in total shock. She only recognised what it was because she had once seen one in a book. Each different gemstone and crystal had been exquisitely cut and framed in intricate settings, the whole joined by delicate gold links.

Stunned, Star looked up and stared at Luc in amazement. 'It's just *gorgeous*…where did you get it?'

'I had it made for you while I was in Singapore. A practitioner skilled in the healing qualities of crystals and gemstones helped me to decide what to include.'

Star slowly swallowed. 'B-but you—'

Luc touched the first gemstone. 'Amber for calm, amethyst for spiritual peace, aquamarine for communication…' he enumerated steadily. 'Azurite to help you find your life path and to trust in your intuition, topaz to protect you through life changes, opal for meditation, tourmaline to heal past traumas, lapis lazuli to change negative views into positive ones…and a rose quartz pendulum for powerful healing energy.'

'I just can't believe this…' Star mumbled, examining each gem with close interest backed by growing appreciation and excitement at the meaning of so very personalised a present. 'This means so much to me, Luc…and that you should have taken the trouble, made the effort when you don't even *believe* in—'

'There is a scientific basis to your convictions. Now that I know that, I can handle the concept better.'

'You mean you don't think I'm a crackpot any more?' Star asked hopefully.

'I never said you were a crackpot.'

'It must have cost you a fortune…not that that counts for anything, with your wealth…but this is just one of those very, very special gifts that speaks so loud…' At that point, Star got up and flung her arms round him, her heart singing like a thousand violins reaching a crescendo. 'You are turning into a really wonderful guy, Luc!'

His arms full of Star, Luc frowned. *Turning into?* From a rat into a wonderful guy. It was a meteoric rise, he conceded. He had known that she would be really surprised by the necklace, but he was astonished that a gift had the power to inspire her with such an emotional response. But then she was very impressionable. Recalling the amount of cool calculation that had gone into that necklace, he suppressed a very slight pang of conscience.

'Put it on for me,' Star whispered.

Taking the necklace from her, Luc undid the catch. She turned round and bent her head for him, felt the cool weight of the jewellery and then, in shock, the hard, sensual promise of his lips pressing to the exposed nape of her neck. Her knees wobbled and every nerve-ending just seemed to sizzle, making her gasp.

'You are so deliciously responsive, Madame Sarrazin,' Luc teased huskily above her head as she fell back into the waiting circle of his arms, every inch of her so tormentingly aware of that lean, hard frame of his that she blushed all over.

He held her fast, the warm, sexy scent of him engulfing her, wiping out all self-discipline. Instinctively she pushed back against him, and he vented a roughened groan at that contact. 'Luc…' she framed with a desperate little shiver.

'Relax…' he urged slumbrously, effortlessly in control when she already felt weak with physical need.

He let his hands roam with sure expertise up over the straining thrust of her urgently sensitive breasts and she jerked and moaned, arching back in a fever of trembling excitement. It had only been a week but it felt like a hundred years since she had last felt his touch.

With a ragged sigh, Luc turned her back to him and stole

one devouring kiss full of a hunger that more than matched her own. Then he dragged his mouth free again and held her tight against him until the fever inside her had subsided to a more bearable level. 'Touching you wasn't the brightest idea...' His own breathing was fractured, his deep voice uneven. 'Particularly not when the bell's already gone for dinner.'

Star hadn't even heard it sounding.

Luc set her back from him with determined but gentle hands. 'Our chef always pushes the boat out when I've been abroad,' he shared ruefully. 'There's probably five courses coming our way. He'll be mortally offended if we don't at least *try* to eat some of it.'

Star touched her necklace several times during the meal which followed. She noticed nothing she ate. She couldn't take her eyes off Luc. She felt buoyant, and full of hope for the future. Luc had used his imagination on her behalf. He had made a real effort to move beyond his own conventional boundaries. Considerable care had gone into the selection of those particular gemstones. And he had done all that purely to please her. From a guy who was at least ninety per cent preoccupied with banking most of the time that was a really impressive gesture, and it touched her to the heart.

They got as far as the dessert during dinner. Then Luc pushed his plate away and held his hand out to her. Her face hot with colour but her body hot with wild anticipation, Star rose from the table to join him.

'Are you feeling happy?' she asked him as they crossed the big hall hand in hand for the very first time.

'It's not a concept I've explored since childhood. What does it feel like?' Luc enquired with amusement.

'I think you'd have to be really *unhappy* before you could appreciate what the reverse feels like.'

'Are you planning to sleep on the sofa tonight?' Brilliant dark eyes encountered and held hers.

'No...' Star muttered breathlessly.

'I am experiencing happiness at this moment, *ma cherie*,' Luc drawled with unconcealed mockery.

Star tensed with sudden discomfiture at the strength of her desire for him. 'A lot of things are more important than sex, Luc—'

'Not to most men,' Luc slotted in softly.

'Is that like a guy thing?'

'Definitely. And, speaking as a male who only planned to marry after his fiftieth birthday—'

Star stopped dead and surveyed him in amazement. 'But why?'

'I didn't want to risk wasting the best years of my life in a bad marriage,' Luc admitted without hesitation. 'It makes sense. Think about it.'

Star didn't want to think about it. She was appalled by such a pessimistic outlook. 'You can't plan stuff like that, Luc.'

'Not with you in the vicinity,' he conceded.

'But didn't it even cross your mind that you might fall madly in love?'

'In lust, yes...in love, no.'

'But I always feel good when I'm in love...well, most of the time,' Star adjusted ruefully.

Sudden silence reigned.

Star glanced at Luc's hard profile and sighed, her eyes veiling. 'You're not comfortable with this conversation, are you?'

Luc tightened his grip on her slender fingers as they began to slide inexorably from his. 'I think the less you think about love the happier we will be,' he stated with flat conviction.

A faraway look of regret in her eyes, Star realised that she was *still* wishing for the moon, and that Luc had just forced her dreams into yet another crash landing. Only a week ago she had been telling herself that she had come to terms with the fact that Luc didn't believe in romantic love. But it was hard to feel optimistic about a potential future with a husband who didn't love her. Particularly when they were such different kinds of people. How loyal would he be to a wife he didn't love?

Now rigid with seething tension, Luc removed his gaze abruptly from her preoccupied face. 'I've got some work to do,' he told her flatly, and released her hand.

Literally exploded out of her anxious thoughts, Star stilled in complete confusion to watch Luc stride away from her and head back down the magnificent staircase again.

She gripped the banister. 'I could keep you company...?'

At the foot of the stairs, Luc swung round, his lean, hard features icily sardonic.

Shrivelled by that look, Star stepped back, the warmth inside her evaporating beneath that chill. 'I guess you don't need company...'

One minute they had been heading for bed, excitement in the air—well, in *her* air anyway. No longer did she feel qualified to say how Luc had been feeling—but the next minute she had become as undesirable as cold tea. Had she said something which annoyed him? She had started talking about love. She groaned, thoroughly irritated with a tongue which frequently ran ahead of her brain in Luc's company. Why did he have to be so touchy? Not just touchy, she conceded heavily, Luc had seem derisive...*repelled*?

Was that her fault? What made a guy go from keen to cold? Too much eagerness? Had Luc been in the act of dragging her off to bed only because she herself had made it so painfully obvious that she could hardly wait for him to make love to her again? Star cringed at that suspicion. No doubt after a couple of sexual encounters she no longer possessed quite the same 'wild' appeal. In fact, maybe now that Luc suspected that in all likelihood she was *always* going to be around, her stock in the desirability stakes had sunk a great deal lower.

After an hour's wakeful twisting and turning in a bed which seemed far too big and far too empty for her, Star sat up with the sense of having finally penetrated the mystery of Luc's behaviour with an explanation that was very slightly less humiliating. For goodness' sake, what an idiot she was! She remembered him admitting that he hadn't planned to marry until he was at least fifty. Now she knew what was wrong. All of a sudden Luc had felt *trapped*, twenty years ahead of his time. In presenting him with two children she had deprived him of the freedom and female variety that all young, sexually active males supposedly cherished. An extra twenty years was a long term to serve for not using contraception, she allowed miserably.

Seated at his desk, Luc sank a brandy in one long, unappreciative gulp. And she called *him* insensitive! He had never been the sensitive type, but Star was getting to him on levels he did not wish to explore. He saw that wistful, yearning expression on her face afresh. His anger got colder and deadlier. Or was it anger? He realised in some surprise that he felt bitter. He felt very, very bitter.

From below her lashes, while pretending to still be asleep, Star watched Luc emerge from the bathroom the next morning.

Stark naked, he was towelling dry his hair. A sensation akin to a tightening knot tugged low in the pit of her stomach. Feeling like a voyeur, she shut her eyes tight in shame. She recalled telling him that there were a lot more important things than sex and decided it was time she learned to practise what she preached. She didn't know what time Luc had finally come to bed. By that stage she had given up hope of him ever appearing and she had dozed off.

'I know you're awake,' Luc remarked lazily.

Her lashes practically hit her eyebrows. *'How?'*

A vibrant smile curved Luc's mouth. 'I spoke and you took the bait!'

She laughed, but it was a challenge. At that instant, his dark, vibrant magnetism just took her breath away.

Wearing only a pair of boxer shorts, Luc strolled across to the bed and sank lithely down on the edge, all bronzed skin, rippling muscles and tangible energy. He handed her a gold credit card and a fat wad of francs. 'You need to do some serious shopping today.'

'Why?'

'Surprise…' His dark eyes gleamed. 'But shop for somewhere hot.'

She sat up with a jerk. 'Are we going away?'

'Late afternoon. You, me, the twins.'

Very slowly Star nodded; she was totally stunned. Luc had once had the same view of holidays as Scrooge had had of Christmas. What was making him so volatile? Why all these inexplicable changes of mood? Last night he had been grim as hell when he'd turned away from her in a very hurtful rejection, and *now*? Like a guy on a mission, he radiated charisma and smiles.

'For a couple of weeks,' Luc added casually.

'What about the bank?'

'I'm tearing myself away from it…but I have to go in today to tie up a few loose ends…OK, *mon ange*?' Lowering his dark head, Luc crushed her parted lips with hungry brevity beneath his, and then rose with unconcealed reluctance again.

'OK…' she said breathlessly.

As he got dressed, Luc listened with the utmost contentment to Star singing off-key in the shower. To think he had actually been apprehensive about the reception he might receive! Storming off last night had been a major misjudgement, he acknowledged. If she had done the same thing to him, he would have been ready to strangle her. Fortunately, Star was happily distracted by the idea of a holiday.

And around dawn Luc had finally seen the error of his ways. Under no circumstances was he prepared to wait until the end of the summer to discover their ultimate fate as a family. And the solution to that problem was so simple that

Luc could not credit he had taken so long to see it. He had to *make* Star fall in love with him again. Then a nuclear bomb wouldn't shift her from his side...

Star spent the morning shopping in Nantes.

In a medieval side-street, she found a fabulous baby shop, and kitted Venus and Mars out with substantial new wardrobes. When cost didn't have to be considered, she discovered to her delight, she could shop at supersonic speed. She bought lingerie by the handful, swimwear and new toe-post sandals in five different colours. In quick succession she went on to purchase T-shirts, two short skirts, five long floaty ones she couldn't choose between, three new dresses and canvas shoes. Stocking up on suncream, a new straw hat and a pair of leopard print sunglasses completed the trip.

With Bertille's organisational ability to hand, and the wonderful knowledge that she could pack the kitchen sink if she so desired, Star had closed the last suitcase and had changed into a fashionably short lemon lace-lined skirt, teamed with a sequinned white T-shirt, when the internal phone rang to inform her that she had a visitor waiting to see her, a Mr Martin. Rory...Rory was here in *France*?

Star flew down the stairs like the wind. Rory was in the hall, looking amazingly elegant in white jeans and a designer T-shirt with a striped cotton sweater casually knotted round his slim shoulders.

As Luc strolled through the imposing front door of his ancestral home, wondering who owned the Porsche with the British registration parked out front, he was just in time to see his wife hurl herself joyously into Rory's arms.

'What a brilliant surprise!' With the ease of long friendship, Star gripped the young blond man's arms, stretched up to kiss his cheek and then held him back from her to subject him to a long, exaggerated appraisal before sounding a low wolf-whistle of admiration. 'Wow! Love those sexy white jeans...don't you look like a really cool dude?'

Rory grinned. 'I brought the Porsche Cabriolet too—'

'Poser!' she mocked, her aquamarine eyes dancing. 'And to think you made me travel round in an ancient old rust-bucket because you didn't want your workmates to know that you were a rich kid.'

'Now, come on, Star…the Morris is a classic British car.'

'I have definitely missed you. Why are you skiving off work and over in France?' she demanded cheerfully.

'I'm supposed to be checking that my parents' villa at Cap d'Antibes is in order for the end of the month… I was worried about you and the twins,' he admitted abruptly.

'Didn't I tell you you didn't need to worry?' Star sighed guiltily. 'Luc and I are—'

'Deliriously happy,' Luc's heavy accented drawl slotted in to spell out.

Star whirled round with a huge but surprised smile. 'Luc, you're home! Come and meet Rory…*properly* this time! He's got to be my best friend in the world.'

From a distance of ten feet, Luc stared bleakly at the young blond man. Rory advanced half a step and then stilled again, acknowledging his host's presence with an uneasy nod.

Star focused on Luc. It struck her that he was remarkably pale, his slashing cheekbones taut. 'Luc, are you—?'

'Look, I'll call in on the way back from the Cap on Sunday.' Rory began.

Star grimaced. 'Oh, heck, we won't be here, Rory. In fact—'

'In just under ten minutes we have to leave,' Luc advanced without the slightest shade of regret.

'Gosh, it's a good thing I got my packing done so quick,' Star muttered in surprise, and some embarrassment. 'We're going away for a couple of weeks, Rory.'

'Possibly even longer,' Luc qualified.

Star glanced at him in bewilderment. 'But, Luc…what about the bank?'

'With a computer, I can work anywhere,' Luc asserted with sardonic bite.

Rory glanced uncomfortably at Star. 'Could I just say hi to the twins before I go?'

'Of course you can!' Star headed for the stairs. 'I feel so awful that you can't stay longer.'

'Luc is a very possessive guy,' Rory whispered on the landing. 'He really doesn't like me being here—'

'Nonsense,' Star said loyally. 'Luc was just surprised to see you, that's all.'

'You seem so happy…'

'I am. So you shouldn't be worrying about me.'

'I went on the pull, like you suggested. I'm going clubbing with a brunette this week,' Rory informed her.

Star grinned approval. 'You could never do anything like that with me because I had the twins…'

'And you'd never agree to a babysitter,' Rory added with a thoughtful frown.

After a brief visit with Venus and Mars, Star walked Rory back out to his Porsche.

'I'll call back at the end of the month. Hell, I nearly forgot… Yesterday, Juno phoned me at work in a real panic because she had left a couple of messages and you hadn't called her back. So I gave her your mobile phone number—'

'Well, she hasn't called yet. Where *is* she?' Star demanded.

'Switzerland…your mother didn't tell me that, but I checked the number after she'd rung off,' Rory admitted.

'Switzerland…what the heck is she doing there?' Star groaned. 'Did you tell her where I was?'

'Yeah…and she got really upset. Then she just hung up again. I'm sorry.' Recognising Star's anxiety, Rory reached for her hand and squeezed it in consolation. 'Do you want that Swiss phone number?'

Star nodded ruefully.

Rory wrote it down and passed it to her. Star dug the piece

of paper into the back pocket of her skirt and wandered very slowly back into the chateau.

Preoccupied as Star had been with concern for her missing mother, she really only noticed how coolly Luc was behaving towards her once the jet had taken off.

'I haven't even asked where we're going,' she muttered guiltily.

'Corsica…'

'Oh, I haven't been there…well, I haven't been *most* places!' she adjusted.

His lean, strong face empty of even a pretence of fleeting amusement, Luc rose to his feet. '*Excuses-moi, mais*…I have work to do,' he drawled glacially.

A heart-stopping vision of French masculine elegance in an unstructured lightweight suit in palest grey, Luc strode off to vanish into the office area of the jet. *Cool?* Luc was acting like the beginning of a new Ice Age. Confused, Star sat on a moment or two before following him. Longing for the light-hearted mood he had been in earlier that day, she perched on the arm of the seat across the aisle from him.

'I appreciate that I've been a bit of a drag since Rory visited—'

Luc kept his attention on the screen of his laptop, but his bold profile hardened.

'I've been worrying about Mum,' she confided.

For a split second a pained light flashed in Luc's narrowed gaze. She wasn't just a poor liar: she was a hopeless one. Having lit up with pure joy at one glimpse of Rory Martin, Star had sunk into silent misery the instant her former lover had departed in his boy-toy car. *Friendship?* All right, so he himself had never had time for close friends, but who did she think she was kidding? She couldn't act for peanuts either. If swarming all over that skinny little twerp in his girly jeans was her idea of friendship, she would be very lonely in the friendship stakes in the future, Luc promised himself wrathfully.

Star cleared her throat awkwardly.

Luc still couldn't bring himself to look at her.

'Juno called Rory from Switzerland and I tried the number, but it was a guesthouse and she'd already moved on without leaving an address,' Star volunteered tautly. 'I know you think she's a…a foolish woman at best and a schemer at worst, but I love her and naturally I'm concerned about her.'

'Naturally,' Luc echoed flatly. 'But to be frank…your mother has a healthy survival instinct. If she's in Switzerland, she must have a good reason for being there.'

'I can't think of any connection, except that that's where she fell pregnant with me,' Star confided.

Luc hadn't known that, but he kept his attention rigidly on the screen.

'You just want me to run along and play…don't you?' Star gathered tightly as the silence stretched.

'*Vraiment!*' Luc flung his arrogant dark head back and subjected her to a sizzling and derisive appraisal. 'After the performance you put on with Rory this afternoon, what more do you expect?'

Her throat caught as she recognised his anger. 'Performance?'

'I have no wish to discuss it further,' Luc ground out harshly.

Star contemplated his rigid profile and it was as if an alarm bell went off inside her head. 'You were jealous…' she whispered, in the tone of one making a fascinating discovery.

Luc slammed his laptop shut with such force it bounced on the desk. He sprang upright. Scorching dark eyes assailed hers in a look of rebuttal as physical as assault. '*Zut alors!* What do you think I am? An adolescent? I found the sight of *my* wife being so familiar with another man very offensive! That is not jealousy.'

He was so much taller than she was that it took courage

not to be intimidated. But Star was now angry too. Rising to her feet, she squared her slight shoulders. 'Whatever you say…but when you're annoyed with me, you'd better learn to face me with it. I won't put up with the deep-freeze treatment. And by the way, if you saw anything offensive in my behaviour with Rory, it was in your own mind.'

'You flaunted your intimacy with him,' Luc condemned fiercely.

'I've never been intimate with him…not intimate in the way *you* mean!' Star returned tartly, infuriated with him. 'And, since you're *not* jealous…I wonder how it was that you *imagined* you saw sexual intimacy where it has never existed!'

Luc froze, shimmering dark eyes suddenly welding to her flushed face. 'Never…?'

Turning on her heel, Star utilised the words he had used with her only a minute earlier. 'I have no wish to discuss it further.'

A lean hand closed over her shoulder to stay her. *'Star—'*

Star pulled away. 'No! I'm really annoyed with you. Why can't you just admit that you have normal human emotions like everybody else? Instead you tried to put me down as if I'd done something wrong! That's what I can't forgive.'

Leaving silence in her wake, Star returned to the twins, happily dozing in their seats like twin angels. Well, their father is no angel, she thought furiously.

CHAPTER NINE

A HELICOPTER took them the last brief leg of the journey.

'That's the villa down there!' Luc shouted above the noise of the rotors.

Star gazed down into a breathtakingly beautiful wooded gorge and saw a villa with a terracotta roof perched just above a stretch of golden sand. A ribbon of road ran down through steep, tortuous bends beneath the trees, but she could see no other houses. A private hideaway...just when she wanted crowds to prevent her lunging for Luc's jugular vein!

Although Star had a quick temper, she usually cooled down again even quicker. But this time she just found herself getting even angrier with Luc. Luc, whom she had once worshipped rather like a god, whom she had unquestioningly accepted was in every way superior to her humble self. Cleverer, stronger, better than her in every way. But Luc had attacked her once too often with her supposed flaws and mistakes.

Descending from the helicopter, clutching Venus, Star studied the rambling, spacious villa. Backed by a grove of tall cypress and beech trees, the weathered tawny stone gleamed like gold in the glowing light of sunset. Even a sourpuss would have been forced to admit that it was an absolutely out-of-this-world setting. And when Luc showed her through the front door it just got better and better. Marble-tiled floors, stylish, comfortable furniture, ornate lamps and vases, beautiful bedrooms and bathrooms, and cots dressed with broderie anglaise bedding awaiting the twins.

'How did you get this place at such short notice...a cancellation?' she heard herself ask, although she had been assiduously ignoring him.

'It's been in the family for a while.'

Star's face took on a jaundiced look. She should have known. Private, exclusive, possessed of every conceivable luxury. 'Was that a Jacuzzi out front?'

'*Oui…*'

'Well, you needn't think you're getting me into that.'

She listened to him audibly exhale, and busied herself with Venus and Mars. She had readied them for bed before they'd left the jet and they were snug in their respective Babygros.

Luc hovered. 'You're not going to have to cook or anything—'

'Oh, I *know* that. You wouldn't want to be poisoned, would you?'

Ignoring that comment, Luc mentioned the maid who would be coming in twice a day, and who would also be available to stay over if they wanted to dine out.

Star put the twins in the cots and thought what truly wonderful babies they were, neither of them one bit bothered by all the different places they had had to sleep recently.

'If you give me the chance, I'll apologise,' Luc drawled levelly.

'Forget it…it would be wasted on me. I'm just sick and tired of you always criticising me—'

'Star…I very much want this to be a special time for us,' Luc said. 'I accept that I spoilt things, but it's not like you to hold spite.'

'No, more's the pity.' Star surveyed him, aquamarine eyes shimmering. It annoyed her right then that he looked so absolutely gorgeous and so absolutely reasonable, as if he was trying to deal gently with a very sulky child. 'I mean, you didn't hang back when it came to censuring my actions, did you? So why did I? And I *did* hold back!'

'If you've got something to say, say it…'

'Have you a pen?'

His black brows pleating, he tugged a gold pen from his inside pocket. Star strolled into the main reception room and espied a notepad by the phone. Sitting down on a sofa, she proceeded to write.

'What are you doing?'

'You're clever when you argue. I want to be sure I'm not knocked off track. I want to be sure I get *everything* out!'

'I think I'll go for a walk on the beach, and maybe by the time—'

'By the time you get back, I'll have cooled off?' Star loosed a driven laugh. 'No chance, Luc. Right, are you ready?'

'Is this really necessary?'

'If you want me to stay married to you beyond the next five minutes, it is very necessary,' Star stated tightly. 'Point one. I do not like being treated like a child. I'm a woman and a mother. I will not be patronised.'

'*D'accord*...OK,' Luc murmured with amusement brightening his eyes.

Star was determined to knock that indulgent look off his darkly handsome face. 'Point two: that winter I fell in love with you, you encouraged me at every turn by not rejecting me. I think you got a kick out of my loving you.'

She had got her wish. His amusement had gone. '*Vraiment*—'

'No, I'm doing the talking here, and then I'm going to bed alone and you are going to *think* about what I've said.'

Luc spread his lean hands wide in an exasperated gesture and strode over to the window.

Star breathed in deep again. 'All that winter, you fed me confusing signals, both before *and* after we were married. You could have shot me down in flames when I said I loved you. If you held back the first time out of pity, it still gave you no excuse to allow me to dog your footsteps, absolutely out of my head with adoration *after* that day.'

Luc swung round, brilliant eyes glinting. 'I didn't want to hurt you.'

'Don't you understand what I'm trying to get you to work

out for yourself?' Star launched at him in frustration. '*Why* did you put up with me? You are not a tolerant, patient guy, and I invaded your space every chance I got. By rights, you should have loathed the sight of me!'

A dark line of colour now demarcated his hard cheek-bones. He said nothing.

Star shook her bright head slowly. 'I mean, just over a week ago I listened to you accuse me of forcing you into situations you didn't want…like you're such a wimpy personality, like you were just totally helpless in the designing paws of a little teenager. You, Luc Sarrazin, chairman of the Sarrazin bank, the guy with the cold, ruthless reputation who doesn't let *anyone* put one over on him!'

'I felt guilty about you…' Luc imparted grimly. 'Whose fault was it that as a child you ended up living with a woman who was a stranger and attending a boarding school? I assumed that my parents would have enough compassion to allow you to stay with us at Chateau Fontaine. As you have cause to know, that was a very stupid and naive assumption.'

'What else could you have done with me? *That* wasn't your fault.'

'I could have tried to help you and your mother. I judged her very harshly on the strength of an hour's meeting.'

'Luc, you were only twenty, and we weren't your responsibility. I was your father's responsibility, and he didn't want to be bothered with me.'

'But I was so angry at the way things turned out that I took nothing further to do with you.'

'You were a little too young to be a father figure…' Star was troubled and frustrated by the direction the dialogue had gone in. But she now saw that Luc had been much more disturbed by events that had effectively been out of his control than she had ever appreciated.

'At the very least I should have visited you—'

'If I made you feel so guilty…I'm glad you stayed away,' Star said woodenly, realising that he had given her another slant on his past behaviour, and really *not* a slant she had had any desire to see. Guilt—a powerful reason to have been unusually tolerant that winter she had fallen in love with him.

'What else is on your list?'

G for Gabrielle. She'd planned to ask him why he hadn't simply told her that he had a woman in his life. With no clear evidence of Luc having an ongoing relationship with Gabrielle, Star had soon dismissed Emilie's confidences about the other woman as being out of date. So it had been a much greater shock to discover on their wedding night that Gabrielle had still been very much a current interest in Luc's life.

'Star…you are sitting there seething,' Luc noted drily.

'I should've gagged you before I commenced attack.' Star emitted a shaken laugh, her triangular face very pale as the point of what he had already told her began to sink in even more deeply and fill her with unbelievable pain. 'I did intend to ask why you went to the extraordinary length of marrying me when you could have just cornered my mother and cleared up the misunderstanding…but you've answered that too. Guilt. Guilt covers everything you ever did, doesn't it? Past, present *and* future.'

Having perceptibly relaxed as her anger visibly waned, Luc now took a hasty step closer. 'What are you trying to say?'

Eyes shuttered, Star stood up, every movement stiff. 'That I've got no plans to forever figure in your mind as that poor deprived child you thought you were rescuing from Mexico. And it's obvious that's all I'm ever going to be. Did you honestly think I'd want to stay around after hearing *that*?'

As she attempted to move past him, Luc shot out a powerful hand to prevent her. 'You misunderstood me…' he gritted.

'No, I asked for the truth and you told me the truth,' Star recited shakily, tiny tremors of reaction starting to ripple through her slender length. 'If it wasn't for the sex, you wouldn't have any use at all for me. It's about the only thing I've got to offer, isn't it?'

Luc closed his hand over her rigid shoulder and spun her round. '*Mais c'est insensé!*... That's crazy!' he launched down at her roughly. 'Why are you talking like this?'

Star focused on the top button of his aqua silk open-necked shirt. Inside herself she felt as if she was dying. 'You really weren't jealous of Rory,' she gasped strickenly. 'My fertile imagination at fault again! But let me tell you one last thing, Luc Sarrazin...you can take your over-developed conscience, your pious outlook and your cruel, unfeeling brain and take a running jump, because I want nothing more to do with you in this lifetime!'

Luc seemed stunned into paralysis by that concluding speech. Star took advantage of his loosened hold to drag herself free and race for the sanctuary of one of the bedrooms.

Crisis. *Serious crisis.* Those two words stood out in Luc's head in letters ten feet tall, but he found that for several deeply disturbing minutes, he couldn't think round them, over them or under them. Then, for a fleeting moment, he recalled the sense of self-satisfaction he had experienced in parrying her questions without even having to think about them. Now he was in shock at the results. He had hurt her, really hurt her.

And you were planning to make her fall in love with you again. A ragged laugh was wrenched from him. The truth was he hadn't a clue where to start. Total meltdown failure now stared him in the face. But the only face Luc could see was Star's...ashen, empty, defeated. As if she had given up on him finally and for ever. Luc endured another terrifying few minutes when he couldn't string two simple thoughts together. He recognised his own instinctive fear for the first time and headed straight for the drinks cabinet, only to freeze. Only a wimpy personality needed alcohol to work out problems...and he hadn't done so well working them out the last time, had he?

The muslin drapes at the window fluttered softly in the light breeze coming in off the Mediterranean. From her bed, Star was watching the sun sink down below the horizon in a crimson blaze of splendour and listening to the soft rush of the surf.

There had been no tears; she felt totally hollow. It was the end, the literal end. Luc's every response eighteen months ago had been prompted by guilt and compassion. She had done all the running; she had *always* done all the running with Luc. Now she was facing the consequences—just as much as he was, she affixed, with a guilt that made her feel even more wretched. Two innocent children were involved now.

As the bedroom door opened, she was jerked out of her reverie. Moonlight glimmered over the paleness of Luc's shirt. Highwire tension was etched in his taut stance just one step inside the door.

'You're right,' he drawled with staggering abruptness, his accent thick as molasses. 'I was jealous of Rory...I was so jealous I felt physically sick. You were ecstatic to see him and you touched him. *Pour l'amour du ciel*...I wanted to beat him up and throw him in the moat!'

Stunned by that blunt confession coming straight at her without warning, Star mumbled. 'Oh...'

'But I did not recognise that I was jealous at the time...' Luc thrust driven fingers through his tousled black hair. 'I thought it was your over-familiarity with him that was making me angry, but when I think back, you might not have done anything I *liked* with him, but then neither did you do anything wrong.'

Star nodded very carefully, as if she was willing him to continue.

Luc moved his hands in an odd jerky motion and then

lunged back against the door, to slam it in a clear burst of frustration. He thrust his dark head back, hands coiled into fists. 'I am very, very possessive of you. I know that's not right, but that seems to be the way I am...'

He sounded really ashamed of that admission. Suddenly needing to see him better than moonlight allowed, Star sat up to switch on the bedside lamp. She collided with staggeringly defensive dark eyes, and her heart ached for him as if he had squeezed it.

'I was very relieved to realise that you and Rory had never been lovers. But that wasn't right either...'

That this was the guy who had told her to go off and experiment with boys her own age was silently acknowledged by the self-derisive twist of his wide, sensual mouth.

'So you've got a dog-in-the-manger side to you,' Star muttered tautly.

'I haven't thought about that...' A flash of dismay showed distinctly in his serious gaze, and even in that tense atmosphere she almost smiled. He looked slightly panicky, as if she had moved off his authorised script and he wasn't equipped to handle it.

'What else have you thought about?' she asked thickly.

'That I interpreted certain events in the manner that suited my view of myself best,' Luc admitted. 'I think I married you because I knew that sooner or later I would lose control and end up in bed with you.'

'But, Luc, when you got me, you didn't want me. I was your wife for six weeks—'

'And I said at the outset it *wasn't* to be a real marriage. I'm stubborn,' he grated with sudden impatience. 'If I slept with you, then it was a real marriage, a serious commitment...a commitment I hadn't even considered making at that stage of my life.'

'So you thought, If I sleep with her, I'll be stuck with her...and that was enough to keep me in a bed at the foot of the corridor,' Star said with flat bitterness. 'Thanks for clarifying that.'

'It was for your sake as much my own. And will you for once acknowledge that that entire six weeks was spent waiting for my father to die...and then burying him?' Luc demanded starkly. 'I know you think I'm unfeeling and cold, but I had a lot more on my mind than my own physical needs!'

Hot, shamed colour washed up over Star's startled face. She lowered her head, unable to comprehend how she could possibly have overlooked that harsh background to those weeks for so long. But then she hadn't loved Roland Sarrazin. He had been a distant stranger to her, a grudging guardian, a man with precious little interest in her. 'Yes...'

'I was under a lot of stress, and you were very appealing, but I didn't want to use you just for...comfort,' he bit out very, very low.

At that, Star lifted her head, aquamarine eyes swimming with tears. 'So you used Gabrielle Joly instead...'

Luc studied her in complete shock.

'Yes...I knew about Gabrielle,' Star confirmed, recognising that that really was a surprise to him.

Striding over to the bed, Luc sank down beside her. 'How did you find out about Gabrielle?' he demanded thickly.

She ignored that question. 'I thought you were finished with her...until our wedding night, when I heard you on the phone to her,' she shared chokily.

Luc lifted his hand and pushed her tumbled hair off her cheekbone, stunning dark eyes full of regret but also considerable bemusement. 'And yet you said nothing...you, who could talk up a storm over a leaf falling, said nothing about something so much more important?'

'You spent our wedding night with her.'

'Don't be stupid...' Luc groaned. 'How could you be *that* stupid?'

'I heard you say you were coming over—'

'To return my set of keys to her house...' Unsurprised, it seemed, by Star's incredulous frown, Luc expelled his breath in a hiss of annoyance. 'That's all the excuse I've got. It was crazy...and she was certainly very surprised to see me on that particular night. But that night I just needed to get *out* and I seized the first flimsy excuse I could come up with and acted on it.'

'To return *keys*?' Star repeated in disbelief. 'On our wedding night? You didn't come home that night...do you think I don't know that?'

'I fell asleep in the car by the riverbank...I never entered her home. I dropped off the keys and realised how open to misinterpretation my call was,' he shared with palpable discomfiture. 'I left again immediately.'

Fell asleep in the car? Luc, within a quarter-mile of a home possessed of thirty-odd bedrooms? Luc dropping off keys that he could have had returned without going anywhere near Gabrielle? It was so unlikely a story that Star simply stared at him wide-eyed.

Dark colour overlaid his fabulous cheekbones. 'It was a mad impulse, foolishly acted on because I didn't trust myself within reach of you that night. I knew you would come to me...'

Star dropped her head. He wasn't wrong about that. That had been exactly what she'd planned to do. But eavesdropping on that call had blown her intentions out of the water and left her high and dry, not to mention paralysed with shock, violent jealousy and very real distress.

'And I wasn't sure I had enough will-power to resist such an invitation. I was *burning* for you that night...possibly even a duck T-shirt wouldn't have held me back.'

'I'd bought a really naff black slinky nightie. It was too big for me. I dumped it.'

'I cannot believe that you said nothing after listening in on that call I made to Gabrielle...' Luc framed her face, forcing her to meet his fiercely enquiring gaze.

'What *right* had I to say anything?' Star demanded shakily. 'You had stated up-front that we weren't going to have a normal marriage…and there you were acting on it. That's how it seemed to me. You were just going to go on with your life like I wasn't there, and if I forced the issue, what would I get out of it?'

'The truth?' Luc prompted hoarsely.

'But I couldn't stop you sleeping with her if you wanted to…' Star reeled off brokenly, still bewildered by the idea that an episode which had caused her so much anguish might never actually have happened in reality. 'You could just have told me that what you did with *her* was none of my business. And once I'd pushed you to the stage of saying something like that, it would have been like something written in stone, and it would have been the end of my hoping to make our marriage a p-proper one!'

Luc felt gutted by the time Star had finished speaking; her pain was still so raw. He clenched his teeth, angry that he had caused her that much pain. She had been too damned scared to confront him about Gabrielle. Like a child unable to cope with unpleasant reality, she had spent the remainder of their marriage pretending to be her usual sunny, cheerful self, and *he* hadn't noticed anything different. But still he could not get his mind around the level of savage insensitivity she had believed him capable of.

'How could you credit that I would spend our wedding night with another woman? What sort of a bastard did you think I was that I would humiliate you like that?' Luc demanded. 'I *knew* how you felt about me. Even if I'd been on fire with lust for some other woman I wouldn't have sunk that low.'

'So instead you slept in your car on the riverbank…like a vagrant in a Ferrari,' Star whispered unsteadily. 'How could you ever think I would have imagined you doing something like that?'

'But now I finally know why you left me and never once

thought of coming back,' Luc conceded in sudden harsh conclusion.

Weary of all the emotions he had put her through, Star let her head flop down on his shoulder, breathing in the achingly familiar scent of his warm skin with a mixture of anguish and tormented hunger. 'You can sleep in here tonight...'

'No...short of you tying me to the bed and raping me. I won't allow you to accuse me again of just using you for sexual release.'

'That night at the castle,' Star reminded him helplessly. 'Stop acting like Mr Noble, Mr High-Minded—'

'I can't explain that night I...I just didn't want to leave you...I could think of nothing else but sex as an excuse. It was all that was *left* after you let me believe that the twins were some other man's.'

His lingering annoyance on that score made her tense. But just as suddenly he hauled her all the way into his arms, devouring dark eyes searching hers. 'Whatever else has changed, you still need me, *mon ange*,' he murmured with unhidden satisfaction.

She went limp against him, but not for long. The fiery demand of his sensual mouth on hers awakened her. And the most consuming impatience seemed to possess both of them. Star helped him to haul his shirt over his head, but was sidetracked when he bared his muscular chest, spreading her palms there, pressing her lips lovingly to every part of him she could reach.

He came down with a groan, struggling to snake his hips free of his trousers while she wrenched at her skirt. But the zip caught, Luc gave it one sharp tug, and when it stayed jammed, he just ripped it apart.

'So I'll buy you another ten,' he muttered feverishly, already engaged in extracting her from her T-shirt and capturing a tautened pink peak with a very vocal male groan of appreciation.

Her excitement was so intense she felt drunk and out of

control, heart racing insanely, every pulse pounding. Her body throbbed with a kind of ecstatic torment of anticipation. He traced the damp heat of her readiness and she twisted and turned, frantic for a more forceful invasion, every sense craving him with shameless, helpless abandon.

'I just want you...I just want you.'

'This is not a very cool start to a honeymoon.' Luc freed her of her last garment with a dexterity that was more driven by desperation than actual skill.

'Honeymoon...? Oh...*oh, please*,' Star moaned, clenching her teeth. 'Talk later?'

'If I'm still alive after this much excitement, *mon ange*.' With a ragged laugh, Luc came down on her and entered her in one powerful thrust. A shuddering groan of pleasure escaped him.

Star wasn't capable of vocalising at that point. The height of her excitement was blinding, silencing, all-consuming. The whole centre of her being was locked into every glorious movement he made. It was like suddenly entering heaven and hoping that heaven was endless. Never before had she experienced such a sense of oneness with Luc; never before had she felt sheer joy rippling through her in concert with the wild high of his possession. An intoxicating combination which sent her spinning into an earth-shattering climax of mindless strength.

He held her so close and tight in the aftermath it was a wonder that she could breathe. In fact she didn't think two adults could ever before have occupied so small a space in so large a bed, and that closeness made her feel so good it brought tears to her eyes. She kissed a loving trail across his shoulder, caressed his damp back.

He held her back about six inches from him, but kept their bodies still intimately entwined. His slashing smile made her heart bang up against her ribs. 'I really *do* get a high from giving you pleasure... I just want to do it again...and again...and...and again,' he teased, punctuating each repetition with tiny provocative and still hungry kisses. 'Rain-check on talking?'

Star studied him with passion-glazed eyes of wonderment, happy, so happy, that if she could have stood being separated from him she might have danced round the room. He hadn't gone to Gabrielle on their wedding night. She decided there and then that he was a god among men; Gabrielle had been incredibly gorgeous, yet Luc had clearly ended that relationship because he was getting married. So, whether he recognised the fact or not, he *had* made a commitment to his teenage bride, Star concluded with a wave of enormous satisfaction.

'You look wonderfully smug,' Luc muttered.

Tact seized a rare hold of her. 'I'm just happy…'

Star opened her eyes and lay sleepily still while a vague memory of Luc assuring her that *he* would see to Venus and Mars slowly surfaced.

For goodness' sake, it was eleven! Luc couldn't possibly have managed the twins on his own! Feeling guilty as hell, Star got up, and, hearing sounds from the lounge area, headed in that direction.

Luc was down on his knees with Venus and Mars propped up against the sofa cushions he had dragged down onto the floor for their benefit.

'Daddy…that's what you call me in English, but if it's French, which you have to learn as well,' he was warning them, 'it is Papa,' he sounded out carefully, and then repeated it, even more slowly.

It was so sweet. The twins made various little sounds like a chorus. Mars was the most earnest in his efforts to acquire this knew knowledge. Venus clutched at her toes, but she didn't take her attention from her father's darkly handsome visage for a second. Star had never seen her daughter stay that still in one place for so long.

'Luc…how the heck did you cope?'

His dark head turned, his eyes gleaming with amusement. 'It was a true learning experience… *Zut alors!* They have some appetite for their breakfast! I forgot to arrange high chairs, so feeding them was difficult, but we managed, and I got them washed and dressed as well,' he pointed out with considerable pride in his achievement.

The twins were only wearing vests. Star swallowed back laughter. 'You washed them too?'

'Of course I did…with a sponge. Venus turned that into quite a game. Watch Papa try to catch me,' Luc shared with a rueful grin of recollection, rising upright as Star bent down to cuddle their son and daughter. 'She found out that I'm clumsy, but persistent! I now badly need a shower.'

There was a fine dust of what just might have been baby cereal in his black hair. He hadn't managed to shave yet either. He paused in the doorway and looked back at her. 'I have very real respect for you now, *mon ange*,' he asserted seriously. 'How did you cope with them on your own? It was *really* hard work. I felt like I needed another set of eyes and at least two extra pairs of hands.'

'You were brilliant, absolutely brilliant,' she assured him softly, her eyes full of warmth.

'*Non*…I was lousy this time around, but next time I'll be better.'

A lot of other men would have been in a bad mood after more than five hours of childcare, and most rich men would have suggested that perhaps leaving Bertille behind had been a major mistake. But Luc wanted to be a hands-on father, not a distant one, and she was impressed that he wanted to rise to that challenge when he didn't have to.

While Luc was in the shower, Star started getting dressed. Her mobile phone buzzed. Realising it might be her mother calling, she lunged for it like a maniac.

'*Star?*' Juno gasped.

'Yes, it's me. Where on—?'

'I am *so* sorry that you've been forced to go back to Luc.

This is all my fault. I feel so dreadful, but, darling, you don't need to stand one more day of that womanising rat! I'm coming to rescue you...OK?'

'I don't want to be rescued, Mum.'

'But—'

'I still love Luc, and we're together again, and you really must stop talking like he's Public Enemy Number One just because he's Roland Sarrazin's son,' Star spelled out steadily. 'And that wedding night stuff? I was *wrong*. He wasn't with Gabrielle.'

'Surely you don't believe that, just on his say so? It's a good thing I'm flying into France this afternoon!'

Star stiffened in dismay, feeling that the last thing her marriage required right now was her mother's enervating presence, and then feeling instantly guilty at even thinking that. 'But we're not at Chateau Fontaine. Luc and I are on our honeymoon, and although I very much want to see you, and hear your side of what happened with that loan Emilie gave you—'

'Star...I've already sent Emilie a cheque in full repayment of that loan.'

'How on earth have you managed to do that?' Star asked weakly. 'Have you borrowed the money from someone—?'

'When will you be back from this honeymoon?' her mother cut in impatiently.

'In two weeks.'

'Well, if you're prepared to wait another two weeks to meet my new husband, I expect I can wait another two weeks to meet my son-in-law again... Luc's got more lives than a cat with you, hasn't he?'

'Mum...did you say what I think you just said?'

'You're just going to have to wait for the exciting details,' Juno pointed out with satisfaction. 'But I can tell you that I am blissfully happy. So I'll see you in a fortnight and you can meet Bruno then too. Bye, darling!'

Star sank down on the bed in shock while the twins crawled round her feet.

She was still staring into space when Luc emerged from the bathroom, just a towel between him and six foot three inches of immodest but gorgeous display. But for once Star had something to deflect her attention from his devastating presence, and couldn't even raise a smile when at first glimpse of Venus and Mars Luc yanked up a dressing robe and hurriedly pulled it round him.

'What's wrong?' Luc demanded the instant he saw her face.

'Mum phoned. She's gone off and got married to some guy she could only have known about two weeks.' Star gazed at Luc in weary apology, her eyes anxious. 'Well, you know it's sure to end in tears.'

Star went on to add that Juno had sent Emilie a cheque in full repayment of the loan.

'This new husband has money...either that or he's parted with his life savings. Not much we can do about this in the short term. Stop being such a pessimist!' His lean, dark features concerned, Luc tugged her up into his arms. 'Why should it be a disaster?'

Star sighed ruefully and rested her troubled brow against his warm bare chest. The tenderness of her mother's too often broken heart did not bear thinking of. 'Luc, you know as well as I do that maybe one man in a thousand could stand Juno's fits and starts...and to get married so quickly she must've fallen head over heels, and she'll be devastated if this Bruno character lets her down—'

'Bruno...and Juno?' Luc strung the two names together and a slight shudder rippled through his powerful frame. 'Seriously?'

'He sounds like a big thug.'

'*Mon ange*...' Luc pushed up her chin, dark eyes bold and level. 'Whatever happens, we will both support her. It's just a little unfortunate that she hates the sight of me.'

'Mostly because she too thinks you went off to Gabrielle on our wedding night,' Star admitted reluctantly.

Luc dealt her a riveted glance.

'And Emilie thinks that too, which is the only reason why she agreed not to tell you about Venus and Mars being born,' Star added in a craven undertone. 'Now I don't have a *single* secret left that you don't know about…isn't that good?'

Luc had the appearance of a male being torn in two different directions. Between strangling her fast and strangling her slowly. Then a muscle jerked at the corner of his hard, compressed mouth and suddenly he gave vent to a grudging groan of grim appreciation.

'You vented your grief liberally…everywhere with every possible person?'

She nodded apologetically. 'Talking helped.'

'But from now on you have to be discreet…you only allow your feelings to overflow in my direction.'

'Of course,' Star hastened to assure him, very grateful to have got over that last embarrassing revelation without an explosion.

'You talk to me about personal things. *Only* me,' he stressed.

'I get the message,' she swore. 'I'll try—'

'Trying isn't good enough. *J'insiste*,' Luc laid down with awesome authority.

'How much do you know about your real father?' Luc enquired casually that evening as they strolled back to the car after dining at a quayside restaurant in Calvi.

Star glanced up at him in surprise. 'Not much, but he really broke Mum's heart. Even eighteen months ago, when I finally got the chance to ask about him, she dissolved into floods of tears. She met him when she was working as a chalet girl in Gstaad. She was only nineteen. He asked her to marry him while neglecting to admit that he was already engaged,' she shared with a grimace. 'Then his fiancée turned up and Juno fled back to London without ever seeing him again.'

'What was his name?' Luc drawled lazily.

'I never asked…it didn't seem important, not when talking about him was upsetting her so much. He really did mess up her life.' Star sighed. 'Mum was brought up by her grandparents, and when they died she inherited nearly half a million pounds—'

'I never knew that.' Luc lifted her up into the four-wheel drive as if she couldn't possibly manage to clamber up on that big step all on her own. But Star was smiling, revelling in the manner in which Luc had been treating her since their first night in Corsica. As if she was spun glass, and so precious. She just loved it.

'Why should you have done? Phillipe had gambled away the lot by the time I was three years old. Mum only married him because she was pregnant with me, and I expect he was tempted by her inheritance.'

'I'm starting to see why Emilie believes your mother has had more than her fair share of bad luck.'

Delighted by that new tolerance, Star gave him a glowing smile in reward.

Two weeks later, Star lay in Luc's arms at dawn.

She was wide awake. They were flying home in a few hours. Wherever Luc was would be home, she acknowledged with complete contentment. Corsica was where they had grown closer than she had ever dreamt possible. It was a gorgeous island, full of spectacular scenery and forests and picturesque villages. This villa would always be a very special place for them.

Deciding to surprise him with breakfast in bed, she eased out of Luc's embrace. She watched his hand move across the bed, as if he was seeking her, as if he could feel her absence even when he was asleep. He would sleep late. He deserved to, she conceded with a grin, admiring the long sweep of his golden back in the soft light filtering through the curtains. He was a wonderful lover, a fabulous father, and shaping up really well as a soulmate. And last night he had spoken heresy…he was planning to *cut* his working hours and reorganise his schedule so that he travelled less.

Over dinner last night she had shared with him the details of the twins' premature birth and the subsequent months of frantic worry and stress. He had been so shocked. He honestly hadn't realised how at risk Venus and Mars had once been. He wished very much that he had been there to support them all, but he didn't blame her for not contacting him. He accepted that what he had said the morning after their son and daughter's conception had convinced Star that he really wouldn't want to know that he was a father.

I love him, I love him, I love him, Star reflected as she thought of that generous understanding and acceptance which had so relieved her. Perhaps tonight she would tell him that she loved him again. While she waited for the kettle in the kitchen, she lifted a glossy magazine which the maid must have been skimming through the evening before. On the front page she saw Luc's distinctive script. A note he had jotted down? Naturally nosy, she turned it upside down to read what he had written. A name and a date. A name that still had the power to drain Star of oxygen and turn her pale.

It *had* to be an old magazine. Not that that quite wiped out the huge sense of hurt she was experiencing. Naturally it was a smack in the face to appreciate that Gabrielle Joly must also have shared a bed here with Luc at one time. Suddenly all her own memories began feeling soiled. She turned the magazine round, just to check the date of it. Only then did she realise in sick dismay that the spoiling of sentimental memories was the *least* she had to worry about!

The magazine was only two months old, so when Luc had jotted down 'Gabrielle arriving' it had been barely a *month* before Star had come back into his life. Star hugged herself, suddenly chilled to the marrow. How could she now have faith in *anything* Luc had told her about Gabrielle Joly?

Luc had allowed her to believe that Gabrielle had been out of his life for a long time. And yet Gabrielle had still been his mistress as recently as two months ago! Star was shattered. Was Luc planning to keep both a wife and a mistress? What else could she believe? If Gabrielle Joly still held his interest after what Star now estimated to be a relationship of several years' duration, the beautiful blonde had to be very important to him. Far more important than Star had *ever* been prepared to consider…

CHAPTER TEN

STAR was gutted by misery.

She would have to wait until they got back to the chateau to confront Luc with her suspicions; it would be sheer madness to embark on what was likely to be a very distressing scene at the outset of a journey home.

So Luc had to make his own breakfast. He had never had to do that before, and it was not an entirely successful operation. When he tried to kiss Star good morning, he got pushed away and snapped at. By the time they boarded the jet, the atmosphere was explosive. Ignoring Luc's repeated demands to know what was wrong, Star concentrated her attention on Venus and Mars.

Ten minutes into the flight, Luc rose from his seat. 'Look at me, Star—'

'I don't want to look at you right now,' she admitted tightly, and lifted her magazine higher.

Luc snatched it out of her hands with a suddenness that shook her into looking up.

'Stand up,' he told her, dark eyes glittering with anger. 'We'll talk in private.'

'No, I—'

'D'accord...' Without warning, Luc simply bent down, scooped her out of her seat and carried her down the plane. 'We are not going to fight in front of the children.'

'Put me down this minute...' she hissed furiously.

Luc dumped her down into another seat and lounged back across the aisle from her.

'We're flying home to a very big party.'

That startling announcement took the wind from Star's angry sails. 'What are you talking about?'

'Being such a romantic guy,' Luc drawled with withering derision, 'I decided to stage the wedding reception we never had as a surprise. Three hundred guests will be waiting to greet us, including your mother and her seriously rich new husband, Bruno Vence. Be warned, Bruno is very small, and he has hair and eyes that are an exact match of yours. And now for the best bit of all. Your wedding dress is waiting for you in the main sleeping compartment.'

'My...my *what*?' Star gasped, already sufficiently thrown by the announcement of the reception and utterly bewildered by the apparent fact that he seemed to know more about Juno's husband than she did.

'You never had the wedding you wanted. Since that was my fault, I have arranged for a church blessing, and this time you get to wear a wedding dress.'

'I can't...I just can't.'

Luc lowered his arrogant dark head. Shimmering dark eyes alight with outrage locked onto hers. 'Oh, yes, you *will*!' he growled. 'You will not embarrass me in front of three hundred people. So ship out, dress up and join the grown-ups. Being in a bad, bad sulky mood is not an excuse for your behaviour since you got up this morning!'

'How about...Gabrielle?' Star whispered raggedly.

Luc stared at her, a pleat forming between his winged ebony brows. 'I don't see the connection.'

'I'll show you...wait a minute.' Star hurried back to her original seat to lift her bag and dig out the magazine cover she had brought from the villa as evidence. Her hands shook. Now the moment had come, she didn't want to confront Luc. Her head was spinning. He had organised these wonderful, wonderful events for her as a surprise, she was now appreciating in shock. They were to have a church blessing and she was to wear a wedding dress and finally be officially introduced to loads of relatives and guests as his wife. And if it hadn't been for the magazine cover she was crumpling between her hands, right now she would have been ecstatically happy.

Luc was poised exactly where she had left him. His darkly handsome face still as glass, he watched her approach. It was a long time since she had seen Luc wear that chilling expression and her skin crawled with foreboding; he had his defences back up. He was guilty; he had to be guilty. He was just waiting to see how much she knew.

In silence, Star extended the magazine cover.

'High drama,' Luc breathed with licking scorn. 'But I don't read this sort of rubbish.'

'It's something you've written on the cover…'

Luc perused his own handwriting. His hard jawline squared. *'So?'*

That undeniably aggressive demand for further clarification wasn't quite the reaction Star had expected. 'Well, it's obvious, isn't it?' she said shakily.

'On the basis of two words and a date I scribbled down the last weekend I spent in Corsica, you decided…what?'

Having to spell it all out somehow made it even more humiliating. A burst of anger pierced the fog of pain and despair which had enveloped Star throughout the morning. 'You're still sleeping with her…you never got rid of her…*all this time* that we've been married, she's continued to be your mistress!' she condemned rawly.

'Are you finished?' Dark eyes as glacial and dangerous as black ice rested on her. 'My relationship with Gabrielle died a natural death several weeks before I even married you! Late last year she got married—'

'Married?' Star stressed in shock.

'During their honeymoon, her husband, Marc, was seriously injured in a road accident. He was only recently released from hospital. When a mutual friend told me of their situation, and of Marc's need for rest and recuperation, I offered them the use of the villa for a holiday.'

Shaken by what he was telling her, Star blinked rapidly. 'But—'

'I haven't seen Gabrielle since she moved to Dijon last year. I was invited to her wedding but was unable to attend.' Luc scanned Star's drawn face with ice-cool eyes.

Star felt awful. 'Luc, I—'

'Gabrielle and I were companions and occasional lovers for a couple of years. It suited both of us. Neither of us wanted to be tied down and we parted just as casually,' Luc informed her grimly. 'I can't understand why you should *still* be so obsessed with her.'

Her face was burning. She could feel the heat of her own severe embarrassment. 'I'm really sorry,' she whispered.

'And I'm really angry with you,' Luc ground out with a newly learned forthrightness which was ironically very unwelcome at that moment.

The thoughts she had thought, the suspicions she had cherished, the very feelings she had gone through over the past hours since reading that stupid note on the magazine now struck Star as rather hysterical.

'For two weeks I've been planning all this behind your back...the church, the dress, the big party...' Luc vented a bitter laugh, a really bleak look in his eyes now, which ripped her to shreds inside. 'And all you've been thinking about all morning is walking out on our marriage again! Tell me, were you looking for a good excuse to leave me?'

White as death now, Star gazed up at him, her tummy flipping with fear. 'It wasn't like that. I got all worked up, and I *was* scared you might still be involved with Gabrielle, but maybe that's because I still feel insecure...Luc, I'm sorry.'

He closed his hands over her slim shoulders in a firm grip. His dark eyes were tough enough to strip paint. 'You are not leaving me again. I don't care if I have to chain you to a wall somewhere...you are *not* leaving me again!' he vented with raw emphasis.

Trembling with reaction, Star watched him stride away. She was deeply shaken by the amount of emotion he had revealed in that last speech. This time around Luc had been so quick, so ready to offer her a commitment to their marriage. But *she* had held back, refusing to give him her trust, making him feel as if he was on trial even though she had denied that. And she loved him so much! So why had she hurt him as she just had with accusations that were patently ridiculous in the light of his behaviour in recent weeks?

Bertille met them at the airport. Enchanted, like Star, when she saw Venus and Mars in the little page boy and bridesmaid outfits Luc had had made up for their children, the young nanny was even more impressed when she saw Star in her wedding gown, wearing a superb Sarrazin diamond tiara in her hair.

'I really *adore* the dress,' Star told Luc in the limo on the way to the church, tracing the beautiful beading sewn into the exquisite fabric. 'How did you pick it?'

'I didn't pick it. I just told the designer that you would want to look like a fairytale princess and, since you're so incredibly talented at embroidery, it had to be of outstanding quality. I only specified that it had to be pure white.'

'You know more about my dreams than I really ever give you credit for,' she acknowledged humbly.

'You'd better read this…' Producing a cutting from a French newspaper, Luc planted it into her hand. 'That's where my information concerning your mother came from. I suppose I should have given it to you yesterday, when I first saw it.'

Still horribly conscious of Luc's distance with her, but feeling she deserved it, Star stared down at the blurry photo of Juno and her male companion. She only then recalled that strange crack Luc had made about the man having her hair and eyes. Bruno Vence was fifty-three years old, described as a Swiss industrialist and a lifelong bachelor. Her mother was described only as an 'old flame'. Obviously the gossip columnist hadn't known her name. But Bruno's friends were supposed to be in severe shock at him racing off to get married to a woman they had never heard of and never met.

'Yesterday…you had this yesterday?' Star frowned, wondering why he hadn't shared it with her sooner.

Luc reached for her hand suddenly, and gripped it very tightly in his, his tension palpable. 'I just have this very strong feeling that Bruno Vence is your father. I met him last year at a business conference. I noticed his eyes were like yours, a very distinctive and unique colour, but I never thought anything of it. *Now* I'm thinking…'

'Luc, what's wrong?'

'Nothing is wrong,' he stated almost aggressively.

'Even if he is my father, and I really do think that's a *very* far-fetched idea,' Star told him gently, 'I won't be upset. Is that what you're worrying about? All I care about is that he should be good to Mum. But, most of all, I don't want anything to spoil this wonderful day.'

'So far it's been a shambles!' Luc groaned.

'No…no, I was very stupid, but nothing's been spoilt for me because I still have you here beside me,' Star swore soothingly, smoothing his tense fingers with her free hand. 'And you are very, very special to me, and so is our marriage. I know now that I want to be with you for ever, Luc, and I'm sorry it took me so long to admit that.'

Luc was very still, and then he released his breath in a sudden hiss. Snapping his arms round her tiny waist, he took her into his arms and kissed her half senseless with an almost desperate passion that just blew her away. He was pleased. She got that message. Probably because he now had the assurance that she was never, ever going to take the children he adored away from him, she reflected, just a little sad that that was the main concern in his mind.

On the steps of the church, with a photographer snapping merrily away, Luc tried to tidy her mussed hair and Star wiped the lipstick off his mouth. It would be pretty obvious to their children some day that a major clinch had occurred on the way to the church.

Heartstoppingly cool, dark and handsome in his formal suit, Luc took her hand and walked her into the little Norman church. The simple blessing that followed recalled for Star her feelings on their wedding day, and by the time they turned from the altar she was feeling full of bridal joy. So intent had she been on the proceedings that she hadn't taken the slightest interest in the fact that the church was packed with guests.

But no sooner did she turn round than her mother appeared in front of her. Comfortably under five feet tall, Juno's youthfully pretty face was wreathed with excitement beneath her cropped blonde curls. 'Star...I have someone here who very much wants to meet you.'

It wasn't the time. It wasn't the place. But then that was Juno, Star acknowledged, feeling Luc's arm tighten round her like an iron band while wondering what on earth was still making her husband so very tense. Surely a church blessing didn't fill a male with the same apprehension as a wedding ceremony?

In her heels, Star was looking eye to eye with the older man who had stepped forward to stand by her mother's side. It was a sharp shock to meet those eyes so like her own, eyes which were unashamedly wet with tears. Bruno Vence shook his greying copper head in mute acknowledgement of his strong emotion before he reached out gratefully to grasp Star's instinctively extended hands.

'I believe you already know who I am...' Her father breathed unevenly.

Five minutes later, in a whirl of confusion, Star found herself sitting in an unfamiliar stretch limousine with Juno and Bruno, not to mention Venus and Mars strapped into conveniently waiting car seats. However, the gathering mysteriously lacked Luc. Star frowned. 'Where's Luc?'

'We can drive straight to the airport and both you and the children will be whisked onto my yacht and out of French territory before anyone can do anything to stop us,' Bruno Vence informed her with impassive calm. 'Your mother believes that your husband must've blackmailed you into agreeing to return to him and that he has used custody of your children as a threat over you.'

'Are you trying to kidnap me?' Star exclaimed in incredulous horror, quite impervious to the fact that Luc had both threatened and blackmailed her at one stage, as he was now entirely forgiven for those sins. 'Juno, how could you *do* this to me? I want Luc...I want my husband!'

'Are you satisfied now, my love?' Bruno Vence asked her anxious mother with a wry smile. 'You see, Star loves Luc. I told you that it looked that way in the church. Our grandchildren are very fortunate to have loving parents.'

'But I wanted to take her and the children away with us,' Juno confided tearfully.

'I'd like to take my daughter away too, so that I could get to know her better,' Bruno murmured with a rueful glance at Star's frowning face. 'But she's an adult now, with a life of her own, and it would be very much simpler if we just made regular visits.'

Star's tension evaporated. 'You gave me quite a fright...'

'Your mother must accept that you are happy in your marriage,' he pointed out apologetically. 'In-laws who are troublemakers are rarely welcome.'

Star leant forward and kissed his cheek without hesitation. 'I think I'll be very happy to get to know you as a father.' She then shifted over beside her disappointed mother and hugged her tight in consolation. 'Now I'd like to hear about your marriage, and don't you dare skip a single detail!' she warned.

Twenty-one years earlier, in Gstaad, Juno had been confronted—*not* by Bruno's fiancée, as the woman had claimed, but by a possessive ex-girlfriend.

'I tried very hard to trace Juno in London,' Bruno shared heavily, holding her mother's hand in his. 'But I failed, because within a couple of months of leaving Gstaad she had impulsively married Phillip Roussel and gone abroad with him.'

'I've always known where Bruno was, but I just assumed he was a married man. Then, the day I had to give up the art gallery, I read a piece in a gossip column that mentioned he was single.' Juno blushed and lowered her lashes. 'But I really only flew out to ask him for a loan, because I was so upset and ashamed at getting Emilie into such a pickle.'

Star immediately knew that the only thing on Juno's mind on that flight to Switzerland had been seeing Bruno again, and she hid a smile.

Bruno was surveying his wife with immense pride and pleasure. 'When your mother walked into my office, I was transfixed. Juno was and is the love of my life. I want you to know that, Star.'

'Your father proposed over lunch an hour later,' Juno proffered. 'It was so romantic, and, you know, twenty years ago he said he *wasn't* a romantic man—but he just couldn't wait to get me to the altar!'

Bruno reddened.

When Star stepped out of the limousine at Chateau Fontaine, Luc was standing on the bridge, seemingly deaf and blind to the greetings of arriving guests.

'We'll see to the children...' Juno called after Star.

For once, the twins were not first in Star's mind. She threaded her passage through the sea of parked cars and headed like a homing pigeon for Luc. The instant he saw her he strode forward, impervious to all onlookers, and pulled her straight into his arms. 'Where the *hell* have you been?' he breathed raggedly. 'And don't you dare tell me you've only come home to pack!'

'No, I'm staying until I'm a skeleton in the family vault.'

'Not funny,' Luc growled, his dark drawl quivering.

'I got to know my father a little. Nice guy, but tough—perfect for Mum. Knows her inside out, adores her, can't believe his luck...they're like a couple of teenagers,' she shared breathlessly.

Luc possessed himself of her hand. 'You won't believe what I was thinking,' he muttered tautly. 'When you and the twins suddenly vanished into that bloody big limo, I suddenly thought I was never going to see you again. I *know* how your mother feels about me—'

'Luc...' A female voice interposed uncertainly.

Luc swung round and then lowered his gaze to focus on his tiny mother-in-law. He froze.

'If Star says you didn't carry on with that Gabrielle on your wedding night, that's good enough for me.'

'We agreed you weren't going to say that,' Bruno groaned from behind Juno.

'But Luc needs to know that I don't believe that any more, and that I intend to like him from now on!' Juno argued.

'Thank you, Juno,' Luc murmured hurriedly.

Her mother gave him a big hug and almost squashed Venus in the process. Hovering in the background, Bertille offered her assistance.

Cradling Mars in one arm, Bruno smiled and extended his other hand to Luc. 'I'm sure you appreciate my daughter.'

'Even *more* since you brought her home,' Luc completed levelly.

Minutes later, Luc closed an arm back round Star. 'You look totally ravishing and gorgeous in that dress, *mon ange*.'

Her heartbeat quickened as she collided with his eyes and she just smiled and smiled.

While drinks were being served, Luc introduced her to loads of people. Star saw Emilie in the crush, but didn't get the opportunity to do more than exchange a brief hug and the promise of conversation at some later stage. A wonderful buffet meal awaited them, delightfully informal and unfussy, just as Star preferred things. Luc stayed by her side all the time. In fact he was like superglue, and her mother had to be quite pushy to manage to share a private word with her.

'I just want to say that I'm sorry that I browbeat Bruno into spiriting you and the twins away from Luc at the church,' Juno confided then worriedly. 'When I saw how distraught Luc was when we brought you back, I was really very ashamed. I never thought he had it in him to really love you as he so obviously does.'

Well, he loves the kids certainly, Star conceded inwardly, too used to her mother's love of exaggeration to credit that viewpoint. As Emilie waved at her, Star passed on from her mother to settle down on a seat beside the older woman.

'I'm overjoyed to see Luc and you together like this,' Emilie told her warmly.

'By the way, that wedding night thingy I thought happened with Gabrielle...' Star whispered urgently. 'I misjudged Luc. It never happened.'

'I'm relieved to hear that, because I always did find it rather difficult to believe,' the older woman admitted gently. 'At the same time, I was very much to blame for what happened between you and Luc that winter.'

Star gave Emilie an amazed look. 'What on earth are you saying?'

Emilie sighed. 'I tried to be a matchmaker and I encouraged you to love Luc. But you were far too young, and Luc was too upset by Roland's illness to concentrate on his own feelings. I should have waited at least another year. I'm a terrible old plotter and planner, Star.'

'No, you're not,' Star told her.

'The main reason I gave Juno all that money was...oh, this is dreadful to have to confess,' the older woman whispered guiltily. 'Star, I *knew* there was a fair chance that the art gallery would fail, and I was praying that if it did it would bring you and Luc and the children together. You have no idea how wretched he was after you left him.'

Star's ears pricked up. Shaken though she was at what

Emilie had revealed, her reference to Luc being wretched superceded all other things. 'Wretched?'

'And not being able to tell him where you were seemed so cruel, but I had given you my promise and you had been badly hurt. However, Luc was dreadfully unhappy as well.'

'Was he? He was worried, of course. I was very childish, not getting back in touch—'

'Star…' Luc intervened from several feet away. 'We get to open the dancing with a waltz.'

'Dancing too?' Star gasped, jumping up and then freezing. 'How do you waltz?'

'You can pick it up.'

'In front of three hundred people?' she yelped. 'Can you jive?'

'No—'

'Fancy picking that up in front of three hundred people?'

'You do have a way of making a point, *ma femme*.' Luc framed her face and kissed her softly, tenderly on her surprised lips. 'I want everybody to go home so that I can be alone with you.'

'Party pooper,' she teased, a shiver of such powerful physical awareness gripping her she blushed. 'OK…I'll try to waltz, but we go slow.'

They drifted round the magnificent ballroom, so enveloped in each other that Star never even noticed what her feet were doing. And when they finally came off the floor, a long while later, Rory appeared with an attractive blonde by his side and apologised for his late arrival. Star was really delighted that Luc had thought to invite him.

Late evening, with only family members remaining, Star and Luc went upstairs. She snuggled up against him and whispered happily and without even thinking about it, 'I *still* love you so much…'

Luc stopped dead outside their bedroom door. 'No, you don't,' he countered. 'I'm still working on that.'

'What are you talking about?' she demanded.

A faint furrow drew his ebony brows together. 'You said *still*…are you saying you never stopped loving me?'

'Didn't I tell you I was going to love you all my life?'

'But then you ran away,' Luc pointed out flatly. 'Stayed away. I had to make threats to get you back, and you didn't exactly grab at the chance to stay married to me—not that I can blame you for that, but—'

'Oh, Luc, I have done a number on you…' Star said guiltily as she opened the bedroom door, thinking that the corridor wasn't the best place to be staging such a personal dialogue. 'I was just trying to be cautious for both our sakes, and I was scared of being hurt again.'

'I don't need to hear you saying you love me again until you can *really* mean it…'

'I mean it now.'

'But how can you?' His dark eyes were very strained. 'I messed up everything eighteen months ago. I didn't even know what was going on in my *own* mind, never mind yours! I drove you away. If I had set out to make a hash of our marriage I couldn't have done better than I have done so far.'

'But you're doing just great…' Star protested.

'I have been trying,' Luc acknowledged—rather touchingly, she felt. 'I took your love for granted when I had it. I liked having you loving me. You were spot-on when you said that. But even when you had gone, and I was bloody miserable, I still didn't grasp *why*! I just thought I was worried about you.'

'I'm here now, and I still love you very, very much,' Star repeated soothingly.

'I had this nightmare last night…and that's how I realised…*finally*…that I love you,' Luc delivered jerkily, a dark rise of colour highlighting his cheekbones.

Star was a little confused. 'A nightmare?'

Luc shrugged, studied his feet. 'It was stupid. I dreamt that Bruno and Juno would take you away. Juno never took to me, so there was no reason why *he* should—and, believe me, if your father wanted you to vanish, he's got the power to do it. It made me feel…sick, knowing that—'

'Oh, Luc.' Star sighed painfully, decided never, ever to tell him that there had been the smallest risk or chance of her vanishing in case he hated her mother for ever.

'So when you got into their car outside the church…and then I saw that the twins were gone too…that's the moment I registered that I loved you…when I thought I had lost the lot of you—my whole family!' he grated, lifting his arrogant dark head and studying her with such powerful emotion that her heart tipped over inside her. 'And I hadn't even *told* you how I felt.'

'Are you sure it wasn't just panic?'

Luc loosed a reluctant laugh at that question. Casting off his jacket, he closed his arms slowly round her. 'I've been in love with you for a very long time—'

'You can tell me anything,' Star encouraged.

He swept her onto the bed and pulled her close. 'First, I lost interest in Gabrielle. Then I just liked you…you fascinated me, and I suppose that's where I should have grasped that I was feeling something I'd never felt before. But I *didn't* grasp it. You have no idea how devastated I was when you left me. It was like the light went out of my life. So I just blamed you for making me feel that bad.'

'Typical…' she said, softly kissing the corner of his beautiful mouth, cherishing that phrase about her being a 'light'.

'And everything with you was *always* devastating.'

'The enemy tank syndrome?'

'Thinking the kids were some other man's, thinking I'd lost your love, not even knowing why I wanted you to still love me and then feeling really bitter—'

'I told you love was messy.'

'Then I seized on the twins as an excuse to hang onto you, so I didn't have to work out how I really felt.' Star removed his tie and began unbuttoning his shirt.

'I'm never going to say all this again,' Luc warned her very seriously, and she smiled against his warm, muscular chest, knowing she would plague the life out of him for any tiny detail he overlooked.

'I planned to make you fall in love with me again,' he explained.

'Nothing like not noticing what you've already got. So that's why I qualified for the honeymoon,' she gathered with amusement.

'I got the honeymoon too, and it felt incredibly self-indulgent,' Luc confided, and lifted her head to steal a passionate kiss. And things just got out of hand, much the way they usually did when they got that close. It was quite a while before they got talking again and, they were sealed together like twin magnets when they did.

'I thought you'd got over me and fallen for Rory,' Luc relived with a shudder of still sensitised recollection. 'I felt threatened, which is why I laid in with all the threats about going to court over the twins.'

'It was a loving friendship, Luc.'

Brilliant dark eyes assailed hers. 'Now you are really and truly and for ever married to me, you're not allowed loving friendships with other men. In all the time we were separated there wasn't *one* other woman in my life.'

'Seriously?' A sudden delighted smile curved her lips, and then she laughed with no tact whatsoever. 'No wonder you wanted one last night with me…oh, Luc, there wasn't anyone else for me either!'

'But you were thinking about it with Rory.'

Star gave him a loving look, recognising in that raw edge to his dark drawl that he was sometimes too clever for his own good. 'I honestly didn't think you wanted me or cared about me at all—'

'I adore you, and I am never letting you go,' Luc swore, with all the fervour a woman in love could ever have wished to receive. 'It took me a very long time to get there, but now that I have I know exactly what I want most out of life and that is you.'

Star heaved an ecstatic sigh.

'I just wish I hadn't missed out on you being pregnant...' Luc admitted ruefully.

'You missed nothing. I was like a small balloon.'

'You *couldn't* look like a small balloon.'

'Just you wait and see—'

'You mean you'd consider extending the family again?' Luc tensed. 'Are you sure it would be safe for you?'

'Don't be silly.' Star smiled at his concern. 'Since you're such a great father, your talents should be fully stretched, so I will definitely think about having another baby some time.'

'We'll talk it over with a doctor first,' Luc asserted with natural caution.

Just ten months later, Star became a mother again. Being Star, she hadn't planned the event, but was incredibly pleased and excited when she found out. Luc spent most of her pregnancy worrying and made her consult several doctors. Star only worried about Luc and enjoyed a perfectly healthy, happy nine months. She give birth to another little boy.

At the chirstening, Bruno admitted covertly to Luc that he was rather grateful they had not taken Juno up on her suggestion that this latest grandson be called Moon. Star's mother lamented that men were so old-fashioned about names and sighed to hear Venus now being called Vivi for short. She was really very shocked when Luc named his second son Orion, and Star's father just burst out laughing.

After putting Vivi and Mars, who were now lively toddlers, to bed that same evening, Star and Luc couldn't resist looking in again at Orion, snuggled in his four-poster cot like a little prince.

'Our genes mingled this time.' Star sighed with satisfaction, for their youngest son had Luc's dark hair and her eyes. 'It's like a sign, isn't it?'

Luc laughed and folded her into his arms. 'I don't need a sign to know that I am very, very happy with you.'

'I know. You were shaping up to be a pretty miserable guy before I came along.' Star gazed up into his stunning dark eyes and felt gloriously dizzy.

'I love you...' he murmured softly.

She curved even closer, reasoning that she needed the support, and whispered the same words back in between kisses. It was a long time before they made it down to dinner that evening.

Duarte's Child

LYNNE GRAHAM

CHAPTER ONE

'WHAT action do you want me to take?' the private investigator enquired.

Duarte Avila de Monteiro let the silence linger and continued to gaze out at his stunning view of the City of London. *She'd been found.* Sudden success after so many fruitless months of searching felt intoxicating. He would retrieve his son. Her too, of course. She was still his wife. He refused to think of her by name. He refused to personalise her in any way.

'Do nothing,' Duarte responded without expression.

His wealthy client was a total emotion-free zone, the investigator decided in fascination. He'd just given the guy the news that he had finally traced his runaway wife and the infant son he had still to meet—and yet nothing was to be done?

'Leave the file on my desk,' Duarte continued in a tone of dismissal. 'There will be a substantial bonus when you present the bill for your services.'

On his way past what he assumed to be the secretary's desk in the ante-room outside, the investigator paused: the secretary was the most stunning Nordic blonde he had ever laid eyes on. 'Your boss is kind of chilling,' he murmured confidentially.

'My boss is a brilliant financial genius and also my lover,' the blonde whispered in a voice as cutting as slashing glass meeting tender skin. 'You just lost your bonus.'

Rearing back in startled disbelief at that poisonous response, the young investigator stared at the beautiful blonde, aghast.

'Shall I call Security to have you removed?' she added
sweetly.

Within his imposing office, Duarte was pouring himself
a brandy and contemplating the immediate future. He had
an overwhelming desire to muster his entire security team
and spring a middle-of-the-night assault on his estranged
wife and child's accommodation. He *had* to move fast before she disappeared again with his son. His mobile phone
gripped between lean brown fingers, he tensed and then
frowned. For an instant, he could not believe that he had
even contemplated such an act of madness. He could wait
until morning... Well, he could wait until dawn at least.

He stabbed out the number for the head of his protection
team. 'Mateus? You will proceed to the address I am about
to give you. There you will find a caravan—'

'A *caravan*...?'

'Which contains my wife and my child,' Duarte admitted
with a grimace at the sheer incredulity he could hear in
Mateus's voice. 'You will ensure that if that caravan moves
so much as an inch it will be followed. You will also be
discreet while treating this as a matter of the utmost urgency and importance.'

'We'll leave immediately, sir,' Mateus confirmed, sounding shaken. 'Your faith in us won't be misplaced.'

'Discretion, Mateus.'

Duarte made a second call to put his private jet on
standby for the next day. Was he planning to kidnap them
both? She was his wife. Kidnapping was a crime. *She* had
kidnapped his son. *Inferno!* A bloody caravan! Duarte gritted his even white teeth, a flash of white-hot rage threatening his hard self-discipline. She was bringing *his* son up
in a caravan while she mucked around with horses. Who
was looking after their child while she devoted her attention
to four-legged animals?

Emily—safe, quiet, humble and as easily read as an open

book—a young woman unlikely to rock any boats. How had he *ever* thought that? With a raw-edged laugh, Duarte drained the brandy. He had picked her quite deliberately for those unassuming qualities. He'd given her everything that would have kept most women purring with delighted contentment. Fabulous wealth, a selection of luxurious homes and glittering social occasions at which she could show off her equally fabulous jewellery. His reward for his unquestioning generosity? She'd betrayed her marriage vows and his trust: she'd got into bed with another man. Obviously quiet women needed to be *watched*.

One of his medieval ancestors had murdered his unfaithful wife and got off scot-free because it had been regarded as an act of cleansing the family honour, rather than a crime. Duarte could not contemplate ever laying rough hands on any woman, even his estranged wife, no matter how enraged he was by her shameless behaviour. Then, Duarte never lost control in any field. He would deal with the situation as he saw fit. Walling her up alive would not have given him the slightest satisfaction and he could only assume his ancestor had been a seriously sick pervert.

There were other infinitely more subtle ways of controlling women. And Duarte knew *all* the ways. Duarte had never practised those arts on his seemingly innocent and shy little wife. So she was in for a surprise or two in the near future…

'I just don't understand why you have to move on,' Alice Barker confessed. 'I can drum up enough eager learners to keep you employed right through the year.'

Stiff with tension, Emily evaded the older woman's questioning gaze. Small in stature and slight of build, she wore her long curly red hair in a sensible plait. 'I don't usually stay anywhere for long—'

'You have a six-month-old baby. It's not so easy to stay

on the move with a young child,' Alice pointed out. 'I need a permanent riding instructor and the job's yours if you want it. My stables would profit from you staying on just as much as you would—'

Feeling the dialogue had gone far enough when there was not the smallest chance of her changing her mind about leaving, Emily lifted her bright head. Her aquamarine eyes were troubled and embarrassed, for she hated to turn down an offer that she would have loved to accept. However, telling the truth about why she had to refuse wasn't an option. 'I'm sorry, but we really do have to leave—'

'Why?' The older woman's weathered face was set in stubborn lines.

Emily's fair complexion was flushed with discomfiture. 'I guess I'm a rolling stone—'

'I don't believe that. I know travelling folk and you don't have that restlessness. You could have a comfortable home and job here with friends—'

'You're making this very difficult for me, Alice—'

The older woman tilted back her greying head and studied Emily with wry eyes. 'Maybe I'm hoping that you'll come clean and admit that you're running from something or somebody…and that the *only* thing keeping you on the road is fear of that somebody or something catching up with you!'

Emily turned very pale at that disturbingly accurate assessment.

'Of course, I suspected that you might be in some sort of fix,' Alice Barker admitted with a sympathetic look. 'You're too reserved and, by nature, I'd say you were a much more relaxed person. You're also too nervous of strangers.'

'I haven't broken the law or anything,' Emily responded in a strained undertone. 'But I'm afraid that's as much as I can say.'

But even as she made that assurance, she wondered if it was *still* true. Had she broken any English law in what she had done? How was she to know when she had not taken legal advice? She'd been on the run for eight months and she'd not got back in touch with her family or indeed anyone else during that period.

'Are you trying to shake off an abusive boyfriend?' Alice was keen to get to the root of Emily's problems. 'Why don't you let me help you? Running away never solves anything.'

Dismayed by her companion's persistence, Emily muttered in a rush, 'You've been really great to us. I'll never forget that but we *have* to leave first thing tomorrow.'

Recognising the sheen of tears in Emily's eyes, Alice sighed and gave the younger woman an awkward hug. 'If you change your mind, there'll always be a bed here for you.'

Closing the caravan door behind her, Alice trudged back down the lane to the stable block to lock up for the evening. Emily drew in a slow, deep, shaken breath. One thing that Alice had said had hit Emily on a very tender nerve. *Running away never solves anything.* That was so horribly true, Emily conceded heavily. Nothing had been solved or settled. It was eight months since she had left Portugal. She had run home to her family for support but her family had treated her like an escaped convict.

'Don't think that we're going to get involved!' Emily's mother had pronounced in furious dismissal. 'So please don't embarrass us with the details of your marital problems.'

'Go home to your husband. You're not staying here with us,' her father had told her in outrage.

'Have you gone out of your tiny mind?' Her eldest sister, Hermione, had demanded. 'What do you think your walking out on your marriage is likely to do to the family business? If Duarte blames us, we'll *all* be ruined!'

'You really are an absolute idiot to come here,' her other sister, Corinne, had said with stinging scorn. 'None of us are going to help you. Did you really expect us to react any other way?'

The answer to that frank question would have been yes but Emily had been too devastated by that mass rejection to respond. *Yes*, time and time again through childhood and adolescence and indeed right up to the age of twenty when she married, Emily had fondly hoped to receive some small sign that her family loved her. That blind faith had sunk without trace for the last time. She'd finally accepted that she was the cuckoo in the family nest, an outsider who was both resented and unwelcome and that nothing was *ever* likely to change that reality.

Why it should be that way she'd never understood. Yet she was painfully aware that had she got the chance to sit down and tell the honest truth about why her marriage had fallen apart, she would undoubtedly have been shown the door by her family even more quickly.

She'd had to face the fact that, whatever she chose to do, she was on her own. So she'd sold her engagement ring. With the proceeds, she'd bought an old car and a caravan and she had hit the road to make a living the only way she could. Travelling around the countryside from one stables to another, she offered her services for a few weeks as a riding instructor and then moved on to pastures new. The longer she stayed in one place, the greater the chance that she would be tracked down.

Of course, Duarte was looking for both her and his child. Duarte Avila de Monteiro, the terrifyingly powerful and even more terrifyingly wealthy banker she had foolishly married. His brilliance in the world of finance was a living legend.

When Duarte had asked Emily to marry him, she had been stunned for she hadn't been beautiful, sophisticated or even rich. Furthermore, her relatives might like to give themselves airs and graces in polite company but, though her family could not bear to have it mentioned, Emily's grandfather had been a milkman. So, understandably, Emily had been overwhelmed that Duarte Avila de Monteiro should decide to marry her humble and ordinary self. That he didn't love her…well, so nothing was perfect, she had told herself. At the outset, she'd been full of cheerful and trusting hopes for the future. Adoring him like a silly schoolgirl, she'd simply marvelled at her own good luck.

Although she had been in awe of her husband, she had never feared him, not the way others did. People were afraid to cross his reserve and offend him. People were afraid of his unapologetic ruthlessness. She'd been stupid *not* to fear him, Emily conceded heavily with the knowledge of hindsight. A wretched light in her troubled eyes, she reached into her son Jamie's cot and lifted his warm, solid little body up into her arms. Eight months ago, Duarte had threatened to take her baby from her as soon as he was born and raise him without her. Within days of being told of that appalling threat, Emily had fled Portugal in a panic.

But unhappily there was no escape from the reality that she had destroyed her own marriage. She had been the guilty partner. It was *her* fault that Duarte had demanded a separation, *her* fault that Duarte had ultimately decided that she ought to be deprived of their child as well. Indeed, in recent months, Emily had started feeling even worse over the fact that Duarte was being deprived of the right to even *see* his own son. Only her terror of losing custody of Jamie and her fearful awareness that she had neither Duarte's money nor influence had triumphed over her guilty conscience.

Now, however, Emily was finally facing the immaturity

of her own behaviour. It was time that she went to see a lawyer and found out exactly where she stood. It was time she *stopped* running…

Yet how did she deal with Duarte? And how would Duarte now deal with her? In spite of herself, she shivered as discouraging memories engulfed her. During their separation, Duarte had exiled her to the country house in the Douro for the winter. She had lived there alone for three months, hoping against hope that he would eventually agree to see her and talk to her again and that the great divide between them might somehow be miraculously mended. But that had been such a naive dream.

For Duarte, Emily thought painfully, would be happy to acquire a son and dispense with the baby machine who had produced that son. For really that was all she had ever been to her gorgeous husband…a baby machine. For what other reason had he married her? Certainly not for love, lust or loneliness. Childlessness was a disaster to the average Portuguese male and Duarte had an illustrious name. The Monteiro family could trace their aristocratic lineage back to the thirteenth century and, naturally, Duarte had wanted a child to carry on into the next generation.

Accustomed to early rising, Emily was up before dawn the following morning.

She'd packed the night before. After feeding Jamie and making herself some toast and tea, she collapsed his cot and stowed it safely away. Living in a small caravan had taught her to be tidy. As she slid into a pair of old navy jodhpurs and pulled on a voluminous grey sweater to combat the early morning chill, she watched her son. Sitting on the carpet in the compact seating area, Jamie was chewing industriously on the corner of a horse magazine.

Emily darted over and detached the magazine from his mouth. 'No, Jamie…here's your ring.'

Presented with the teething ring which had been chilled specially for his use, Jamie dropped it again and his bottom lip came out, brown eyes filming over with tears as he tried without success to reach for the magazine again. Sweeping her son up into her arms, Emily cuddled him and wondered why he loathed the teething ring which would have been so much kinder to his sore gums.

As always the warm baby smell of Jamie sent a great wave of love through her and she hugged him tight. He had Duarte's black hair and golden skin and the same shape eyes as her. Right now, because he had another new tooth on the way, he had pink flushed cheeks and he looked absolutely adorable in his red sweatshirt top and tiny jeans.

Checking that she had secured everything moveable, Emily decided to put Jamie out in his car seat. She had said her goodbyes the night before and all she still had to do was hitch up the caravan to the car.

It was a fresh spring day and the breeze blew back the Titian red curls from her brow. With Jamie balanced on her hip, she unlocked the passenger door of the car. Strapping her son into his seat and stowing the baby bag of supplies that went everywhere with them, she chatted with greater cheer than she felt to him. 'I timed this so that we would see the six o'clock train passing at the crossing. Choo-choo, Jamie—'

'Choo…' he seemed to sound out but she was prepared to concede that it might have been the wishful thinking of a proud mother.

Another day, another place, Emily reflected wearily and it was no longer the smallest thrill to contemplate the unknown that lay ahead. She had stayed longer than was wise at Alice Barker's stables, not only because she liked the older woman but also because she had been in dire need of a period of regular employment and earnings. Running even an old car was expensive; she had recently had to renew her insurance and replace the whole exhaust system. So, once again, she had little cash in reserve.

As she stuck her car keys in the ignition and turned, intending to hitch up the caravan, she heard an angry shout and then another. It sounded like Alice. Frowning in dismay, Emily hurried past the caravan to see what was happening. At the rear entrance to the stables, she saw a sight that shook her. Alice Barker was standing with a shotgun trained on a man.

'Just you tell me right now what you were doing!' Alice was demanding furiously.

As Emily rushed automatically to support the older woman, she heard the man speak and she caught several words. Alice's trespasser was striving to apologise in Portuguese. Emily froze in her tracks. *Portuguese?*

'I caught this chappie trying to creep up on your caravan!' Alice called to Emily with patent disgust. 'One of the peeping Toms, one of those filthy perverts…that's what I've caught. Just as well he doesn't seem to speak a word of English. I shouldn't think he's saying anything any decent woman would want to hear! Reach into my pocket and get my phone, and we'll ring the police!'

But Emily did not move an inch. Every scrap of colour draining from her slanting cheekbones, she stared at the stocky, well-built Portuguese male in his smart city suit. It was Mateus Santos, Duarte's security chief. Her tummy churned, her brain refusing to move at speed. The older man was as white as his own shirtfront, evidently not having expected to be greeted by a very angry woman with a shotgun when he came snooping.

'*Emily!*' Alice barked impatiently.

Mateus's strained gaze swerved to Emily's stilled figure with perceptible relief. '*Doña Emilia…*' he greeted her and followed that up with a hasty flood of Portuguese.

Emily understood a little more of the language than she

could actually speak and she caught the gist of his appeal. Mateus was asking her to tell Alice that he was no danger to anybody. Only that wasn't quite true, Emily decided in sudden total panic. If Mateus was at the stables, it meant that Duarte had tracked *her* down and that Duarte now knew where she was. 'I know this man, Alice. He's no threat, but please keep him here until I can get away—'

'Emily…what on earth is going on?' Alice demanded in bewilderment.

But Emily was already speeding back towards her car. Where Mateus was, Duarte would soon follow. She jumped into the driver's seat and then realised that she had still to hitch up the caravan.

With a gasp of frustration, she began to reverse the car and then dashed out again to haul at the caravan with frantic hands. The task accomplished, she was in the act of swinging back into her car when she saw the bonnet of a big silver vehicle filter into the mouth of the lane she needed to go down to make her exit.

Heart thumping somewhere in the region of her convulsing throat, Emily stared in absolute horror at the limousine. Duarte! It could only be Duarte behind those tinted windows. Just as suddenly, she unfroze again and flung herself into her own car. The ground siding the lane was unfenced and reasonably level. She could drive *around* the limo! Firing the engine, she slammed the door. Within six feet of the long luxury vehicle seeking to block her escape, she turned the steering wheel and took her car off the lane on to the rough grass verge. The caravan bounced in protest and the vibrations shook the car but, within the space of thirty seconds, she was back on the concrete lane again, the caravan still in tow.

She would go to a lawyer, Emily told herself frantically. She would stop at the first legal firm she saw and beg for an appointment and advice. She was not going to risk fac-

ing Duarte alone in case he simply took Jamie from her
and flew him out to Portugal. Hadn't she read horror stories
about disaffected foreign husbands taking that kind of action when their marriages to their British wives broke
down?

And, worst of all, wouldn't Duarte have grounds to argue
that *she* had virtually pulled the *same* stunt on him? Jamie
was six months old and his own father had yet to meet him.
What right did she have to keep them apart? An agony of
conflict and guilt in her gaze as she questioned what she
was doing, Emily pulled out of the lane on to the twisting
country road that lay beyond.

Duarte would attempt to follow her but she was at an
advantage for she knew the area. How could she take the
chance of trusting Duarte when he might take Jamie away
from her? She would be lucky to ever see her child again.
Where she was concerned, her estranged husband would
not be feeling the slightest bit sympathetic or reasonable.
Why, oh why, oh why had she waited this long before
acknowledging that it was past time she sorted out the
whole mess?

Rounding a corner on the road, Emily had to start immediately slackening speed. A shaken laugh shorn of any
humour was torn from her tight throat. The railway crossing
lay ahead. The warning lights were flashing and the auto-
matic barriers were coming down signifying that a train was
about to pass through. She was trapped for a good five
minutes by the very train she had promised Jamie he would
see as a treat. By the time the express finally thundered
past the barriers, Emily was studying her driving mirror and
watching the silver limo appear behind her on the road.
Caught! Fate had not been on her side. In a gesture of
frustrated defeat, Emily lifted one of her hands from the
steering wheel and struck it down on the dash board.

She felt a prick like a sharp stinging needle in the side

of her hand. Blinking, she glanced down and gaped in dawning horror at the big bee crawling away. It wasn't the season, a little voice screamed inside her, it wasn't the season yet for bees! She hadn't replaced her allergy kit when she had mislaid it over the winter. She dropped her hand down to open the driver's door. Already she felt like she was moving in slow motion; already she could feel the sensation of her heartbeat starting to race.

She lurched out of the car. She struggled to focus on the formidably tall and dark male striding towards her but she raised her hands to her face instead, feeling the tenderness and the heat there, knowing that her skin had probably begun to swell and redden. 'Sting…bee!' she framed jerkily.

'Where's your adrenaline kit?' Duarte demanded, instantly grasping the crisis and reacting at speed.

With enormous effort she blinked and connected momentarily with stunning dark golden eyes that she would never have dared to meet had she been in full control of herself. 'Lost…'

'*Meu Deus!* The nearest doctor?' Duarte caught hold of her as she doubled over with the pain piercing her abdomen and vented a startled gasp. 'Emily…a hospital…a doctor?' he raked down at her with raw urgency. '*Where?*'

It was such an effort for her to concentrate, to speak. 'Village through the crossing,' she wheezed.

She was conscious of movement as he carried her, the roar of car engines and raised voices in Portuguese but she was in too much pain to try to see what was happening. She opened her swollen eyes with a grimace of discomfort, for her whole body was hurting. She registered that she was lying in Duarte's arms inside an unfamiliar car and was suddenly terrified that everyone had forgotten about her baby. 'Jamie…?'

'*He* will be OK…'

Even in the state she was in, the sense that she was now

hearing his voice from the end of a long dark tunnel, she picked up on that stress. *She* might not be OK. She had been fifteen years old when it was impressed on her after an adverse reaction to a bee sting that she must go nowhere without her adrenaline kit. She had been too scared not to be sensible but, as the years passed without further incident, she had gradually become rather more careless. 'If I die…' she slurred with immense difficulty because the inside of her mouth and her tongue were swollen, 'You get Jamie…only fair—'

'*Por amar de Deus*, you are *not* going to die, Emily,' Duarte cut in savagely, lifting up her head, rearranging her with careful hands because she was starting to struggle for breath. 'I will not allow it.'

But before she lost consciousness, all she could think about was that it *would* be only fair if Duarte got Jamie. It was a punishment for her to be near Duarte again. It made it impossible for her to evade her own tormenting memories. Eleven months ago, one instant of hesitation had cost Emily her marriage—Duarte had found her in the arms of another man.

She'd let Toby kiss her and she still couldn't explain why, even to herself. At the time she had been desperately unhappy and Toby had astonished her when he had told her that he loved her. In her whole life, nobody had *ever* told Emily that they loved her and she had never expected to hear those words. Certainly, she'd given up hope of ever inspiring such high-flown feelings in her gorgeous but essentially indifferent husband.

While she'd been frantically wondering what she could say that would not hurt Toby's feelings, Toby had grabbed her and kissed her. Why hadn't she pushed him away? She'd not been attracted to Toby, nor had she wanted that bruising kiss. Yet she'd still stood there and *allowed* him to kiss her. She'd been unfaithful to her husband and there was no justifying that betrayal of trust to a male as proud and uncompromising as Duarte. In the aftermath, she'd been so distraught with shame that she had made a total hash of convincing her husband that that single kiss had been the *only* intimacy she had ever shared with Toby. Convinced that she'd been having an affair, Duarte had demanded a separation, even though she was four months pregnant with their child.

Emily's eyes opened and she snatched in a great whoosh of oxygen to fill her starved lungs.

The injection of adrenaline brought about an almost instantaneous recovery but she was severely disorientated and she didn't know where she was. As she began to sit up, scanning the unfamiliar faces surrounding her and recognising a nurse in her uniform, she gasped, 'What...*where*?'

'You just had a very narrow escape. You were in anaphylactic shock.' The older man gave her a relieved smile. 'You're in the cottage hospital. I'm the duty doctor. We administered the adrenaline jab in the nick of time.'

'Take it easy and lie down for a minute,' the nurse advised. 'Do you feel sick?'

As Emily rested back again, she moved her swimming head in a negative motion. After that initial buzzing return of energy which had revitalised her, she now felt weak as a kitten. She was on a trolley, not a bed, and as the cluster of medical staff surrounding her parted because the emergency was over she saw Duarte looming just feet away. She raised trembling hands to her still tender face, felt the swelling that was still there and knew that she had to look an absolute fright. In addition, the very minute that foolish thought occurred to her, she became aware of her own demeaning vulnerability.

For a split second, it was like time stood still. Her dazed aquamarine eyes wide above her spread fingertips connected with his spectacular dark golden gaze. His eyes were rich as the finest of vintage wine but utterly without expression. She could feel her heartbeat quicken, the wretched inescapable burst of liquid heat surge between her slender thighs. He came, he saw, he conquered, she misquoted, shaken to her depths by her own helpless response. From the first moment it had been like that with Duarte.

There had been a wild uncontrollable longing that had nothing to do with sense or caution. Something that had come so naturally to her, something that had been rooted so deep in her psyche that only death could have ended her addiction to him. He'd drawn her like a magnet and, what was more, he had known it from the first instant of their eyes meeting.

But their marriage had been a disaster for both of them, she reminded herself miserably. The more she'd loved him, the more she had become agonised by his inherent indifference. Impervious to her every attempt to breach that barrier, he had broken her heart. She had even been hurt by his satisfaction when she fell pregnant, for it was a satisfaction he had never shown in her alone. The old sick shame filled her as she recalled that fatal kiss which had cost her everything that mattered to her. She had finally broken through Duarte's reserve only to discover that *all* she could touch was his pride and his honour.

'I could strangle you for your carelessness, Emily...' Duarte breathed in a curiously ragged undertone.

'What *you* need is a good cup of tea. You've had a nasty shock too,' the middle-aged nurse informed Duarte in a brisk and cheerful interruption. Unaccustomed to being addressed as if he was a large child, he looked sincerely startled.

A porter began to wheel out the trolley on which Emily lay. As the nurse had spoken, Emily had finally recognised the ashen quality of Duarte's usually vibrant skin tone and the sheen of perspiration on his sculpted dark features. She closed her eyes, acknowledging the truth of the older woman's assurance. She had almost died on him. Evidently, he was relieved that she had survived. Maybe he did not hate her *quite* as much as she had assumed he did.

But then hatred meant a strong emotion where the target was concerned, didn't it? And Duarte had never felt *any* particularly strong emotion in her direction. A pain that felt almost physical enclosed her and she shut her eyes in self-defence. She knew that she had never had the power to hide her feelings from him and she had not the courage to meet his eyes levelly.

'Your husband has had the fright of his life,' the kindly nurse soothed her in a small empty side ward. 'When your child runs out in front of a car, you shout at him afterwards because you're angry and afraid that you almost lost him.'

'Yes…' Emily was rolled gently into a bed. She did not like to say that Duarte's most likely feeling now was one of complete exasperation and contempt. In her position, he would never have made the mistake of being without that life-saving adrenaline kit.

'Why am I being put to bed?' Emily asked, finding herself being deftly undressed.

'The doctor wants us to keep you under observation for a few hours just to be sure that you have no adverse reactions.'

Helped into a hospital nightdress in a faded print and left alone, Emily lay back against the pillows, anxiously wondering who exactly had charge of Jamie and how her baby was coping with her sudden disappearance. Almost at the same moment as she was thinking that the nurse reappeared, cradling Jamie, who was howling at the top of his lungs. 'I believe this little soul is yours and he wants his mum!'

Emily opened her arms and Jamie grabbed on to her the

instant he was brought within her reach. 'Who was looking after him?'

'The older man, who arrived just after your husband brought you in. He doesn't speak any English. He was out at Reception trying to calm your little boy down.'

Mateus Santos, she assumed, a committed bachelor who was probably pretty useless with young children. Jamie snuffled into weary silence against her shoulder just as Duarte appeared in the open doorway. He stilled when he saw the child in her arms and the nurse slipped out, leaving them alone.

Her tummy twisting, her eyes veiled, Emily muttered awkwardly, 'Have you seen Jamie yet?'

'No…Mateus brought him here in your car. My time was taken up tending to you,' Duarte admitted curtly.

Jamie had a death grip on her. He was going through that stage of disliking strangers that many babies went through around his age. He resisted being turned round and pushed his dark head under her chin. He'd had quite enough of excitement and strangers for one morning. It was anything but the best moment for Duarte to meet his son for the first time.

'Duarte…I'm *so* sorry!' Emily heard herself admit with her usual impulsiveness, a sob catching in her aching throat. 'I am so very sorry for everything…'

'That cuts no ice with me,' Duarte responded with eyes that were as hard and bright as burnished steel, cold derision etched in every line of his starkly handsome features as he studied her shaken face. 'How dare you drag my son round the countryside in a caravan like a gipsy? How dare you put me in the position where I have to answer to the police merely because I attempted to *see* my own child? And how dare you look at me now and insult my intelligence with that pathetic excuse of a word, "sorry"?'

CHAPTER TWO

'THE... police?' Emily stammered even more aghast.

'Since I married you, you have brought me only shame and dishonour.' Duarte breathed starkly, his controlled lack of volume far more dramatic than any shout.

'The police?' Emily whispered again shakily, her sensitive tummy tying itself into sick knots.

'Your employer, Mrs Barker, reported your great escape from her property *and* my natural pursuit. She expressed concern for your safety. Two police officers are now waiting outside for my explanation.' Duarte drew himself up to his full imposing six-foot-four-inch height and squared his broad shoulders with all the fierce pride of his ancestors in his bearing, but sheer outrage glittered in his condemning gaze.

'Duarte—'

'If you dare to lie and suggest that I have abused you or mistreated you in *any* way whatsoever, I will fight you for custody of my son! Is that quite clear?'

As crystal. Chilled to the temperature of ice by that announcement, Emily trembled. Her arms wrapped more tightly still round Jamie. Impervious to that old chestnut that children were always disturbed by maternal tension, Jamie had dropped off to sleep against her shoulder. With that single threat, Duarte had deprived Emily of voice, breath and hope that their differences could be resolved. She was in shock and could not have said why. After all, if Duarte had been prepared to separate her from her child the instant he was born, he could only be even keener to do so after the months that had since passed.

23

But then, eight months ago, Duarte's words of threat had *not* been spoken to her face. It was only thanks to her friend, Bliss that Emily had learned of Duarte's plans. Bliss had overheard Duarte state his punitive intentions to his lawyer and had forewarned Emily of her estranged husband's intentions.

Now quite unable to dislodge her arrested attention from Duarte, she scanned his fabulous bone structure for some sign of softening and found none. He meant what he was saying. Standing there straight and tall and unashamed and more beautiful than any male had the right to be. Like a dark angel. Even emanating aggressive vibrations, he was absolutely gorgeous, possessed of the kind of sleek, dark, bronzed good looks that turned female heads wherever he went. Why the heck hadn't she smelled a rat the size of the Titanic when he proposed marriage to someone as ordinary as she was? And why on earth had he neglected to mention his tragic first marriage? For any heart that Duarte ever had was buried in the grave with his childhood sweetheart.

'Is that understood, Emily?' Duarte prompted lethally.

Dully she nodded, dredging her attention from him in shrinking apprehension. To think that on several occasions recently she had anxiously wondered if she had misjudged him! No, there was no room to suspect *now* that Bliss might have misunderstood what she'd overheard or that Emily herself had overreacted to something said in anger and never ever intended to be acted upon. After the way she'd behaved, Duarte did not believe she *deserved* to have their child.

'Yes…' Emily turned her pinched face away and rested her cheek against Jamie's soft, sweet-smelling baby skin to comfort herself. Every which way she looked, she had done wrong, and there was no point offending even more by seeking to defend herself.

'I have no wish to part you from our son,' Duarte stated in a grim undertone. 'He needs you very much.'

'Do you really think that?' she whispered shakily.

'I say nothing that I don't mean. Give me Jamie now that he is asleep,' Duarte urged moving forward. 'Mrs Barker followed my security team here. She has offered to take care of our son until you are released from hospital. I understand she is familiar to him.'

Taut with suspicion, Emily held fast to Jamie's precious weight, but then she saw Alice appearing in the doorway with a look of discomfiture on her face. The older woman was carrying Jamie's baby bag. 'I'll look after Jamie, Emily. It's the least that I can do.'

'I will leave you both and deal with the police,' Duarte delivered coolly.

Alice grimaced and sank down at the foot of the bed. 'How was I to know he was your husband? I thought Mafia hitmen were descending on us and I was really frantic when they took off after you!'

'You didn't know what was happening…and I was totally stupid,' Emily groaned in remorse. 'I made things even worse by trying to run again. I just panicked and then I got stung—'

'And your husband, whom I thought was a dead ringer for the Godfather at his most glamorous, *saved* your life.' Alice winced. 'I feel so awful now for calling in the police and now they *won't* go away until everyone's explained themselves about twenty times over.'

'It's OK… It's all my fault. I always do the wrong thing,' Emily mumbled heavily. 'Particularly around Duarte—'

'Not much of a husband if he makes you feel like that. Maybe, to make me feel a little more relaxed about all this, you could tell me that he is really wonderful.'

'He *is*… I was the one who wrecked everything.' Emily sighed.

By wanting more than Duarte had ever offered, she'd made herself unhappy. She'd had a hunger to be loved and, if not loved, at least needed. But Duarte had not needed her either. She had just felt like another one of his many possessions with no true existence or purpose without him. She had never had much confidence but, flung in at the deep end of a world so very different from her own, she had sunk like a stone, becoming even more shy and awkward. By the time of their separation, she'd gone from having low self-esteem to having no self-esteem at all.

Alice left with Jamie. Then a very weary-looking police sergeant made a brief visit to Emily's bedside to confirm that she had no complaint to make against her husband. Having made that assurance while cringing at the thought of what Duarte must have undergone, Emily fell asleep and did not awaken until lunch arrived on a noisy trolley. The doctor called in to have a brief word with her and tell her that she was free to leave. As she had no appetite for food, she slid straight out of bed. Removing her clothes from the cabinet, she got dressed again.

Mateus Santos was waiting at Reception to escort her out to the limousine.

Duarte was seated in the back of the limo. Emily climbed in and sat down at the furthest point from Duarte that she could contrive. 'What now?' she asked tightly.

'We'll pick up Jamie and then we're going home.'

The silence lay between them, deep as a swamp and twice as treacherous.

Emily swallowed hard. *Going home?* She had not yet given him a direct look. Now she turned her head, her throat tight, her sea-green eyes strained. 'Just like that?'

'Just like that,' Duarte confirmed, skimming her a veiled glance from his dark, deep-set eyes. 'I had your possessions cleared from the car and the caravan and packed. I also told Mateus to dispose of both vehicles as you will have no further use for them.'

That was the moment that Emily appreciated that she now possessed only the clothes she stood up in. Her fingers closed over the ragged cuffs of her old sweater in an effort to contain an almost overwhelming sense of being trapped. 'It would have been nice if you had asked me what I wanted to do with them.'

'But then, all that concerned me was what I wanted,' Duarte murmured with velvet soft cool, reaching forward to sweep up the car phone as it buzzed.

Going home? He was taking them straight back to Portugal. From below her lashes, she studied him, nervous as a cat on hot bricks. The hard smooth line of his high cheekbones in profile, the classic perfection of his arrogant nose, the tough angular jawline slightly blue-shadowed by the hint of returning stubble. He was incredibly good-looking and sexy and she found it very difficult to resist the urge to stare when his attention was distracted from her. She listened to him talk in Portuguese, as smooth and cool as if he had not just dramatically reclaimed his runaway wife and child. No, indeed, it might have been any ordinary day and she might have been any woman.

'Duarte...' she framed jerkily as soon as he had replaced the phone. 'I'd like to stay in England—'

'That's not possible unless you insist on a divorce.'

Emily did not feel that she was in a position to insist on anything. Duarte had slaughtered all the protest in her the very instant he had threatened to fight her for custody of Jamie. She'd already spent far too many months fretting about how poor a parent she might seem in comparison to him in any courtroom. Her evident lapse in fidelity, her flight to England, her fear-inspired failure to deal with matters like an adult which had forced Duarte to mount a search. Nothing that she had so far done would impress a judge. Nor would her case be helped when it came out that she had been raising Jamie in a caravan while she roved around taking casual employment. In a Portuguese court, she had not the slightest doubt that Duarte would win custody of their child.

She curved her trembling hands together to steady them. 'I thought you would want a divorce.'

'Not at present.'

Emily wanted to scream. He was shutting her out. He had always done that, depersonalising every encounter, holding her at a distance…except in bed. Her fair complexion reddened to ferocious heat at that inadvertent thought. Just then, she could not bear to recall the physical intimacy which she had once cherished as evidence that he must care for her to some degree. Now it pained her to recall her own humiliating naivety. They had had separate bedrooms from the start. Sex had always seemed to have a faint aura of the forbidden. But it also had been wildly exciting…for *her*. The only time she had dared to touch him had been in the privacy of her own bed. In daylight, Duarte had been way too intimidating.

In a fierce struggle to control her wayward mind, Emily made herself focus on the child's car seat anchored opposite. Jamie's seat. Duarte was taking them both back to Portugal. Duarte was not thinking of a divorce. Duarte was not currently planning to deprive her of her son. Those facts were the *only* facts that mattered right now, she told herself urgently. She was tired of running and exhausted by living on her nerves. All these months, she had had no real life. What lay ahead could surely be little worse than what she had experienced in the past…

'Are you going to have other women…again?' Emily heard herself ask and almost died on the spot because that dreadful question had just come out of nowhere and leapt on to her unguarded tongue.

The silence seemed to flex like a stranglehold ready to tighten round her slender throat.

Slowly, Emily looked up, aquamarine eyes aghast.

Duarte gazed back at her as if she had just dropped down through the car roof, a fully fledged alien with two heads. 'What do you mean by...*again*?' he prompted very softly.

Emily connected with electrifying dark golden eyes and gulped. 'I didn't mean anything...I...I just wondered.'

'You made an accusation,' Duarte contradicted with razor-edged cool. 'A specious feminine attempt to justify your own behaviour by implying that *I* played away—'

Emily was backtracking so fast she was literally into full-throttle reverse. Not because she was a coward but because she could not afford to antagonise Duarte, lest he change his mind and decide that Jamie did not need his mother as much as he believed he did. 'No, I didn't...I didn't—'

'Don't try it again,' Duarte warned steadily, shimmering eyes resting on her like a slowly uncoiling whip lash.

Turning away in turmoil to stare fixedly into the middle distance, Emily only then appreciated that the car had already pulled up outside Alice's farmhouse. The chauffeur opened the passenger door and she leapt out like a rabbit with a fox on her tail. The older woman was already coming outside with Jamie clasped in her arms. 'Will you and Duarte join me for coffee?'

Emily reclaimed Jamie, her heart beating very fast. She didn't want to get back into the limo. She wanted to run again and she knew that this time there was no place to run. 'I'll ask Duarte if we've got time—'

But Duarte was right behind her. He greeted Alice with a courteous charm which Emily had only got to enjoy briefly during their even more brief courtship. Emily stared at her husband, marvelling at the tone of regret he contrived to employ as he refused an invitation he could not have had the slightest desire to accept. She said goodbye in a dulled little voice and got back into the car to fix Jamie into his seat.

'Stop cringing around me,' Duarte instructed grittily as the chauffeur closed the door on them again.

At least the previous unfortunate subject which she had opened was forgotten. But she noted that he had given her no answer. Not that she cared any more, she told herself. They would hardly be living together again but wasn't it peculiar that he wasn't talking about what they were going to be doing? Or was exerting that kind of power over her part of the punishment?

Becoming only slowly aware of the silence, Emily turned her head. Only then did she recall that Duarte was really only now having his first meeting with his son. Duarte was studying Jamie with an intensity she could feel. Jamie was kicking his feet, smiling and in the mood to be admired. Emily watched Duarte. The tension etched in his bold bronzed features, the movement of the lean brown hand he semi-raised and then settled back on a long powerful thigh again.

He wanted to touch Jamie. He wanted to connect; naturally he did. Her throat thickened in the weighted quiet. She slid Jamie's little blue teddy towards Duarte, nudging his braced fingers with the toy. 'You could give him that—'

'When I need your advice, I'll ask for it.' Lean strong face clenching hard, Duarte dealt her a flaring glance of bitter hostility. 'It's not a lot of fun wondering whether my own child will scream if I try to touch him.'

Emily paled. 'I know…I'm sorry—'

A tiny muscle pulling tight at the corner of his hard jaw-line, Duarte thrust his broad shoulders back against the seat.

'I've got plenty of time to get to know him. I'll do it without an audience.'

He was so incredibly proud. Had she not seen the yearning in Duarte's body language as he contemplated his infant son, she might have believed that he felt nothing.

'I was scared to get in contact with you...I was scared of losing him—'

'I'm not about to discuss your behaviour in front of him. You're his mother. You sound distressed. Look at your son...he's listening to your voice and watching your every move and you're *scaring* him,' Duarte condemned.

Emily saw the truth of that censure in Jamie's anxious air and her strained eyes stung, forcing her to blink rapidly. She compressed her lips on all the words that wanted to spill out of her but which Duarte did not want to hear. And could she really blame him? She *was* making excuses again. Right at that moment, Duarte's sole interest was in his son. She was just an adjunct, along for the ride because Jamie needed her. However, it was painfully obvious to Emily that Duarte was barely tolerating her presence.

From the instant they entered the crowded bustling airport, Emily became conscious of her scuffed shoes, faded jodhpurs and ancient sweater. The outfit had been practical for the long drive she had expected to have but she felt like a tramp beside Duarte, immaculate in a charcoal grey suit exquisitely tailored to his tall athletic physique.

'I could have done with getting changed,' she said uneasily. 'But I don't really have anything suitable.'

She had left all her expensive clothes behind in Portugal. Not that that much mattered, she conceded ruefully, for that wardrobe had rejoiced most in fashion accidents. If she got the colour right, she invariably got the style wrong. Growing up, she had been a tomboy, living in jeans and riding gear. Her attempt to experiment with a more feminine look had been squashed in her sensitive teens by her sisters' scorn. It had been poor preparation for marriage to a rich man and entry into a daunting world in which her appearance really seemed to matter.

'You can buy an outfit here and change,' Duarte pointed out.

To Emily those words were confirmation that she looked an embarrassing mess. Her throat thickened and her eyes stung and she reddened fiercely for she had no money either. She hovered over Jamie's buggy with a downbent head.

Through swimming eyes, Emily focused on the gold credit card extended in silence by her husband. The most enormous bitterness and pain seemingly rose out of nowhere inside her and she whispered helplessly, 'You should've married some fancy model, a real fashion plate...not someone like me!'

'It is a little late now.' Duarte's deflating tone was more than equal to capping even the most emotional outburst. 'And this is not the place to stage an argument.'

Emily swallowed hard. When had she ever had the nerve to argue with him? Yet it was odd how much she now wanted to argue but she was far too conscious of being in public where angry words would be overheard. Accepting the credit card without looking at him, she released her hold on the buggy and headed for the closest dress shop. There she scanned the packed displays. Choose really bright colours, Bliss had once advised Emily, saying that such shades flattered Emily's pale skin tone and balanced her red hair. Emily sped over to a rack of cerise dresses but they were way too plain in design to conceal a figure that Bliss had gently pointed out was more boyish than lush. Browsing at speed, she picked a jazzy orange handkerchief top with bell sleeves and a big glittery lime green motif on the front. Nobody was likely to notice her lack in the bosom depart-

ment under that, Emily thought gratefully. She teamed the
top with a long orange skirt that had the same fancy hem.

Both garments matched in colour and style, she reflected
with relief, thinking that that should definitely ensure a pre-
sentable appearance. She picked up a pair of high-heeled
leopard-print mules because she knew they were the height
of fashion. Her purchases made, she made harried use of a
changing cubicle. Emerging from the shop again, hot and
breathless, she saw Duarte and his security men standing
around Jamie's buggy in the centre of the wide concourse.

Mateus and the rest of his team focused on her and momentarily stared before lowering their heads. Then Duarte
glanced in her direction and froze. Not a single betraying
expression appeared on his darkly handsome features but
he seemed to breathe in very deep and slow. And she knew
right then that she had got it wrong again. Her heart sank
right down to the toes of her horribly uncomfortable mules
and she despised herself for her own weakness, her pathetic
attempt to please and win his approval in even the smallest
way.

'Sorry I took so long,' she mumbled, reclaiming the
buggy without glancing back up at him but conscious of
his brooding presence with every fibre of her wretched being.

'No…problem,' Duarte sighed.

In the VIP lounge, she caught an involuntary glimpse of
herself in a mirror and she was startled. She looked like a
fluorescent carrot, she decided in stricken recoil. Flinching,
she turned away from that mortifying reflection. Sitting
down, she tried to disappear into herself and her own
thoughts in the manner she had begun to practise within
months of marrying Duarte. He never had been any great
fan of idle chatter. She just wanted to sink into the wood-
work, sitting there in an outfit that he most probably

thought was ghastly. So why did she care? Why did she *still* care?

Emily had always been conscious that she was neither pretty nor beautiful. Her mother and both her sisters were tall shapely blondes with classic bone structures. Even in appearance, she had not fitted her family. At the age of ten, she had asked her mother where her own red hair came from in the family tree as even her father was fair. Her mother had dealt her a angry look as if even asking such a question was offensive and had told her that she owed her 'unfortunate' carroty curls to the genetic legacy of her late grandmother.

Seeing no point in bemoaning what could not be altered, Emily hadn't ever really minded being short, red-haired and small in the chest and hip department. But the same moment that she first saw Duarte Avila de Monteiro, she had started minding very much that she would never have what it would take to attract him. Of course, it had not once occurred to her that a male of his calibre and wealth would look twice at her anyway but she still remembered her own foolish feelings of intense sadness and hurt that it should be that way. That Duarte should be so utterly detached from her when her own senses thrilled to even his presence a hundred feet away.

And she still recalled the very first moment she had laid eyes on Duarte and very much doubted that *he* did…

CHAPTER THREE

BY THE time she was nineteen, Emily had qualified as a riding instructor.

Her two older sisters had found lucrative employment in their father's wine-importing business but Emily had not been offered the same opportunity. Indeed, urged by her mother to leave home and be independent long before she was earning enough to pay a decent rent, Emily had finally given up on the job she loved. She had taken work as a live-in groom at Ash Manor, Duarte's English country house.

The stable manager had hired Emily and, working at the manor, she had had an interesting insight into the lifestyle of a super-rich and powerful banker. Aside from his private jet, his fleet of helicopters and luxury cars, Duarte owned half a dozen palatial homes, superb horseflesh and a priceless art collection. He was the guy with everything, the target of endless awe, speculation and envy. But the one thing Duarte Avila de Monteiro did not have, it seemed, was the precious *time* to enjoy his innumerable possessions.

It had been weeks before Emily actually saw her wealthy employer in the flesh but she had already been told what he was like. Cool, polite, distant, formal, not the type to unbend with lesser beings, very much the product of a Portuguese aristocratic lineage said to stretch back to the thirteenth century.

His incredible silver sports car pulled up one afternoon while Emily and another female groom were cleaning tack. The stable manager hurried from his office to greet Duarte.

'That car's a MacLaren F1, worth six hundred grand,'

Emily's companion groaned. 'And just wait until you see *him*. When I first came here, I assumed the banker boss was some old geezer, but he's only twenty-eight and he's pure sex on legs. If you got him on his own without his bodyguards, you'd lock him in your bedroom and throw away the key!'

Even more than two years on, Emily still remembered that first shattering sight of Duarte. Sunlight gleaming over the luxuriant black hair stylishly cropped to his proud head as he climbed out of his car, a crisp white shirt accentuating his bronzed complexion but most of all she had noticed his stunning eyes, deepset and dark as sable at first glance but tawny gold as a hunting animal's the next. She was shocked and bemused by the unfamiliar leap of her own senses and the quite ridiculous stab of loss which assailed her when he turned away to open the passenger door of his car.

In place of the beautiful woman she had expected to see in Duarte's passenger seat was an absolutely huge shaggy dog curled up nose to tail into the smallest possible size.

The other groom backed into the tack out of sight. 'I'm not going to get stuck with that monster again. That dog's as thick as a block of wood, won't come when you call it and it's as fast on its feet as a race horse!'

Before the other girl even finished speaking, the stable manager called Emily over and told her to exercise the dog.

It was an Irish wolfhound. Unfolded from the car, it had to measure a good three feet in height and Emily was just one inch over five feet tall herself. But although Emily had not been allowed to have a pet as a child, she adored dogs of all shapes and sizes.

'Be kind. Jazz is getting old,' Duarte's rich, dark, accented drawl interposed with cool authority.

Emily angled a shy upward glance at him, overwhelmed by his proximity, his sheer height and breadth and potent masculinity. She had to tip her head right back to see his lean, dark, devastating face. She collided with sizzling dark golden eyes and for her it was like being knocked off her feet by a powerful electrical charge. She trembled, felt the feverish heat of an embarrassing blush redden her fair skin, the stormy thump of her heartbeat and the most challenging shortness of breath. But Duarte simply walked away from her again, apparently experiencing no physical jolt of awareness, feeling nothing whatsoever, indeed not really even having seen her for she had only been another junior employee amongst many: faceless, beneath his personal notice.

And, no doubt, had not fate intervened, her acquaintance with Duarte Avila de Monteiro would never have advanced beyond that point. However, in those days, Duarte had left Jazz behind at the manor when he was out of the country. The dog should have stayed indoors but the housekeeper had disliked animals and as soon as Duarte departed, she would have the wolfhound locked in the barn. Exercising Jazz fell to Emily for nobody else wanted the responsibility.

'The boss is fond of that stupid dog. If it gets lost or harmed in some way, well it'll cost you your job,' the stable manager warned Emily impatiently. 'That's why we just leave it locked up. I know it seems a little heartless but the animal's well fed and it has plenty of space in there.'

But Emily was too tender-hearted to bear the sound of Jazz's pathetic cries for company. She spent all her free time playing with him in a paddock and she gave him the affection he soaked up like a giant hungry sponge. So, the evening that the barn went up in fire, when everyone else stood by watching the growing conflagration in horror, Emily did not even stop to think of her own safety but charged to the rescue of an animal she had grown to love.

Although she contrived to calm Jazz's panic and persuade him out of the barn, she passed out soon afterwards from smoke inhalation. Surfacing from the worst effects, she then found herself in a private room in the local hospital with Duarte stationed by her bedside.

The instant she opened her eyes, Duarte sprang up and approached the bed, his appearance startling her out of what remained of her scrambled wits. 'Risking your own life to save my dog was incredibly foolish *and* incredibly brave,' he murmured with a reflective smile that in spite of its haunting brevity had more charm than she had believed any smile might possess.

'I just didn't think,' she mumbled, transfixed by the drop-dead gorgeous effect of him smiling.

'You are a heroine. I contacted your family.' His strong jawline squared. 'I understand that they are very busy people and, of course, I told them that you were already re-covering. I am not sure whether or not they will find it possible to visit.'

Paling at that sympathetic rendering of her family's ev-ident lack of concern at the news that she had been hos-pitalised, Emily veiled her pained gaze. 'Thanks...'

'It is I who am in debt to you. One of the grooms had the courage to confess that, but for you, Jazz would have spent every hour of my absence imprisoned in that barn,' Duarte admitted grimly. 'You are the only one in a staff of almost twenty who had the kindness to take care of his needs.'

Embarrassed by that unsought accolade, Emily muttered, 'I just like animals and Jazz may be a bit daft but he's very loving.'

The forbidding look on his lean dark features dissipated and he vented a rueful laugh. 'Jazz has a brain the size of a pea. He was my sister's dog. After her death, he should have been rehomed but I did not have the heart to part with him.' His face shadowed again. 'Perhaps that was a selfish decision for I am often away on business—'

'No. He just adores you. I couldn't get him to settle at

night until I got the housekeeper to give me an old sweater of yours to put in his bed,' Emily volunteered in a rush.

There was an awkward little silence. Faint colour now scored his superb cheekbones. He studied her through black lashes lush as silk fans, palpably questioning why he had unbent to such an extent with her. A minute later, he had been the powerful banker again, politely taking his departure, having done his duty in visiting her. A magnificent bouquet of flowers and a basket of fruit had been delivered soon after his departure. She had not expected to see him again except at a distance when he was at the manor.

But the next day when she was released from hospital, Duarte picked her up and insisted on driving her home to convalesce with her family. She spent the whole journey falling deeper and deeper in love with a guy so out of her reach he might as well have come from another galaxy. There was only a little conversation during that drive for Duarte was often on the phone.

Her family took one astonished but thrilled look at Duarte and his chauffeur-driven limousine and invited him to stay to dinner. Billionaire single bankers were hugely welcome in a house containing two young, beautiful single blondes. Indeed, her sisters Hermione and Corinne had competed for Duarte's attention with outrageous flattery and provocative innuendoes. Sunk in the background as usual by their flirtatious charm, Emily had felt painfully like the ugly duckling amongst the swans.

Emily was sprung back to the present by the necessity of boarding the jet. Soon after take-off, she realised that Jamie was overtired and cross. The steward showed her into a rear compartment where a special travel cot already waited in readiness for its small occupant. It took Emily a good twenty minutes to settle Jamie and then, with pronounced reluctance, she returned to the luxurious main cabin again.

Duarte rose from his seat and straightened to his full commanding height. 'Is Jamie asleep?'

Emily nodded jerkily, her tension rising by the second.

'Verbal responses would be welcome,' Duarte added drily.

Encountering brilliant dark golden eyes, she reddened hotly. 'Yes, he's asleep but maybe I should sit with him for a while in case he wakes up again.'

'Trying to impress me with maternal overkill? Tell me, who looked after Jamie while you were giving riding lessons?'

'Nobody—'

'Nobody?' Duarte queried with hard emphasis.

Emily frowned in surprise. 'It really wasn't a problem. I was only instructing a couple of hours a day and I would park Jamie's buggy outside the paddock. He was never more than a few feet from me and he usually had the company of parents watching their child's lesson.'

As Duarte listened, his lean powerful face tautened, his wide sensual mouth compressing. 'Usually? A working stables is no place to leave a baby unattended. You know as well as I do that riders can't always control their mounts and that your attention must've been on your pupil—'

Under that attack, Emily had stiffened and lost much of her natural colour. 'Jamie was always safe. I did the very best that I could—'

'But your best wasn't halfway good enough,' Duarte cut in with biting derision. 'You left my son at the mercy of passing strangers instead of ensuring that he received proper care—'

'I wanted to spend every minute with him that I could and you're making this sound much worse than it was,' Emily protested defensively. 'Everywhere I worked, Jamie got loads and loads of attention. Most people like babies, especially happy ones—'

'That's not the point,' Duarte said coldly.

Emily worried at her lower lip and then said heavily, 'Even if I had wanted to, I couldn't have afforded to pay someone to look after him—'

'And whose fault was that?'

As her tension climbed, Emily trembled and her tummy churned. Thinking straight had become a challenge; she had never been much good at confrontations. However, on this occasion she found herself struggling to speak up in her own defence. 'Whose fault was it that I left Portugal in the first place?'

Far from looking impressed or indeed startled by that comeback, Duarte inclined his arrogant dark head to one side and levelled his incisive gaze on her in the most formidable way. 'Presumably you are about to give me the answer to that strange question?' he prompted.

'I only left Portugal because I thought that you were planning to try and take my child off me the minute he was born!' Emily countered in an accusing rush.

Duarte angled an imperious brow. 'What kind of a nonsensical excuse is that? Before this morning, I never made a threat in that line. To be frank, my patience with you came to an end today. But who or what gave you the idea that I might have been considering such a dramatic move last year?'

Emily flinched and dropped her head, shaken at how close she had come in her turmoil to revealing Bliss's role in events eight months earlier. Had she done that, she could never have forgiven herself. Bliss had been the truest of supportive friends during Emily's troubled marriage, cheering Emily up when her spirits were low while offering helpful advice and encouragement. Although Emily had not contacted the other woman since leaving Portugal, she assumed that her friend still worked as Duarte's executive assistant. Bliss had eavesdropped on that confidential dia-

logue between Duarte and his lawyer and had forewarned
Emily. Were Duarte ever to discover that a member of his
own staff had been that disloyal, Bliss's high-flying career
would be destroyed.

'I just got the idea…at the time, the way you were treating me—well, er…it seemed to make sense to me and I
was afraid that you were planning to separate me from my
child—'

'So you chose to separate our son from *me* instead. Is
that how this sorry story goes?' Duarte dealt her a look of
shimmering challenge that made her breath trip in her already tight throat. 'This convenient angle that continually
seeks to turn you into a poor little victim? Well, I have
news for you—I'm not impressed, *querida*.'

'I'm not trying to impress—'

'No?' Without warning, Duarte sent her a sudden slanting golden glance as hard and deadly as an arrow thudding
into a live target.

Feeling the sudden smouldering surge in the atmosphere
but unable to comprehend what had caused it, Emily un-
twisted her laced hands and made a jerky move with one
of them as if she was appealing for his attention. 'I know
I've made mistakes—'

'Mistakes?'

'—but now I'm just being open and honest—'

'*Open*…and *honest*,' Duarte repeated with a brand of
electrifying soft sibilance that danced down her rigid spine
like a fullscale storm warning. '*Que absurdo!* An honest
whore you were not!'

Emily's lips parted company and she fell back a faltering
step in dismay at the proclamation and that particular word
being aimed at her. Even in the aftermath of finding her in
another man's arms, Duarte had not employed such an
emotive term. 'B-but—'

'But what? You were carrying my baby when you slept

with another man. How many women have affairs while they're pregnant with their husband's child?' Duarte demanded in a derisive tone of disgust that nailed her to the spot. 'But no such fine sensibilities restrained *you*. You even dared to introduce me to your lover. You also brought him into my home. Only a whore would behave like that.'

Forced to recognise the extent of the sins being laid at her door, Emily gasped strickenly, 'Duarte, it wasn't like that and Toby was *never* my—'

'Do you really think I'll listen to your pathetic excuses? You are nothing to me.' Duarte made that wounding statement with a savage cool that bled all remaining colour from her shaken face.

You are nothing to me. That he should feel that way was hardly news but spoken out loud that acknowledgement cut Emily in two.

'But you belong to me. *Minha esposa...*you are my wife,' Duarte completed with sardonic bite.

Under the onslaught of that ultimate putdown, Emily felt something curiously akin to a re-energising flame dart through her slim tense body and she flung her head back. 'No...I don't belong to you like your cars and your houses and your wretched art collection,' she heard herself asserting. 'I may be your wife but I'm not an object without any thoughts or feelings or rights—'

Although she had no recollection of him moving, Duarte was now a step closer, threateningly close. Even as she was still fighting to understand quite where her own unusually spirited defence had come from, she was awesomely conscious of the expanse of all that lean, taut masculinity poised within inches of her own much smaller frame.

In the electrifying silence that had fallen, shimmering golden eyes sought and held her scrutiny, all the powerful force of will he possessed bearing down on her. 'You have no rights in this marriage.'

'I don't believe you mean that...you couldn't,' Emily reasoned, tearing her gaze hurriedly from his as her heart rate speeded up. 'You're just very angry with me—'

'I am not angry with you,' Duarte growled like a leopard about to spring on an unwary prey. 'But I cannot and will not trust you with the kind of freedom I gave you before.'

'*That*...was freedom?' A startled laugh empty of humour was wrenched from Emily's working throat, for she had found her duties as a Monteiro wife as rigid a constraint to her days as a prison cell. Every daylight hour had been rigorously organised for her with a weighty yoke of responsibilities that took no account of her own personal wishes.

Hard dark colour scored the hard set of Duarte's proud cheekbones. 'So you find my former generosity a source of amusement?'

'Oh, you mean your money...' Emily very nearly let loose a second nervous laugh as comprehension finally sank in and her soft mouth tensed. 'Well, it wasn't much consolation when you were never around and I never did take to shopping, although I did try hard to like it. You see, I wasn't the sort of woman you should have married and I still can't really understand why you *did*...'

Duarte stared down at her with eyes as dark and fathomless and deep as the midnight witching hour. As he ensnared her fraught gaze afresh, she forgot what she was saying at the same time as she forgot to draw another breath. The atmosphere surged around her like a slow smouldering fire closing in, using up all the oxygen. But still she stood there, plunged without warning into a welter of physical sensations she had never been able to fight. As a wave of excitement as terrifying as it was thrilling washed over her, her heart thumped like a frantic bird trapped inside her, every tiny muscle tensing in reaction to the rush of liquid heat burning between her slim thighs.

'Can't you?' he murmured huskily.

The very sound of that silken dark drawl sent a responsive shiver down her spine. She snatched in a stark audible breath to flood her depleted lungs. She was tormentingly aware of the stirring heaviness of her small breasts and the painful sensitivity of her swollen nipples pushing against the bra she wore beneath her top.

'Aside from my wealth, I had nothing to offer you but you appeared to want very little.' Duarte studied her with spectacular dark golden eyes that had the most scorching effect on her already heated flesh. 'Apart from me…and you wanted me like you wanted air to breathe. At the time it seemed a fair exchange.'

Her mind a mess of jumbled and inane thoughts, Emily quivered as she literally struggled to concentrate on what he had just said. Understanding came in a trickle and then a gush and almost washed her away in a floodtide of pain and humiliation. Like an accident victim, she reeled back a step from their proximity, aquamarine eyes shattered, shame over her own weakness where he was concerned following fast.

You wanted me like you wanted air to breathe…

It was the most hurtful but demeaning truth she had ever had to swallow. Momentarily it threw her back into the past and a time when she would have done anything, accepted anything on any terms just to be with him. And all this time *he* had known that, a little voice of horror wailed inside her head. She was appalled and then shaken by her own refusal to accept that he had recognised from the very outset just how deep his hold over her was. All the shameless heat he had awakened without even trying drained away, only to be replaced by a fiery surge of hot colour that dwindled equally fast.

'You shouldn't have asked,' Duarte murmured, smooth as glass.

'Once...you wouldn't have answered,' Emily parted numb lips to respond and her own voice emerged all bumpy and broken.

'That was then. This is now and much has changed.' Duarte surveyed her with hard dark eyes of satisfaction. 'But, sadly for you, not, I think, your hunger for me.'

'Well, that's where you're dead wrong...' A sudden revivifying burst of bitter anger powered through Emily's quivering length. 'As you said, that was then and this is *now* and I got over my stupid crush when you got me pregnant and then decided to forget I even existed!'

'Did you really get over it?' Duarte reached for her with such a complete lack of warning and such shattering cool that she stared up at him in a wide-eyed daze, a frown just beginning to form between her brows. Before she even had the chance to blink, his hard sensual mouth came down on hers with all the explosive force and expertise of a heat-seeking missile.

Since that onslaught was the very last reaction she'd expected, she had no time to even try to muster her defences. She was blasted from angry shame straight into stunned and helpless response, a muffled gasp torn from her throat as he crushed her into the steely contours of his hard powerful physique. She couldn't breathe, didn't want to, couldn't think, didn't want to. Her whole body seemed to surge up and into his, instantly fired by the burning heat of desire he could unleash. He pried her lips apart, let his tongue delve in carnal and provocative exploration of the tender interior of her mouth and she shuddered and moaned as the upswell of electrifying sensation became more than she could bear.

'Duarte...' she gasped feverishly. 'Duarte—'

'Jamie's crying. You should go to him.'

Like a woman lost in a dream she let him set her back from him. Her brain felt befogged and her body was still gripped in the talon claws of an excitement she had never expected to feel again.

'Jamie...' Duarte said again.

And, in the same instant, her wits returned and she emerged from the grasp of the sensual world which had betrayed her with a sudden nasty jolt. Blinking rapidly, she pressed a trembling hand to the tiny pulse flickering like mad above her collarbone and she stared up at Duarte in resounding shock. His lean, dark, devastating face was cool as ice, his brilliant dark golden eyes challenging.

Jamie! Finally recognising the faint cry that she normally reacted to within seconds, Emily hurried away, pale as death and all knotted up inside with maternal guilt and self-loathing. Jamie had mislaid his teddy but he calmed down the instant his mother reappeared. The teddy restored to his grasping hand, his sleepy brown eyes pinned to her face and then slowly began to drift closed again. Emily sat down on the bed by the cot.

She was still trembling and her body ached from that elemental surge of hunger which she suppressed for so long. Of course, it had been so much easier to deny that side of her nature when Duarte was not around. Reliving the immediacy with which she had fallen into his arms, she squirmed and hated herself. She should have had more pride. But on another level she was simply stunned that Duarte should actually have *touched* her again. Duarte who, eleven months ago, had said he could not even stand for her to remain beneath the same roof.

Yet, he had touched her again and she had made a fool of herself. But then, she ought to be used to that by now, she conceded heavily. Hadn't her gorgeous sophisticated husband always specialised in running rings around her besotted self? And her mind slid back again into the past when just a glimpse of Duarte had lit up her world...

A month after the fire in the barn, Emily had been informed that Duarte wanted to see her. Fresh from the morning exercise run with the horses, Emily had been cringingly conscious of her messy hair and muddy clothing but too worried about *why* he should want to see her to waste time getting changed.

For the first time, she set foot *inside* Ash Manor to see the beautifully restored Georgian interior that lay beyond the imposing front door. Jazz raced across the hall to throw himself at her with his usual exuberance. She got down on the floor to give him a hug that turned into a mock wrestling session—and then discovered that Duarte was standing watching her childish antics with his dog.

Momentarily his rare smile glimmered on his lips and he said something but she didn't catch what he said. The visual effect of Duarte after four weeks of deprivation had bereft her of all rational thought and concentration. In strong embarrassment, she'd scrambled up and he had shown her into a library where he invited her to sit down.

'I'm pretty dirty.' Emily had scanned the watered silk covering the indicated chair, preferring to look at it rather than at him as her wretched face burned scarlet. 'I'd be better standing.'

'As you wish. I won't be keeping you long.' Duarte lounged back against a polished desk, the very picture of polished elegance in his tailored business suit. 'When I entertain here, my friends and business associates often bring their families with them. I believe you're a riding instructor. I'd like you to start giving lessons to my younger guests. Naturally I'll raise your salary. Are you interested?'

Emily glanced up with a surprised but pleased smile. 'Very much.'

That winter, Duarte spent a remarkable amount of time at Ash Manor. Her duties gradually extended to generally supervising and entertaining any visiting children. At the end of the first month, Duarte said that it would be more convenient if she moved out of the flat she shared with the other grooms and into the manor itself. Dismayed to then be told that she was expected to take her meals in the dining room, she had ducked that challenge on the first night. Settling down to her evening meal in the kitchen, she had been aghast when Duarte strode in.

'What are you doing in here?' he had demanded in exasperation, startling her half out of her wits. 'You eat with my guests now.'

But everyone but Duarte and the children had ignored her in the dining room. Content to be ignored in a gathering of so many wealthy and important people, she had been taken aback when Duarte continually attempted to drag her into conversations.

'I heard Mr Monteiro tell Mum that you're marvellous with children and animals,' one of her temporary charges told her chattily one rainy evening while they worked on a horribly complex jigsaw. 'And very kind… Can I stay up until we finish this?'

Crumbs to a starving heart, she'd thought at the time, hugging those few words of approval to herself but secretly wishing that those words had been more personal. But much much later, when she was Duarte's wife, she had finally grasped that she had been under observation during that period, marched out like a reluctant-to-perform animal so that he could see how she behaved, how she thought, how she reacted in different situations. And quiet and shy had ultimately been fine with him. After all, what qualities does a male look for in a low-maintenance wife?

For that was the starring role for which she had been carefully picked with the minimum of required effort on his part. A low-maintenance wife, dead keen on soppy things like kids and dogs, unlikely to require much attention.

'You've done a terrific job,' Duarte informed her some weeks later. 'Let me take you out to dinner.'

Paralysed to the spot, she had stared at him. 'Oh, there's no need for that—'

'Emily—'

'Really, I wouldn't be comfortable imposing on you like that,' she had gabbled, distressed and embarrassed at the idea that he believed that he owed her some sort of treat for admittedly working very long hours.

'But I insist. Dinner… Eight,' Duarte had stated curtly.

So he took her out to dinner and she sat looking at him like a hypnotised rabbit, mumbling responses, spilling her wine and, due to the fancy menu couched in French, ending up with raw steak when what she had really wanted was a well-done one.

'Why are you so nervous?' he had finally asked with an air of imperturbable calm that just might have been laced with concealed exasperation.

'I'm just not comfortable,' she told him miserably.

'But we have often talked before this.'

'This is different—'

'So it is…' Duarte had given her a wry look. 'I don't believe I've had a date this disastrous since I was a teenager.'

'A…a *date*?' she had stressed in considerable shock.

'Why not? I like you, Emily. What more is required?'

After marrying him, she could have told him exactly what was required. But that evening, offered the substance of her wildest fantasies she had had no such caution and commonsense. She had simply gazed back at him, transfixed by a sensation of wondering joy and gratitude. 'I like you too,' she'd said inanely.

'Excellent,' Duarte had pronounced as the plate of raw steak was discreetly removed at his instruction to be replaced some timeless period later by a cooked one.

'In fact, I like you a lot,' Emily had heard herself adding like an eager schoolgirl.

'Even better,' Duarte had asserted valiantly.

But he hadn't kissed her that week or the next. In fact if she hadn't hovered one night during the third week in the most humiliatingly suggestive way, she honestly believed that he might not have bothered to kiss her at all until he married her. Evidently registering that some lusty enthusiasm was required to impress even the most shy and inexperienced of women, he had got it all over with at once. He had taken her to bed the same night. In the dawn hours, while she was lying on the far side of the bed, wondering frantically whether she ought to be sneaking back to her own room, Duarte had opened his stunning dark golden eyes and rested them on her blushing face and murmured with grave quietness, 'Will you marry me, Emily?'

And she had not asked why. Nor had she or he broached a single one of the questions that she imagined people usually exchanged on such a momentous occasion. She'd just nodded like a marionette having her strings pulled by expert hands. And those expert hands had reached for her again in reality as he breathed lazily, 'I may already have got you pregnant. We'll get married very soon.'

Emily was sprung from her introspection by an announcement over the tannoy that the jet was soon to land. With a groan at the necessity, she lifted her sleeping son from the cot and returned to the main cabin.

CHAPTER FOUR

WHEN Emily emerged from the jet with Jamie in her arms, she saw two limousines waiting on the tarmac to greet them. A slim svelte female, clad in an elegant suit the shade of eau-de-nil alighted from the first car. As the woman's pale golden hair glinted in the evening sunlight, a warm smile relaxed Emily's tense mouth and she hurried down the steps in Duarte's wake.

Bliss was *still* working for Duarte! As Bliss finally spotted Emily and the baby she was carrying, her face froze and she momentarily stilled. Naturally Bliss would be stunned to see her back in Portugal, Emily reflected, and then hurriedly ditched her own smile in an effort to be more discreet. Bliss had said that Duarte would never approve of his wife embarking on a close friendship with one of his personal staff and, naturally, Bliss had not wanted to risk damaging her career prospects.

'Mrs Monteiro...' Bliss acknowledged coolly, her clear blue eyes skimming off Emily just as quickly again, her exquisite face expressionless.

Bliss was being really discreet, Emily decided but she felt just a bit cut off by that greeting and anxiously wondered if she had offended the other woman with her silence in recent months. If she had, it would be ironic for she had stayed out of touch rather than subject her friend to the stress of further divided loyalties.

'Wait in the car, Emily,' Duarte instructed in an arctic tone.

Reddening as Mateus surged ahead of her to open the passenger door of the rear limousine, Emily climbed in and gazed back out at her husband and his executive assistant where they remained about thirty feet away. Duarte looked very grave but, as always, stunningly handsome. All tall and dark and sleek and bronzed, command and authority stamped into every hard line of his lean powerful face. Bliss, who had always reminded Emily of a fairytale princess brought to life, looked curiously frozen and a bright swathe of pink now burned over her delicate cheekbones.

Striding over to the limo, Duarte swung in beside Emily and the car moved off. Surprised that the jet had landed at Lisbon rather than at Oporto, Emily wondered if Duarte was heading to a business meeting. Certain that Duarte intended to send both her and his son back to the house in the Douro, Emily contemplated the very long car journey which lay ahead for her and Jamie.

At least it was spring, she thought ruefully. She had spent the winter of their separation in the country house and it had been dismal. These days the Monteiros only ever used the property for a rustic summer break or during the *vindima*, the grape harvest when the Portuguese enjoyed getting back to their roots. In winter, the villa had been shrouded in the thick grey mists that rose above the dramatic high banks of the Douro river and day after day it had rained heavily and got colder. Emily shivered at those depressing recollections.

'Perhaps I could spend the winters in England,' Emily proposed in a small taut voice.

Duarte moved a lean, silencing hand for he was talking on the car phone. He frowned at her, winged black brows drawing together above clear golden eyes. Biting at her lip, Emily turned away again. The limo had already left the motorway. They were on the outskirts of the pretty hilltown of Sintra and within a startling stone's throw of her former marital home, the Quinta de Monteiro. She assumed that Duarte was being dropped off home first.

Dense forest covered the hills above the ancient winding streets of the tiny village below the *quinta*. The verges of the road were carpeted with a colourful riot of naturalised crocus and scilla blooms. It was beautiful. But gooseflesh rose on Emily's arms as she found herself studying the narrow corner building where Toby had once had his artist's studio. The window shutters now bore a faded 'for rent' notice.

'I assure you that you won't be spending the winters or indeed, any other season in England,' Duarte imparted that news with a gritty edge to his dark deep drawl. 'I could not trust you that far from my sight.'

Emily twisted her head back with a bemused look. 'I beg your pardon?'

'From now on, everywhere you go you will be accompanied,' Duarte murmured.

'Wh-what on earth are you talking about?' Emily stammered as the opulent car glided below the imposing turreted entrance of the Quinta de Monteiro.

'You heard me.' Spectacular golden eyes tough as granite settled on her with unnerving force. 'If you go riding, you will take a groom, and for all other outings, you will have a driver and a bodyguard. At any hour of the day, I will expect to know where you are and what you are doing—'

'But I never went riding in the Douro...' Emily was having huge difficulty in comprehending the necessity for such excessive arrangements and her bewilderment was visible.

'I spend precious little time at our country house,' Duarte said drily. 'I was merely pointing out that there is a price to pay for my generosity in taking you back.'

'Taking me back...' Emily mumbled in repetition. 'Taking me back...*where*?'

'If I did not know you better, I would believe you were drunk,' Duarte delivered a split second before his chauffeur opened the door beside her. 'We will continue this discussion indoors.'

With an enervated flick of her eyes in the direction of the Quinta de Monteiro, a vast sixteenth-century building as monumental and impressive as a castle, Emily repeated uncertainly, 'Indoors? You want me to come inside?'

'No matter how much one might feel like it, one does not leave one's wife to sleep in the car,' Duarte framed with considerable sarcasm.

Emily sat bolt upright, finally pausing to consider that phrase 'taking you back' in a different light. Not just back to Portugal, it seemed, but back to sharing the former marital roof. True, it was an exceptionally large roof, beneath which the most bitter enemies could probably live separate lives, but even so Emily was shattered by the concept. With an effort, she parted her lips, keen to clarify the matter. 'Duarte…I—'

Springing out on to the gravel, he swung back and grasped her hand in an impatient movement to urge her on. 'Come on… Victorine is waiting to welcome us.'

Emily ducked down her head and peered round him in dismay. There stood Victorine like a door sentinel, a middle-aged woman clad from head to toe in unrelieved black, her face set like an ancient Egyptian grave mask. Welcome? Victorine *welcome* the head of the family's unfaithful wife back to the hallowed ground of the Monteiro ancestral home? Was he joking? Even in the early days of their marriage, Duarte's former mother-in-law had been unable to conceal her antipathy towards Emily.

'I'm not going in,' Emily argued in a feverish undertone. 'I had no idea you were bringing us here. I thought I was going back to the house in the Douro—'

'Then a geography lesson would appear to be in order,' Duarte gritted without hesitation. 'Get out of the car, Emily.

For once in your life behave as I might reasonably expect my wife to behave.'

Every scrap of colour drained from her complexion at that wounding statement which reminded her of her every past failure. Then redemption and release came from a new discovery deep within her pain. 'I'm sorry...I really don't want to be your wife any more,' she whispered and her voice might have shook but somehow that admission made her feel stronger than she had felt in a very long time.

'Meu Deus!' Duarte bent down and scooped her out of the passenger seat with powerful and angry hands. 'That I should lower myself to the dishonour of taking back an adulterous wife and that you should *dare* to display such ingratitude in response!' he growled down at her with enraged golden eyes.

Emily gasped in disbelief when Duarte lifted her bodily from the car with the ease of a male sweeping up a small recalcitrant child. She could not credit that her controlled and reserved husband, who was no fan of public displays, should behave in such a way while Victorine was watching them. But then, never had she seen Duarte's anger before, for he'd not allowed her to see it, and what he'd just said to her was burned like letters of fire into her memory banks. 'Put me down,' she gasped in stricken recoil but her request was ignored.

When they were still several feet from the tall front doors which were spread wide on the huge hall behind her, Victorine spoke. 'I am sorry to say it but if that trollop enters the *quinta*, I will leave, Duarte.'

'That would be a great pity,' Duarte murmured without expression as he lowered Emily down on to the step in front of him. 'But this is my home and within my home no one will tell me what I may or may not do, nor will anyone abuse my wife.'

Emily was as shattered by that tough comeback from

Duarte as the older woman appeared to be. Victorine's thin
features betrayed incredulous resentment.

'Duarte...' Emily began in an agony of discomfiture.

'If my daughter Izabel could see you now with *her*...'
Victorine condemned with a bitterness she could not hide.

Every muscle in Duarte's big powerful body went rigid
and his dark deep voice carried an edge of reproach. 'Let
your daughter rest in peace.'

As Victorine stalked back indoors in high dudgeon, it
was Emily who broke the strained silence that she had left
in her wake. 'Jamie's still in the car—'

'He's asleep. The staff will see to him for the moment.'
Signalling the housekeeper hovering at the back of the hall,
Duarte gave an instruction to that effect. Then, resting a
hand to Emily's taut spine, he pressed her into the superb
salon with its tall gothic windows and thrust the door shut
behind them again.

The wall at the foot of the room was dominated by a
huge full-length portrait of Izabel, an exotic brunette in a
fabulous blue ball gown. Emily tore her gaze from that
familiar but oh, so daunting image. Izabel, Victorine's beloved only child and Duarte's first wife. Five years earlier,
Izabel had died in a ghastly car wreck that had also claimed
the life of Duarte's twin sister. *Rest in peace?* Emily's sensitive tummy clenched. One way or another, she had been
haunted every day of their marriage by Izabel, the ultimate
of impossible acts to follow. Even now, Duarte could not
bear to mention her name and the Quinta de Monteiro remained stamped by the spectral presence of its former mistress.

'Please go and speak to Victorine before she does anything foolish,' Emily urged wearily. 'I don't want to stay
here anyway, so there's not much point giving her the impression that she has to move out to avoid me.'

'This is my home. Here you will stay.'

That abrasive intonation made her lift her head again and she clashed with smouldering dark golden eyes that could have splintered a lesser being at a hundred paces. She gulped. 'I *can't*… If that's how Victorine feels, what about the rest of the family and your friends?'

Duarte flung back his arrogant head and vented a harsh laugh of derision that ripped through the tense atmosphere like a knife blade. '*Inferno!* Do you think I took out a full page ad in the newspapers to spread the word that the village layabout had been screwing my wife?'

White as milk, Emily stared back at him and cringed. He'd never used such language around her before but in its use she finally recognised the savage anger he was containing and she quailed from it. 'But I never slept with him,' she argued in desperation. 'All that *ever* happened between us, you saw for yourself—'

'Saw and will never forget.' Duarte swore with a raw force that chilled her. 'Don't insult my intelligence. While you were in the Douro, I was foolish enough to reconsider your explanations—but then I received confirmation of your guilt from a third party. It was not *only* I who saw you acting like a slut.'

Emily had backed away several steps. Rigid with stress, she could not stop trembling. 'What third party? How could there be a third party who witnessed something that *never* happened?' she exclaimed in appalled protest. 'Was it your mother-in-law? I don't think Victorine would lose much sleep over lying about me.'

'You wrong her.' Duarte's contempt at that suggestion was unconcealed. 'She may not like you but she was not involved. Nor is your sordid affair common knowledge. Fortunately, that third party I mentioned is not a gossip.'

Emily lifted unsteady hands to her drawn face. It was a warm evening but her skin felt like ice and she dimly registered that she was suffering from the effects of shock. She was devastated to learn that, during their separation eight months earlier, Duarte had been fair enough to think over afresh whether or not she might have been telling the truth about Toby. Then, sadly, he had had his mind made up for him by some hateful person, who had either lied or seriously misinterpreted something they had seen. But who?

But just as suddenly the identity of that mysterious third party no longer seemed of immediate importance to Emily. She had let Toby kiss her and it was little wonder that, having seen that display, Duarte should have no faith whatsoever in her pleas of innocence. 'Obviously you're going to think what you want to think...'

Duarte strode forward and reached for her arms to hold her still when she would have spun away. '*Meu Deus!* What I *want* to think? Do you honestly believe that any man wants to think of his wife in another man's bed?' he raked down at her with charged incredulity, his lean, powerful hands biting into her elbows before he thrust her back from him.

Rage and aggression. That's what she was seeing. Two traits that Emily had once believed that her immensely wealthy, cool and sophisticated husband did not possess. Was he not one of the legendary *baroes*, a baron of Portuguese industry? Not just a banker alone. Duarte had interests in biotechnology, textiles, timber and cork, not to mention ownership of a world famous vineyard that produced wine to die for. One of the old money elite, it was true, but also innovative, tenacious and ruthless as all hell let out. Not a male with a problem in the realm of self-control.

Duarte thrust splayed brown fingers through his luxuriant black hair and breathed in slow and deep. His stunning eyes were veiled by spiky black lashes almost long enough to hit his superb cheekbones which were now scored with faint colour. 'If I frightened you, I'm sorry. It is difficult for me even to look at you in this room.'

Her face flamed and she studied the exquisite handmade pastel rug that adorned the polished floor. The night of that dreadfully boring dinner party she had walked out through the French windows on to the terrace with Toby to enjoy the breeze. How could she have forgotten that location? It did not suggest that she was the world's most sensitive person. *He* remembered—of course he did. But then she had greater cause to want to forget. Her strained eyes burned with tears and she mumbled, 'What can I say?'

'Nothing. The more you say the angrier I become. It is like a chain reaction.'

She couldn't look at him but there was no escape from her own despairing regret. One brief moment in time, one failure to react as her husband had naturally expected her to react with instantaneous rejection, a fatal hesitation that had cost her everything she had, everything she valued. And what a terrible truth it was that people never really appreciated what they *had* until it was taken away without any hope of return, Emily acknowledged painfully.

'I must speak to Victorine. She deserves greater consideration than I granted her on our arrival,' Duarte drawled with a grim lack of intonation. 'I lashed out at her then because I could not defend you against the charge of being what she calls a trollop.'

'You called me a whore…' Emily squeezed out the word from between compressed lips and swallowed hard.

'If I apologised, I'm afraid it would not be with sincerity,' Duarte admitted and the door thudded shut on his departure.

Emily snatched in an uneven breath. Sharing the same house with Duarte promised to be a nightmare, no matter how big the *quinta* was and no matter how infrequent their meetings. He despised her. He was never ever likely to believe that she had not been intimate with Toby. Indeed, Duarte could hardly stand to be in the same room with her. Yet he had kissed her on the flight—well, not at all the way he used to kiss her, she conceded wretchedly. There had been a dark, almost derisive lack of tenderness in that brief encounter and a cold calculated passion she'd never felt in him before. He'd sought out her weakness and exploited it without pity. Duarte had a streak of cruelty she'd never dreamt he possessed.

The housekeeper came to invite Emily to inspect Jamie's nursery. She went upstairs to find a whole bunch of admiring female staff gathered round a beautifully carved wooden cot in the centre of an airy room. Wearing an unfamiliar white sleepsuit, Jamie lay in his crisp blue and yellow bedding and continued to sleep like a log. Emily remained in the doorway, taking in surroundings in which she herself had had no input. Colourful ducks marched round the wallpaper border and bright curtains hung at the windows. The surface of every piece of nursery furniture was packed with waiting toys, many still in their packaging.

Her throat thickened as she appreciated that the room had been prepared long before Duarte had even found his son. Had he bought those toys himself? Gone into a shop, selected them in an act of positive thinking, determined to believe that he would eventually find them and get to bring his child home? Guilt ate her alive and she turned away shame-faced from the sight.

'It's a lovely nursery,' she said in careful Portuguese and she managed an appreciative smile.

The housekeeper led her further down the corridor and spread open the door of a large and beautifully furnished bedroom. Recognising the clothing being carefully put away by a maid as her own, Emily realised that she was now being shown her new quarters. On the other side of the *quinta* from the vast interconnecting bedroom suite she had once shared with Duarte. Just about as far as he could exile her and still keep her within the same walls—but at least she would be close to Jamie, she reminded herself, striving to keep up spirits sagging low enough now to hit the level of the wine cellars.

No sooner had the maid departed than a knock sounded on the door. Hurriedly composing herself, Emily opened the door to find herself facing a uniformed nanny, eager to proclaim her many childcare qualifications, her ability to speak English as fluently as she spoke Portuguese and her family's history of devoted service to the Monteiro family. Emily smiled and nodded repeatedly for not much else seemed to be required from her but she was taken aback and dismayed that Duarte should already have engaged a nanny for their son.

Jamie already had the entire household staff hanging over him like he was the seventh wonder of the world. But then, Duarte himself had been the last infant in the *quinta* nurseries and the Portuguese adored children—her son's arrival was a major event. But Emily felt that the immediate hire of a nanny when she herself had now nothing to do *other* than look after their son was a clear demonstration that Duarte did not consider her responsible enough for the task. Using the internal phone by the bed, she requested her evening meal in her room. She might as well get used to staying out of Duarte's way. He didn't want to see her, speak to her, have anything to do with her—and, in the mood she was in, she did not feel she could even blame him.

It was not as if she had *ever* had any actual proof that Duarte had slept with other women when he was away on business. But he had not come to her bed again after her pregnancy had been confirmed. After a while, pride had demanded that she lock that connecting door between their bedrooms and let him think that she wasn't one bit bothered by his lack of interest.

He was the man who had once murmured to her in the dark of the night and in the oddest tone of self-discovery, 'I have to confess that sex is very important to me.'

The man who had stood straight and tall and said, the day after his marriage proposal had been joyously accepted, 'I'm not in love with you and it is only fair that I should be frank on that score.'

Even after almost two years, the pain of hearing that admission spoken out loud still hurt her. She hadn't wanted him to pretend but she hadn't wanted him to speak those words either. Knowing in her heart of hearts had been one thing, a stark confession almost too much for her to bear. She had adored him and *still* adored him but she'd been so miserable in their marriage that now she could no longer see any point in their continuing such a charade. Just for Jamie's sake? Jamie, the precious child whose father had broken her heart.

When her evening meal arrived on a tray, she ate with no great appetite. Then she freshened up in the en suite bathroom and unravelled her hair from its constraining plait to brush out the tangles. She searched her reflection in the mirror. Emily Monteiro, unwanted, unloved wife. Major failure in the wife stakes, she added fairly. And on *his* terms he had given so much. The wedding ring, the name, the wealth, the security. So what if he had never ever returned her phone calls? So what if he had muttered Izabel's name on several occasions while he slept by her side? So what if he had got bored with her skinny, flat-chested body and engaged in a little discreet infidelity with more exciting and beautiful women?

Well, actually, she registered in the midst of her growing turmoil, Duarte Avila de Monteiro might still be the love of her life but she had pretty much hated him as much as

she loved him once it became clear that her pregnancy concluded his interest in her. Once he had impregnated her,
that had been that. Duty done, mission accomplished. She
closed her aching eyes. The low-maintenance wife project
had gone belly-up when he least expected it.

Sick and tired of her own emotionalism, Emily headed
for the nursery. Jamie was sure to be close to waking and
hungry by now. The door stood ajar and, hearing Duarte
laugh, Emily hesitated in surprise. Then she heard the
nanny issuing serious advice on how best to hold a baby
and just had to sneak a look. She saw Duarte sprawled in
a chair, long powerful legs extended as he held Jamie cra-
dled in his arms and struggled to coordinate a feeding bottle
held at an awkward angle.

'I need another hand,' he groaned in Portuguese.

Yet his lean, boldly masculine profile was relaxed. There
was even the hint of a rueful smile at the corner of his
expressive mouth as he dealt with the unusual experience
of not being an immediate brilliant success at something.
Evidently, he did not mind the young nanny as an audience
to his efforts to get acquainted with his baby son. But he
would not have turned to Emily for similar advice and support. Cut to the bone by that humiliating awareness, Emily
crept back to her room, feeling like the most hated woman
in the world. Even Jamie wasn't crying for her, she reflected painfully.

An hour later when she dared to emerge from her room
again, Jamie was sound asleep in his cot. Emily was dying
to lift her son and hold him close but there was a baby
listener beside the night light. If Jamie cried, the staff would
come running and she would look like an irresponsible
mother. That warning image sent her into retreat.

She was leaving the nursery when Victorine intercepted
her.

'You have Duarte's son. You must be feeling very

pleased with yourself,' the older woman condemned bitterly.

'Please don't feel you have to leave. This is your home,' Emily pointed out, ignoring that opening sally.

The older woman pursed her lips. 'It hasn't been *my* home since you first came into it. When Duarte put someone like you in my daughter's place, he...'

At the sound of that all-too-familiar refrain, Emily suppressed a groan. Once the centre of her mother's world, the late Izabel had been a renowned beauty as famed for her style as her effervescent charm. Unable to come to terms with Izabel's premature death, Victorine had deeply resented Duarte's remarriage.

As the older woman paused for breath in what had grown into a rant freely interspersed with spiteful comparisons, Emily simply sighed, 'Your daughter is no longer here but you're still part of Duarte's family and he's fond of you.'

Frustrated by Emily's lack of reaction to her gibes, Victorine dealt her a look of boiling resentment and hurried back the way she had come. Sticks and stones can break my bones but words can never hurt me, Emily rhymed to herself. But, feeling in dire need of some fresh air, she went out to the charming courtyard at the back of the *quinta*. There she sat on a stone bench in rueful appreciation of the superb box-hedged herbal gardens designed by her talented predecessor. The light was fading fast and using the same service staircase she had employed earlier, she returned to her room to have a shower before bed.

She'd already shed her top and skirt when someone turned the handle on her bedroom door and partially opened it. Freezing in dismay, she heard Duarte's deep drawl as he addressed one of the staff in the corridor and she dived into the bathroom in a panic to snatch up a towel.

'Emily?' Duarte breathed, a raw edge to his dark, rich voice that sent a current of foreboding through her.

She emerged with pronounced reluctance from the bath-room. 'Yes?'

Shimmering golden eyes raked over her shrinking figure and the death grip she had on a towel that was just a little too small for its purpose. She had one unpremeditated clash with his smouldering gaze and she hastily looked away again, her heart jumping as if she had jammed a finger in a live electric socket. The anger she had seen in him earlier was no longer contained. It leapt out at her like a physical entity and radiated around him like a dangerous aura. From the fierce set of his lean dark devastating face, the rigidity of his broad muscular shoulders and the clenching of his long brown fingers into fists, she read a level of unholy rage she'd truly never ever expected to see in a male as self-disciplined as he was.

'How *could* you?' he demanded wrathfully.

'How could I…wh-what?' she stammered, tummy churn-ing at the terrible tension in the atmosphere.

'Don't play games with me unless you want to get hurt…' Duarte ground out. 'Victorine came to me in great distress to tell me how you had taunted her with her daugh-ter's death…'

Emily's knees were locked together and her legs gave an involuntary wobble, the high-heeled mules she still wore providing a far from stable support. 'I didn't taunt her. All I said was that her daughter was no longer here—'

'I don't believe you. It's a very long time since I've seen Izabel's mother in such a state and you cannot even look me in the face.'

Emily could feel herself beginning to *feel* guilty even though she knew that she had said nothing that could have upset the older woman. Nor could she help but recall how enraged Victorine had looked when she'd realised that Emily was no longer a soft target on which to vent her spleen. She lifted her chin, raising strained aquamarine eyes to meet a gaze as stormy as the threatening glow inside a volcano about to erupt. 'She can only have misunderstood what I said—'

'Don't push me on this. Shock is written all over you. Shock that Victorine told tales and your unpleasantness has been exposed for me to deal with—'

'I did not taunt her with Izabel's death. Why would I do that, for goodness' sake?' Emily prompted on a rising note of protest.

'Because, as the mother of my son and my wife, you might well feel that you have a great deal of power in this house.'

A nervous giggle bubbled up out of Emily's constricted throat. 'Power? *Me?* I was less important than the most junior housemaid the last time I lived here! Victorine was always picking out my mistakes in front of the staff, embarrassing them, humiliating me…' As Emily's voice ebbed in recollection, it then gathered renewed steam. 'Nothing I ever did pleased her *or* you. I spent hours trying to make up menus, only to have them rejected. I got to the stage where I didn't care if you never ate again! I let her march me out to the endless coffee mornings, the polite social visits, the charity functions, the dinner parties for which you never turned up and I changed my clothes at least four times a flippin' day—'

'Emily,' Duarte gritted.

'Do you know something?' Emily proclaimed with the fierce bitterness that assailed her when she recalled how desperately hard she had worked to fill her role as a high society wife. 'I'd have had an easier ride down a nineteenth-century coal mine than I had being your wife!'

That last phrase dropped into a silence so deep that a feather could have fallen and sounded out a resounding crash. Duarte surveyed her with hard dark eyes. 'You condemn yourself with every word you say. It's obvious that you've *always* resented Victorine's presence here and would very much prefer to see her move out.'

Emily's lips opened and then very slowly closed again, her eyes widening in dismay as she realised what Duarte had extracted from her unfortunate outburst. Suddenly she could have bitten out her own impulsive tongue but innate honesty prevented her from lying. It was true—no way could she put her hand on her heart and say that she had *not* resented his mother-in-law in the past. Regimented by Victorine into a lifestyle she loathed and then continually criticised and shown up in front of others as she failed to fill the hallowed shoes of her superhuman predecessor, Emily had often wished that Victorine would magically vanish from her horizon.

'But it wasn't like that tonight, Duarte,' she argued vehemently. 'I *know* you're fond of her and I reminded her of that and asked her to think again—'

'I have more trust in her ability to tell the truth than I have in yours. If you ever do anything like this again, you will pay a high price. *Don't* turn away from me like that!' Duarte raked at her, making her flinch.

So now as well as being the most hated person in the house and a trollop and that other word which she could bear to recall even less, she was also a nasty shrew and an outright liar. Emily kept on turning away, for she had too much pride to let him see how savaged she was by his refusal to place even the smallest trust in her word.

Long powerful fingers settled on her slight shoulder and flipped her back again with a masculine strength that was far from reassuring. 'When I say jump, now you say, "How high?" Haven't you got that message yet?'

'No...and I won't,' Emily told him, her gaze glimmering with angry tears. 'You are not going to make me feel any worse about myself than I already feel!'

'So *you* feel bad?' Duarte loosed a derisive laugh that

broke the surging tension with the disturbing effect of shattering glass. 'But I bet not one tenth as bad as *I* felt about bringing you back into my home this evening…'

Emily dropped her head and tried to swallow the great fat lump of guilt in her throat. She was in turmoil, wanting to scream and sob and attack him all at one and the same time. Once again she'd been her own worst enemy. Why, oh why had she been foolish enough to even *speak* to Victorine? Why hadn't she just minded her own wretched business and walked away? But she knew why, didn't she? She had not wanted to feel that the older woman's departure was yet one more sin to be piled up at her door.

'But now you're about to make me feel much better about that difficult decision,' Duarte completed in a charged undertone that sent the oddest tremor down her responsive spine.

'Oh…and how am I going to do that?' she prompted chokily, fighting to hold the tears back until he left her again. He hated her, he absolutely hated her and she could not imagine how she had ever managed to persuade herself that Duarte had no truly strong emotions where she was concerned.

'Sex.'

Engaged in an apparently enraptured scrutiny of his soft leather loafers, Emily blinked rapidly in receipt of that explanation. Mentally she strained to persuade herself that he had not uttered that single unexpected word with the smooth cool of a male who had already overcome his anger while she was still struggling even to *think* like a rational being.

The silence seemed to rush and eddy around her like a high wind.

She raised her gaze to the well-cut beige chinos sheathing his long, long powerful length of leg and lean hips, up more slowly still to the belt encircling his narrow waist and the casual white shirt open at his bronzed throat.

'Sex…?' Emily almost whispered as if it physically hurt her to say the word.

Duarte lifted a lean hand and pushed up her chin. Volatile golden eyes set between spiky black lashes inspected her disbelieving face. *'Sim, querida.'*

Yes, he said in confirmation but her brain refused to credit the evidence of her hearing.

CHAPTER FIVE

'S-SEX?' Emily stammered helplessly.

'The concept appeals and intrigues,' Duarte murmured silkily.

Emily drew in a very ragged breath but still her voice was faint. 'Does it really? Tell me, when did this sudden attack of lust occur to you? Is this like…your equivalent of that ancestor of yours who bricked his wife up alive in a wall?'

'Such a very insightful question, *querida*.' Duarte surveyed her with brilliant dark eyes alight with hard amusement. 'But rather naive. I don't need to explain myself to you and why would I?'

As Duarte narrowed the distance between them, Emily went as rigid as a porcupine going on the offensive. 'Don't you dare touch me!'

Duarte scanned the flushed oval of her delicate face, his strong jawline hardening. 'Perhaps I want to remind you that you're mine. Perhaps it *is* that basic…I don't care.'

'Basic's not me,' Emily framed unevenly because she trusted herself even less than she trusted him. She could feel his proximity with every skin cell she possessed. In her mind's eye she could even visualise every shameless skin cell sitting up and begging and that made her cringe. For what had always lain at the very heart of Duarte's total irresistibility had been the simple truth that her *own* resistance was nil.

He hooked a lean brown finger into the towel she was still clutching. 'Overkill, don't you think?'

She trembled, a liquid sensation of heat pooling deep

71

inside her, her legs welding her to the spot. He was so close
she could smell the warm male scent of his sunwarmed
skin, so close she could feel deliciously threatened by the
sheer size differential between her and the potent masculinity of his lean hard physique.

'You signed up for your own personal punishment plan
while we were still airborne,' Duarte delivered in a tone as
smooth as silk.

She was staring up at him, wholly enveloped in her own
growing reaction to him. It had always been that way,
which was why when things were wrong between them she
just never looked directly at him, out of fear that he would
guess how great his power was. Only now, she'd reached
the point where she could not stop staring, drinking in every
taut angle of that strikingly dark and handsome face of his,
the proud arrogant jut of his nose, the fabulous cheekbones
that lent his features such pronounced strength and defini-
tion, the fine grain of his skin that roughened round his
hard jawline. And still she was not satisfied; still it was not
enough to satiate that need within her.

'S-sorry? Punishment plan?' she echoed a whole ten seconds after he had finished speaking and only after frantically plundering her memory.

'My kind of punishment,' Duarte spelt out with measured
satisfaction.

Stunning dark golden eyes held hers as he finally jerked
loose the screening towel so that it drifted down into a heap
on the rug. Strong hands lifted to snap round her wrists and
prevent her startled attempt to stoop and retrieve it.

'Duarte…?' Emily gasped, very much taken back by his
behaviour.

He held her back from him and let his intent gaze roam
at a leisurely pace over her slim, slight figure. She tried to
curve away from him, curl in protectively on herself while
still standing, but he held fast to her. Visually exploring

the rise and fall of her small breasts beneath the barrier of her bra, his attention strolled down to her tiny waist and the swell of her hips where a pair of white cotton panties that were not of the diminutive variety shut off his view.

'The cotton look was fine when sweet and wholesome was the draw but it's not to my taste now,' Duarte confided while Emily's pale skin coloured up like the rising sun beneath an appraisal that was reducing her to agonies of embarrassment. 'And since pleasing me must necessarily *be* your top priority—'

'*Why*? Why would it be?' she broke in, wild in her humiliation.

'Security of tenure,' Duarte specified in cool warning. 'And please let's ditch the I'm-so-shy routine I used to respect because I don't respect it any more.'

Her heart was thudding so fast, she could hardly catch her breath. 'It wasn't a routine—'

'But it must have been,' Duarte asserted in interruption as he backed her inexorably in the direction of the bed. 'All those hot afternoons you spent in *his* studio in pursuit of a surprise portrait supposedly for me? At a time when you had locked the door between our bedrooms you were attending all those sittings purely for my benefit? And you're *still* trying to persuade me that the same lout that I personally heard swearing eternal devotion to you never laid a finger on you?'

Emily nodded jerkily, conscious of how very unlikely he made her being innocent sound but still ready to argue. 'I was hardly ever alone with him. He had a girlfriend—'

Duarte elevated a winged dark brow. 'Get a better story. Or even better, tell me exactly what you *did* do with him—'

As he swept her up into his arms and settled her squarely down on the centre of the big bed and stepped back from her, she said feverishly. 'Nothing, absolutely nothing.'

'I beat the hell out of him,' Duarte informed her with chilling exactitude.

Suddenly the atmosphere was sizzling like a stick of dynamite ready to blow. In considerable shock, Emily gazed back at Duarte, all her colour ebbing—for the very last thing she would have expected from Duarte was that kind of violence.

'That was my right,' Duarte stated soft and low and dark, watching her like a hawk ready to pounce, smouldering dark golden eyes welded to her sincerely shaken face. 'Do you think that I didn't know that he followed you to the villa in the Douro? That he repeatedly attempted to see you? And that when that failed, he kept on phoning?'

A pin could have been heard dropping in her appalled silence.

Duarte studied her with a hard force she could feel in every atom of her being. 'If you had encouraged him then, if you had *once* spoken to him or seen him, you would not be here now.'

So throughout that winter she'd passed at the country house, nothing that happened there had gone unreported to Duarte. Emily was genuinely shattered by that discovery. 'We…we were separated,' she whispered shakily.

Savage anger flared in his blazing look of challenge. 'You were still my wife and what is mine stays mine until *I* choose to relinquish it!'

Before her she saw a male with traits she had failed to recognise before. The male that existed behind the deceptive patina of sophistication and cool courtesy. A more primitive breed of male, every bit as aggressive and possessive of what was his as any backstreet fighter. She'd never been so shaken in her whole life—for only then it occurred to her that naturally, Duarte used the same forceful drives for his personal life that he used every day in a more civilised way in business—in that field his ruthlessness was a living legend.

'Turning him away in the Douro was the only thing you did right,' Duarte pronounced grittily.

Emily was now realising that the only reason that Duarte had left her alone on the bed was to undress. She lay there with the curious sensation of being weighted to the mattress while she watched him finish unbuttoning his shirt. As he bent to remove his shoes, the shirt hung loose, disclosing an enervating glimpse of a broad chest the colour of living bronze, with dark curling hair emphasising his powerful pectoral muscles and the hard flat contours of his stomach. Her breath locked in her throat. As he straightened to his full six foot four inches, she couldn't take her eyes from him. He was a stunning vision of raw masculinity and it had been so long since she had seen him like that. Indeed, it was over a year since they had shared the smallest intimacy, she reminded herself, dimly seeking excuse for her total absorption in him.

'There will be no separate bedrooms this time, *no* locked doors,' Duarte spelt out, sending the zip rasping down on his chinos, angling his narrow hips in a slight movement that she found inexplicably but hugely sexy.

Her fair skin coloured up hotly on that straying thought and, dredging her eyes from him in severe embarrassment, she focused on the edge of the linen sheet already neatly folded down by a maid in readiness for an occupant. *Two* occupants, she reflected, her brain moving at a tenth of its usual capacity. Duarte was going to make love to her. It occurred to her that saying 'no' was still an option and that she really ought to say something.

'I really don't want this,' Emily told him.

'Just who are you trying to kid?'

Aghast at that blunt comeback, Emily blinked in dismay and was betrayed into a sudden upward glance. Duarte surveyed her in flagrant challenge, sardonic amusement gleaming at her shaken expression. He stood there naked and magnificent, his hard shaft fully erect.

'You are not chained to the bed but you're not running anywhere. Why?'

For a timeless moment, she simply stared at him, seriously wrongfooted by that enquiry. Throwing her a look of irredeemably male logic, Duarte came down on the bed and reached for her so fast, she gave a stifled gasp of fright.

'Let me tell you *why*,' he urged, knotting long fingers into her tumbled red-gold hair as he brought her up against his hard muscular chest. 'I can turn you on just by looking at you!'

Crushed into the unyielding strength of him yet forced to maintain an eye contact that she would have done just about anything to avoid, Emily felt as if she was fighting for her last ounce of pride. 'No…not any more—'

He tugged her head back, shimmering eyes scorching down into hers. 'So what was that little demonstration of total surrender on the jet, then? One last fling?'

Her whole body was already reacting to the steely contours of his with insidious little quivers of heat and a drowning weakness that was even more dangerous to her self-discipline. The fresh warm scent of him was in her nostrils with every breath she drew, achingly familiar, achingly erotic. 'You…you took me by surprise—'

'*Nâo te acredito*… I don't believe you,' Duarte derided, his breath fanning her cheek and then his hot hard hungry mouth claiming hers with a raw assurance that made denial impossible.

It was a shattering kiss, full of explosive demand. His tongue stabbed into the tender moist interior of her mouth and plundered the sweetness with an invasive force that made her heart hammer as fast as if she'd run a three minute mile. She trembled beneath that onslaught, her hands clenching, nails biting into her palms as she attempted to withstand the raw sexual enticement of his expert mouth on hers. But the little kernel of nagging heat he had already awakened low in her belly was too seductive. She started shifting in his grasp, pushing into him in a helpless surge and all the time, Dear heaven, I want him, want him, *want him*, was running like a charged mantra through her mind.

'Indeed, belief would be a great challenge,' Duarte husked, ungenerous in victory as only a rogue male can be—and then he did something that truly shook her. Taking her hand, he curled her fingers round his bold erection. 'That's more like it...'

He felt like hot steel sheathed in silk. Her hand shook a little and her face burned scarlet at being asked to do what she had previously only done in darkness and beneath concealing covers. But an undeniable excitement gripped her and she stroked his hard masculinity, feeling the inexorable surge of answering heat between her trembling thighs.

In response, he caught her back to him and mated his mouth to hers with ferocious hunger. Then he drew back from her when she was clinging to him. Her hands dropped from him and she was disorientated by the sensation of her breasts coming free from her bra without her having had anything to do with it. She glanced down at herself to see that the front fastening had already been undone. Even as she whipped up her hands to cover herself, Duarte was ahead of her, imprisoning her fingers in his own, forestalling her.

'Stop it...' she gasped, embarrassed by the sight of her own bare flesh because she felt that she could not compare to other women with the small pouting swells crowned by rosy distended nipples.

Duarte used his superior strength to flatten her back on to the bed and stared down at her with hot hungry eyes of appreciation. 'You can't hide the evidence of your own desire,' he breathed, lowering his head to capture a swollen, throbbing tip between his lips.

Her entire body jerked, for she had always been almost unbearably sensitive there. Her hands flexed within the hold of his and he released them but she dug her fingers into the sheets beneath her instead. Excitement was like a damburst inside her, pressure building up with every second and she could not withstand her own intense need to be touched. A low keening sound was torn from her as he tormented the rosy crests with the kind of skill that drove her absolutely wild. So somehow they got to the stage where he was holding her down purely to keep her still and her hands had, seemingly without an input from her, risen to lace into his luxuriant black hair, urging him on in helpless writhing yearning.

'So tell me you're not mine now, *minha pequena esposa*,' Duarte invited, a roughened edge to his dark, deep drawl as he lifted his head from the glistening buds still begging for his attention.

'Don't stop…*please*,' she heard herself beg like a supplicant and even as she said it she knew she would cringe for herself later, but just then the sheer craving he had unleashed took precedence.

'Was it like this with Jarrett?'

For a split second she could not think who 'Jarrett' was. Toby, Bliss's cousin. Toby Jarrett. The name stood out in her mind's eye and made her tummy clench. She gazed up at Duarte, suddenly as terrified as an animal knowing it was about to be slaughtered, and knowing that there was absolutely nothing she could do about it because he wouldn't believe her.

'You are just sick with shame,' Duarte bit out, studying her as if he had her under a microscope and could read every nuance of expression.

She shut her eyes on the hot scorch of threatening tears.

Even while her wretched body leapt and burned for him and her every thought was at bay, *he* was still in sufficient control to attack.

'Much good that does either of us,' Duarte growled in an oddly ragged undertone and then suddenly he was gathering her back into his arms, reclaiming her mouth with a kind of blazing fiery desire that went through her quivering body like sheet lightning. He shuddered against her and then he stilled and, for a split second of horror, she thought he was about to pull free of her and instinctively she wrapped her arms round him as tightly as she could.

And then she felt a long forefinger stroking her cheek where a tear had escaped and left a telling trail and he cursed in Portuguese. He claimed her lips again at the same time as his exploring hand teased the aching points of her breasts. That instant of all too painful self-awareness was sent into oblivion by the renewed force of her own response.

'Duarte…' she moaned at the peak of an almost agonised gasp as his stroking fingers discovered the dampness of the triangle of fabric stretched taut between her restive thighs.

He stripped away that last barrier and found the hot moist core of her femininity. Her heartbeat seemed to thunder in her own ears as her body writhed without her volition. There was only wild sensation and overwhelming hunger for anything that would ease the tormenting ache of pressure clawing at her. She could feel him against her thigh, hot and hard and rampantly aroused and just knowing that she could still have that effect on him intensified everything that she felt.

'I can't be gentle…' he groaned, rising over her and parting her thighs with impatient hands to haul her back to him.

'Doesn't matter…'

Nothing mattered then but the driving thrust with which he entered her. Her body was just one gigantic source of longing and then he was there, dominantly male, stretching her with his strength and fullness and there was so much intense pleasure she cried out against it.

'Emily, *meu bonita…*'

My beautiful one, she savoured in stunned surprise and gazed up at him to register the hard-edged need etched into his lean dark devastating face but saw the concern in his hot golden eyes. 'I hurt you?' he prompted.

She shook her head, beyond speech, and even if she could have spoken she could not have thought of any way to tell him that that much pleasure came close to pain. But it seemed he understood, for a flash of raw male amusement flared in his spectacular eyes and he came into her again, hard and fast and not to be denied. She arched her hips up to him in helpless encouragement. He set a raw sensual rhythm that heightened her excitement to a level she could not control. There was nothing but him and the wild surging rise of her own excitement, her own primal delight in his erotic dominance. Every pulse racing, his name on her lips, she reached the dazzling instant of release and cried out in ecstasy at the explosive charge of sensation pulsating through her in waves. She clung to him as he shuddered over her and vented a ragged groan of intense satisfaction.

Happiness was bubbling up inside her now. To be so close to Duarte again, to feel so at home, to feel needed, wanted, *secure*. As he freed her of his weight, she followed him across the bed to stay close. She buried her face in a smooth brown muscular shoulder and drank in the hot, husky scent of him like an addict. One arm sliding round his neck, she lay across him, happy but engaged in frantic thought. Intimacy was the foundation stone of any normal marriage. My goodness, what had possessed her when she had briefly believed that she ought to be saying no?

In fact, so strong was her sense of joy and relief that she

had not made that foolish mistake, she found herself muttering feverishly, 'You're just so fantastic…'

Part of her cringed for herself even as she said it and then she noticed how rigid he was under her and how silent. Not that in the aftermath, Duarte had ever been exactly chatty. But she also became agonisingly aware that he did not have his arms round her and that she was the one making all the effort to be cosy and close and warmly intimate. About then, she just started wanting to die.

'And you're so affectionate, *querida*,' Duarte breathed a little stiltedly and then he finally curved an arm round her slim, still length and smoothed warm fingers down her taut spinal cord.

'Stop it…' she whispered.

'Stop what?'

'I can feel you thinking,' she mumbled, sensing his mental distance from her with every atom of ESP she possessed.

'I am thinking that I need a shower,' Duarte said drily.

And why was he thinking that? A shower would get him back out of bed again, away from *her*, she reflected miserably, a mass of insecurities unleashed inside her again. But he couldn't stay in the shower forever, could he? Slowly she edged away from him again, hoping to be snatched back; it didn't happen. He rolled lithely over and sprang out of bed. All potent male, hair-roughened skin and rippling muscles. Absolutely gorgeous but never hers, never really hers even at the beginning and even less likely to be now after what had happened eleven months ago.

Emily pulled herself up against the tumbled pillows, reading the raw tension in his wide shoulders but unable to silence her own desperate need to be heard. 'Duarte?'

'What?' he growled like a grizzly bear.

He was *so* volatile, she registered in amazement. How had she never seen that in him before? Had she been so wrapped up in her own self-pity that she'd never appreciated that she was married to a male who literally seemed to boil beneath the surface of that cool front with dark, deep, dangerous emotion?

'I've got to say it...I'm sorry,' she muttered feverishly, plucking nervously at the corner of the sheet beneath her hand. 'No matter how bad it looked, I never felt anything for Toby and I never had an affair with him either—'

Duarte swung back to her with the speed of a lion ready to spring. Angry golden eyes struck sparks off hers in a look as physical as a slap on the face. 'Don't you know when to keep quiet?'

Shrinking back into the pillows and pale as death, Emily whispered, 'I *need* you to listen—'

Duarte threw up both hands in a violent gesture of lost patience and strode on into the bathroom.

She listened to the shower coming on full gush and a sense of defeat engulfed her. It was swiftly followed by the conviction that she was the most stupid woman in existence. Why was she always so naive with him? *Sex*, he had said before she succumbed to her dream of how she wanted it to be. And so lost had she got in that delusion that, in the aftermath of passion, she had swarmed all over him as if nothing had ever been wrong between them, but it had been only sex as far as he was concerned, not making love, not a meeting of minds. Incredibly exciting sex, in her opinion, but then what did she really know about what it was like for *him*?

Just the slaking of a physical hunger on the nearest most available female body? Well, she'd certainly made herself available. Exactly as he had expected. *I can turn you on just by looking at you.* She stuffed her hot face into the cooling linen. Her own personal punishment plan, he had said—and what had he meant by that? And why hadn't she asked? Her sated body told her where her mind had been. Lost. Wanting him, wanting him much more than common sense. She'd had no restraint. She had so desperately wanted to believe that physical intimacy could fill the terrible emptiness that losing him had filled her with, could provide the first bridge between them, could give her back *hope*. Her nails raked down the smooth sheet beneath the pillows, self-hatred burning her like poison.

Suddenly, she pulled herself up and back on her knees, thrusting her wildly tangled hair back over her shoulders. Her strained face taut, she leapt off the bed, looked around for something to pull on to hide her nakedness and snatched up his discarded shirt. She came to a halt on the threshold of the bathroom where Duarte was already towelling himself dry.

'I suppose you think everything you ever thought about me has been proven now...I suppose you think I *am* a whore!' she fired at him jaggedly.

Duarte raked a driven hand through his damp tousled hair and rested dark deepset brooding eyes on her in the tension-filled silence. 'Leave it,' he warned and tossing the towel aside, he strode past her.

Her legs felt horribly wobbly. She leant back against the bedroom wall to steady herself. A tight hard knot of pain was building inside her, threatening to take control of her entirely, no matter how hard she tried to get a grip on herself. 'Sleeping with me was like a power play, was it?' she mumbled sickly. 'A case of finding out how high you could make me jump? And just how desperate I would be to please you?'

'I told you to *leave* it...' Duarte ground out, the long sweep of his muscular golden back rigid with stormy tension as he hauled on his chinos.

Emily felt she'd already been reduced so low that nothing else could hurt her. However, it belatedly dawned on her that he was getting dressed again and that he wasn't

staying the rest of the night and that seemed the lowest
blow of all. 'Where are you going?'

Duarte swung back round to face her, his lean strong
features ferociously set. 'Any place I don't have to listen
to you getting it all wrong—'

'How am I getting it wrong?' she pressed in desperation.
'Duarte?'

Brilliant eyes grim, he let a harsh laugh escape. 'Do you
think this is so easy for me? I'm thinking about you with
Jarrett almost all the time. I can't get it out of my head...'

Her tummy twisted, her drawn face tightening.

'So all kudos to me for pulling off a fantastic performance between the sheets.' His derision, whether angled at
her or himself made her flinch. 'Two years ago, I was your
first lover and that meant something to me. Now it's all
gone and I am just so bloody angry with you that I don't
know why I brought you back here!'

She felt dead inside because he had killed her hopes. She
was being rejected again. 'It was only a kiss and I didn't
even like it...' she framed strickenly.

'If you open the subject one more time... Where the hell
is my shirt?' he demanded in raw completion.

Realising that he had yet to notice what she was wearing,
she peeled off his shirt and threw it back at his feet.

Duarte stared at her with pronounced intensity. She stood
there like a statue, her hair falling round her like tongues
of fire against her fair skin but for once she made no move
to cover herself.

'Take your blasted shirt and get out!' she suddenly
gasped.

He flicked it up, the movement all grace and derision
somehow perfectly combined. She yanked open the door,
spread it wide.

Duarte threw her a sardonic look. 'If you were looking

for a guy who turns the other cheek, you shouldn't have married a Monteiro.'

She slammed the door shut on his exit, turned the key in the lock and then ran all the way back to the bed to throw herself facedown on the mattress.

Almost simultaneously it seemed the noise of a sudden jarring crash sent her rolling over in shock to glance back in the direction of the door. She was just in time to see it smash back against the wall. She focused on Duarte, who had kicked it open, with shaken eyes of disbelief. He stood there with clenched fists, breathing heavily, all powerful and quite unashamed masculinity.

'You lock a door against me again and I'll break it down every time!' Outraged golden eyes assailed hers with pure aggressive force. 'Do you understand?'

Very slowly and carefully, she nodded.

CHAPTER SIX

HAVING scarcely slept during a night of emotional turmoil, Emily was up early the following morning and in the nursery with Jamie.

When his nanny found her there, the young woman smiled in understanding and left them in peace. Given lots of cuddles, Jamie was in the sunniest of moods, but soon his big brown eyes turned sleepy again. His every need met, Jamie had an enviable capacity to be as happy in Portugal as he had been in England.

Emily had a shower and put on a denim skirt and tee-shirt. A maid brought her breakfast and she had it out on the balcony—white coffee and wonderful fresh-baked bread served with home-made honey. She was told in answer to her enquiry that 'Don Duarte' had left for his Lisbon office shortly before eight.

It promised to be a glorious day. Surrounded by woods of pine, eucalyptus and oak, the gardens were lush and tropical, full of spiky palms and superb flowering shrubs, the extensive lawns already being industriously watered by the gardeners. Beyond the trees stretched the extensive *quinta* estate of orange and lemon and olive groves. Against the backdrop of the purple green mountains, the tiny village houses sprinkled the hillside like toys. In every direction the views were breathtaking.

Emily had missed Portugal so much during her absence yet, two years earlier, she knew she'd severely underestimated the challenges of marrying a male who not only did not love her but also whose world and expectations were so very different from her own...

Even their wedding had not been what she had wanted. Duarte had desired neither frills nor fuss and, as she loved him, she'd suppressed her longing for a wedding gown and worn a suit. Lunch had followed at an exclusive hotel but it had been attended only by her family and a handful of Duarte's business acquaintances.

'I'd call it a bit shabby,' her sister Hermione had said with a sniff. 'Are you *sure* this isn't a shotgun do?'

From the instant she'd told her family that she was marrying Duarte, the humiliating suggestion that he might only be marrying her because she had fallen pregnant had been repeatedly raised. When her denials were received with cynical disbelief, it had done nothing for her self-image.

Duarte had even been too busy for a honeymoon and they had been married for a week before she discovered that she was *not* his first wife. Studying their marriage certificate with dreamy eyes, she'd finally noticed that he was described as a widower.

'Why didn't you tell me?' she had asked in astonished hurt.

'It wasn't relevant,' Duarte had told her flatly.

Pressing for further details, she had naturally been shocked to learn of the car crash that had killed both Izabel and his twin, Elena. But she'd also noticed that that night, for the first time, Duarte didn't make love to her. Early on, she had learnt that trying to talk about Izabel drove Duarte from her. That same evening, sadly, Jazz, the dog she had adored and whom she had credited with bringing her and Duarte together, had passed away in his sleep and that concluded their stay in England.

Duarte had brought her home to the *quinta* and that very first day, Victorine had invited Emily to her private sitting room where there were framed photographs showing her late daughter Izabel, glorious in her fabulous wedding gown, Izabel on her Caribbean honeymoon, Izabel enter-

taining royalty…Izabel…Izabel…Izabel. Emily had learnt
right then that she was a second-best wife.

A knock on the bedroom door forced Emily from her
introspection. Victorine was trying not to look at the lock
which Duarte had broken the night before. Emily flushed
for naturally the older woman would know that she and
Duarte had had a row. The whole household would be
buzzing with the sheer shock value of Duarte doing something that much out of character.

'May we speak?' Victorine asked stiffly.

Emily was dumbfounded to see tears glistening in the
older woman's shadowed eyes.

'I've seen your son. He is a very beautiful baby…' Victorine told her heavily. 'I feel great guilt that I lied about
what you said to me last night and I could not sleep. I told
Duarte the truth at breakfast.'

That astonishing confession froze Emily to the spot. At
the same time, however, she could not help thinking that
if what Victorine was telling her was true, Duarte had certainly not hurtled upstairs to offer *her* an apology for mis-
judging her.

'I am sorry for the way I have treated you,' Victorine
continued doggedly. 'When I saw your son, who is the
future of this family, I asked myself how much my un-
kindness might have contributed to your separation from
Duarte last year—'

'Never mind, it's over…forgotten,' Emily broke in awkwardly, finally recognising that Victorine had indeed faced
the results of her resentment and had emerged much chas-
tened from the experience.

In revealing discomfiture, Victorine looked away from
the damaged door. 'I've made trouble between you and
Duarte but it won't happen again. The maids are packing
for me.'

As Victorine turned away, looking old and frail and forlorn in her unhappiness, Emily touched her thin arm in a sympathetic gesture. 'You don't need to leave for my benefit.'

'Duarte said I must. He is very disappointed in me and very angry—'

'He'll get over that,' Emily asserted as Victorine began to sob, her fragile self-control splintering at the prospect before her. 'So you and I got off to a bad start but I just can't imagine this place without you and where are you going to go anyway?'

'Two years ago, Duarte said to me, "Emily is so sweet, so kind, you will love her"…and I *hated* you before I even met you!' the older woman wept.

Emily took Victorine back to her own rooms, knowing how much she would dislike any of the staff seeing her in tears. She began to understand that it had been her own change in attitude the night before which had ultimately led to the present situation. Unable to bully Emily as she had once done, Victorine had lied to Duarte and had then been horrified by her own behaviour. It was odd how good could sometimes come out of bad, Emily was thinking as she went downstairs after calming the other woman down.

It seemed to be a day for surprises: Bliss was in the main hall speaking to the *quinta* housekeeper. Clad in a simple navy dress that was a marvellous foil for her blonde beauty, Bliss moved to greet her.

'I had no idea you were here!' Smiling, Emily asked the housekeeper to serve coffee.

'Strictly in a business capacity, I'm afraid, so I can't stay for long.' Bliss sank down gracefully on a silk-upholstered sofa in the salon. 'Duarte has a big party arranged for this weekend. I was just checking the final arrangements. I've been acting as your husband's hostess since your departure.'

Unsettled by that news and quick to pick up on the brittle

quality of her friend's manner, Emily said in surprise, 'Didn't Victorine object?'

'That hateful old cow?' Bliss laughed. 'Oh, not being a softy like you, I soon settled *her*! I let her know that her ideas about entertaining were fifty years out of date and an embarrassment to Duarte. Ever since then, when there are guests, she takes an early night.'

That unfeeling explanation filled Emily with uneasy distaste. Victorine had her flaws but Emily would never have dreamt of referring to the older woman in such terms. 'Bliss—'

Bliss merely talked over her. 'Mind you, I never thought I'd see *you* back here again either. I was very annoyed when you did your vanishing act last year.'

Grateful for that honesty, Emily spoke up immediately. 'I'm really sorry I didn't keep in touch but—'

'That's not what I'm talking about. When I told you about that little chat I overheard between your husband and his lawyer, I was warning you to get your own legal advice instead of sitting on the fence, hoping all that nasty divorce stuff would go away. I wasn't expecting you to flee the country and put everybody into a loop trying to find you!'

Emily paled at that censorious clarification.

'In tipping you off, I felt like I had *personally* deprived Duarte of his child,' Bliss admitted in no more comforting continuance. 'What on earth possessed you? And now to come back here, regardless of how Duarte feels about you—'

'What are you saying?' Emily faltered in growing shock at what she was hearing.

'Come on, Emily…all Duarte cared about was getting his son back and resident in Portugal. Now he's got him, he won't let you take him away again. In a marriage that was failing from day one, where does that leave you?'

'I've never discussed Duarte or our relationship with you,' Emily reminded the other woman uncomfortably.

Her exquisite face an icy mask, Bliss rose to her feet. 'Well, excuse me for presuming on our former friendship—'

Emily flew upright in distress. 'No, Bliss...I didn't *mean*—'

'Don't come crying to me when you find yourself divorced and without your precious son!' Bliss told her scornfully. 'Can't you see the bigger picture here? Doesn't it occur to you that Duarte may already have another woman in his life?'

Emily's tummy gave a sick somersault and she could barely credit that the blonde was a woman she had once believed was a true friend. 'Why are you behaving like this?'

'Maybe you should have settled for my cousin, Toby, while you had the chance,' Bliss derided dulcetly before she departed, leaving Emily standing in the salon in a stricken daze.

Had Duarte met someone else? Well, why not, a little voice demanded. Wouldn't he have felt he had every excuse to find solace elsewhere? She could feel herself inwardly coming apart at the seams under the new stress which Bliss had imposed on her already overwrought system.

She'd just heard Bliss's car driving off when a phone was brought to her.

It was Duarte on the line. 'Will you meet me for lunch?'

Emily blinked in disconcertion. Duarte was neither in the habit of phoning her during his working day nor of inviting her to meet him for lunch.

'I have something to tell you,' he murmured tautly.

A woman who drove him to smashing locked doors open was *not* for him. He regretted bringing her back to Portugal,

recognised his mistake. No, more probably he planned to
tell her that he had met someone else. Slow, agonised tears
started trekking down her cheeks.

'Emily?' he prompted. 'I'll send a car for you. Please
come.'

He rang off without another word. She went upstairs to
see if the more dressy clothes which she had left behind
when they separated were still intact in the room she had
once occupied. They were. She fingered through the many
options available. Cerise pink, fire-engine red, fluorescent
orange, traffic-stopping purple. Picking the jazzy pink
which hurt her aching eyes, she got changed. He was going
to dump her again. She *knew* he was. Last night, he had
more or less said right out how hard he had had to push
himself to go to bed with her again. Mind you, at the time,
he'd *seemed* fairly enthusiastic!

The car ferried her the thirty-odd kilometres into Lisbon.
Duarte had a superb apartment on the Avenida da Libertade
and, as she ascended from the car in the long tree-lined
boulevard, sick butterflies were dancing in her tummy.

Ushered into the imposing drawing room where she'd
once fallen ingloriously asleep during a supper with his
friends, following an evening at the opera, she focused on
Duarte. Her heart started behaving as if someone was playing football with it and her mouth ran dry.

Poised by one of the tall nineteenth-century windows,
black hair gleaming in the sunlight, his elegant light-grey
pinstripe suit cut to fit his broad shoulders and long powerful thighs, Duarte looked absolutely spectacular. Studying
those lean, darkly handsome features of his and hurriedly
evading those all-seeing, all-knowing, stunning golden
eyes, she ran out of breath. Suddenly, all she could think
about was the passion of the night hours and all she could
feel was the intimate ache that still lingered at the core of
her own body as a result.

'Thank you for coming,' Duarte said with grave quietness.

'I'd never have the nerve to stand you up,' Emily confided, her fingers biting so hard into the clutch purse she was holding that her hands were hurting. 'Where are we going for lunch?'

'I thought we could eat here.'

Instantly, she felt trapped. True, a public place was hardly suitable for the delivery of any revelation likely to *upset*. But couldn't he just have waited until he came home for dinner? Instead, she'd been summoned like a schoolgirl to hear her fate and that felt distinctly humiliating.

'Do I have to eat?' she enquired brittlely. 'I'm not hungry.'

'As you wish. Would you like a drink?'

'A brandy...' She glanced at him while he dealt with her request, seeing the tension etched in the hard cast of his bronzed profile. The atmosphere was so strained, she felt an unwary word might snap it in two.

Sitting down on the edge of an opulent antique sofa, she sipped nervously at the brandy.

'This morning, Victorine admitted that she'd deliberately mislead me about what you said to her—'

'I know. She also spoke to me and apologised,' Emily responded.

Duarte paced forward from the window and moved his hands in a very expressive gesture of regret. 'I misjudged you and I owe you a very big apology for I have never known you to be cruel.'

Emily shrugged jerkily, unable to reap the smallest satisfaction from that acknowledgement. 'It was just another metaphoric stick to beat me with, wasn't it?'

Dulled colour rose to accentuate the strong slant of his high cheekbones. 'You may be right. However, when my former mother-in-law then went on to confess that she'd resented you from the very hour that I married you, I was very much shocked.'

Surprised though Emily was that Victorine had gone that far in her need to ease her conscience, Emily simply sighed. She was more concerned about what he might have to say next.

'I was foolish to believe that Victorine would easily accept another woman as my wife,' Duarte stated with a harshened edge to his dark, deep drawl. 'Had I not had a board meeting early this morning, I would've come to speak to you immediately.'

'Well, business first and last,' Emily breathed helplessly. 'There's nothing new in that.'

'No…but I think today business came first because it was easier to handle,' Duarte conceded, startling her with that frank admission. 'Naturally I feel guilty. Our home should have been the one place where you could feel relaxed and content but Victorine's spite must've made you very unhappy.'

Emily felt like a stone. Old resentments and bitterness had hardened her usually soft heart. 'I always blamed *you* more than I blamed her…'

Duarte's golden eyes zeroed in on her and narrowed. The taut set of his jawline revealed his surprise at that condemnation. 'But you never once complained about Victorine—'

'And why would I have?' Emily got up in a sudden movement, powered by angry defensiveness at that suggestion that she ought to have spoken up sooner. 'Why would I have thought that complaining would have got me anywhere with you? After all, you are not the world's most sensitive person either, are you?'

A sardonic black brow quirked. 'Meaning?'

'Those portraits of Izabel in the salon, the dining room and the main hall…' Emily illuminated tightly. 'I could've understood that if you'd had children with her but you didn't. How was I supposed to feel that the Quinta de Monteiro was *my* home?'

Duarte was studying her with frowning intensity but a faint perceptible pallor was spreading round his taut mouth. 'I never *thought*…I was so used to them being there—'

'Well, you know…your first wife may have been a great beauty and the paintings may be wonderful art, but you should've had them moved to less prominent places. I felt intimidated by them. And although I'm not terribly interested or indeed gifted in any way at fancy interior design and stuff like that,' Emily admitted flatly, 'I would've appreciated the freedom to redecorate just one room and feel that it, at least, was mine.'

Every bone in Duarte's lean dark devastating face was rigid by the time she had finished speaking. 'I cannot excuse myself for my lack of sensitivity.'

'No, you can't,' Emily agreed with very little in the way of satisfaction. Then nothing he said could touch or ease the hard knot of pain inside her. Even while she railed at him, she was thinking how pointless her reproaches were. Those oversights had merely spelt out his basic indifference to her feelings. He'd never been in love with her and only a man in love would have considered such things. But she'd said enough, knew that if she said anything more, he might realise just how jealous she'd been of his first wife. Not very nice, she reflected guiltily. Izabel had proved to be an impossible act to follow.

'It's all water under the bridge now.' Emily drew in a slow steadying breath, for she knew exactly what she needed to find peace of mind—her freedom. Freedom from such demeaning comparisons between herself and a dead woman. Freedom from wanting the love she could never have because that wanting was self-destructive. 'So, before you start telling me things you would much prefer not to tell me, *I* have something to say.'

'You have mý full attention,' Duarte drawled in the most insidiously discouraging way.

'How do you do that?' Emily found herself asking. 'How do you manage always to make me feel that I shouldn't say what I'm about to say? I mean, you don't even *know* what I'm about to say!'

Duarte reached for her tense hands and unlaced them to hold her taut fingers in his. A bleak look had darkened his amazing eyes to a midnight glimmer of light as he gazed down at her. 'I'm not planning to smash any more doors down, *minha esposa*. Is that what is worrying you?'

The warmth of his hands on hers was a subtle entice-ment, as was the endearment. Pinned to the spot by those brilliant, dark, sexy eyes of his, she shivered, every tiny muscle she possessed tensing. That close, she could feel the heat of his lean powerful body, smell the evocative scent of him, composed of warm male laced with a faint hint of some exotic aftershave. All so familiar, all so devastatingly familiar that her senses reacted to him no matter what she did.

'I'm sorry if I frightened you. I lost control of my temper but it will not happen again,' Duarte intoned huskily, the very sound of his dark, deep voice setting up a quiver at the base of her spine.

'Stop it…' Emily urged shakily, desperately seeking to muster her defences against that wholly seductive onslaught of sensations.

'Stop…*what*?' Duarte probed with a sincere incompre-hension that infuriated her.

Her teeth gritted behind her compressed lips. She saw just how weak she was. It seemed she never learnt where he was concerned. He got close and her brain seemed to go into free fall—and yet he was still being cool and precise and he was not deliberately striving to set her wretched body alight. That knowledge just made her feel so horribly humiliated by her own lack of control that she dragged her hands free of his and stepped back.

'What's wrong?' Duarte murmured levelly. 'Are you still angry with me?'

Angry? Was she *still* angry? Mulling over that question, Emily conceded that she'd started being angry with Duarte within weeks of marrying him. Even while loving him to distraction, she'd been angry from the instant she laid her devastated eyes on Izabel's gorgeous photogenic face. Angry because she wasn't loved the same way, angry that her only value to him seemed to lie in supplying him with the child he wanted but angrier still that she was so hopelessly and helplessly obsessed with a man who neither needed nor loved her. In one way or another, she'd been made painfully conscious of that reality almost every day of their marriage.

'There's nothing wrong...' Emily said, not quite levelly. 'I just want a divorce.'

Duarte stilled the way people did when they got an entirely unexpected response. 'And you don't think that comes under the heading of there being something wrong?'

'Right now...' Emily breathed, colour highlighting her heart-shaped face, 'I do not want you getting clever with me.'

'Clever...' Duarte flung his proud, dark heard back.

Her fingers coiled into fists by her side as she forced herself on. 'I told you yesterday...I told you I didn't want to be your wife anymore—'

'Last night...' Duarte trailed out those two words until she felt like her face was burning, 'you gave me a rather different message.'

'I didn't know what was going on last night. I wasn't myself,' Emily stated between compressed lips of mortification. 'But that mistake is not going to make me change my mind about what's best for me—'

'Jamie?' Duarte slotted in, smooth as a stiletto.

Emily paled. 'I'm willing to live in Portugal so that you can see as much of Jamie as you like—'

'All right, you move out and I keep Jamie.'

Emily's lower lip parted company with her upper in sheer shock.

'Now I wonder why you aren't into that solution when it is only the reverse of what you are suggesting that *I* should accept,' Duarte pointed out without remorse. 'Only twenty-four hours after I get to meet my son, you want to deprive me of him again and you somehow expect me to be cool about it?'

'All right, you're making me feel horrible…' Emily muttered, unable to avoid seeing the unlovely comparison he'd put before her. 'But feeling as you do about me, you have no right to expect me to live with you just for Jamie's sake.'

'Haven't I? You were perfectly happy last night until I blew it,' Duarte reminded her without hesitation. 'Now, had you said then that you could not bear me to touch you, I would have agreed that at the very least we should separate.'

Emily caught on fast to that argument. Hugely aware that he could talk semantic circles round her and tie her into knots to the extent that she would soon not know where she was in the dialogue, she grasped hurriedly at the getout clause he had put before her. 'Well, I'm saying it *now*. I can't bear for you to touch me!'

'Where do you get the nerve to say that to me?' Duarte derided, reacting to that statement with a level of incredulity that was seriously embarrassing.

Flushed to the roots of her red-gold hair, Emily backed off several steps. 'I'm not taking back a word of it…'

Like a leopard on the prowl, Duarte followed her retreat.

'I don't have to justify wanting a divorce—'

'Yes, you do,' Duarte overruled with infuriating logic.

'OK...' Trapped between the wall and Duarte's lean powerful physique, Emily came to a halt with her shoulderblades up hard against the plaster. 'When I married you, I was too young to know what I was doing. You took advantage of the fact that I was in love with you. I had a lousy hole-in-the-corner wedding and I didn't even get a honeymoon!'

Duarte elevated a winged black brow with pronounced disbelief. 'That's...*it*?'

'That's only to *begin* with!' Emily slung, her temper firing up fast at his refusal to take her seriously. 'Then you brought me home to a house ruled by your ex-mother-in-law, who hated me on sight. After that, you hardly bothered to notice that I was alive—'

A charismatic smile began to form on Duarte's wide, sensual mouth. 'I seem to recall noticing that you were alive so often and with such frequency that I once fell asleep in a board meeting!'

Chagrinned by that literal interpretation of her words, Emily changed tack to suit that line of argument as well. 'So you *admit* that all you ever shared with me was a bed—'

'If you wanted to share the board meetings too, you should have mentioned it.'

Pure rage filled Emily. 'When I phoned you during the day, you never once returned my calls!'

Duarte frowned. 'What calls?'

'I daresay there was a time or two when you were much too busy to speak to me but there is just no excuse for you never once phoning me back—'

'I never refused a call of yours in my life,' Duarte interrupted with a palpable edge of masculine annoyance. 'I have better manners. We Portuguese are not so taken up with business that we overlook either courtesy or family during working hours.'

'Well, I was overlooked time and time again until I got the message!' Emily raked back at him in a growing fury at her inability to make any charge stick and draw blood. 'And where were your precious manners when you failed to turn up for the dinner parties I arranged in my deadly boring, dutiful role of being your wife?'

'Again you are making false accusations, not one of which you have ever mentioned before,' Duarte condemned with chilling bite. 'Where is all this nonsense coming from and why have you wandered from the point?'

'*My* point is—' Emily stabbed the air between them with a raised hand and, even in the grip of her temper, was rather pleased with the effect.

Without warning, Duarte moved forward and brought his hands up to plant them on either side of her startled face, long fingers meshing into the strands of her fiery hair. Shimmering golden eyes that had the flashfire charge of lightning clashed with hers. '*Your* point is non-existent or else you might have said something worth listening to by now,' he grated rawly, half under his breath, as he gazed down at her. 'I asked you here so that we could talk in private and I could express my regrets for my behaviour last night. But you have refused to listen. Instead you have done nothing but sling lies at me!'

'Lies…?' Intimidated in a very physical way by the manner in which he had her cornered, Emily was nonetheless conscious of a sudden maddening and truly insane need for him to touch her in exactly the way she had told him minutes earlier that she could not *bear* to be touched.

'Desire is not a one-way street. I know when I am wanted by a woman,' Duarte spelt out in the same dark dangerous undertone that was playing merry hell with her awakened senses.

'Really? Absolutely always?' Emily framed doggedly but no longer quite sure of what she was saying and why.

Other reactions were taking over at mind-bending speed:
the steady acceleration of her heartbeat, an alarming shortness of breath, a sensation of exhilaration and awareness
so intense it was like standing on a razor edge.

Duarte laced his hand into a whole hank of fiery red-
gold strands to hold her fast and then he brought his hot
hard mouth crashing down on hers. Fire in the hold, she
thought crazily, every inch of her jolted by the surge of
wild excitement charging her. He dropped his hands and
inched up the skirt of her dress, long sure fingers gliding
up over her slender thighs with a knowing eroticism that
only added fuel to her response.

She was shaking, clinging to him. She did not know how
or when her hands had crept up to grip his wide shoulders
but only by holding on to him was she staying upright.
With a sudden hungry groan, Duarte cupped his hands to
her hips and lifted her against him, pushing her back against
the wall, letting her feel the full force of his arousal. Any
grip Emily had on reality vanished at that point.

She heard herself moan under his marauding mouth like
an animal. With every invasive stab of his tongue he mim-
icked a infinitely more primal possession and stoked her
desire to more electrifying heights.

'Duarte… Please,' she gasped.

'Please what?' Duarte probed huskily, pushing her thighs
further apart, letting his expert fingers linger within inches
of the throbbing core of her shivering body.

'You're torturing me!'

Duarte let her slide down the wall on to her own feet
again and one of her shoes had fallen off, making her blink
in confusion at the lopsided effect of her own stance.

'If I was a real bastard, I'd make you beg,' Duarte spelt
out in a roughened undertone, spectacular golden eyes
scorching over her as she struggled somewhat belatedly to

haul her dress back down from her waist. 'But I'm far too excited to deny myself that long!'

'What are you *doing*?' Emily squeaked as he swept her up into his arms with more haste than ceremony.

'Emily…' Duarte groaned as he strode out of the drawing room and down the corridor towards the bedrooms. 'What do you *think* I'm doing?'

CHAPTER SEVEN

'BUT we were talking about getting a divorce!' Emily protested, sufficiently reanimated by the change of surroundings to say what she should have said five minutes sooner.

'Correction, *you* were talking on that subject. When you can put up some convincing resistance to my advances, I'll consider talking about it,' Duarte proffered with a wolfish and very male downward glance of challenge.

'I am not getting into bed with you again… It would be wrong!' Emily argued frantically as she shouldered open the door in a luxurious bedroom.

'Wrong at this juncture would be playing the tease and why should you want to?' Duarte enquired, lowering her to the carpet, bending down to pluck off the remaining shoe she wore so that she could stand normally and then spinning her round to unzip her dress.

As he spun her back like a doll and gave the sleeves of the garment a helpful tug to assist it on its downward journey, Emily stood as though transfixed. 'Duarte…I'm being serious—'

'So am I,' he swore, watching the dress slide down with satisfaction and shrugging out of his beautifully tailored jacket to let it fall on the carpet as well. 'I want you. Here. Now. Fast…'

'But you haven't even told me yet what you brought me to tell me…' her voice faltered and trailed away altogether as she thought of that 'here…now…fast' bit he had threatened and a truly unforgivable dart of liquid heat forced her to lock her knees together.

'I've done all the talking I want to do for one day. I've

apologised. I've owned up to gross insensitivity. You were as receptive as a rock-face but you didn't complain about anything I can't fix,' Duarte asserted on a very single-minded tack as he shed his tie and wrenched at his shirt with pronounced impatience.

'All right, I was lying when I said I didn't want you to touch me,' Emily owned up in desperation. 'But please keep your shirt on. If you take it off, I'm lost.'

Momentarily, Duarte paused and cast her a gleaming glance of vibrant amusement. He slid out of the shirt with the fluid grace of a matador in the bull ring. 'This is one battle you're destined to lose—'

'But I can't... We can't. This...*this* is not the answer!' Emily surveyed him with guilt-stricken intensity as he stood there poised, all hair-roughened bronzed skin and lean hard muscle. Him looking like a Greek god was not exactly the biggest help she'd ever received in her belief that she had to put a lid on what was happening between them.

'Isn't it?' Duarte reached out and hauled her into his arms, smouldering dark gaze roaming over the rise and fall of her breasts. He unclipped the bra, found a pouting swell of tormentingly sensitive flesh and rubbed his thumb over the throbbing tip. 'I want you so much I'm in agony...'

She leant into him even though she tried to stop herself. She could feel the same want mounting like a hungry, conscience-free flood inside her. Last night might never have happened. She was shocked at the strength of her own yearning, shocked by the overpowering surge of excitement awakened by the sight of his lean hand cupping her breast.

'This is what we need now, *minha esposa*,' Duarte asserted, pulling into him and lifting her to bring her down on the side of the elegant sleigh bed. 'Talking is too dangerous. Talking when there is no solution is just stupid.'

'earing those sentiments pronounced with such unquenchable masculine conviction should have sent her leaping from his arms in angry frustration. But he was arranging her on the bed with the care of a male about to extract the utmost from the experience and she could not take her eyes from his. Dear heaven, those wonderful eyes. He just had to look at her and her own thoughts just dwindled and yet somehow she felt secure about that, safe. That was all wrong and she knew it was but when Duarte loomed over her like every fantasy she'd ever had, self-control was not an option her overheated body wanted to consider.

'Talking is supposed to *be* the solution,' she murmured in a last attempt to place head over heart.

'It put us in separate beds last night. It made me kick in a door. You think that's healthy?' Duarte challenged as he stripped down to a pair of black silk boxer shorts that were the very last word in sexy apparel. 'No, my way is better.'

My way is better. Not exactly the last word in compromise, was he? But she gazed up at him and the most enormous swell of love surged through her and, all of a sudden, nothing else mattered.

'Once, you used to look at me like that all the time.' Duarte came down on the bed like a predator, taking his time, and a helpless little shiver of anticipation rippled through her taut and restive limbs. 'I became accustomed to it…'

Most men would be pretty content to be uncritically adored by their wives, Emily reflected. And the ironic truth was, while she'd remained content to settle for less on her own behalf, she had been happier. Whether he knew it or not, the wild card that had upset the balance had been the very unsettling discovery that he had loved Izabel. No, nobody had told her that; even at her worst, Victorine hadn't been that cruel. She had seen it in that wedding photograph of Izabel and Duarte together, the love, pride and satisfaction he had had in his acquisition of his beautiful bride.

'I want it back,' Duarte said lazily and he pressed his wide, sensual mouth to the tiny pulse below her ear, a sensitive spot that seemed to overreact with blinding enthusiasm and sent her momentarily haywire with hunger.

Gasping for breath and trying to sound cool, Emily looked up at him and trying to sound dry but actually sounding very stressed, she said, 'I don't do adoration any more. I grew up.'

Duarte let a provocative hand roam over her distended nipples and her back arched as if he had burned her. 'But you can regress,' he murmured smooth as silk.

Regressing felt so darned good, she thought helplessly. He pushed her flat again with a husky laugh of amusement and lowered his carnal mouth to her tingling breasts where he turned torment into a new art form. Control evaporated about there for Emily. Her body was all liquid burning heat powered by a hunger that was steadily overwhelming her.

'You want me?' Duarte demanded, fierce control etched in his dark features.

'Now…' she begged.

He spread her thighs like a Viking invader set on sexual plunder and it still wasn't fast enough for her. He came over her, into her, in a shocking surge of primal male power and she almost passed out at the wave of intense pleasure.

'You feel like hot silk,' he groaned with raw sensual appreciation, plunging deeper still.

And from then on in, she gave herself up to voluptuous abandonment. The hot sweet pleasure just took over and she could only breathe in short agonised gasps. In the steely grip of that mounting excitement, her heart thundering, her blood racing like wildfire through her veins, she whimpered and arched her hips to invite his urgent thrusts. She cried out at the peak of a climax of breathtaking power, her entire body wrenched into the explosive hold of that erotic release.

Afterwards, it was like coming back to life after a long time somewhere else. Where else, Emily could not have specified at that precise moment, but it didn't seem to matter for she felt this glorious sense of unquestioning contentment and delight. Her needs felt few; she was with Duarte and Duarte was with her. Life felt wonderful.

Duarte rolled over, carrying her with him, and gazed down at her passion-stunned face with brilliant golden eyes of satisfaction. 'I think that settles the divorce question for the foreseeable future.'

Disorientated by that sudden descent to the prosaic and the provocative when her own brain was still floating in euphoric clouds, she blinked and stared up at him. Duarte pushed her head down into his shoulder, dropped what felt like a kiss on the crown of her head and held her close in silence.

'Duarte?' she mumbled, trying to ground her brain and focus.

'I'm going over to London on business next week. You and Jamie can come and we'll visit your family…OK?'

Thrown by that suggestion, Emily began to lift her head.

'I was bloody furious when I discovered you'd gone there and they'd thrown you out again,' Duarte stated, startling her even more, his strong jawline clenching. 'Not very sympathetic, were they?'

Emily had paled. 'I hadn't got around to telling them about us being separated…or anything else,' she mumbled, shrinking from any mention of that episode with Toby. 'Mum and Dad just didn't think it was right that I had left you and they probably thought that showing me the door again would send me back to Portugal more quickly.'

'Or maybe they thought that helping you might offend *me*,' Duarte drawled very quietly. 'And that if they offended me, I might not be just so generous in putting new business in the way of the family firm. Have you even considered that angle?'

Emily regarded him with shaken reproach. 'Is that how you think of my family? That's an *awful* thing to suggest!'

'I'm an appalling cynic but, obviously, you would know your own flesh and blood best...' Duarte murmured, relieving her with the ease with which he made that concession.

Emily relaxed again.

'It's just that most parents would think twice before they threw a married, very pregnant and distressed daughter back out into the snow,' Duarte continued, dismaying her with his persistence. 'They also took my side. They didn't even *know* what my side was but they took it all the same—'

'People don't always react the way you expect them to...especially when you take them by surprise, as I did,' Emily pointed out defensively.

'I can certainly second that.'

He didn't like her parents. Why had she never realised that before? Emily lay there in his arms, forced to reluctantly concede that, if anything, the emotional distance between her and her parents had only grown since her marriage and had been almost severed altogether when she turned up on the doorstep without her husband in tow eight months earlier. Her family had visited her only once in Portugal. Although Emily had bent over backwards to ensure their every comfort and provide every possible entertainment, true enjoyment had seemed to elude her relatives. Her mother and her sisters had seemed to band together in a trio of constant criticism which had made Emily feel about an inch high. The couple of invitations she had made after that had been turned down with no great effort devoted to polite excuses.

'Let's have lunch and then go home and spend the rest

of the day with Jamie,' Duarte suggested, taking her mind off her regret over her uneasy relationship with the family she loved.

'That's a lovely idea,' she said warmly.

Only then did it cross her mind that she'd come to the city apartment expecting to hear some ghastly revelation that had never transpired. Desperate to conserve her own pride, she'd started rambling on about getting a divorce when a divorce was probably the very last thing in the world that she wanted. Sometimes, she worked herself up into such a state, she acknowledged shame-facedly. Duarte had made passionate love to her twice in twenty-four hours. Was that the behaviour of a man interested in another woman? And wouldn't she have made the biggest mistake of her life in saying no? They had achieved a closeness that had entirely eluded them the night before.

They lunched in the elegant dining room and were just finishing their coffee prior to departing when the door opened without any warning and Bliss strolled in carrying a document case.

'I'm sorry, Duarte. I didn't realise that your wife was here. Mrs Monteiro…'

'Miss Jarrett,' Emily muttered, barely able to look at the blonde after the unpleasantness of their meeting earlier in the day.

But Duarte was already rising from his chair, his charismatic smile lighting up his darkly handsome features. 'My apologies, Bliss. I changed my plans and neglected to inform you.'

A dewy smile free of her usual mockery fixed to her exquisite face, Bliss sighed softly, 'I really ought to be used to that by now.'

'I'm going home for the rest of the day.'

Emily watched the little tableau playing out in front of her with wide eyes of disconcertion. She saw Duarte stride to greet Bliss and receive the document case rather than wait for her to come to him as he once would have done. Duarte was, as a rule, formal with his employees and un-given to addressing them by their first names. When had he decided to relax his formidable reserve with Bliss?

'I'll see you out,' Duarte assured Bliss.

As they left the room together, Emily sat like a stone in her chair for several seconds. Just when had such a staggering change taken place in Duarte's relationship with his executive assistant? Unable to sit still, she found herself getting up and walking restively over to the window. She recalled Bliss's low soft voice, a tone she'd never heard the blonde employ before and she'd never seen her smile like that either, like an infinitely more feminine version of the harder-edged Bliss she herself had got to know. Out of nowhere, a tension headache settled round Emily's temples like a tightening circle of steel. Thump, thump, thump was her body's enervated response to the mental alarm bell going off at shrieking decibels inside her head.

Duarte and Bliss? Were her suspicions insane? Was she even thinking straight? But hadn't Bliss carefully ended their friendship only a few hours earlier? Hadn't Bliss made it clear that her sympathies now lay squarely with Duarte? And, finally, hadn't Bliss venomously pointed out that Duarte might already have another woman in his life?

Was Bliss that other woman? Her tummy churning at the very thought of such a development, Emily struggled to get a grip on her flailing emotions. She felt like a truck had run over her. She felt cold inside and out. Why shouldn't Duarte be attracted to Bliss? Bliss was beautiful and witty and clever. Bliss was exactly the kind of wife Duarte should have picked to replace Izabel. Was he sleeping with her? *Had* he slept with her? Exactly when had his relationship with his executive assistant become so familiar that he smiled at her like that? Smiled with warmth and approval and intimacy?

Was she crazy to be thinking these kind of thoughts? There they were, calling each other by their first names and exchanging smiles, and suddenly she had them tucked up in bed together? She was not going to leap in and say anything to Duarte. She was *not*. Any such questions would be very much resented.

And while she stood there, fighting to put a lid on her emotional turmoil, she found herself thinking back to her friendship with Bliss Jarrett. Within months of her marriage to a male who worked very long hours, Emily had become very lonely. Although she'd been dragged out everywhere by Victorine on social visits and had met several women whom she might have become friendly with, the language barrier had reigned supreme. She'd met very few people who spoke fluent English and it had taken her a long time to master even the basics of Portuguese.

When she had phoned Duarte's office, she had always been put through to Bliss. She would leave a message with Bliss but Duarte would never call back. Once or twice in those early days, she had phoned just to check that her message had been passed on to him. With an audible suggestion of embarrassed sympathy on Emily's behalf, Bliss would gently assure her that her husband had received the message.

Eventually they had begun chatting and Emily had confided that she hated shopping alone. Bliss had offered to accompany her and then hastily retracted the suggestion with the apologetic explanation that Duarte would not approve of his wife socialising with a mere employee. Desperate for company, Emily had pointed out that what Duarte didn't know wouldn't hurt him.

And so the friendship that she had valued had begun, a friendship that was a breath of fresh air to someone as lonely and insecure as she had been then. Shopping trips, lunches and, on several occasions when Duarte was abroad on business, Bliss had invited her to her apartment for a meal. There she had met Toby and there she had come up with the stupid childish plan to have her portrait painted in the forlorn hope of displacing an image of Izabel from even one wall of the *quinta*.

'Are you ready?' Duarte asked from the dining room doorway, making her jerk and return to the present.

Emily breathed in deep, steadying herself. She would make no comment; she would say nothing. There was probably nothing whatsoever in what she had seen. It was only her own insecurity playing tricks on her imagination. Crazily she pictured herself standing up at a divorce hearing and saying 'Duarte *smiled* at her...that's my evidence.'

In the lift that took them down to the ground floor, Emily stole a glance that spread and lingered to encompass every visible inch of her tall, dark and absolutely gorgeous husband. She loved him. They were back together...weren't they? He was making an effort to repair the great yawning cracks in their marriage, wasn't he? So what if most of the effort he was putting in was bedroom-orientated? Did that matter? Did that make him less committed? Had he *ever* been committed to her?

Engaged in such frantic and feverish thoughts, Emily tripped over a metal bin to the side of the exit, skidded across the floor and came down on her bottom.

'*Meu Deus!*' Duarte exclaimed and immediately reached for her to help her to her feet again. 'Are you all right?'

'So...s-so,' she stammered, refusing to massage the throbbing ache assailing her bruised hip.

'Didn't you see it?' Smoothing her down, Duarte focused on the bin which was about four feet tall and hard to miss.

Emily clambered into the limousine on wobbly legs. She would keep her tongue between her teeth for the whole drive home. Just then, she recalled that odd little scene she had witnessed at the airport between Duarte and Bliss. The way he had taken a few extra minutes to speak to Bliss in private before joining Emily in the car, the tension she'd witnessed between them. What had he been saying to Bliss to make her freeze and turn red? Exactly how intimate were they?

'When did you get so friendly with Bliss Jarrett?' That demand just erupted out of Emily's mouth and she was horrified at herself, at the clumsiness of that leading question, not to mention its undeniably accusing tone.

There was one of those truly awful laden silences.

Duarte elevated a sardonic brow and his spiky black lashes partially screened his dark deepset gaze. 'I don't think that's a subject we should open.'

What the heck was that supposed to mean? An evasive response was the very last thing she needed, in the mood she was in, but she really did try very hard to let the subject stay closed. She bit down on her tongue so hard, she tasted her own blood. She told herself that she ought to trust him but, the trouble was, she knew she no longer trusted Bliss. And even though Duarte was emanating sufficient vibes to warn her off, she ignored them.

'It's natural for me to be curious.'

'I'm not sure that you'll be grateful for my explanation. Bliss was very embarrassed when she realised that you had had an affair with her cousin and she offered to resign,' Duarte advanced in a glacial tone.

'Did she really?' Emily whispered shakily, feeling like he had just dropped a giant suffocating rock on top of her.

'After those developments, it would have been a little difficult for us to return to our former working relationship as though nothing had happened. I have great respect for Bliss both as an employee and a personal friend. I would appreciate it if you would keep that fact in mind.'

'I'm not really sure what you're saying,' Emily mumbled although she was dreadfully afraid that she did. She was also horribly tempted to say that, in terms of personal friendship, Bliss spread herself around behind other people's backs, but it sounded mean and petty and she stopped herself just in time.

Duarte angled his proud dark head back and viewed her with chilling dark eyes without the smallest shade of warmer gold. 'You have no right to question me. You had an affair. You broke up our marriage. You then vanished and it was seven months before an investigator even picked up on your trail—'

'Duarte...' she broke in jaggedly, her voice breaking under that onslaught.

'Throughout those months I didn't know whether you were dead or alive or even whether or not I *was* actually a father. It was a very difficult time for me. During that period, Bliss became something more than just an employee—she became a supportive friend.' His beautiful dark eyes were like a card-player's eyes, remote, cool, but disturbingly challenging.

She wanted to kill him. Then she wanted to strangle herself. He was telling her the cruellest thing. He was telling her that her own behaviour, her stupid immature vanishing act and all those months of silence had laid the foundations of what he termed a 'friendship'. Was he telling her that Bliss was his mistress and that he wasn't giving her up? And was it unjust and melodramatic of her to suspect that Bliss might have a far more ambitious agenda than mere friendship in mind? Hadn't Bliss frightened Emily into leaving Portugal and then made use of that opportunity to increase her own standing with Duarte? Or was, Emily asked herself, she trying to justify her *own* mistakes and blame Bliss for the fall-out?

At that point what felt like the last piece of a bewildering puzzle seemed to fall into dismaying place and Emily stared at Duarte in sudden horror. 'Bliss is that third party you mentioned, *isn't* she? That discreet person who confirmed that I was carrying on with Toby when I *wasn't*—'

'I won't dignify that accusation with an answer,' Duarte countered drily.

It was as if he was slamming a door in her face without conscience. She wanted to ask him how intimate his relationship with Bliss had become but was not entirely sure she could stand to hear an honest answer at that moment. He would not feel that he had to defend himself. After all, didn't he believe that she had betrayed him with Toby first? She could feel his anger, contained but always there between them, awakened by the reminder of her supposed affair, his attitude hardened by the manner in which she had questioned him about Bliss.

'Tell me,' she muttered dry-mouthed, feeling that no matter where she turned she was in a no-win situation and always in the wrong, 'would you even have considered bringing me back to Portugal had I not had Jamie?'

'The jury's still very much out on that one,' Duarte drawled with freezing cool. 'Right now, I'm changing direction like a metronome.'

Neither of them said another word for the remainder of the drive back to the *quinta*.

After they arrived Duarte strode off with the terse explanation that he had an important call to make, Emily went upstairs to fetch Jamie and scooped him out of his cot with eager hands. After stopping for a chat with the nanny and discussing at some length the reality that her son needed more clothes, she cuddled Jamie all the way down to the ground floor again. There she set him on a rug in the salon to talk to him.

'Your father doesn't like me very much right now but that's OK,' Emily informed her six-month-old son with a rather wooden bright smile, destined to reassure him that she really wasn't sad. 'I'm just warning you that whenever you do anything stupid, it will come back and haunt you for a good hundred years. It will smack you in the face at every turn and leave you feeling awful—'

'I think you're taxing his concentration span...' Duarte murmured from somewhere behind her at the same time as she noticed that Jamie was kicking his feet and demonstrating definite signs of excited welcome at the approach of someone he liked.

'I didn't know you were there!' Emily was seriously rattled by his appearance.

'Put on the fake smile again. Jamie's not very discerning.' Duarte hunkered down by her side to grasp their son's extended chubby fingers. 'He wouldn't know a pity-fest from a celebration.'

'If that's supposed to make me feel better—'

'No...but *this* is...' Anchoring one powerful hand into her tumbling hair, Duarte tugged her head around and captured her startled lips under his. Instinctively, she began to tip towards him. That slow-burning kiss awakened a bone-deep yearning inside her for the pure reassurance of physical contact and acceptance.

And then something funny happened. Her memory threw up a perfect recollection of his last words before they vacated the car. Just as quickly, she found herself pulling back from him for the first time in her life and she caught the flash of surprise in his stunning gaze before he veiled it.

'If I'm only here for Jamie's benefit, we'd better not stretch me too thin,' she said tightly.

Duarte reached forward and lifted their son with the same carefulness he might have utilised in handling a bomb. And her heart twisted because she knew it was her fault that he was still afraid of being rejected by Jamie. Emily being

Emily, she then felt immediately horrible for not allowing Duarte to kiss her as much as he wanted to.

'Victorine tells me that you invited her to stay on,' Duarte murmured while he struggled to get Jamie into a comfortable position on one raised, lean, powerful thigh. 'In the circumstances that was extremely generous of you. However, she's asked me if she can move into a house on the outskirts of the estate which is currently unoccupied. I've agreed.'

'With me in charge, prepare yourself for a sudden slump in staff efficiency,' Emily told him apprehensively.

'If there's a problem, you come to me and I will deal with it.'

Meanwhile Jamie chortled and dug delighted hands into Duarte's luxuriant black hair and pulled hard.

'He's not scared of me any more,' Duarte breathed with a sudden grin.

Duarte took Jamie upstairs to the picture gallery which was lined with distinctly gloomy canvases of Monteiro ancestors and gave their infant son a potted history of the family with a perfectly straight face.

'Don't you think he's just a little young for this?' Emily remarked.

'This is our family. Nothing comes before family. Not business, not anything,' Duarte imparted with considerable gravity. 'My earliest memory is of my father bringing me here and telling me what it means to be a Monteiro.'

Not noticeably impressed, Jamie went to sleep draped over Duarte's shoulder. When Emily came back downstairs from settling their son for a nap, three estate workers were engaged in removing Izabel's giant portrait from the wall in the salon. The whole room would have to be redecorated. She wondered where the painting was going, looked at that gorgeous sultry face and sighed to herself. For so long, she had tormented herself with pointless comparisons between herself and Duarte's first wife. Now she was receiving what would seem to be her just reward. She now had live competition that struck her as much more threatening.

Nothing comes before family, Duarte had stated with unequivocable conviction. Finally he had answered that loaded question she had shot at him in the car. Jamie came first, so therefore Jamie's needs would take priority over more personal inclinations and mothers were not interchangeable. But where did Bliss fit into that picture?

That night she lay in her bed watching the door which had been expertly repaired stay resolutely closed. She was not one whit surprised. Duarte had been angry when she turned away from him during that kiss. Duarte would sooner burn alive than give her a second such opportunity. He was so damnably proud and stubborn.

So there you are, once again you did the wrong thing, Emily told herself wretchedly. Here she was worrying that the man she loved might be, at the very least, seriously attracted to a woman who was on convenient call for him throughout his working day. And what had Emily done? Angry with him, striving to protect her own pride, she had rejected him and she could not have picked a worse time to do it...

CHAPTER EIGHT

FIVE days later, on the afternoon of the party which Bliss had organised, Emily was fiddling in desperation with a vast floral arrangement in the main hall.

Victorine had been creative with flowers. Emily was not. In spite of all her efforts, the blooms looked like they'd been dropped from a height into the huge glass vase and persisted in standing like soldiers on parade when what she really wanted them to do was *bend*.

The past five days had been an ongoing punishment. The long-awaited removal of Izabel's portraits had left ghastly marks on the panelling in the main hall and on the wallpaper in the dining room and the salon. As there wasn't time for redecoration, she'd attempted to move the furniture around, which hadn't worked very well. In the end she'd taken paintings from other places to try and cover up the damage. At one stage she had been tearing her hair out to such an extent she had even seriously contemplated approaching Duarte and begging for Izabel's wretched portraits to be brought back from wherever they had gone...on a temporary basis. Only the prospect of his incredulity at such an astonishing request had prevented her.

Her mood was not improved by the reality that she and Duarte were existing in a state of armed neutrality in which her bedroom door stayed closed and might even be left to gather cobwebs. That was not good for her nerves. Last night she'd decided that even having it smashed down in what now seemed like true *heroic* style wouldn't make her bat an eyelash and would indeed be welcomed.

Meanwhile, Duarte was being teeth-clenchingly courteous and charming, his entire demeanour that of a male wholly untouched by anything so uncool as a desire for the smallest physical contact with his wife. She knew he would not break...at least, not in her direction. At the same time she had the dubious comfort of knowing that Bliss was rarely out of his reach. At her lowest moments, Emily wondered if he was already slaking his high sex-drive with the glamorous blonde and even if Duarte and Bliss could have been secret lovers long before Toby came into Emily's life...

Indeed, her imagination had taken her to the outer reaches of her worst nightmares. In those worst-case scenarios, Duarte figured as the biggest four-letter word on planet Earth and behaved with Machiavellian cunning and cruelty to deceive his dumb, stupid wife. Now she was finding herself recalling her own trusting friendship with Bliss's cousin, Toby Jarrett.

'It's so simple,' Bliss had laughed. 'You want Izabel's portraits out of the way, you have yourself painted and present your husband with the canvas as a gift. He is certain to take the hint.'

But Bliss had had an uphill battle persuading Emily that she was worthy of being painted. To sit for her own portrait had required a level of self-esteem that Emily did not possess. However, in the end Emily had allowed herself to be convinced and, by then, Toby had already been renting a tiny house and studio in the village below the *quinta*.

They had first met at Bliss's apartment. He'd had his girlfriend with him, a wealthy and possessive divorcée who did not trust other women within an inch of Toby's blond good looks and easy boyish charm. But Toby had never flirted with Emily when she went down to his studio for sittings. His lady friend had soon tired of superintending Emily's visits like a suspicious chaperone.

With Toby living so close to the Quinta de Monteiro,

Emily had felt it was only polite to invite him to dine with her and Duarte one evening. So she had told her first lie to Duarte and had pretended that she had just got talking to the young Englishman in the village. Prevented from revealing her friendship with Bliss, how could she possibly have told the truth? And, since she'd wanted the portrait to be a big surprise, she had had to keep her visits to Toby's studio a secret.

After a meal during which her husband and Toby seemed to radically disagree on virtually every subject under the sun, Duarte had drawled, 'Try to bury him in a larger gathering of guests if you invite him again. He's as argumentative as a rebellious teenager and, if he's such a wonderful artist, why did he drop out of his art college in England?'

Duarte had been extremely unimpressed by Toby. Emily, by then in the early stages of pregnancy and suffering from horrible morning sickness and a distinct feeling of abandonment because Duarte had not made love to her in weeks, had felt defiant. Whatever else, Toby might be, he was, in Emily's humble opinion, an incredibly talented painter. As far as she was concerned, any artist who could make her look almost beautiful was gifted beyond belief. She'd looked forward to the prospect of Duarte being forced to eat his own words.

Nobody had been more astonished than Emily that fatal night when Toby suddenly broke into an impassioned speech on the terrace beyond the salon. Telling her that he loved her, that Duarte did not deserve her, that if she ran away with him, he would cherish her forever and never neglect her as Duarte did. Since Emily had seen no warning signs of Toby falling in love with her, she'd been transfixed by shock. The most enormous self-pity had engulfed her when she appreciated that, for the very first time ever, someone was telling her that they *loved* her. Duarte, she'd thought in an agony of regret that evening, would never

ever look at her that way or speak to her as though she was some unutterably precious being whom he could not live without.

'*Meu Deus*...' Duarte breathed without the smallest warning from behind Emily.

Dredged at dismaying speed from her miserable recollections of the past, Emily turned scarlet because even *thinking* about Toby made Emily feel ultra-guilty. She spun round to find Duarte, sleek and sophisticated in a superb dark business suit, engaged in studying her floral arrangement with raised dark brows.

'Was the vase knocked over?' Duarte enquired.

Emily paled and surveyed the results of her creative efforts with tragic eyes and a sense of injustice. Bad had gone to worse. Several stems had broken beneath her too-rough handling and the blooms now hung forlorn.

'No, the vase didn't fall,' Emily admitted in a small, wooden voice devoid of any human emotion. 'I was trying to arrange the flowers.'

Beside her, she heard Duarte draw in an audible breath. 'I was looking at it from the wrong angle. It's one of those trendy displays...right?'

'Oh, shut up!' Emily launched at him, shocking him as much as she shocked herself with that outburst that rejected his face-saving excuse. She dashed a defensive hand across eyes that were now filled with stinging tears. 'It looks blasted awful and you *know* it does! I'm no good with flowers—'

'Why should you be?'

'Because other women are and I'm no good at *anything*!' Emily lamented bitterly and went racing for the stairs before she broke down altogether. On the first wide landing, she glanced back over her shoulder. Towards the back of the hall, Duarte's uniformed chauffeur, who was holding a pile of fancy-looking gift boxes, stood like a graven image.

Duarte was just staring up at her with stunned dark eyes that seemed to suggest that not only was she lousy in the feminine creativity stakes but also decidedly unhinged.

Emily fled on up the stairs like a lemming gathering speed to jump off a cliff. Why not? A night of horrible humiliation stretched before her. Playing hostess with Bliss smirking on the sidelines at her awkwardness. The even more horrendous challenge of choosing what to wear. The crazy but superstitious conviction that having her predecessor's portraits banished had been the kind of move calculated to bring serious bad luck.

Therefore, it was decidedly disorientating for Emily to race for the sanctuary of her bedroom and find the bed stripped, the wardrobe doors hanging open on empty spaces and two maids engaged on a thorough clean-up. Slowly she backed away again, only to find something or someone very solid blocking her retreat. She whirled round, trembling, shaken, bewildered by what she had just seen.

'Calm down,' Duarte spread eloquent hands in a soothing motion.

'Calm down? Where am I being moved to now? Out the front door? Or down to the cellars with the rats?'

'Let's not get totally carried away, Emily. There are no rats in the Monteiro wine cellars.' Duarte made what she considered to be a totally unnecessary contradiction.

'But there *is* one upstairs!'

Duarte frowned. 'You are joking, I hope—'

'Why are you always so literal? I'm referring to you!' she hissed in frustration.

Duarte tried to reach for her hand. She folded her arms but he was persistent. Unfolding them by the means of gentle pressure, he imprisoned one of her hands in his. Then he dragged her down the corridor, across two landings and all the way over to the other side of the house. Nothing short of thumbscrews would have squeezed a demand to know where he was taking her from Emily's mutinously compressed lips.

Duarte cast open the door of his own bedroom, indeed threw it dramatically wide. Emily stalked in, seething with so many uncontrolled emotions she was afraid she might explode.

'Now look around you,' Duarte suggested, sounding just a little taut.

Her teddy nightshirt was spread across one corner of his bed like a major statement. 'But...b-but, we've *never* shared a room—'

'Any reason why we shouldn't?'

Straying away from him, thrown into a loop by this unexpected development, Emily plucked her nightshirt off the bed, embarrassed that it had been put on show when it was so very unworthy of public display.

'Is that a...no?'

Emily shrugged and rubbed the fringe on the rug with the toe of her canvas-shod foot. But in the depths of the eyes she kept tactfully lowered lurked surprised satisfaction. Indeed, it was amazing how powerful she felt at that moment. He would have done *anything* sooner than ask up front. She could feel his tension. A non-verbal invitation to share a marital bed was quite a proclamation of intent on his part and a none-too-subtle step in the right direction. Suddenly the past five days of dreadful stress she had suffered while attempting to seem unconcerned by the divisions between them seemed very worthwhile—ultimately, *he* had come to *her*.

'It's a big bed,' Emily acknowledged softly. 'I suppose we can be as frigidly polite in that bed as we are at the dinner table.'

'OK,' he murmured with a level of cool that almost made her smile. 'By the way, I've bought you a present.'

Emily was stuffing the nightshirt into as small a ball as

possible and endeavouring to lose it discreetly by pushing it with a prodding toe below the bed. 'A...*present*?'

Duarte indicated the gilded boxes now stacked two feet high on the dressing table.

'For...*me*?' Emily hurried over to the stack to investigate with great curiosity. Never before had Duarte given her a surprise gift.

She hauled all the boxes over to the bed. The lid of the biggest one went flying and she ripped into the tissue paper and was astonished to emerge with some sort of garment. 'You bought me...something to wear?'

'For the party tonight.'

'Why would you buy me something to wear?' Emily asked in sincere bewilderment.

Duarte elbowed back his well-cut jacket and dug two lean hands into his trouser pockets and shifted a wide shoulder in an understated shrug. 'A whim...'

She shook out the incredibly tiny garment. 'But it looks like...' She bit back the tactless word, 'underwear', and studied the fine glistening fabric with wide questioning eyes.

'A dress?' he suggested.

'A...d-dress?' she stammered, striving valiantly to conceal her horror at the prospect of appearing in public with bare arms, legs on display and nothing whatsoever to draw attention away from her non-existent bosom. 'But it's too small to be a dress...'

Duarte breathed in deep.

'And it's so *pale* in colour.' A sort of delicate palest blue that was certain to make her naturally fair skin look washed-out and ghostly.

'Maybe this wasn't one of my better ideas,' Duarte remarked in a rather strained undertone.

Dear heaven, she was being so cruelly tactless! He finally made the effort to go and buy her an unexpected and personal gift and she stood around moaning about it like an ungrateful brat. If he wanted her to appear with every skinny bone accentuated, she would do so. If he wanted her to wear a dustbin bag, she would try to wear it with a smile. It was the thought which counted, not the actual gift.

With forced enthusiasm she dug into the remainder of the boxes, terrified of what other horrors awaited her. Shoes to match but so flat, she would disappear; only two-inch high heels, she noted in dismay. Lingerie fine enough to flow through the proverbial wedding ring alongside the dress but at least while she was shivering, she would be benefiting from an extra layer. An unpadded bra…how *could* he? Was nothing sacrosanct?

Strolling over, Duarte extended a large jewel case. 'Sapphires to go with the dress.'

She froze as if a spectral hand had danced down her spine. As he flipped open the case to display a gorgeous necklace and drop earrings, Emily exuded discomfiture rather than pleasure. 'Did Izabel…ever wear them?' she whispered haltingly.

'No…I have *never* asked you to wear anything worn by Izabel!' Duarte grated in a seriously rattled response.

'But I thought…you know? All that jewellery you shoved at me just after we got married…I thought it had belonged to her.'

Duarte looked heavenward as if praying for self-control. 'Izabel only ever wore diamonds and Victorine has them now. I gave you the family jewellery, not one piece of which Izabel liked.'

'Well, I wish you'd told me that a long time ago…' Emily admitted tremulously, now willing to stretch out a shy fingertip to touch the gleaming beauty of a single sapphire. For her, just for *her*. She could hardly believe it. She swallowed the great fat lump forming in her throat and blinked back tears.

'I may have my flaws but I am not *that* insensitive.'

They were talking about Izabel quite naturally, Emily registered in surprise. He was finally talking about Izabel instead of going horribly silent and bleak and avoiding the subject.

'I'm really touched that you should go to all this effort just for me,' Emily said chokily but she hoped, where the dress and the bra were concerned, he wasn't planning to make a habit of spontaneous shopping trips on her behalf.

'It's an effort that I should have made a lot sooner than this,' Duarte breathed almost harshly.

'Better late than never...' Emily mumbled, pretty much stunned by that admission of fault. She felt even guiltier that she had never worn any of the jewellery he had given her after their marriage because she'd honestly believed it had all been Izabel's. She must have seemed so ungrateful, she thought now.

She took a deep breath. 'I think I ought to admit that I've always been terribly jealous of Izabel.'

'Jealous?' Duarte awarded her a startled look.

Emily winced. 'She got the wedding dress and the honeymoon. She was so beautiful and really gifted at decorating—'

'She hired top designers—'

'And being a hostess—'

'She hired the best caterers—'

Emily frowned, for he was denting the mystic myth of Izabel and she could not understand why he should be so disloyal to her predecessor's memory. 'Obviously, she was special. You fell in love with her when you were only a teenager—'

Duarte vented a grim laugh that silenced her. 'Please don't tell me that you listened to Victorine's story about Izabel and I having been childhood sweethearts!'

'Well, yes...but—'

Seeing her confusion, Duarte groaned out loud, his lean strong face bleak. 'You really don't know the truth even now, do you? But then, who would go out of their way to tell you the sordid details? I didn't want to relive them and Victorine always preferred to inhabit a dream world where her daughter was concerned.'

'Sordid details?' Emily queried in bewilderment. 'What are you talking about?'

'Izabel was a drug addict and not one who had any desire to be cured.'

Feeling the bed hit the back of her knees, Emily dropped down on it in a state of shock. 'You're not serious…'

Recognising her disbelief, Duarte expelled his breath on a hiss. And then he told her about Izabel. Yes, he had first met her when he was sixteen but Izabel had been five years older and quite out of his reach. Indeed he had not met her again until he was in his twenties. An heiress in her own right, Izabel's father had died when she was a child and she'd been raised by her adoring mother and allowed unlimited freedom from an early age.

'Unfortunately, I didn't move in Izabel's world, nor did I know her circle of friends. While they were partying, I was studying and then working eighteen-hour days in the bank. When I met her again six years later, I was mad for her,' Duarte admitted bluntly. 'I couldn't believe that she was still single. I couldn't wait to marry her; I just couldn't believe how *lucky* I was…'

Emily studied the rug at her feet. She really didn't want the intimate details, but they washed off her again because her mind was still fighting to handle the concept of the glamorous Izabel as an addict.

'I caught her with cocaine on the second day of our honeymoon. She just laughed, called me a killjoy and said I had better get used to it because that was how she lived. I was shattered,' Duarte confessed with grim exactitude. 'Before the wedding, I *had* seen her in a very excitable state but I didn't recognise her behaviour as abnormal or suspect the truth. She did have a very lively personality…and she was a tremendous show-off.'

'A…show-off?' Emily's own misconceptions about Izabel were sunk into final obscurity by that almost wry label.

'Izabel craved attention and publicity. No matter what it took, she had to be noticed and admired. She was the ultimate party girl.'

'Couldn't you persuade her to accept professional help?'

'Four times in three years she was rushed into hospital with overdoses. Neither the doctors, nor I, nor even her mother could talk her into entering a rehabilitation clinic or even considering a treatment plan. Mentally, she went downhill fast—but addicts have a distorted grip on reality—'

'Surely other people must've realised she was taking drugs?'

'When she did anything crazy, her friends would cover up for her because they had the same habits to protect and conceal. She had her own money, dealers in every port of call and any relationship we had fell apart within months. My sister Elena died because I was unable to control Izabel.'

Duarte's restive hands moved in a small silent motion that just screamed guilt and more pain than Emily had ever witnessed in another human being.

'I don't believe that. I *don't* believe it was your fault!' Emily protested fiercely.

'When I was abroad, Elena would try to watch over Izabel, for Victorine was quite unequal to the task. My twin made the fatal mistake of getting into Izabel's car and letting her drive. The car went off the road at the most phenomenal speed…' he completed thickly.

'Please don't think of this or talk about it any more,'

Emily begged, humbled by the agony he could not hide and appalled by what she had learnt. She was devastated that he had contrived to bury what could only have been a three-year-long nightmare behind that formidable reserve of his.

'Not exactly a story calculated to put either of us in a party mood,' Duarte remarked broodingly.

'If you would like to put her pictures back up, you can,' Emily mumbled, that being the biggest sacrifice and apology she could conceive at that particular moment.

Duarte dealt her a look of sheer bewilderment.

'I feel sad for Izabel and you now. Poor Victorine too...all those pathetic tales she fed me about her perfect daughter and I can even understand why she did it now—'

'An alarming inability to deal with reality?' Duarte suggested.

'No, she wanted to remember Izabel as she might have been without the drug abuse—remember the good things, not the bad. Maybe you would feel better if you copied her a little...' Emily muttered awkwardly.

'There *were* no good things,' Duarte grated with sudden savage impatience. 'Why do you think I married you?'

'I'm not sure I want to know, in the mood you're in,' Emily said gently.

But Duarte was determined to tell her. 'After Izabel, I swore that no woman would ever have that kind of power over me again,' he breathed with stark bitterness.

Oh, well, that was really not news, Emily reflected, understanding that he was in an explosively emotional frame of mind after finally rising to the demeaning brink of admitting that his first marriage had been a disaster. Perhaps he might eventually reach the healthy point of wondering why his second marriage had run into rough waters as well.

For Emily could now see that *she* had paid the price for the amount of pain, humiliation and disillusionment that the self-destructive Izabel had inflicted on Duarte. Once bitten, forever shy. She also understood there was much that he'd *not* said, for she could read between the lines. He had really loved Izabel because he had not given up on her. How many times had he struggled to help Izabel and had his efforts thrown back in his face?

Somewhat put out by Emily's stoic and seemingly unresponsive silence, Duarte drove a not quite steady hand through his black luxuriant hair. Baulked of a further outlet, he said bossily, 'You should be getting ready for the party.'

And display body parts she much preferred to conceal beneath long skirts and sleeves and loose tops that hinted at more than she possessed. Like a lamb to the slaughter, she gathered up his gifts and went for a shower to freshen up.

When it crossed her mind that if she wore her hair down with that brief dress and low heels, she might look like she was mostly hair and vertically challenged, she decided to put her mane of red-gold hair up instead. Show off her neck. Why not? All else was going to be bared. Having donned the dress, an hour later, there was no temptation for her to examine her reflection in the mirror.

As she came downstairs she noticed that some gifted person had worked wonders with the floral disarrangement she'd abandoned earlier. Duarte strode out of one of the ground-floor reception rooms. Clad in a well-cut dinner jacket, he looked devastatingly male. Her heart skipped a beat but now there was a kernel of resentment.

Duarte focused on her with intent dark golden eyes and stilled as if someone had yanked an off switch inside him.

Emily started backing up the stairs again. 'I could have told you…I look like you don't feed me. Give me two minutes and I'll be covered up again!'

Duarte strode forward. 'You look breathtaking…'

Full marks for stunned stare of appreciation, she thought

and waited on the punchline that she was sure was about to come and then she would be a good sport and laugh.

'Gorgeous, *minha jóia*.'

Emily winced. 'No, I'm not.'

Duarte grabbed her hand and practically carried her over to the giant gilded mirror on the paneled wall. 'What do you see?'

'I'm not looking. I don't like my legs, my arms, my—er—other bits.'

'I love them,' Duarte husked bending over her. 'You have beautiful legs—'

'They're too short,' she hissed.

'Very shapely ankles, dainty arms, a neck like a swan's—'

'It's not long enough—'

'*Everything* in perfect proportion and you look distinctly ethereal in that shade of blue—'

'Spectral and gaunt?' She inched up her eyelashes.

'Ravishing. You grew up with two sisters jealous that you outshone them entirely in the looks department. Stop tormenting yourself with your non-existent flaws,' Duarte urged with a frank exasperation that had a much more powerful effect on her confidence than his compliments.

Finally studying her reflection, Emily saw herself as she had never seen herself. Elegant, slim and small it was true but not scrawny. Putting her hair up had been a good idea for now she could see that her face had a shape and her eyes looked all bright and starry. She turned ever so slightly sideways to check out the bosom profile. No improvement there but my goodness that dress flattered her, particularly the colour!

She looked in the mirror and met Duarte's intent gaze. He dealt her a hot, sizzling appraisal that spoke lustful volumes and made her quiver in helpless response. Well, she was ravishing him, anyway. 'My sisters aren't jealous of me—far from it,' she told him ruefully.

'Why else would they always be putting you down and cracking jokes at your expense?'

She sighed. 'It's just always been that way…their sense of humour, I suppose.'

'And your mother either acting as if it's not happening or even joining in. I know you care about your family but I think you need to assert yourself and make them treat you with respect.'

At that point the front doors were opened wide to greet the arrival of their first guests. There was no time for further conversation but she was disconcerted by what he'd said. It hurt that he had noticed her family's lack of respect but she was touched that he was concerned enough to advise her. Unfortunately, she could not imagine standing up to demand anything from her far more assertive elder sisters.

The party was in full swing by the time Bliss arrived and made an entrance. Every male head turned to watch Bliss glide across the room, her shapely figure enhanced by a scarlet silk sheath dress that was a far cry from her discreet business suits.

Her heartbeat accelerating, Emily watched Duarte cut through the crush to greet his executive assistant and she turned away again. There was *nothing* going on between Bliss and Duarte, she told herself firmly. They had become friends. She would just have to learn to live with that.

Duarte was not acting like a male involved in an affair. Duarte was behaving very much like a male who wanted to keep his marriage intact. She'd actually made it to that holy of holies once denied, a shared marital bed! He had told her about Izabel. He was entranced by their son. He had bought her a whole outfit and it did seem to do something special for her. Then there were the sapphires which had attracted many admiring comments and every time she said 'Duarte gave them to me,' she felt like a million dollars.

So she was looking on the bright side, refusing to dwell on murky suspicions for which she had no proof. Bliss Jarrett had always been a man's woman and very ambitious. It was hardly surprising that she should have ditched her covert friendship with Emily and chosen to shift her allegiance to Duarte instead. And, to be fair, Emily reflected ruefully, possibly Bliss *did* thoroughly dislike her now for what her foolish flight from Portugal had done to Duarte.

While she talked herself mentally into that state of calm and security, Emily drank her way through two glasses of wine. She rarely touched alcohol, for she did not have much of a head for it, but she felt in dire need of a little Dutch courage.

'Emily…?' called a bright familiar voice.

It was Bliss, all smiles and self-satisfaction. 'I've arranged a terrific party, haven't I?'

'Yes…absolutely.' Emily plastered what she hoped was a serene smile on to her lips and prayed for an interruption.

Across the room, she glimpsed Duarte, his brilliant eyes centred on both women. Emily smiled so hard at Bliss her face hurt.

'He's mine. Just you watch me in action,' Bliss invited.

'I trust him…' Emily didn't know if she did but it sounded good and strong. What she really wanted to do was lock Duarte up somewhere very secure, just to be on the safe side.

'When Duarte found you, he was about to instigate divorce proceedings.'

Emily widened her eyes in the desperate hope that that made her look incredulous. 'I asked for a divorce. He said no.'

'I don't believe that for a moment!' Bliss derided with

blistering scorn. 'We're lovers. Haven't you worked that out yet?'

Emily froze. Her heart divebombed to the soles of her feet. Her tummy performed a sickening somersault. 'I don't believe you.'

'Suit yourself.' Bliss simply laughed and walked away.

Emily finished her wine with a shaking hand. *Lovers!* That announcement was not a cue to panic, she instructed herself. In dismay, she watched Duarte move out on to the dance floor with Bliss. Emily wriggled through the clumps of chattering guests round the edge of the floor. Peering under arms for a better view and stretching her neck and standing on tip toe, she kept Duarte and Bliss under close surveillance.

She lifted another glass from a passing tray and watched Bliss press her lithe body into intimate connection with Duarte. But a moment later, Duarte backed off from that contact. Bad move, Bliss, he's not into intimate displays in front of audiences, Emily thought angrily. But then, when had Bliss ever been able to resist a challenge? Hadn't Bliss once told her that a clever woman could easily manipulate any man into doing her bidding? Now Bliss was whispering coyly into Duarte's ear. Duarte flung his arrogant head back and laughed and Emily felt stabbed to the heart and her bravado curdled at source.

If he fell for an Izabel, he could fall for a Bliss. *Lovers?* While she herself had been in England? Emily didn't know what to believe. One minute she was suffering agonies of jealousy but the next, she was telling herself that she could not trust anything that Bliss said. Forcing herself to stop spying on her husband and his 'friend', Emily turned on her heel.

Only minutes later, Duarte curved an imprisoning hand to her elbow and tugged her back against him to murmur ruefully, 'The one drawback of those shoes is that I can't see you in the crowd. Where have you been?'

'Oh...around.'

Now it seemed it was her turn to be whirled round the dance floor. She snuggled up so close to his lean hard body that a postcard could not have squeezed between them. Duarte tensed a little in surprise.

'If you push me away, you're *dead*,' Emily swore. 'It's bad enough having to smell *her* perfume on you.'

'Isn't jealousy hell?' Duarte imparted with a silken lack of concern that was just about the last reaction she had expected to receive.

'What would you know about it?' Emily snatched in a charged breath and then just stormed right to the heart of the matter. 'Bliss told me that you were lovers!'

Assailed by that dramatic contention, Duarte responded in the most withering of tones, '*Que absurdo!* Why would Bliss say such a thing? That is not my idea of a joke, Emily.'

'Are you saying you don't believe me?' Emily's voice rose in volume at the same velocity as her temper.

Duarte tightened the arm he had curved to her rigid spine like a restraining bar. 'No comment—'

'If you don't give me a straight answer, I'm walking off this floor!'

'You've been drinking...you're upset—'

Emily flung her head back and studied him with tormented aquamarine eyes. No. He didn't believe her. He was being smooth, evasive, possibly even extremely *cunning*.

'Bliss said that you weren't comfortable with her being here,' Duarte murmured very drily. 'Even at a distance of a hundred feet, I could see that too. You really don't need to make up childishly silly stories as well.'

Emily wrenched herself free of him with a sudden movement that took him by surprise. She felt violent, furious, incredibly bitter. Bliss and her games, always one step ahead. Duarte? If he was innocent, nothing short of a tape-recording would convince Duarte that Bliss had said such a thing. If he was guilty, all he had to do was accuse his wife of being intoxicated and jealous!

Concentrating on avoiding Duarte, Emily circulated. Every time he came within twenty feet of her, she moved on and plunged into animated conversation with someone else. At last their guests began to take their leave but it was a slow process. Then an elderly woman announced that her handbag had gone missing and immediately became very upset. Emily could have done with her husband's calming presence—her own level of Portuguese was unequal to the challenge of soothing the poor woman. Unfortunately, Duarte was nowhere within view and Emily had to martial the anxious and weary staff into an ordered search. The bag was finally found intact in the cloakroom. Telling the servants just to go to bed and clean up the party debris in the morning, Emily ushered their volubly apologetic guest out to her limousine with great relief.

As Emily walked back indoors, the big house felt eerily silent and empty. Had Duarte just gone up to bed? From the amount of light reflecting on the landing window, Emily realised that the lights had been left on outside in the court-yard garden. With a groan, she went back downstairs to switch them off. She frowned when she saw that the garden doors were still open and then she stopped dead in her tracks: Duarte and Bliss were outside.

Even as Emily looked, Bliss made a sudden almost compulsive movement and tipped forward into Duarte's swiftly extended arms. They were locked together like two magnets in the split second it took Emily to surge forward and gasp strickenly, 'You rotten, lying bastard!'

CHAPTER NINE

DUARTE thrust Bliss hurriedly back from him and wheeled round, his lean strong face startled, his whole demeanour one of almost exaggerated incredulity.

'Did you think I'd gone to bed?' Emily's voice broke on that rather meaningless demand but her brain was locked on that intimate image of them together and the sheer horror of the discovery that her very worst fears should have been proven right before her eyes.

Bliss strolled forward, her scarlet dress shimmering in the lights, her exquisite face offensively cool and collected. 'This is rather embarrassing but I do assure you that you misunderstood what you just saw. I simply stumbled and Duarte saved me from a nasty fall—'

'Do you honestly think I'm s-stupid enough to swallow that old chestnut?' Emily stammered, half an octave higher, utterly thrown by the blonde's reaction until she worked out that Bliss was assuming yet *another* role and this time for Duarte's benefit. That of supportive lover engaged in a tactful cover-up!

Duarte studied Emily's drawn and accusing face and he squared his broad shoulders. 'Don't be silly, Emily,' he urged in the most galling tone of authority. 'It's a warm night and Bliss was feeling faint. She almost fell and I steadied her. *End of story.*'

Duarte rested expectant dark deepset eyes on his wife.

Instantly, Emily looked away, away from both of them. She was trembling and sick with shock at their behaviour. Why were they doing this to her? Couldn't Duarte, at least, have come clean? Instead, they stood united against *her*, both of them making the same stupid excuse and both of them treating her as if she was an hysteric making wild childish allegations!

'I think I ought to go home, Duarte. I'm so sorry about this,' Bliss sighed with regret.

Enraged by the other woman's composure, Emily spun back. 'Tell me, what role are you playing now, Bliss? You're a very good liar but I have to admit that my head's spinning tonight!'

'Get a grip on yourself, Emily,' Duarte grated.

Emily couldn't bring herself to look at him. She kept on staring at Bliss. 'Have you told my husband about what a great friend you were to me before I left Portugal?'

'I really don't know what you're referring to,' Bliss responded drily.

'Oh, really?' Emily marvelled that she herself did not simply spontaneously combust with rage and sheer violent frustration. 'You mean you don't remember all those cosy lunches we shared at the Faz Figura restaurant in the Alfama? You don't recall the dozen shopping trips either? Not even my visits to your apartment?'

Bliss directed a marvellous look of sublime discomfiture at Duarte as if she was listening to the ravings of a very confused and drunken woman.

'Well then, if I never *visited* your apartment, tell me how I know that you have your dining room chairs covered in fake zebra skin?' Emily asked fiercely, determined to corner and entrap Bliss in her own lies. 'How come I know that you have a grandfather clock that belonged to your parents in your sitting room? Leather seats, glass tables—?'

As Emily's desperation to expose the blonde's lies rose to a charged peak, Bliss expelled a weary sigh. 'Well, I *do* have a leather suite but then so do many people and I would *adore* a grandfather clock but I've never owned one. As for the fake animal fur seats?' Bliss grimaced. 'I have rather better taste.'

Emily's rigid shoulders slumped. Evidently it would take someone a great deal cleverer than she was to catch Bliss out.

'Please go home, Bliss,' Duarte urged in an electrifyingly quiet request. 'I'm sorry you had to witness this.'

Bliss strolled past Emily like a queen and walked back indoors.

Duarte swore in driven Portuguese, and strode over to Emily, who was staring emptily into space. He gripped her by the arms to force her round to face him. 'What the hell has got into you? A friendship with Bliss? Since when? Are you paralytically drunk and delusional? How could you make such an ass of yourself?' he demanded with savage incredulity.

Emily was in a daze. 'Bliss *does* have a grandfather clock,' she protested shakily. 'And we were friends and I'm not drunk but I'm beginning to *feel* delusional!'

His smouldering dark golden eyes narrowed and he converted his hold on her limp arms to a supportive soothing hold. Looking distinctly at a loss, Duarte expelled his breath in a slow hiss. 'Look, I think you need to get some rest…OK?'

'You think I'm crazy. Or do you? Maybe you're as big a deceiver as *she* is! If that's how it is, fine. I don't care any more.' Emily raised her arms in an abrupt movement to shake free of his lean hands. Turning away from him, she set off down the corridor.

'I'll be upstairs in five minutes…' Duarte called after her. 'Do you want me to come up with you?'

'No, thanks.' If he thought she was going upstairs to share a bedroom with a male who thought she was only one mental step removed from a nervous breakdown, he had better think again.

Emily trudged back across the echoing main hall and out the front doors just in time to see the tail lights of Bliss's sleek silver sports car disappearing down the winding drive. Naturally one grandfather clock would now be speedily disposed of or possibly Bliss had got rid of that parental legacy months ago, Emily reflected numbly, for the clock had not suited the ultra-modern decor of Bliss's city apartment.

Unable to bear the claustrophobic silence of the house or the prospect of another confrontation with Duarte, Emily wandered out into the moonlit gardens. The dew-wet grass crunched beneath her feet. The palms cast spiky, mysterious shadows that faded the further she moved away from the house. She saw the domed bulk of the building the Monteiros called a summerhouse glimmering in the darkness beneath the trees. A grand eighteenth-century folly built of white marble, it was large enough to house a full orchestra. Mounting the steps, Emily dropped down on to a hard marble bench. Just then, the folly had a great deal more appeal than any bed containing Duarte.

Her husband thought she was nuts. He had gone from outraged disbelief to sudden grave concern. Right now, he was probably ringing one of his many medical friends to ask for some serious advice and book her an appointment with a psychiatrist.

In the quiet of the folly, Emily skimmed her shoes off to flex her crushed toes and willed herself to be calm. She saw that once again she had been set up by Bliss. Having seen Emily watching her with Duarte, Bliss had staged a pretend fall. No other explanation made sense. If Duarte wanted to snatch Bliss into a passionate embrace, he was highly unlikely to do so in a well-lit courtyard in full view of more than forty windows.

So, in that sense, she *had* made an ass of herself, Emily acknowledged grimly. But it was difficult to care when she was truly at the end of her tether. Bitterness was rising inside her like a dam surging to break its banks. Assert yourself, Duarte had told her when he was telling her how to deal with her own family.

But when had she ever asserted herself with *Duarte*? She was Mrs Doormat Monteiro and it was little wonder that Bliss was able to best her at every turn. Eleven months ago, Duarte had demanded a separation and he had dispatched her to the house in the Douro and she had gone without a murmur. She had behaved as if she *was* an unfaithful wife!

Why? She had been consumed with guilt over a kiss that she had neither invited nor enjoyed. Why had she beaten herself up for so long over that stupid episode? She had not been unfaithful and she had not betrayed her husband. But, totally intimidated by Duarte's chilling rage and his even more appalling conviction that she had actually been sleeping with Toby Jarrett, she had become so distraught that she had been incapable of offering a convincing self-defence.

As Emily sat there ruminating on her cold marble bench, she began to see that she had spent most of the twenty-two years of her life blaming herself for every bad and unlucky thing that had ever happened to her. When her parents didn't hug her as a child and her older sisters bullied her, she had assumed that the fault was in her and not in them. She had felt guilty and ashamed that she wasn't sufficiently loveable and had just tried harder and harder to please in the hope that somehow matters would improve. Only they never had improved, she conceded sadly.

Then she had married Duarte. Duarte with his domineering force of will and powerful personality. She had put up with everything thrown at her. Victorine, Duarte's endless absences on business, a lifestyle she disliked. Had she ever complained? No! She had blamed herself for not being content with what she had and for wanting too much.

Instead of putting the blame squarely where it belonged on Duarte's shoulders.

Hearing a twig snap somewhere nearby, Emily froze into stillness.

'Are you trying to play hide-and-seek now?' Duarte derided as he strode into view from below the screening darkness of the trees. 'It is three o'clock in the morning. Do you realise how long I've been searching for you? How concerned I've been? If I hadn't found your tracks across the grass, I'd have been turning the staff out of bed to look for you!'

Emily studied him with a glorious sense of calm and not the smallest desire to apologise for her lack of consideration. In moonlight, Duarte was a dramatic study in black and white. So tall, so dark, so handsome. Always in control, preferably in control of *her*—yet he was losing his reserve at a staggeringly fast rate this time around. Why? She wasn't the same woman she had been at the time of their separation, eleven months ago.

'You really have been a lousy husband,' Emily sighed. 'And I don't need to be hysterical or intoxicated or nuts to tell you that—'

'You can abuse me all you like *indoors*,' Duarte stated icily. 'I refuse to stand around in the garden at this hour listening to this nonsense.'

'Fine. Goodnight,' Emily said quietly.

'Look, you're overwrought—'

'You're not at the bank, Duarte...so drop the command tone of voice. I won't be bullied or browbeaten—'

'But you might just be strangled,' Duarte intoned, mounting the steps at an aggressive pace. 'Now, I understand that you feel threatened by Bliss and that it may even be my fault that you feel jealous and insecure—but no way are you going to make a major event out of that stupid incident in the courtyard!'

'Am I not?' Emily sat up a little straighter and raised her chin.

'It's outright nonsense for you to pretend that you suspect me of infidelity!' Duarte delivered in the same thunderous tone. 'And, in your heart, you *know* it is—'

'Do I?' was all Emily said and not in a tone that suggested she was greatly interested in the subject.

'I would not have an affair with an employee—'

'I thought she was your friend…and wasn't I once an employee? And in a much humbler capacity than Bliss has ever been.'

Duarte dealt her an electrifying look of smouldering frustration. 'That was different!'

'So maybe Bliss was what you call different, too—'

'Are you *trying* to wind me up?' Duarte demanded incredulously, staring at her expressionless face with probing intensity.

'Why would I do that? Bliss need not be a problem, Duarte…providing that you can prove to my satisfaction that you are innocent.'

'What the hell is that supposed to mean?' he launched at her.

'That this evening I witnessed something suspicious between you and Bliss,' Emily reminded him in the same reasonable tone that seemed to be making his even white teeth clench. 'I don't need to justify my expectation that you should now immediately convince me beyond *all* reasonable doubt that you are blameless.'

'And how am I supposed to do that?' Duarte bit out furiously.

Emily lifted a slight shoulder and dropped it again. 'I don't know. It's not my problem, is it?'

'I've had enough of this!' Duarte growled and, taking a sudden step forward, he bent down and scooped her off the bench and up into his powerful arms. 'You've gone haywire since last night! You're trying to play games with me—'

'By demanding that you prove yourself innocent? Was it a game when you did the same thing to me after seeing Toby kiss me?' Emily asked dulcetly.

Duarte froze. 'So *that* is what this is all about...'

Imprisoned in his arms and as limp as a rag doll, Emily looked up at him. 'And I've been much kinder to you than you were to me in the same circumstances—'

'Just keep quiet or I'll lose my temper!' Duarte seethed, arms tightening round her slight figure as he strode down the steps and headed back towards the house.

'I mean, you can't say that I sat you down, stood over you like a hanging judge and frightened you to the extent that you just fell apart at the seams...can you?'

'Shut up!' he roared.

'You see, I'm not a bully—'

'What did you say?'

'I think you heard me—'

'*Inferno!* I am bloody well not a bully!' Duarte raged, jawline rockhard. 'How dare you accuse me of being a bully?'

'Well, if carting me back indoors without my consent is *not* bullying, I don't know what is.'

Duarte jerked to a very abrupt halt. 'I'm looking after you, not bullying you,' he framed, in such a rage he could hardly get the words out.

'But I don't want to be looked after. I can look after myself and I can walk on my own legs.'

With hugely exaggerated care, Duarte lowered her to the grass. Only then did she realise that her shoes had been left behind in the folly. Duarte had been well aware of the fact. He gave her a sardonic smile.

'Thanks,' she said compressing her lips.

'That night I saw you in Jarrett's arms, I controlled my

temper. How many men would have done that?' Duarte demanded rawly.

'I was very upset and I felt guilty even though I hadn't done anything and you scared me—'

'I didn't lay a finger on you!' Duarte bit out.

'No,' Emily agreed unevenly. 'But I was scared that you might—'

'When have I *ever* hurt you?' His bronzed features very pale in the light still cascading from the *quinta*, Duarte stared at her in fierce reproach.

'Never. But that night I was scared—and, because I was scared and very upset, I made a hash of explaining myself to you. You didn't listen anyway. You were already convinced that I had betrayed you. Yet what did you see?' she prompted tautly. 'You saw him grab me and kiss me—'

'I was around long before that,' Duarte cut in grimly. 'I heard him begging you to run away with him and a whole hell of a lot of other juvenile rubbish!'

'Until Toby spoke, I had no idea that he believed that he was in love with me. I was in shock and I didn't want to hurt him and I didn't know what to say—'

'So you just stood there and let him kiss you. If that's as good as your story gets, don't waste your breath trying to raise the subject again!'

'Well, I'm looking forward to seeing how you plan to convince me that you have been one hundred per cent faithful to me for the whole of our marriage,' Emily countered in a slightly strained voice as she picked her way painfully across the gravel fronting the house in her bare feet.

'I expect you to trust me' Duarte informed her without the smallest hesitation.

'I expected you to trust me and look where it got me,' Emily countered without hesitation. 'So please don't expect me to be more generous than you were.'

On the steps of the house, she stopped to brush off the

gravel embedded in the stinging soles of her feet. That task achieved, she headed straight for the sweeping staircase.

'Emily...this is ridiculous,' Duarte breathed wearily. 'When you vanished for eight months, I thought it would serve you right if I did find another woman but I didn't *do* it!'

'Prove it,' she said without turning her head.

'How the hell can I *prove* it?' he raked at her rigid back. 'Call in character witnesses?'

Emily was so exhausted after the effort it had taken to stand up to Duarte's towering personality, she was beyond any further thought or action. In any case, since she had long since sent the staff to bed, Duarte was going to have to douse lights and lock up, which was likely to take him quite a while. In the bedroom that she'd never shared with him before, she dug her teddy nightshirt out from under the bed, padded into the bathroom and stripped where she stood. Donning the nightshirt, she freshened up and pulled the clips out of her piled-up hair, letting it fall round her in a wild tangle. On her passage to the bed, she remembered the sapphires she still wore. Setting the earrings and the necklace down on the cabinet, she slid between the sheets and lay there, barely able to keep her heavy eyes open.

Had she got anywhere with Duarte? Had he seen the point that she'd been trying to make? That he had judged *her* on superficial evidence? Where had his trust been? Had he ever trusted her? It was not as if she'd ever been a femme fatale, who flirted like mad with other men and gave him cause for concern.

Duarte strode into the bedroom like a threatening storm ready to rain down thunder and lightning. As his attention settled on the slight bump she made in his bed, some of his high-voltage tension visibly ebbed.

Emily sighed, tucked her hand under the pillow and

turned on her side to go to sleep. 'G'night,' she mumbled sleepily.

'Right...so now I'm getting the big freeze!'

She thought about that and sighed again. 'I'm just tired.'

Ten minutes later, he tugged her across the bed into his arms and she groaned out loud while surreptitiously snuggling back into the hard heat of him. He turned her round to face him, brilliant dark golden eyes still ablaze with vibrant energy.

'Bliss *did* have a grandfather clock,' he murmured with the air of a male expecting a burst of applause. 'And no, I have never been in her apartment but I do recall her telling me a long time ago that the only thing her father left her when he died was an ugly big clock. An appraiser had advised her to keep it as an investment and she had it shipped out here.'

'Congratulations,' Emily mumbled, eyes dropping closed again.

'You can't go to sleep now, *minha jóia*,' Duarte ground out incredulously. 'Did you hear what I said?'

'Talk about it in the morning—'

'It *is* the morning and we're flying over to London in precisely six hours' time,' Duarte reminded her with considerable impatience and he shook her shoulder slightly, lifted and dropped her limp hand, striving to rouse her again.

But nothing short of a fire alarm would have wakened Emily or persuaded her to take the slightest interest in anything other than sleep.

'Anyone ever tell you that you sleep like the dead?'

'You.' Glancing up from the magazine she was pretending to read, Emily noted anxiously that once again, Duarte was staring at her from his seat opposite. He had been doing that ever since she came down to breakfast two hours earlier and yet he had barely spoken to her. The drive to the airport had been similarly filled with unspoken tension and in half an hour the jet would be landing in London.

'Tell me, do you remember what I said to you last night just before you feel asleep?' Duarte enquired with studied casualness.

Emily chewed at her lower lip and silently shook her head. It was a lie. She did have a vague recollection of him accusing her of giving him the big freeze but that was not a subject she was particularly keen to reopen, for she was all too well aware that when she had wakened around seven in his arms she had *not* given him the big freeze. Reddening at that mortifying awareness of her own drastic lack of control, Emily returned to her fake perusal of the magazine and wondered why she'd dreamt about Bliss's grandfather clock during the night. Quite where and how the clock had figured in her dream, she could not recall.

'You're just so quiet,' Duarte remarked.

'Last night drained me,' she muttered honestly.

'You made your point. You more than made your point,' Duarte extended. 'But I assure you that I have *never* been intimate with Bliss Jarrett.'

Emily nodded, much as if she was listening to a weather report.

'At least *look* at me...' Duarte intoned in low-pitched frustration, evidently as aware as she was of the presence of the nanny nursing Jamie at the other end of the cabin.

Slowly Emily raised her head, aquamarine eyes full of strain.

She encountered stunning dark golden eyes that made her own instantly sting with tears and hurriedly she dropped her head again.

'Please don't cry...' Duarte leant forward and grasped her knotted fingers between both his hands. 'I feel enough of a bastard as it is.'

Emily gulped.

'I've really screwed up our marriage,' Duarte muttered half under his breath, startling her into looking up again— but there was nothing to be gained but a view of Duarte's gleaming dark springy hair bent over their linked hands. 'I don't want you to argue with me about that.'

Emily surveyed his bent head in growing wonderment. She had no intention whatsoever of arguing with him on that score. There was a moment of awkward silence while he gave her a chance to argue in his defence. His wide shoulders emanated ferocious tension when the silence remained unbroken.

'In the future I will do a lot of things differently,' Duarte swore, practically crushing the life out of her fingers, every word emerging stilted and raw with emotion. 'I'm not the most liberated guy around but I can change. Ordering people around just comes very naturally to me...'

'I know,' Emily whispered. 'It's just I'm not really sure why you're talking like this—'

Duarte lifted his proud head and his incisive dark golden eyes glittered over the bemused expression on her face. 'I didn't sleep last night. I kept on getting flashbacks of you cowering in a chair in front of me after I caught...*saw*,' he adjusted hastily, 'you in Toby Jarrett's arms that night. I don't think you got out a single sentence that I didn't interrupt—'

'I didn't—but maybe I was a bit tough on you last night because understandably, you were very, very angry with me after what you saw—'

'Emily, shut up,' Duarte groaned. 'You probably weren't tough enough. I need you to stand up to me—'

'I don't like confrontations but I'll try.' Emily watched Duarte breathe in very deep and slow. 'You don't need to say anything more. I know why you're saying all these things...'

'You *do*?' Duarte looked dubious.

'You're afraid that I'm planning to get off this plane and take Jamie and refuse ever to come back to Portugal but I wouldn't *do* that to you again,' Emily assured him heavily.

'Actually…' Duarte released her hand and flung himself back into his own seat. He surveyed her with bleak dark eyes. 'That *wasn't* why I was saying those things. For once in my life, you are ahead of me. Believe it or not, I hadn't considered that possibility.'

'I won't part you from Jamie,' Emily reaffirmed a second time.

'If you come back to Portugal with me this evening, you can have the dress, the honeymoon and the very moon itself if you ask for it,' Duarte asserted with brooding darkness. 'Whatever you choose to do, I will not issue any threats.'

Emily was hurt that he had so little faith in her promises. She just could not fathom what was going on inside that darkly handsome head of his. He was like a man suffering from ever-growing shock. His moods were all over the place. He was as tense as a rumbling volcano. He was talking like she had never heard him talk before in his life. Was he really so scared of losing Jamie? Then why wouldn't he be? Without very much thought at all, she had denied him any contact with his son for many months. How could she blame him for doubting her?

'Duarte…there's a couple of things I'd like to say,' Emily admitted in a rush. 'Please listen, even though you don't believe what I'm telling you…'

'I'm listening…'

'I never told you that I had become friendly with Bliss because she said that you'd think it was inappropriate and that it might damage her career prospects with you,' Emily related, deliberately not looking at him lest she lose her nerve. 'I met Toby in her apartment and she persuaded me

to let him paint me. The portrait was supposed to be a
present for you—'

'I don't really want to hear any more,' Duarte incised in
a charged undertone.

Emily ignored him and started talking even faster so that
she could finish. 'When I left the house in the Douro eight
months ago, it was only because Bliss phoned me to warn
me that she had overheard *you* speaking to your lawyer and
discussing your chances of taking my baby away from me
as soon as he was born.'

The silence simmered like a heatwave about to explode
into violence.

Emily mustered her courage and glanced at Duarte. His
attention carefully pinned to some point in the middle distance, his bronzed skin was stretched super-taut across his
hard bone structure. Pallor was stamped round his set
mouth, the pallor a male restraining and containing rage.

'Is there any more?' he almost whispered.

'Nothing important.' Shrivelled by his silent, smouldering reaction to her revelations, Emily grabbed up her magazine again, grateful the jet was coming in to land.

Thirty minutes later, in the crowded concourse inside the
airport, Emily turned to say to Duarte, 'I'm leaving Jamie
with you…OK?'

Her husband emerged from his extreme preoccupation
and frowned at her. 'But we're going to see your family
together—'

'I thought you had a business meeting—'

'I had it rescheduled.'

Emily interpreted that sudden announcement as confirmation that he did not trust even *her* out of his sight, never
mind Jamie. 'It's just I'd prefer to see my family alone—'

'I'm coming with you,' Duarte informed her in a studi-
ously level tone. 'We'll let Jamie and his nanny go straight
to Ash Manor and join them there later.'

'You're not listening to me. I want to speak to my mother alone. I want to talk to her in private. I don't want company.'

'When I said I could make changes, I did not mean I could turn into New Age man overnight,' Duarte drawled. 'Your mother will walk all over you and upset you. She always does. If I'm there she stays within certain limits.'

'I don't want New Age man, Duarte…I just want you to respect my wishes.'

'Don't say you weren't warned, *minha esposa*.'

Odd how he could boss her about with such sublime cool himself but react like a caged lion at the mere prospect of anyone else taking advantage of her easy-going nature. It was a kind of territorial possessiveness, she supposed vaguely. Feeling sympathetic, she allowed him to arrange for a limo to take her to her family home when she could perfectly well have climbed on the train and got there much faster.

CHAPTER TEN

'I SUPPOSE you had better come in,' Lorene Davies said grudgingly when she found her daughter on the doorstep of her smart detached home.

Nervous as a cat, Emily watched her mother's slim, straight back disappear into the kitchen. An attractive blonde woman well into her fifties, she looked a good decade younger. Following her disinterested parent, Emily hovered in the kitchen doorway while Lorene continued to stack her dishwasher with plates. Not much of a welcome after her eight-month absence, Emily thought tautly. But then, had she really expected anything different?

'Been in touch with your husband recently?' the older woman asked with her first flicker of curiosity. 'He came here looking for you last year and he seemed to blame us for not keeping you here. It was really very embarrassing and, I can tell you, I was very annoyed about it. You've always been a problem, Emily.'

Emily stiffened, thinking she'd been the quietest, tidiest and most helpful child in the household but had only ever earnt criticism in return for her best efforts.

'Look, I'm sure you don't want me taking up your time when you're so busy. I won't keep you long,' Emily murmured, her nails digging into the palms of her clenched hands as she willed herself on. 'I'm only here for one reason. I hope you can give me an honest answer and I promise not to hold it against you—'

'What on earth are you rambling on about?' Lorene Davies demanded angrily, unaccustomed to her timid daughter addressing her in such a manner. Emily forced her chin up and stood as tall as she could. 'I have a right to know why you don't like me—'

'Don't be ridiculous! Don't like you? What's that supposed to mean?' Her mother said scornfully. 'You have such odd ways, Emily.'

Emily lost what little colour she had. 'If I'm odd, you made me odd. I need to hear a reason from you and then I'll leave you in peace.'

Tight-mouthed, Lorene studied her for a long timeless moment of tension. 'All right. Before we moved up here from Cornwall, I had an affair and lived with another man for a while. That man was your *real* father...'

'What are you telling me?' Emily mumbled, her skin coming up in gooseflesh.

'What you said you wanted to know.' Lorene folded her arms, looking defiant and bitter. 'His name was Daniel Stevenson. He owned a big stud farm. Daniel said he was going to marry me when my divorce came through but he changed his mind when I was about seven months pregnant. He told me to go back to my husband and he slung us out—'

'My father—Peter Davies *isn't*...my father?' Emily said sickly.

'No, but when I went back to Peter he said he'd raise you as his child and we moved up here to make a fresh start. That's more or less it.'

'This Daniel Stevenson...I look like him, don't I?' Emily prompted chokily.

'You're the image of him,' Lorene confirmed grimly. 'He died about fifteen years ago. A riding accident. I can't say that I grieved when I heard about it. He was a creep. I really loved him but I was only one in a long line of foolish women—'

'I'm sorry...' Emily saw the core of her mother's hardness in the bitterness in her eyes. Lorene had been hurt, humiliated and abandoned.

'I'm sorry too,' the older woman muttered wearily. 'But I could never feel for you what I felt for your sisters. It wasn't your fault but I still can't look at you without remembering Daniel and I couldn't forgive him for what he did to me.'

'I can imagine. Thank you for finally telling me,' Emily managed to say and then she turned on her heel and walked straight back out of her childhood home. Her sisters had probably known the truth for years, she thought strickenly, possibly even recalling something of that time when their mother had taken them to live with Daniel Stevenson. Why had she been excluded from the secret?

For an instant she hovered on the outside step, struggling to get a hold on the shock consuming her. Duarte, where are you when I need you? The craving for Duarte was so strong she could've cried. Was she really going to tell him that sad little story? The unfaithful wife and the womaniser? Duarte with his incredibly respectable family tree and aristocratic background?

The front door behind her opened again. 'Would you like to come back in?' Lorene asked awkwardly.

'Thanks for the offer but no,' Emily muttered in harried surprise and without looking back she hurried back out to the limousine parked and screened by the high hedge.

Hurried steps sounded behind her. A hand briefly touched her arm. 'Emily, I'm sorry...' Lorene Davies suddenly sobbed.

In any other mood, Emily would have been astonished by that display of emotion in her direction but just then she could not deal with it and all she wanted was to escape. As she flew through the garden gate and back on to the pavement, the rear passenger door of the limousine opened and Duarte stepped fluidly out in front of her.

'What are you doing here?' she gasped chokily.

He scanned her pasty, white face and opened his arms and she threw herself against him with a strangled sob. She'd never been so glad to see anybody. It felt so good to be held. Nothing else seemed to matter. Nothing seemed to hurt so much. He lowered her into the car and nudged her along the seat to climb in beside her.

'How did you g-get here?' she stammered in bewilderment.

'Cab. I suspected that you were planning to confront your mother and I thought I should be within reach just in case it didn't pan out the way you wanted it to.'

She wiped her streaming eyes with the tissue he supplied. 'It didn't. I asked her why she didn't like me and I thought...I thought maybe she would deny it. Or say I had been an extra child she'd never wanted 'cos my sisters are so much older...or that I was a bad pregnancy or a very difficult baby—'

As the limo moved off, Duarte pulled her back against him and curved his arms lightly round her. 'And instead?'

'It turned out I'm the family's dirty secret—'

'Stop exaggerating,' Duarte urged, smoothing her tousled hair back from her damp brow. 'Come on...'

'Mum had an affair with a real creep and he was my father—'

'I suspected something of that nature,' Duarte confided quietly.

Emily tensed and tipped her head up to squint up at him in the most awkward way. 'You...*suspected*?'

'You don't resemble any one of your relatives, *minha jóia*. That in itself could have been simple genetics but, taken in tandem with the manner in which they treated you, it did make me wonder.'

Looked at from upside down, Duarte really did have the most incredible long lashes, Emily conceded absently. She sighed. 'I feel like I've just lost my whole life...like I'm not the person I thought I was—'

'You're Emily Monteiro,' Duarte reminded her instantaneously. 'We'll do some research on your true father if you like. A few details that did not relate to him being a "real creep" might help you come to terms with this.'

'My mother got so upset after telling me...but when she started telling me she was so hard about it.'

'She's probably been dying to get it off her chest for years but I'm sure she didn't get much of a kick out of confessing when it came to the point. Especially as, knowing you, you probably said thanks in your politest voice before tottering away.'

'Pretty much... How do you know that?'

'If you could thank me after I demanded a separation, you could certainly thank your mother for hurting you.'

Emily was so shaken by that statement that she pulled away from him and turned round to face him levelly. 'Did I say thanks that night after you had said you wanted a separation?'

Duarte nodded in confirmation. 'I took it to mean that you had decided that you *did* want to be with Toby Jarrett—'

'Oh, no...you misunderstood!' Aquamarine eyes aghast, Emily shook her head. 'How could you think that?'

'Emily...what I saw and heard that night was a major, not minor shock to my system and you weren't the only one of us saying things you hadn't thought through.'

'Oh... What did you want me to say?'

Duarte gave her an almost wry smile that tugged at her heartstrings for a reason she could not define. 'You were supposed to get down on bended knees and plead for a second chance. Instead you went upstairs and started packing.'

Emily shut her eyes and slumped back against the seat.

Duarte had just told her something she would rather not have known, for it tore her apart. She might have got all that nonsense about Toby cleared up there and then and they might never have separated at all!

'Why is it that you *seem* to be such a predictable woman and yet you never ever give me the response I expect?' Duarte demanded in rampant frustration.

'Sorry…'

'Forget it. I'll go back to my bad old ways. Easy as falling off a log,' Duarte assured her smooth as silk. 'We're going to embark on our honeymoon at Ash Manor. Agreed, it's *not* the Caribbean but the Caribbean does not have good associations for me—'

Duarte had her attention now. 'Honeymoon?' she parrotted.

'Bliss and Toby are off the conversational agenda for the moment,' Duarte decreed, warming visibly to the bad old ways of command.

'How can they be?'

'I'm logical, *minha jóia*. No controversial discussions equals no arguments. We can have a church blessing in Portugal and you can trot down the aisle in a rainbow of clashing colours—'

Emily fumbled to find her voice. 'Are you sending me up with all this?'

'Trying to take your mind off your newly discovered family connections.'

'You don't need to go that far—'

Duarte quirked a sardonic black brow. 'I admit that giving you the moon, if you ask for it, is likely to prove a problem—'

'But why…why would you do all this for me?'

'I want to stay married, *querida*. Much as I would like to, I can't chain you to the marital bed or force you to live with me. Basically, I'm endeavouring to launch a rescue bid on our marriage.' Duarte rested his spectacular dark eyes on her shuttered and still tear-stained face. 'If, at any point, you feel moved to offer even an ounce of enthusiasm for that venture, feel free to speak up.'

Emily tore her gaze from the undeniable enchantment of his and thought of how much she loved him, even when he was being unspeakably smart at her expense. 'This is all about Jamie...can't you just admit that?'

Duarte settled himself fluidly back into the far corner of the limo and scorched her with his golden eyes in challenge. 'Is that what you want?'

'Yes!'

'OK...it's about Jamie. I won't tax your patience with all the pros and cons of a child having two parents.'

Given the honesty she had believed she craved, Emily felt dreadful. He was willing to do *anything* to keep their marriage afloat for Jamie's benefit. 'I appreciate your honesty,' she said woodenly.

'Happy now?' Duarte prompted with what she considered to be sheer cruelty.

'Ecstatic...' she mumbled.

It was so strange to be back at Ash Manor as Duarte's wife. Those few days after their wedding, two years earlier, she'd still not felt like his wife. Duarte disappeared into the library to make some phone calls and she went off in search of Jamie. He greeted her with a little shout of pleasure and held out his arms to be lifted.

'Because you're a Monteiro, I'm going to stay one too,' she told her son mournfully but she could not stay down for long in his company.

Duarte loved his son. Duarte had experienced instant love and acceptance where his child was concerned. What did she get in comparison? She got the name, the wealth and now she was going to have the stupid dress and the stupid honeymoon rammed down her throat, whether she wanted them or not! On the other hand, whatever else Duarte was doing, he was not pining for Bliss, was he?

Why did she always want what she couldn't have? Duarte valued their marriage and that should be enough for her now. She'd grown up a lot—she'd stopped living in cloud cuckoo and hoping he might suddenly fall passionately in love with her. But at the same time, she should also be making demands. He was never likely to be more approachable or more willing to listen to her again.

She took Jamie out for a walk in his pram. It was a high coach affair purchased in Lisbon and totally impractical for country conditions. But while she bounced the pram down a grassy laneway beneath the trees, she was considering the demands she felt she ought to make. Having returned to the house and passed her sleeping son over to his nanny, she went into the drawing room and found writing paper and a pen. Then she wrote and she wrote and she wrote.

Duarte was still on the phone when she entered the library. He gave her a slow smile, brilliant eyes roaming over her tense pink face, skimming lower, lingering in provocative places as though he was touching her. He filled her with an awareness that was so strong she was embarrassed by her own susceptibility.

'I want you...' he murmured huskily as he tossed the phone aside and reached for her.

'I think you should read this first...' Emily slid her demand sheets across the polished surface of his desk.

'What's this, *minha jóia*?'

'My blueprint for the rescue bid,' she told him tautly.

Duarte laughed with vibrant amusement, tugged her down on to his lap and started to read. Then he gently and firmly lifted her off him again. 'I work no more than eight hours a day, the only exception being an emergency? That's not possible—'

'You could try it.'

'If I go abroad, you come too?'

'You could try going less often—'

'"For every day you spend away from me, I will spend a day away from you,"' Duarte read out loud in disbelief. 'That's blackmail. We would never see each other!'

'I need a life too—'

'*Do homemes a praça, da mulheres a casa,*' Duarte quoted that well-known Portuguese proverb with gravity. Men out and about, women at home.

'The rescue bid is off—'

He paled. 'OK. You win but have you ever heard of the art of compromise?'

'I did nothing but compromise the first time around and I was miserable and lonely.'

Looking grim, Duarte made it on to the second sheet and then he smiled at her with that sudden flashing charisma that could make her heart sing. 'Truthfully—you don't really want me out of your sight for longer than eight hours at a time?'

'If you want to think that, that's fine by me.'

His smile vanished. He skimmed through all the minor requests, even chuckled a few times and then, without any warning, he suddenly slung the last sheet aside and sprang upright. 'You don't want any more children with me? What kind of a condition is that?'

He looked so hurt, so full of reproach and incomprehension.

'You made me feel that I had to give you a baby when we first married and the truth is, I felt too young and I wasn't ready to be a mother then,' Emily admitted awkwardly.

'I never ever demanded that you give me a baby—'

'No but you took if for granted that I would.'

'If that is how you feel…didn't you *want* him?' Duarte shot at her in sudden emotive appeal.

'I adore Jamie but if ever I have another baby, it has to be because *I* want another baby.'

'All I can say is that I believed you felt the same way as me about having a family…'

She saw the sincerity in his eyes as he made that claim and felt terrible.

'Obviously I won't make the same mistake again,' Duarte drawled flatly. 'No wonder you were so miserable when you were pregnant—'

Emily's eyes shimmered. 'I was unhappy because after I became pregnant you just…well, I mean, you never touched me again—'

'Did you expect me to disregard the doctor's advice?' Duarte demanded in astonishment.

'What advice?' Emily frowned.

'Emily, you were present when the doctor advised us to desist from marital relations for the first few months!'

'I never heard him say that…' She sank down in the chair behind her. Thinking back, she remembered that during the first antenatal examination she had had, she had refused to have Duarte present and the nurse had translated the doctor's comments because the older man had not spoken English. When Duarte had been called back in the nurse had gone out and the doctor had talked at length to them both, but Emily hadn't paid much heed for she had trusted Duarte to translate anything of any further importance.

'You honestly didn't know?' Duarte raked an impatient hand through his black hair and stared at her. 'If you didn't understand, why didn't you ask me to explain afterwards, if not at the time?'

'I couldn't wait to get out of there! The whole time the doctor was examining me he was telling me off for being so thin and underweight and he was upsetting me. You never even mentioned it to me,' she condemned in turn.

'What was there to mention? Who wants to discuss a blanket ban on sex?'

'I misjudged you. I'm sorry. I wouldn't have locked the bedroom door if I'd known we were supposed to be desisting, or whatever he called it,' she lamented, feeling foolish. 'I felt so rejected.'

'I wasn't exactly celebrating either.' Reaching down, Duarte tugged her upright, his lean, strong face taut. 'We were like strangers when we first got married. I believed I could take a wife and that we could be content without being very close—'

'You chose the wrong woman—'

'I deserved a gold-digger.' He gazed down at her with rueful, dark-as-midnight eyes. 'I made you very unhappy.'

'I need closeness...'

'I'm working on it—but I'm really good at the physical end of the scale...' Duarte cupped her cheekbones, spread his fingers and drew her mouth under his with a hot, hungry urgency that nonetheless contained a vein of tenderness she had never felt from him before.

And suddenly she was kissing him back with the most desperate surging need powering through her, her slim body quivering at every contact with his. Breathing raggedly, he lifted his head. 'Let's go to bed—'

'It's barely tea time—'

'Let's go to bed—'

'What about Jamie's bath?'

'Our son has a nanny, and I can't wait and neither can you,' Duarte assured her with mesmeric intensity, shifting against her to acquaint her with his bold arousal, cupping her hips in the same sinfully erotic way to pull her up to him.

They got to the bedroom without meeting anyone, which had been Emily's only fear. Duarte brought her down on the bed fully clothed and came down on top of her and kissed her breathless. The need in her was so intense she was raw with it, shaken by her own desire. She just wanted him so much and his passion more than matched hers. He was wild for her and the more she recognised that, the more she threw off her inhibitions. She raked her nails down his back at the height of fulfilment and looked in stricken dismay at the marks she had left on his beautiful back in the aftermath.

Duarte just laughed and hugged her to him with easy strength. 'You just used me, *minha esposa*. As a vent for a very upsetting day. I'm not complaining but if I ever call back home at lunchtime and grab you off your feet and pin you flat to the nearest horizontal surface, you have to promise to be equally understanding.'

As Emily could not picture him dragging himself from the bank at lunchtime, she just pressed a kiss to a muscular brown shoulder and drifted off to sleep, satiated and secure.

CHAPTER ELEVEN

EMILY spun slowly round in front of the cheval mirror, admiring herself from every angle.

It was the wedding dress of her dreams. Romantic, filmy, the colour of champagne and the most superb fit. Her tiny waist was accentuated which had the miraculous effect of lending her the illusion of a fuller swell in the bosom department. Not that it mattered to anyone but her, for Duarte seemed to have a genuine passion for her just as she was.

Humming under her breath, she feasted her eyes upon herself. He would love the dress. She knew he was bracing himself for the clashing rainbow of colours because he was not to know that dear Bliss had convinced her that that was what most flattered her. But it had only taken one glimpse of herself clad in palest blue for Emily to see the light.

They had spent three weeks at Ash Manor, returning to Portugal only the night before. Three of the happiest weeks of her life. There was a kind of magic in the air between them. No doubt that was her romanticising his erotic and intense absorption in making love to her at every possible opportunity but they had had a lot of fun out of bed too. With Jamie. Out riding together. And all the time she'd been learning that she had spent a long time married to and living with a male she had never really got to know. But then, Duarte had not really wanted her to get to know him then.

'I thought you would be the kind of wife whom I would always find in the stables with the horses,' he had confided only the week before. 'Instead you were always out socialising and shopping and, when you were at home, you threw constant dinner parties. It reminded me of life with Izabel. I hated it.'

Instead of pleasing him with her efforts to fit the role she had assumed he wanted her to occupy, she had actually been pushing him away. The more she discovered, the more she loved him for what he was really telling her was that they were much better matched than she could ever have believed. He liked to entertain friends and family at home but he very much preferred to keep business connections out of their home.

He gave her flowers every day and laughed at the way her arrangements turned out. He gave her true affection that did not always lead to passion. He gave her everything but his heart. And she had pretty much given up on his heart. As she finally came to understand just how much Izabel had hurt him, she knew why he had had the reserve and that desire to control. His heart had brick walls round it except where Jamie was concerned and if she ever told him that all that was wrong with him was his gigantic unconfessed fear of being hurt again, he would never, ever forgive her.

After all, she'd already hurt him with Toby, hadn't she? She had dwindled into a poor little victim instead of forcing him to recognise that she was telling the truth.

As for Bliss, well, Emily believed that she'd already worked out the most likely scenario on that score. Duarte was probably going to admit to her that he had slept with Bliss during the difficult months that he had been searching for his wife and child. She was going to have to deal with that and she didn't know how she would. But that explanation made sense as to why Duarte should have insisted on not talking about Bliss for a few weeks, didn't it? Duarte had decided that if he had risked telling her the truth first, their marriage had no hope of surviving.

An impatient knock sounded on the door. 'Emily…?'

She smiled, suppressing the pained regret roused by her most recent thoughts. She opened the door a chink. 'Close your eyes...'

'No. I want to see you,' Duarte overruled. 'I've waited long enough.'

She opened the door wide and let him look.

His brilliant eyes shimmered over her. 'You look amazing. I was a selfish bastard two years ago—'

'I don't think you meant to be,' Emily told him forgivingly.

'That's right, Emily. Encourage me to be like that again.'

'What time do we have to be at the church for the blessing?' she prompted.

'We've got plenty of time—'

'Why won't you tell me what time?'

'I have a couple of people waiting downstairs and we need to deal with them first.' Duarte banded an arm to her spine as they reached the first landing.

'What people?'

'Had I had the option, I would've staged this weeks ago but I couldn't track the guy down. He was hiking round South America.'

'Who are you talking about?' Emily frowned.

Dropping his hand to her waist, Duarte ushered her towards the salon. 'Toby Jarrett.'

'*Toby?*' Emily gasped in pure horror. 'I don't want to see *him* again!'

However, a bigger shock awaited her within the salon. Not Toby, whom she was expecting, but Bliss. Bliss turned from the window with a saccharine smile that froze when she registered in visible bewilderment that Emily was wearing a wedding dress.

'We won't keep you long, Bliss,' Duarte drawled. 'To save us all a long trawl through murky waters, you could just confess to being a scheming, vindictive woman.'

Bliss blinked and stared at Duarte. 'I beg your pardon?'

'You weaseled your way into a fake friendship with my wife so that you could cause trouble. You never ever told me when Emily called the office and tried to speak to me. You also forgot to fill in my diary for the dinner parties—'

'I don't believe I'm hearing these terrible accusations,' Bliss said in a mortified tone of reproach.

Emerging from her own shock that Duarte should even have made such very accurate accusations, Emily's head turned as the door that connected with the dining room pushed open and framed Toby Jarrett. Emily's face reddened fiercely. Tall and fair and lanky, Toby moved deeper into the room.

'What are you doing here?' Bliss demanded sharply.

'I'm here to call your bluff,' Toby sighed, his frank open features grim. 'You offered me several thousand pounds to try and seduce Duarte's wife last year. I was broke but even I wasn't that low. I was quite happy to settle for the portrait commission—'

'He's telling outright lies!' Bliss snapped. 'Surely you don't believe this rubbish, Duarte?'

'Why *should* Toby lie?' Emily murmured tightly, focusing on the blonde with shaken eyes of revulsion after what the younger man had revealed. 'What has he got to gain from lying now?'

Duarte studied his executive assistant with chilling cool. 'I cannot blame Emily for trusting you when I made the mistake. You're sacked, Bliss—and, by the way, if you keep on telling people that I slept with you, I will take you to court for slander—'

'And how are you ever going to prove that you *didn't*?' Bliss slammed back at him and she gave Emily a cold look of triumph. 'You're never going to know for sure, are you?'

'I think the fact that you pulled the same stunt with your

last employer would go a long way to vindicating me,'
Duarte remarked very quietly.

Stilling at that response, Bliss turned white and then she
stared at her cousin in furious condemnation. *'Toby?'*

'Sorry—but when you came out to Lisbon to work on
the strength of a fake reference issued by one of my father's
friends, you promised that you were making a fresh start.'

'You did something like this *before*?' Emily demanded
of Bliss.

'Her last boss was married, too. She told a couple of
people in confidence that they were lovers and got the ru-
mour mill going,' Toby explained ruefully. 'Then she tried
to blackmail him by threatening to lie to his wife as well.
But he went to the police. Bliss got off with a police caution
but only because she managed to convince a doctor that
she had had a nervous breakdown.'

'Were you planning to blackmail Duarte too?' Emily
asked the blonde in horror.

Bliss seemed oddly diminished in stature but her eyes
were as hard as ever. Without troubling to respond—indeed, accepting that her every malicious act had been exposed—she just walked out of the room.

'I think she was hoping to *marry* Duarte,' Toby told
Emily gently. 'But to achieve that, she had to get you out
of the picture. She went mad with rage when Duarte re-
married—'

Duarte looked shaken by that information.

'I'm sorry I was such a jerk last year, Emily.' Toby
shrugged awkwardly and hovered in front of her where she
could no longer avoid looking at him. 'But to know you is
to love you and I'm a hopeless romantic. There you were,
the neglected wife—'

'She's not neglected any more,' Duarte slotted in faster
than the speed of light. 'And you told me that you fall in
love *very* easily—'

'I suppose that's true. Blame the artistic temperament.' Toby grinned at both of them, quite untouched by the smallest shade of embarrassment.

'I just wish you'd come clean with me about what Bliss was up to,' Emily censured helplessly.

'He wanted you for himself. Why would he have told you the truth about his cousin?' Duarte remarked flatly.

'I was ready to talk about Bliss after you and Duarte separated because that did make me feel bad, as it was pretty obvious that you weren't remotely interested in me. But you wouldn't talk to *me* when I trekked out to the Douro to try and sort things out,' Toby reminded Emily.

'And then I beat you up to make you stay away from her,' Duarte conceded in the thwarted undertone of someone trying to regret an action but not succeeding that well. 'You did try to get me to listen to you but I wasn't prepared to give you a hearing.'

'And after that,' Toby said with a feeling shudder, 'I was totally out of charity with you and too scared to try and talk to Emily again.'

Duarte thanked Toby for lending him his support and in doing so, ushered the younger man to the door where he urged him to enjoy his flight back to Peru.

'You're darned right I will—in your jet!' Laughing, Toby strolled out looking as if he hadn't a care in the world.

Emily watched Toby depart and felt very much like taking him by the collar and shaking him. He had caused so much trouble but it had really washed right back off him again. Easy come, easy go, that was Toby. Yet, in spite of that, Toby *had* made the effort to try and set her straight about Bliss. It was just unfortunate that she had refused to speak to him.

'I'm grateful that Jarrett was willing to provide the back-up for exposing Bliss.' Duarte shot her stilled figure a veiled glance. 'I was afraid that, without his support, you would remain suspicious.'

Emily coloured and spun away, afraid that what she was thinking would show in her face and rub salt in the wound. Duarte was so proud. Yet he had tracked down Toby and asked him for his help. She cringed inwardly at what that approach must have cost Duarte in terms of pride.

'When did you realise that Bliss was lying?' she asked uncomfortably, in one way feeling guilty that she had forced him to such lengths but in another feeling hopelessly upstaged. She had demanded proof and, no matter what the cost to himself, Duarte had supplied her with proof of Bliss's true nature. It might have taken him three weeks to track down Toby but Duarte had not called off the search. Nor had he hesitated to confess that he had been equally taken in by the other woman. Emily was extremely disconcerted by his behaviour.

'The grandfather clock…I did tell you that I had a vague recollection of Bliss once telling me about the clock—'

'No, you didn't,' she argued.

Duarte awarded her a wry smile and reminded her of how tired she had been at the end of that party three weeks earlier. 'You didn't take in what I had told you. As soon as I recalled the clock reference, I appreciated that if Bliss could lie about that, she was most probably lying about *everything*—'

'So why didn't you tell me that, the next morning?' Emily demanded.

'I still had no proof to offer that I hadn't had an affair with her,' Duarte pointed out. 'And, to be frank, I had shot myself in the foot, trying to make you jealous of her—'

'Say that again…' Emily was frowning at him, struggling to understand that sudden confession.

Duarte moved expressive and fluid hands. 'I—'

'Tell me that bit again about trying to make me jealous,'

Emily cut in a second time. 'I just want to be sure that you actually *said* that—'

Duarte was very taut. 'That conversation we had in the car after you had come to the city apartment. You had been talking about divorce again. I was angry with you. It was the impulse of a moment to exaggerate the less formal terms of my relationship with Bliss—'

'To…make…me…jealous,' Emily echoed afresh as if she was having a great deal of trouble coming to terms with that concept. 'You mean, you *lied*—'

Duarte winced at the bluntness of that term. 'At that stage, I didn't think it would do you any harm to wonder exactly what I *might* have been doing while you were staying lost in England for months on end—'

Emily folded her arms and stared at him with accusing aquamarine eyes. 'I don't believe I'm hearing this—'

'At that stage I was still suffering from the conviction that I was making a very generous gesture in trying to put our marriage back together again—'

'So you told me what was most likely to undermine it? You let me think you had got so close to Bliss—?'

'*Meu Deus*…I lived to regret my impulse, didn't I?' Duarte countered with feeling fervour. 'All I did after you went missing was work and search for you—but to confess that seemed weak!'

Emily pivoted away from him to hide a sudden helpless smile. He'd wanted to make her jealous. He had not had a clue what a nest of intrigue he was naively stirring with his behaviour. His pride had been hurting. He had been foolish but in a manner that now struck her as quite ridiculously sweet. Where was the man whom she'd once believed was so utterly indifferent to her feelings? It occurred to her that that man had never existed.

Bliss had found a fertile playground in the emotional distance between Duarte and his new wife and Emily's own shy insecurity had been the other woman's greatest aid. The blonde's first tentative efforts to cause trouble would have been swiftly concluded had Emily ever turned round and asked her husband why he never returned her phone calls.

'I have never found Bliss attractive. I was always aware of her cold nature but. I did not require anything warmer from an employee whom, even now, I must concede *was* an exceptionally efficient assistant,' Duarte asserted heavily.

'When I began telling you on the flight to London about the other things she had done, you were furious with her, *not* with me...' Emily registered, turning back to look at him again, relishing that reference to Bliss as being cold.

'Of course I was furious—but more with myself even than Bliss, *minha jóia*' Duarte admitted with bleak, dark eyes of regret. 'I was bitterly angry that you had been manipulated to that extent and that I had exposed you to her malice. If I had treated you as I should have treated you, Bliss would have been powerless.'

'Yes. Just one more thing,' Emily framed with curiosity. 'The first day I came back. At the airport, you stayed with Bliss to talk to her...what about?'

'I took exception to the way in which she looked at you and spoke to you,' Duarte admitted without hesitation.

'You were telling her off.' Emily tried very hard not to laugh but for a few seconds, it was a fight she thought she would lose. She swallowed hard. She thought back to some of the things he'd said to her that same day and compared it to the speed with which he had turned on Bliss to rebuke her for what he had evidently seen as a lack of respect; she could only be amused.

'I assure you that I never ever discussed either you or our marriage with Bliss. Our more relaxed working relationship did not embrace any true confessions. I do not discuss private matters with anyone—'

'I know...' Emily conceded, fully convinced. 'Until recently, not *even* with me.'

'Right...OK, I walked right into that one,' Duarte agreed, but dark colour had risen to outline his high cheekbones.

'I just want you to appreciate that not telling me the truth about Izabel was taking confidentiality a giant step too far,' Emily murmured gently.

Duarte snatched in a sustaining breath and squared his broad shoulders. 'I believed you would think a great deal less of me if you knew what a mess my first marriage had been.'

Distressed by that patently honest admission, Emily closed the distance between them and reached for one lean brown hand. 'It wouldn't have been like that. I would have understood you much better—'

Duarte gazed down into her hugely sympathetic aquamarine eyes and murmured with brilliant golden eyes that had a rueful tinge, 'I should admit that I also rather enjoyed being treated like an omnipotent god.'

Emily blinked in disconcertion.

'It enabled me to feel in control...and I'm not in control at all!' Duarte groaned out loud with startling abruptness as he glanced at his watch and registered the time. 'We're running late for the church!'

Emily sighed. 'Look, you don't have to go through with this simply to please me. When it comes down to brass tacks, stuff like this dress and the church blessing, well...I'd much rather not have them if you really don't want them.'

'Of course I want them, *minha esposa*...' Tightening his hold on her fingers, Duarte hurried her out to the waiting limousine with quite indecent speed. 'This blessing will signify a new beginning to our marriage and a proper commitment on my part to make you happy—'

'You mean you *never* had any intention of making me happy two years ago?' Emily muttered painfully.

Duarte tucked her and her skirts into the car with careful hands and sank down beside her. 'Then the only thought in my head was making *me* happy.'

'Oh...' Only somewhat soothed by that contradiction, Emily decided that she would have to think that confession over in greater depth. 'You're saying you were totally selfish...'

Duarte vented a reluctant laugh and closed his hand over hers again. 'I was striving to evade using exactly those words.'

The limousine drew to a halt mere minutes later outside the little village church. As Emily stepped out of the car, she was taken aback to find Victorine moving forward to present her with a beautiful bouquet of flowers and proffer stilted but evidently genuine good wishes. Emily smiled with true pleasure and thanked the older woman.

'That was so sweet of her, Duarte,' Emily enthused as her husband led her into the church, which was filled to overflowing with more flowers and lit only by candles. 'Oh, this is really lovely...'

The blessing was simple but sincere. Emily listened to every word with the happy and grateful sense that indeed she and Duarte had already found their new beginning. Her eyes damp with unashamed tears of emotion, she was startled when Duarte closed his arms round her and kissed her breathless in the shadowy darkness of the tiny church porch.

Emerging from that unexpectedly passionate clinch, Emily was flushed and in need of being guided back to the car.

'I want you to know that I have rearranged my work schedule and delegated a good deal of the business that formerly took me abroad,' Duarte informed her, studying her with intent dark golden eyes. 'This is the optimum right moment for you to make further demands, *querida*.'

Emily's mind was a terrible blank. She was in awe of this male so determined not to fall into the mistakes of the past again. Indeed, she felt just a little like a new project being enthusiastically attacked and could not help but worry about the effect of what so many sacrifices would be on him in the future. Would his first fine flush of courageous effort wear off and leave him feeling that life with her was just one big pain?

'You really don't need to *do* any more to please me. I'm not going anywhere. I'm not going to leap on the first plane back to England when we have some stupid row,' Emily assured him carefully. 'You can stop worrying.'

'I also want to admit that I totally overreacted over Toby Jarrett because, from my point of view, there was some horrible truths in what he said about my not deserving you,' Duarte ground out like a male set on an unstoppable course to tell all whether he wanted to or not. 'It was bad enough seeing him kiss you but it was worse thinking that I drove you into his arms!'

'Oh, dear...' Emily glanced at his darkly handsome profile as they walked back into the *quinta*, registering his pronounced tension with dismay.

'In fact, the weeks you were in the Douro were not exactly the best weeks of my life,' Duarte framed with charged difficulty, striding straight past the assembled household staff apparently without seeing them and carrying her with him towards the stairs. 'You see, you were still in Portugal. I had seen off Toby, dealt with him. You were still within reach...'

'Hold it a minute...' Emily urged weakly and hurried back a few steps to accept the flowers that the housekeeper was proffering and thank the older woman and their staff for the kind chorus of best wishes being offered.

Darting back to Duarte's side, breathless with her arms full of flowers, Emily prompted him helpfully, 'You were saying that while I was still within Portugal you thought of me as being still within reach…?'

Lean, powerful face rigid with tension, Duarte frowned and carried on up the stairs with Emily scurrying in his wake. 'Duarte?'

'When you vanished I was on the brink of coming to see you and asking you to come home,' Duarte completed in a charged admission.

'Please don't tell me any more…' Emily urged in a wobbly voice as tears clogged her throat. 'It's only going to make me hate myself for running away even more than I already do—'

'No. I think you had to do a vanishing act before I could admit to myself how much I loved you. And, having admitted that to myself, it sort of got it out of the way and you can be sure I didn't think about it again until very recently,' Duarte confided.

On the threshold of their bedroom, Emily surveyed him with very wide eyes of shock.

Duarte removed the flowers from her arms and settled them on the nearest piece of furniture.

'You can't leave them lying there. They'll die out of water,' Emily mumbled, no longer sure what she was saying. 'You just said that you loved me…'

Duarte closed both hands over hers and pulled her over the threshold and closed the door with a well-aimed kick.

'That is so bad for the wood,' Emily rebuked, feeling distinctly dizzy.

Duarte drew her close and splayed his fingers to her cheekbones. 'I wanted you the minute I laid eyes on you—'

'I bet you don't even *remember* the first time you laid eyes on me!' Emily objected, regarding that lesser claim as an equally contentious subject and wondering dismally if he thought that he needed to pretend that he loved her to make her happy.

A winged dark brow climbed. 'Don't I?'

'No way do you remember,' Emily told him a second time.

'You were wearing ancient jeans with holes in the knees and an old green sweater,' Duarte recounted with a certain amount of self-satisfaction. 'Your gorgeous hair was tied back with a piece of baling twine—'

'You remember...' Emily acknowledged in open disbelief at the accuracy of that description. 'But you didn't even seem to look at me—'

'So I'm subtle, *minha jóia*,' Duarte teased with glancing amusement brimming in his gaze as he absorbed her continuing shock. 'I thought you were very fanciable but I wasn't planning to do anything about it—'

Emily was hanging shamelessly on his every word. 'What changed your mind?'

'You dragged my dog out of a barn on fire and I was hugely impressed. There you were, not only sexy but nice into the bargain and so modest. Then I took you home to your family and realised you were Cinderella in disguise. All my protective instincts were roused—'

'Were they?'

Having begun, Duarte was now eager to tell all. 'I thought up that job so that I could get to know you better—'

'Without committing yourself to anything more,' Emily slotted in helplessly. 'And after you had looked your fill on me being kind and helpful with little children and animals, you asked me out to dinner with a view to what?'

'Marrying you. What's wrong with that?' Duarte went on the defensive, bright golden eyes clinging to her taut expression and troubled eyes with forceful intensity. 'OK, so I was terrified of making another mistake and I didn't rush in to asking you out—'

'It's all right. You may not have rushed in to asking me out but you did rush in to asking me to marry you,' Emily conceded but somehow still contrived to make it sound as if she had received the consolation prize.

Duarte hauled her into his arms, troubled eyes colliding with hers. 'And doesn't the fact that I couldn't wait to make you my wife tell you something?'

'You decided you'd wasted enough time observing me?'

'Inferno!' Duarte groaned as he stared down at her in frustration. 'I was in love with you. I just didn't want to admit that even to myself!'

She searched his lean powerful face and the intensity she met in his stunning eyes set her free forever from the belief that he did not love her. Her heart went off on a roller-coaster ride that left her breathless. 'So when did you appreciate how you felt?'

Perceptibly, Duarte winced. 'When we were separated and I started thinking that maybe I should give you a second chance—'

'It took you that long?' Emily probed unimpressed.

'Slow learner...' Possibly feeling that they had dwelt enough on his reluctance to face the strength of his feelings for her, Duarte claimed a slow deep kiss that made her pulse race.

'Just one thing you haven't explained,' Emily recalled as she surfaced. 'I assume Bliss *was* the third party who confirmed that I was supposedly having an affair with Toby—'

Paling, Duarte gave her a look of deep regret. 'Who else? She said that Toby had confided in her and that she had urged him to break off the relationship—'

'That conniving little shrew—and you couldn't see the wood for the trees!' Emily condemned hotly.

'If it hadn't been for that kiss I witnessed, I wouldn't

have been so easily convinced,' Duarte argued. 'But, at the time, as far as I was concerned, Bliss had no axe to grind and every reason to avoid referring to the fact that her cousin had seduced my wife!'

'You should have had more faith in me—'

'After Izabel, trust was a problem for me. As for having more faith,' Duarte continued, deftly closing his hands to her waist and lifting her off her feet to deposit her down on the bed. He followed her down with easy grace and studied her. 'I still haven't heard an explanation of why you asked me the day I found you and Jamie if I was intending to have other women *again*?'

'Oh...that!' Her own ire doused by a dose of the same medicine, it was Emily's turn to look uncomfortable. 'Bliss never once said that you had other women but she used to sort of hint that she suspected that you strayed when you were away on business—'

'Never *once*,' Duarte delivered. 'I always valued our marriage. I would not have risked it—'

'Even when the bedroom door was locked?'

'I put that down to your being pregnant...just not being in the mood,' Duarte confided huskily. 'But when I saw you with Toby, I put a very different construction on that locked door.'

Raising a newly confident hand, Emily let her fingertips stroke down over one hard sculpted cheekbone in a loving caress. 'I love you loads and loads and loads but please don't ask me why it took me so long to decide I wanted a divorce.'

'Are you kidding?' Duarte groaned, the last of his tension dissipating as he heard those words and studied her hectically flushed face with intensely appreciative eyes of gold. 'Every time you mentioned divorce, I went into panic mode. I thought I was going to lose you again. When we were flying into London and I was facing the fact that Bliss was lying and I had got everything wrong, I felt like I was fighting for my life—'

'So that was why you were behaving that way. Sort of desperate...' Emily recalled with a heady sensation of having more power than she had ever dared to hope over the male she loved.

'And you were *so* convinced that my sole objective was hanging on to Jamie, I saw that if I told you I loved you then, there was no way on earth you were likely to believe me,' Duarte confessed with a ragged edge roughening his dark deep drawl.

'You're probably right. On the other h-hand,' Emily stammered slightly as a lean hand glided in a possessive sweep from her waist to her breast.

'You were saying, *minha jóia*?'

'I forget...' And she looked up at him, her fingers lacing into the thick black hair she loved to touch, her aquamarine eyes shimmering over him with wondering satisfaction while he slowly lowered her down on to the pillows.

Duarte frowned and abandoned her with startling abruptness. 'That reminds me.'

Emily sat up in shock and watched him stride through to his dressing room. 'Reminds you of what? Where are you going?'

Duarte emerged again with a large parcel which he balanced on the foot of the bed while he ripped off the packaging.

As Emily focused on the painting of herself which she had last seen at Toby's studio, her soft mouth opened in considerable shock.

'You were right. Toby *is* one hell of an artist. I took the painting from him because I felt that he had no right to keep an image of my wife,' Duarte informed her loftily, a possessive glow in his gaze as he surveyed her. 'I intended to destroy it but, when I looked at the canvas, I could not bring myself to commit such an act of destruction.'

Emily's eyes stung. 'Now I *truly* believe that you love me—'

'Never doubt it, *minha esposa*. I will never stop loving you,' Duarte swore, abandoning the canvas to gather her back into his strong arms and claim her mouth with hot and wholly appreciative fervour.

Eighteen months later, Emily tucked Jamie into his bed. Their son had learned to walk early and at supersonic speed he'd demonstrated extraordinary persistence at escaping from his cot. A little bed shaped like the toy cars he adored had seemed a safer option for their miniature mountaineer.

Smoothing his tumbled black hair from his brow, she watched him slide into the sleep of exhaustion, contentedly clutching his faded blue teddy and looking impossibly angelic. Throughout the day Jamie ran on pure livewire energy and Emily was very grateful to have not only the assistance of a nanny but also of Victorine, who had become one of Jamie's most devoted slaves. Emily adored her son too but she was already recognising many of Duarte's traits in their son. The try, try again determination, the bone-deep stubbornness and the hot temper—and she was equally grateful that Jamie had a father willing to exert loving but firm control.

There had been quite a few changes in their lives over the past eighteen months, she reflected with the lightness of heart that had become second nature to her. No longer did she worry herself sick about imminent disaster. Knowing that she was loved and valued and very much needed by Duarte had made a huge difference to her self-esteem. Even her Portuguese had improved by leaps and bounds, enabling her to overcome her former shyness and enjoy company and make proper friends.

After exchanging stilted taut phonecalls with her mother the year before in an effort to ease the tension between them and visiting again, Emily had finally acknowledged that she and her mother were never likely to be that close. Her mother's husband, Peter Davies, had never had any interest in her and that had not changed but, now that she understood why that was so, it no longer hurt her.

However, it had been a very welcome surprise when both her sisters, initially shaken by the effect of Emily finally asserting herself, had slowly come round to seeing her as she *was* rather than as the illegitimate kid sister whom they had pretty much been taught to despise. Only then had she realised how easily families could all sink into the same bad pattern of behaviour. She had finally appreciated that neither Hermione nor Corinne were that close to Lorene either but over the past year her sisters had steadily become closer to Emily.

'They just copied your mother. It wasn't until you made them stand back and question their attitude that they saw how it had been. They're adults now and they've started thinking for themselves,' Duarte had asserted with immense approval, no longer referring to them as the ugly sisters and indeed making much-appreciated efforts to introduce them to eligible men.

And Duarte? Emily crossed the corridor into their bedroom—the nursery had been moved to a more convenient location. Emily smiled as she noticed the adrenalin kit in the bedroom—Duarte had insisted they had one in every room.

Duarte strolled out of the bathroom, still wet from the shower, only a towel wrapped round his lean hips. 'Is Jamie asleep?'

He still took her breath away, Emily conceded, striving not to stare like a teenager at all that potent masculinity on display. 'Out like a light—'

'It'll be the five o'clock start he had today.' Duarte gave a slight shudder at the memory of being bounced into rude wakefulness at dawn by his energetic son.

'Oh, well,' Emily said wickedly. 'You are the man who once wanted a really big family and I have reached a decision—'

Duarte had tensed. 'What about?'

'I want another baby—'

'Two to bounce on us at dawn?' Duarte tried to tease but shock was written all over him at that announcement. 'Emily, you really *don't* have to make the kind of sacrifice for me. There's a lot more to family than numbers. I'm perfectly happy with Jamie—'

'But I'm not and this has very little to do with you,' Emily told him with dancing eyes, touched by his efforts to dissuade her when she knew how much he regretted never having had the opportunity to really share her last pregnancy with her. 'I just have this yen for another child—'

Duarte searched her smiling face with a frown and he argued, 'I don't want you being sick and miserable—'

'But it's not going to be like that again—'

'How do you know?'

'I *know*,' Emily told him with an air of feminine superiority. 'I just know…OK?'

He reached for her and drew her lazily up against his big powerful body, sending her temperature rocketing. Stunning golden eyes glittered over her with possessive heat. 'It's just we come first and I want you to be happy—'

'You're the man who promised me the moon,' Emily said plaintively, lashes cast down. 'I'm *still* waiting…'

Duarte vented a deeply appreciative laugh and backed her down on the bed. 'Are you ever going to let me live that down, *minha esposa*?'

'Probably not.' She smiled up at him, her heart in her eyes, luxuriating in the adoring look he could not hide, thinking how lucky she was and how gloriously happy. It had not taken the gift of the moon to bring about that transformation. All it had taken was love.

'I love you more every day,' Duarte groaned hungrily against her extended throat, feeling her quiver and arch in instant encouragement. 'You've got me flying home for lunch now. You make me insatiable—'

'Hear any complaints?' Emily teased, inching off his towel like a shameless woman set on seduction. 'Instead of some boring working lunch, you get me—'

'And the more I get of you, the more I want you,' Duarte confided, stringing a trail of tormenting kisses across her delicate collarbone. 'OK…we'll think about another baby when we've really talked over the idea in depth.'

Arabel Monteiro was born nine months and two weeks later and their daughter's conception never was discussed in depth. Emily was neither sick nor miserable during her second pregnancy and Duarte presented her with a very beautiful diamond-studded moonstone pendant and earrings.

'You're not getting off the hook that easily,' Emily warned him cheerfully.

'I think you finally know me, *minha esposa*,' Duarte pronounced with loving eyes and his wonderful smile.

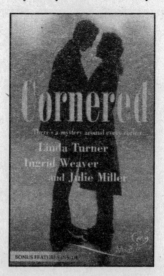